THE BROKEN TOWER SAGA

A Single Brutal Fate

A SINGLE BRUTAL FATE

THE BROKEN TOWER BOOK 2

LEE PAIGE O'BRIEN

AMULET BOOKS · NEW YORK

PUBLISHER'S NOTE: This is a work of fiction. Names, characters, places, and incidents are either the product of the author's imagination or used fictitiously, and any resemblance to actual persons, living or dead, business establishments, events, or locales is entirely coincidental.

Cataloging-in-Publication Data has been applied for and may be obtained from the Library of Congress.

ISBN 978-1-4197-6517-9
eISBN 978-1-64700-852-9

Text © 2025 Lee Paige O'Brien
Jacket illustration by Corey Brickley
Book design by Deena Micah Fleming

Published in 2025 by Amulet Books, an imprint of ABRAMS. All rights reserved. No portion of this book may be reproduced, stored in a retrieval system, or transmitted in any form or by any means, mechanical, electronic, photocopying, recording, or otherwise, without written permission from the publisher.

Printed and bound in the United States
10 9 8 7 6 5 4 3 2 1

Amulet Books are available at special discounts when purchased in quantity for premiums and promotions as well as fundraising or educational use. Special editions can also be created to specification. For details, contact specialsales@abramsbooks.com or the address below.

Amulet Books® is a registered trademark of Harry N. Abrams, Inc.

ABRAMS The Art of Books
195 Broadway, New York, NY 10007
abramsbooks.com

TO THE TRANS KIDS WHO'VE HAD TO MAKE
THEMSELVES AT HOME IN THE DARK,
BUT STILL HOPE FOR DAYLIGHT.

YOU DESERVE TO EXIST IN THE SUN.
YOU DESERVE EVERYTHING.

CHAPTER ONE

RAT DIDN'T THINK THEY'D EVER GET USED TO THE EERIE quiet. Frost crunched under their shoes as they picked their way across the ruins, and the sharp chill in the air was the edge of a knife.

They settled against the curve of the weathered staircase and slid their phone from their pocket to check the time. Overhead, the night was already fading, the last stars faint above the dark rise of the mountains in the distance.

It was almost morning, and if Isola had any intentions of meeting them, she would have been there by now.

"It's fine," they said to themself. The cold had bitten through their gloves half an hour ago, and their fingers were numb.

They shouldn't have gone to Ashwood. Anything to do with Isola was always a mistake and a dangerous one. To have come here more than once—to have come without telling anyone—was worse.

But Rat had been dreaming about the tower, and they hadn't been able to get back to sleep. Somehow, even though each time they swore they wouldn't, they'd ended up here again, their coat pulled on over their sweatshirt and their hair still messy from sleep.

Just to keep an eye on her, they reminded themself. They needed her close, and they needed to be in her good graces. Nothing else.

But Isola hadn't been there in days.

Rat put their phone away and looked up at the ruins. The bones of the estate rose up around them, the bare rafters and fallen beams black against the still-dark sky.

"Okay, then. Don't come," Rat said under their breath.

Certain they were alone, they raised their hand to a casting position. They drew in a breath and thought of the tower rising out of the field of weeds. Rat pictured the faint dusting of stars, naming each one like they could draw it into being. Slowly, their power uncoiled in their chest, waking in answer as they traced a spell sign on the air.

"*Open*," they breathed, the word taking on the cadence of a spell. The world shivered around them, and for a moment Rat could sense every corner of the ruins and every gap in the world where the pieces didn't quite come together. The cracks that something could slip in through and all the out-of-sight places they could hide.

Sometimes Rat still thought of finding dead passages that way; like the world was a puzzle box, and if they turned it the right way, they could feel the space between the pieces and all the places where it might give way completely if they pushed.

Sometimes it was even easier than that, like nudging open a door that had been left ajar or slipping behind a curtain.

Sometimes it felt like nothing at all, as if Rat was simply noticing another hallway or an extra staircase that had been there all along.

Rat focused on the spell, holding the image of the tower in their mind. Aether glinted on the air, curling like dust, and the scent of mugwort and autumn slithered in under the bite of ice. Then, like always, the spell collapsed, and whatever they'd glimpsed was gone again.

Rat's chest fell. With a sigh, they traced another spell, this time back to campus. They cast a final glance around the ruins and then stepped through the passage, the crumbling shell of Ashwood giving way to the familiar boards of the widow's walk over Mallory Hall.

The darkened sprawl of the Bellamy Arts spread out below them: the long, low shape of the library, snaking around one edge of the main lawn; the steeply pitched roofs of the campus skyline; and the now-crooked silhouette of the clock tower rising up in the center of everything.

Letting out a breath, Rat dropped down against the rails. It had been six weeks since the wards had come down. They'd already taken their last exams, and after tomorrow, the semester would end, and the campus would close until the new year. In all that time, Rat still hadn't gotten any closer to reaching the Ingrid Collection and returning Isola's heart to her. They hadn't even managed to open a passage back to the tower.

After all the months they'd spent trying to stay away, now that they wanted to find it again, it wouldn't let them through. They could open the way to almost anywhere else, but no matter how hard they tried, whatever paths led to the tower remained firmly shut.

Rat slumped back, tilting their face up to the sky. Absently, they traced their thumb over the cuff of the sweatshirt beneath their coat to the burns that were left over from when it used to belong to Harker.

It wasn't really the tower they were after.

A cold wind swept across the widow's walk, and Rat shoved the thought away before it could finish forming. They refused to think about Harker Blakely at all.

"*Open*," they said to the empty air. Nothing happened.

Finally, the morning breaking around them, Rat picked themselves up and headed back inside.

CHAPTER TWO

BY THE TIME RAT MADE IT DOWN TO THE MAIN CAMPUS for their final class of the semester, the last stars had faded out of the sky.

After everything that had happened during the fall, Fairchild had given Rat a list of conditions if they were going to stay on campus. Private casting lessons to learn to control their powers had been at the top.

Frey had scheduled them first thing in the morning in a practice room hidden on one of the upper floors of the library. Aside from magic, mornings and libraries where probably two of Rat's least favorite things, but they hadn't argued. The early lessons meant the building was still empty, and it saved Rat from having to explain to the rest of the school why they'd suddenly begun casting after so many years of insisting they didn't have any powers.

It had been a long time since Rat had actually tried to learn magic, and longer since they'd had any kind of real training from anyone besides Isola. A part of them had hoped that maybe once they started casting again, they would suddenly know what to do, but they'd quickly realized that wasn't going to be the case.

If Harker was there, he probably would have been ridiculously smug that no amount of being special, and powerful, and an Evans had made Rat good at magic.

"One more and we can call it a day," Frey said, motioning for Rat to try again.

Rat leveled their gaze at the votive candle positioned on the table at the center of the room. Carefully, they balanced their weight, shifting into a casting stance.

"*Light*," they said under their breath, tracing their fingers through the air the way they'd been taught.

The wick smoldered pitifully.

"Raise your elbow," Frey told them.

Heat rose in their face as they adjusted their stance. Harker had always made it look effortless. He could have lit the candle just by glowering at it.

"*Light*," they said again, louder this time. Rat cut their hand bluntly through the air, willing the spell to take, but nothing happened.

Frustrated, they drew the spell again. "*Light*." A spark the color of sunlight nipped their fingertips, singeing them. With a yelp, Rat jerked their hand back. "Fuck," they muttered, pressing their fingers to their mouth.

Beside them, Frey lifted his eyebrows, and Rat ducked their head as they abruptly remembered where they were. With a flick of Frey's wrist, the candle flared to life, the spellfire burning hot and bright.

Rat looked back at him, and Frey extinguished the flame with a wave of his hand. "You're new at this," he said. "It's alright if it takes time."

"I was going to get it," Rat said. "Eventually."

"Next time." Frey traced a retrieval spell, and the candle rose from the table and drifted back to him as if carried on an invisible current. Smoothly, he picked it out of the air and held it out to them. "I remember Elise saying you might spend a few days at the Council Chambers with her this year," he said, but as he spoke, a small, worried frown tugged at the corner of his mouth. "Is that still the plan for the break, then?"

"Oh, I . . . no," Rat said. "I'm probably just going to go back home."

As far as the school was concerned, Isola had been responsible for taking the wards down, and the Council's presence on campus had only been to help. In that version of the story, Rat had been the powerless heir to the Evans family. Nothing that had happened had been their fault, and Evening had arrived right in time to save them from being taken back to the tower.

Rat was never sure how many people actually believed that. But with only Rat's word to go on, any other suspicions had remained just that.

Frey gave them a small smile. "I suppose it's just as well. It's been a long semester for everyone. To be honest, I'm glad you might finally get some time away," he said. "Maybe you'll even get a chance to practice."

"I'll try," they said. They gave their best attempt to smile back as they moved to put the candle away, but all over again, it hit them that they were really leaving. Without meaning to, they thought of the empty ruins, quiet around them in the predawn chill, and the scent of aether on the morning air. They hadn't even come close to opening a way back to the tower yet.

Rat turned back to Frey. "Sir. Could I ask you something?"

Frey considered them. "I'm not sure if I'll be able to answer, but I can try."

"Do you know anything about places that can't be reached?" they asked. "Not a ward, but like, if you needed to seal off another world completely, so a wayfinder couldn't get there? How would you do that?"

"That's a very specific question."

"But it could be done," they insisted. "Right?"

Frey thought for a long moment, and then his face softened. "You remember the terms of our lessons. I believe it was made very clear that I'm teaching you on the condition that you don't attempt to go to the tower. This is meant as a defensive measure only."

"But what if I couldn't find it anymore?" Rat said before they could stop themself. Another part of the official story—the version the school still believed—was that Rat had never actually set foot at the tower before. In that version, Isola had sent her messengers to them, but Rat hadn't gone to her. Never as far as the field of fallen stones, and never willingly. Rat wasn't supposed to know where to find it at all.

Frey's brow drew together over the top of his glasses, and Rat sunk back a little. He looked more concerned than surprised, but somehow that was worse.

"I just . . . hypothetically," they said, knowing how weak it sounded. "If I'd looked for it before. Not to go there, or anything, but just to see if I could. And it wasn't there now. What would that mean?"

He laced his fingers together like he was considering how much damage Rat could do. Finally, he said, "You mean a banishment."

"A banishment," they repeated.

"I'm saying this so you'll understand what you're dealing with," he said slowly, choosing his words. "It's powerful magic. This isn't the kind of spell you can batter yourself against expecting it to break. And even if you could, I don't think it would be wise to keep trying."

"But what if there was a way? I just—I mean, it could be done. Couldn't it?"

Frey studied them, and then shook his head. "I know you and Blakely were close, but you need to let this go," he said gently. "We'll find a way to bargain with Isola, but the goal of your studies—"

"Is to ensure my safety."

Frey let out a breath. "For your own sake, I'm asking that you let the school handle this. I know Isola might have made it sound like there was a chance she'll still give him back if you cooperate with her, but I've seen this game play out before, and it always ends badly."

"Yeah. I . . . You don't really need to remind me."

"All the same. I've been at Bellamy Arts for a long time," he said. "I've seen what she's capable of, and I don't think she's going to retreat this time. Something tells me we haven't reached the end of this."

Rat hesitated. "No?"

"No," he said. "Not even close."

After Frey let them go, Rat made their way back downstairs. The campus had already begun to empty out over the last few days now that the term was coming to an end, and the building was quiet as they headed into the stacks.

Tomorrow morning, they'd be leaving Bellamy Arts until January, and they still had nothing to show for the last six weeks.

They thought of Harker the last time they'd seen him, rain-soaked and shivering on the floor of the clock tower, coughing up blood and starlight as Evening's spell had slowly undone him. Of the cold brush of the death working that had driven the school's wards, before Rat had torn it apart and nearly brought the whole campus down. Of Isola, at the end of the night, coming back to collect payment for the help she'd given them in the fight.

Harker had been missing since November. Even if no one would say it to them, Rat already knew there wasn't any amount of patience or negotiating that was going to bring him back to Bellamy Arts. Harker wasn't the first student who'd been taken to the tower, and each one Isola had chosen over the years would have been just as clever and ruthless as he was. Capable enough that Isola could use them on campus. Ambitious enough to toy with before she grew bored and did away with them. If she'd let Harker survive this long, it was only because as far as Isola was concerned, the real game had always been getting to Rat.

"A banishment," they said under their breath, shoving the thought away. They traced their finger over the spines of the books, even though they already knew they weren't going to find anything. They didn't know where to look, and even if there was something that could help them, it still wouldn't be any use, because they didn't actually know how to read spell diagrams.

Harker had always been the one who understood magic. Rat was the heir to two archives, and for all the good it did, they might as well have taken the books down and built a fort out of them.

Rat reached up to rub the dryness from their eyes as they came to the end of the shelf, and their phone buzzed. They slid it from their pocket as a new text from Jinx lit up the screen.

war room, half an hour

Rat tapped their fingers against the screen and then put their phone away again without responding. Jinx had never texted them a full sentence in all the time they'd known her, so they doubted they were about to get an explanation now.

Jinx was also one of the few real friends Rat had at Bellamy Arts, but even she didn't know the full truth about the deal they'd made with Isola.

Jinx knew Isola's still-beating heart was locked away somewhere beneath the school in the confines of the Ingrid Collection, and she knew Rat had promised to get it back for her in exchange for Harker's freedom. She didn't know Rat had sworn to return to the tower when all of this was finished. Except for Harker, no one did.

I'm going to figure it out somehow, Rat reminded themself. They turned from the shelves and came up short as they nearly crashed into someone.

"Sorry," the boy said, catching them. "I just—Rat Evans, right?"

Since the night wards had come down, Rat had been repeatedly reminded of the fact that almost the entire campus knew them. By this point, Rat had heard at least a dozen different stories about what had happened. As far as they could tell, no one seemed sure of the events except that, somehow, Rat was at the center of it.

But there were other rumors, too. Quieter ones, about the way the supposedly powerless heir to the Evans family had spent the better part of the semester with one of the most ruthlessly gifted students in their year at their throat, and when the dust had settled, Harker had been gone, and they hadn't.

"Yes, I killed him," Rat said flatly, pulling away.

"Wait." The boy turned after them. "I'm not here for gossip. I need you to sign for some books."

They eyed him warily, taking him in for the first time. He looked a bit older than they were, sharp-featured and fair-skinned, hair pushed back from his face. There was something put together about him, if a little windswept, like he'd just come in from outside. He was vaguely familiar, but only in the way almost all of the old blood kids in the New York crowd were familiar, and Rat couldn't place him.

"Allister," the boy said, reading their expression. "I work in the library. The front desk asked me to find you."

A flush crept up the back of Rat's neck. They considered opening a dead passage and just vanishing into the stacks.

"Look." Allister exhaled deeply. "We found some of your books when we were getting Blakely's things out of the staff room. We were going to call you to come in and pick them up, but I thought you might still be here."

Rat straightened. "What?"

"Spellbooks," he said. "They had your family's archival stamp. I'm not going to guess how he got them, but they're down at circulation for you."

"Can I . . . ?"

"I can take you. It's this way." He motioned for them to follow, and they started after. He took them back down the main staircase. "Is it that bad?" he asked after a moment, breaking the quiet of the empty library. "The rumors?"

Rat gave him another wary glance. "You haven't heard?"

"People tend to talk. I hear a lot," he said.

"And do you believe any of it?"

He looked back at them as he came to the landing. "Do with this what you will, but everyone loves a mystery, Evans. If you don't give them a story, they're going to make their own."

Allister paused like he was giving them a chance to speak. When they didn't, he started down the next flight, to the bottom of the stairs.

He headed back into the reading room at the front of the library, past the deserted rows of tables. When they reached the circulation desk, Allister slipped behind the counter. "Everything's back here. I just need to find them," he said, ducking down to rummage through a pile of things.

Rat craned their neck. "Are those his?"

Allister hesitated, and they knew they were right.

"Could I see?" they asked before they could stop themself.

He chewed his lip like he was deciding something. Then, maybe because Rat sounded desperate, he took a stack of books and notes from under the counter, an age-worn flannel shirt folded up beneath them. "Just be careful with them," he said, sliding it toward Rat. "The books are mostly holds that came in. Everything else is supposed to go back to the main office."

Rat traced their thumb down the spines of the books, coming to stop at the shirt. They touched the burn marks on the sleeve.

"That's everything we had here," Allister said "Or everything we found, at least. Blakely had a way of disappearing. I assumed he'd claimed a reading room somewhere, but you'd probably know his hiding places better than I do."

"Did you know him?"

"Honestly? Not that well. We spoke a few times, but that was really it."

If they knew Harker, *we spoke* was probably an incredibly generous assessment of whatever had actually happened. Before Rat could ask anything else, though, Allister held up another stack of books.

"Here," he said. "These are the ones I'm supposed to give you."

"Thanks," Rat said, then hesitated. Anything that had come from their archives was proprietary. If Elise knew the books were there, she would probably come pick everything up herself. "Do you know if anyone contacted my family yet?"

"That's the thing. They're not Evans books. We're supposed to release them to you."

Rat's chest tightened as they reached for the first volume, but they already knew what they would see. A set of familiar, age-worn reference books lay in front of them, each one bearing the Holbrook family's archival stamp. Their senior year of high school, Rat had stolen the books out of their father's study, desperate to find a spell that would keep Isola from finding them again. Back then, they'd still thought there was a chance she might let them go.

Even if they couldn't read spellbooks, Rat still knew these ones from back to front. They'd forgotten Harker hadn't returned them.

Rat opened one, riffling through the pages. They stopped as they came to a loose sheet of paper tucked between a set of spell diagrams. Frowning, Rat slid it out, but instead of Harker's usual notes, the paper had been folded around something.

Their pulse skipped as a heavy silver coin slipped into their hand.

"Is that a draub?" Allister asked.

They looked up like they'd just remembered he was there.

"Sorry," he said quickly. "I just didn't think anyone still had those anymore." He frowned. "What kind of spell is that?"

A sigil had been etched into the silver, breaking the crescent moon printed on one face of the coin, but the lines of the spell looked rough, and it was missing Harker's usual details, like it was still in progress.

Rat's chest fell. They hadn't realized until that moment just how badly they'd been holding out to find something that could help.

"It's probably nothing," they said. "Thanks, though. For the books, I mean. Really." Rat closed their hand around the coin, then paused, unsure if they were allowed.

Allister waved them off. "If anyone asks, I didn't see anything."

They gave him a last, grateful nod, still feeling like they'd breathed in a handful of ashes. Then they slid the coin into the pocket of their sweatshirt and swept the books into their backpack.

As soon as they made it outside, Rat slumped against a tree and sunk to the ground, the cold air stinging against their skin. Harker had been gone now for the better part of two months, and somehow, they still expected him to have all the answers.

Probably, if it was him at Bellamy Arts, he would have found the Ingrid Collection and slain Isola twice by now. Since Rat had gotten to school, all they'd managed to do was make enemies and break the campus in half.

Rat pushed their hand through their hair, then felt their phone buzz in their pocket. They slid it out to see another text, this time from Will. *Hey, are you still coming?*

Then *We're figuring out times for the train tomorrow morning. Can you be at the student parking lot at 6:45?*

Rat stared at it for a long moment.

I actually, they typed, then stopped as they realized they'd run out of plans and the dorms were closing.

A gust of wind blew across the path, carrying with it the scent of coming snow. Rat looked up to see a black bird watching them from the low branches of one of the trees that lined the path.

Letting out a breath, Rat looked back at their phone. *Sounds great,* they typed. *I'll see you there.* They cast a last glance over their shoulder, the bird still peering down at them, and then sent off the text and started back toward the dorms.

☠

Rat stopped back at their room for a lantern and then took the winding route down to the sunken campus.

In their first few weeks at Bellamy Arts, Rat had learned the school was full of passageways and hidden doors—not just the dead passages they saw everywhere they went, but entrances into the network of tunnels that snaked beneath the school. At one point, setting foot in the tunnels alone would have been unthinkable, but Rat knew their way now. More or less.

The tunnels had changed since the wards had come down. Even though the debris had been cleared from the campus proper, something below the school had broken. The rough stone corridor that led the way to the War Room was dusted with rubble now, the ground uneven where it had shifted when the wards came apart, and the air was thick with the smell of aether. Weeds and grass spilled out between the broken stonework, sprouting impossibly down the length of the corridor in a riot of mugwort and yarrow, like the tower had bled in through the cracks.

A horrible longing twisted in Rat's chest, but they shoved it back down before they could think too hard about what it was. They hated how much closer the tower felt here, like if they shut their eyes, they could have been back in its outlying fields.

They hated the part of themself that wanted that.

At the end of the hall, the doors to the War Room had been left open, and they found Jinx kneeling by the coffee table in the center of the ring of mismatched chairs, her leather jacket draped across her shoulders like a cape.

Since the War Room had been trashed last year, they'd managed to set most of it right again. A few of the chairs had been patched up, restoration spells stitched into the upholstery, and the broken lanterns had all been repaired or replaced.

Sorting through all the books and papers had taken longer, though. They still hadn't taken full stock of everything, but even though Evening had torn the room apart searching for the Holbrook Map, Rat couldn't help the creeping suspicion that some of their other notes on the tunnels might never turn up again.

"Hey," Rat said, settling against one of the chairs. "Am I late?"

"You just missed everyone," Jinx said. "I was about to finish up, but I could use some extra hands."

"What is all of this?" Rat asked, peering over her shoulder at the clutter of notes. A rough map was spread out across the uneven stacks of books, made up of a patchwork of sketches and floor plans that Rat had done, lined up to create the shape of the old campus.

"I don't know. Maybe nothing," Jinx admitted, still studying the papers. "I was down here to pack up and I had to go over everything again before we left. I feel like I'm missing something." She furrowed her brow, and the light caught the frame of her glasses. "What do you think, Evans?"

Rat leaned in, taking in the winding passageways, and their gaze settled on a sketch they'd done of a set of doors, tucked into the clutter beside the maps. Their mind went back to the clock tower, the stairs beneath the seal leading down into the dark. They'd returned there more than once. Since the night the wards had come down, the protection spells that had once kept them out of the building seemed to recognize them now, but the doors at the bottom of the stairs hadn't budged.

Over the last six weeks, every moment that was left over from lessons and exams, Rat had spent working down here in the tunnels, poring over their maps, but they didn't even know what they were looking for anymore.

"Fuck," Rat said, half to themself. They sank to the floor beside Jinx, slumping against the foot of the chair. "We're really leaving."

With a sigh, Jinx settled back on her heels. "We are."

They were all taking the same train out tomorrow, but everyone was parting ways once they reached the city. If Rat was honest, they probably didn't need to travel together. It was just that no one had wanted to leave the school before they had to.

"I just . . . There has to be something we're not seeing." Rat tipped their head back. "Do you think we're making a mistake?"

"I think that whatever we've been doing, we're not going to solve it like this," Jinx said.

Rat sighed deeply. Even if they didn't want to admit it, she was right.

"The offer still stands, you know. If you don't want to go home," Jinx said. "I bet there's some detective work we could do up at my grandparent's place."

"I think Elise might disinherit me if I don't go home." Rat flashed a weak attempt at a smile, but their chest fell. They didn't have a next move. It had been almost four months since they'd been back to the Evans place, and they hadn't let themself think about what it would be like once they were back in the empty house behind all of its layers of wards and protection spells.

"Consider it an open invitation," Jinx said. "I'll be there all break if you change your mind."

"Thanks," Rat managed.

Quiet settled over the War Room again. Finally, Jinx pushed herself back up and snapped a picture of the maps, then tucked her phone back into the pocket of her too-big leather jacket. "Come on. We should get this stuff upstairs," she said, sweeping the papers back into a pile. "Cromwell and I put up some door wards, but as long as we're off campus, we're probably better off being safe." She paused to nod to a pile of books. "Can you take those?"

Rat picked them up as Jinx got to her feet.

As they climbed up after her, she took a lantern, then traced a spell on the air. The rest of the lights winked out around her, dropping the War Room back into darkness. "We already sealed the other exit. I can close this one up before we go."

Rat cast a last glance around the room, then, with nowhere else to go, followed her out into the hall.

CHAPTER THREE

RAT KNEW THEY WERE SUPPOSED TO PACK THEIR BAGS, but when they finally got back to their room, they dropped everything on their bed, curled up on top of the blankets, and pulled their pillow to their chest. They didn't know when they drifted off, but once they did, their sleep was shallow and restless.

Rat used to dream about the cool press of Isola's gloved fingers to their cheek and the whisper of wind through the tall grass, but more and more, they dreamt about Harker instead. Sometimes he died in the clock tower, coughing up blood and magic. Sometimes by Isola's hand, with his throat torn out or her sword between his ribs. Sometimes he was simply gone, and Rat just knew with a horrible certainty that he'd been taken somewhere they could never bring him back from.

Always, though, they lost him.

It was already dark when Rat jolted awake, their heart beating hard. They rolled over, still clutching their pillow. Harker was alive. Even if he was at the tower now, and even if they couldn't get to him.

Rat forced themself to breathe, the phantom scent of fire and magic still fresh in their mind. All over again, they remembered Harker in the clock tower, clutching their sweatshirt, heat pouring off him in ragged waves as his power slipped away from him.

"Please stay here."

Their eyes stung. Suddenly Rat couldn't get enough air. "God, fuck you, Blakely," they hissed.

The quiet of the building settled heavily around them.

"Fuck." Rat shoved themself out of bed and jammed their feet into their shoes.

They hated him. They wished he was here. They wished they'd just gone with Isola from the beginning instead of dragging him into this.

Before Rat could think about where they were going, they grabbed their cloak from the foot of their bed and clasped it over their sweatshirt. They couldn't be in their room anymore. They needed to be somewhere they could breathe. Rat took their gloves from the nightstand and started into the darkened hall, the dorm silent around them as they made their way down to the lobby.

Outside, it had started to flurry, snow curling through the air in drifts. The sharp bite of the cold cut through their cloak, but they started down the main path anyway.

Out of all the enemies Rat had managed to make, they still thought of Harker Blakely as the worst. He was ruthless and clever and ran on an ungodly combination of black coffee and ambition. Before Isola had taken him, he'd sworn himself to her service and stolen one of Rat's father's maps from the school archive, and he'd come closer than anyone else she'd ever tasked with finding her heart.

Rat was also pathetically in love with him.

The jagged line of the main campus's rooftops rose up ahead of them, but Rat followed the trail toward the edge of the tree line and the low, rolling slope of the hills beyond that. They thought about going back to Ashwood, but they already knew they wouldn't. Wherever Isola had been the last few weeks, they would figure this out without her. They were done waiting for her to come find them in the ruins.

They didn't care if they hadn't found the Ingrid Collection yet, or if they hadn't fulfilled their end of the deal. They just needed to get to Harker.

They refused to leave things like this.

Rat thought of the crooked rise of the tower, and the field of fallen stones, and Harker the way they'd last seen him, the faint scent of smoke still clinging to him.

Rat cut their hand through the air, tracing one of the only spells they knew. "*Open,*" they said, breaking the quiet of the empty campus. They felt the world give, and a dead passage opened ahead of them.

Rat stepped through, and the path gave way to the east woods. The trees rose up dark and barren around them, the pitched roofs of the campus just visible in the distance.

Magic pulsed under their skin, and for a moment, they could sense the familiar path to the tower, tugging at them.

The tower had been theirs from the moment they'd first seen it in one of their father's sketches, and they'd always been meant to end up there. Rat knew the way in every hollow of their bones. It was the one place they couldn't escape, and no matter where they went, they'd always found their way back to it.

They thought of Isola, her voice like cold water. *"Just imagine you're coming home."*

Another passage opened ahead of them, glinting between the trees, and Rat started toward it. They came through to somewhere deeper in the woods, where the trees grew closer together and the darkened shape of the school was barely visible in the distance. The scent of frost and mugwort hung heavily in the air, and the earth was frozen beneath their shoes.

Rat's heart beat in their mouth as they shoved themself forward, following the thread of their powers. Instinctively, they found the next passage, and the frozen soil turned to brittle, snow-dusted grass.

Then the next.

They cut their hand through the air. "*Open!*"

Their voice echoed across the clearing, and for one terrible instant, the world shuddered around them. Then something pushed back, and like always, the spell slipped away from them.

Rat slowed, catching themself. There wasn't another passage.

They'd come to the far edge of the woods. The last time they had been there, it had been just after the Whisper Ball, when a search party had been combing the woods for any trace of where they'd gone, and Harker had been in the infirmary, hating them. It hadn't occurred to them that things could get any worse than that.

Now, a light dusting of snow blanketed the ground ahead of them, and the air had turned bitter. An impossible quiet hung over everything.

Rat cut their hand through the air again, drawing the same spell. "*Open!*" Nothing. "*Open!*" They raised their hand to cast it again.

"No?"

Rat spun around. Behind them, Isola had appeared in the low branches of a tree. Snow dusted her shoulders and stuck in the dark snarls of her hair.

"Were you going somewhere?" she asked lazily, dangling her leg over the branch. Her cloak draped behind her, open to reveal the line of her sword.

"You can't set foot on school grounds."

Isola canted her head, like she was waiting for them to produce a school from somewhere. "Do you see your stars?"

With a chill, Rat remembered how far from campus they really were. Without looking, they knew the skies had changed overhead.

"All the stars are mine," they told her, stalking past.

"Bold tonight, aren't we?" Lightly, Isola slid down from her perch, cloak billowing after her as she dropped to the ground. Frost crunched under her boots. "I'm curious, though. You haven't told me what brought you here."

Rat scowled at her.

"Should I guess?" Isola started after them, her long strides easily closing the distance. Her eyes gleamed as she drew ahead of Rat, weaving into their path. The woods opened into fields ahead of them, the frozen overgrowth still poking through the snow. "You spent so much time running away, I never thought I'd see you this eager to go back."

Rat bristled. "Maybe I'm here for the quiet. If you can find me here, you could have found me at Ashwood."

She dipped into a mocking bow. "If you don't want to hear where I've been, say the word and I'll be out of your way."

They sharpened, and immediately hated themself for it. "What do you want?"

Isola's mouth curved. "You know, it's curious how I always seem to find you by yourself. Your friends don't know you still speak to me, do they?"

"Did you want to talk or not?"

Isola looked up, her gaze traveling out past the edge of the trees. A bird circled low overhead, dark against the slowly fading sky. "My messengers hear things, but I needed to see for myself. Someone's been breaking into the archives of some of the oldest families." She tilted her head. "Four in the last six weeks, all of them ransacked."

Rat came up short. *Evening.*

It had to be. Even if the spells that sealed off the clock tower answered to Rat now, they'd known they weren't going to have long before Evening made his next move. They turned toward Isola, forgetting themself. "What was taken?"

"Nothing," she said, her voice keen with interest. "Or at least, nothing that anyone will say. I would have looked further, but there are places in your world where I can't easily maneuver."

Rat suppressed a shiver. Something about the whole situation raised the hairs on the back of their neck.

"Whatever it is," she said, her breath warm on their cheek, "if I were you, I would make a point of finding out."

They looked up at her. This close, she towered over them, her shoulders broad under her cloak. The faint autumn scent of the tower clung to her, and her eyes were sharp and bright in the predawn gloom.

"I'll keep that in mind," Rat said.

"You should. In fact." Deftly, Isola drew her hand through the air, and a small, round mirror appeared between her fingers, like a trick of the light. "I brought you something. Think of it as a reminder of what you have to lose."

Before Rat could ask what she was doing, she exhaled, her breath fogging on the glass. When it cleared, they were looking at a narrow ruin of a room, the stonework weathered away. A single window slit the wall like a wound, crumbling where weeds had grown up between the bricks.

Without asking, Rat knew they were looking at the tower. Even if they'd never set foot inside, they still saw its wild overgrowth and broken stone in their dreams. They were sure that if they tried, they'd be able to name each constellation that shone in the almost-dark sky.

Harker sat perched on the ledge of the broken window, his knees drawn to his chest. His cloak draped heavily over the bony ridge of his shoulders to pool on the stonework around him like a second shadow. Beneath it, he wore a set of plain, dark clothes that Isola must have given him. His hair was longer than Rat remembered, left in loose snarls like it hadn't been worth the effort of tying back. In the half-light, he seemed to belong there, ragged and sharp-edged, like another one of Isola's creatures.

He shifted, and fresh bruises peered out from the collar of his shirt on the little skin Rat could see. Everything in Rat went cold.

"What did you do with him?"

"Nothing yet." Isola tilted her head, but they couldn't miss the threat in her voice. "In fact, given all the trouble he's caused, I think I've been rather hospitable." Rat's chest tightened, but before they could answer, Isola lowered the mirror again and pressed it into their hand. "Consider it a gift."

Isola drew back again, and her gaze tracked across the sky, like she was plotting her route to leave.

"Wait," Rat said in a rush. Their voice rang out across the clearing. "Let me go back with you."

Isola gave them a small, cruel smile, and they realized their knees were shaking. Delicately, she cupped their jaw, tilting their face up to hers. "Someday," she promised. Then she released them and took a step back, her form already shifting as she moved. The next moment, she was a great black bird, her wings spread wide to catch the air.

Rat stared after her, desperate and furious as she took off into the waning night.

Before this was over, Rat swore to themself, they were going to raze her to the ground.

CHAPTER FOUR

BY THE TIME RAT MADE IT BACK TO CAMPUS, THE SNOW had let up again and the sky had begun to fade. They packed their things without letting themself think too hard about where they were going.

Every winter, when the nights were at their longest, the Council of Hours held a Revel to mark the season. Rat had never actually been to one. All they knew was that it ran until morning, and that most of the oldest families used the event to broker the kind of deals that weren't spoken of in the daylight. That was where Elise would be spending the beginning of the break, to shore up her alliances and probably run damage control, to protect the Evans name from the unfortunate fact that Rat happened to share it.

It was also the last place Rat should be, since showing up at the Council Chambers would put them firmly in Evening's territory, surrounded by his allies.

Their invitation had arrived weeks ago, but they'd been planning to throw it away.

"*If I were you,*" Isola's voice echoed in the back of their mind, "*I would make a point of finding out.*"

Rat got to their feet and went to their desk.

Most of the guests arrived the day of the Revel, but there were always a handful who came earlier. Rat knew how this game worked now, enough to know that they wouldn't be turned away. Evening wouldn't pass up the chance to have them there, and the rest of the Council would have to allow it, because Rat was an Evans.

They opened their drawer and dug out the envelope and RSVP card, printed on the same heavy cardstock as the invitation and marked with a simple telegraph sigil that twined across the back in gold ink.

Rat took a pen and marked down their attendance. *Please inform the Council I'll be accompanying Elise as a personal guest of Edgar Cromwell and the High Office of Evening*, they wrote underneath.

Before they could think better of it, they signed their name and slipped it back into the envelope. There was the faint charge of magic on the air as the spell took.

"No turning back now, Evans," Rat said under their breath. Steeling themself, Rat turned to get their bag, then stopped as they caught sight of the mirror Isola had given them resting where they'd left it on their bedside table.

Harker had finally gone to sleep, curled on the floor of his room in the tower, his cloak draped over his narrow frame. Outside the crumbling window, the sky had slowly grown lighter, and the stars Rat could see had shifted overhead.

Rat picked up the mirror, tracing their thumb over the edge of the frame. "Blakely, you burning wreckage," they said into the glass. "Just hold on, okay?"

The alarm on Rat's phone chimed. They slid the mirror into their coat pocket, tucking it beside their compass, and gathered their things to go.

CHAPTER FIVE

RAT SENT OFF A MESSAGE TO THE OTHERS WITH THEIR new plan before they headed down the stairs. The sun still hadn't fully risen, and the building was deserted as they made their way to the lobby of Mallory Hall.

Will was already waiting, leaned against the arm of an empty couch, his face flushed from the cold and his usually neat hair mussed like he'd just rolled out of bed.

"Rat. Hey." He picked himself up, concern etched across his face. "Jinx wanted her car at the train station, so I told her we'd meet her in town," he started. "I got your text about the Revel. Are you really planning to . . ."

He trailed off, and Rat realized they'd been awake most of the night and probably looked like it. Mud had dried on their shoes, and they hadn't had a chance to shower off the traces of the deep woods.

"I'll explain when we have everyone," they said, but their voice came out hoarse. "We should get going. We have a train to catch."

For a moment, Will looked like he might press them. Then, with a gentleness that made Rat suspect they looked even worse than they felt, he let it go. "Here," he said, taking their bag before they could protest. "I already put my things in the car last night. I pulled it around from the student parking lot, so it's close by."

Outside, the morning was just beginning to break, the day cold and bright. Rat trailed after as Will drew ahead, leading them in the direction of Armitage Hall.

Will Chen was probably Rat's oldest friend, and they'd known him since before either one of them could cast. He was one of the few people who knew about their powers, even before they'd come to Bellamy Arts, but he'd been a late addition to the group. Jinx had taken to him right away, though, maybe because he was one of the nicest people Rat knew, or, just as possibly, because his hobbies included being really good at defensive casting and ignoring his better judgement.

Rat kept close behind him as the path cut toward a small lot close to the tree line, tucked away behind the building. Frost glinted on the grass, and almost all the other cars had already gone.

"Hey," Will said. The same note of concern from before slid into his voice, and Rat realized they'd come to a stop at the edge of the path. "Ready to head out?"

Rat looked back at the sharp peaks of the school's rooftops, rising up against the pale expanse of sky. Something in their chest fell at the thought of leaving now, but the answers they needed were at the Council Chambers. "Yeah," they said, hiking up their backpack. "We should get going."

The town of Bellamy, New York, was only a couple of minutes from the school by car. The entirety of the town center was made up of a small grid of tree-lined streets and red-brick shopfronts, with the post office at one end and a train station on the other.

During the year, Rat imagined it was probably overrun with students, but it was winter break now, and they'd arrived early enough that the streets were still deserted.

Jinx was already there, leaned against the side of a battered pickup truck that had to be older than she was and looked like it ran entirely on arcane magic and hope. Agatha perched on the hood beside her, dressed in a long coat that was cut a bit like a cloak, her hair left loose down her back in long, dark waves.

Jinx waved as she caught sight of Rat and Will. "Evans! Chen! You're late."

"I voted to leave without you," Agatha said, propping her chin on her knuckles.

Jinx gave her a look and turned back to Rat. "I assume we've got a lot to talk about."

Rat opened their mouth to answer, and then realized everyone's attention had shifted to them. "Yeah. A couple of things."

"We should start moving," Jinx said. "Cromwell wanted to grab breakfast before we left. There's a bakery around the corner that has pretty good coffee." She paused, studying Rat, and they realized how tensely they were holding themself. "I was thinking of splitting off to find some seats on the train. Come with me?"

They nodded, relieved, and Jinx turned to Will and Agatha.

"Alright if we meet you there?" she asked.

"Of course," Will said as Agatha slid down from the hood of the car. "Text me your order."

As soon as the others had gone, Jinx said, "Okay, Evans. How are you really?"

"Fine," Rat managed.

Jinx let out a breath and tipped her head toward the train station building. "Come on," she said, motioning to Rat. "It's freezing out here. We can talk on the train."

They followed her through the parking lot and up the steps to the platform, where the train was already idling on the tracks. It was significantly warmer inside, and aside from a handful of commuters and the last Bellamy Arts students returning to the city for the break, there was almost no one there.

Jinx led the way to an unoccupied car and lifted her bags on to the overhead rack, then dropped into an open booth.

"Alright. What's actually going on?" she said as soon as Rat had tucked away their luggage.

"I don't know," they said, sliding in across from her. "We might have a lead."

"Yeah. I got that part from your texts," she said. "I don't like any of this."

"I don't either," Rat admitted. "But . . ."

"But you think Evening is up to something."

"You don't?"

Jinx leaned in, folding her arms over her lap. "If it looks like he's searching for something, he probably is. It's a bold move to go after the other old families like that, but after last semester, I'm not sure there are that many lines he wouldn't risk crossing," she said. "I just think we need to be careful with Isola."

"She doesn't get anything from sending us in the wrong direction. She wants her heart back."

"It's never one thing with her," Jinx said.

Rat opened their mouth to argue, and Jinx leveled her gaze at them.

"You know her. She's playing a game, Evans." Jinx shoved her hand through her curls. "Look. I'm never going to repeat this, but Blakely is clever, and he's relentless. If Evening hadn't shown up first, there's a real chance he could have gotten to the Ingrid Collection before us. Your powers are rare, but we both know that with a couple of years and the right books, Blakely would be right on your heels. All Isola had to do was wait, and he would have become whatever she needed him to be."

"Maybe," Rat said grudgingly. They wanted to protest more, but they'd had the exact same thought.

"Cutting you off from him when the two of you finally had a common enemy? Making herself your only source of information about him? Giving you missions?" Jinx gave them a pointed look. "It's the same thing she's been after from the beginning, Rat. She's trying to keep you close. You have to know that nothing good is going to come from this."

"It's Isola. Nothing good ever comes from dealing with her," Rat said. "If Evening is up to something, I'm not sure if we have much of a choice."

Jinx settled back against her seat. "It's really wolves on all sides, isn't it?"

Rat flashed her a shaky attempt at a grin. "I'm starting to think that's kind of all we do here."

Jinx's mouth tugged at the corner into a wry not-smile. "Don't sell us short. Sometimes it's terrors."

Before Rat could come up with something to say to that, Jinx glanced behind them, and Rat turned to see Will and Agatha in the aisle.

"We've returned victorious," Agatha said, flopping dramatically into the seat beside Jinx, a paper bag from the bakery in her lap. "Please feel free to commend me."

Will slid in beside Rat, carrying a drink holder with three paper to-go cups. He lifted one up and held it out to Jinx. "Earl Grey, two sugars, one milk."

"I'm in your debt, Chen," she said, taking it from him.

He shot her a winning smile, then turned back to Rat. "You never actually texted me an order, so I guessed," he said, passing the next cup to them. "Coffee, but like, it's mostly half-and-half?"

"Thanks," Rat mumbled, suddenly exhausted. It was too early in the morning for them to be perceived, they decided, sinking back against the seat.

Somewhere behind them, a bell dinged as the doors slid shut. A moment passed before the train hitched into motion, the platform falling away behind them as they pulled out of the station.

"So," Agatha said, dropping her head gracelessly into Jinx's lap. "I heard we need a new plan for the Revel. Can we talk about it yet?"

Jinx looked down at her, unamused, and Agatha offered her the bag of pastries. Resigned, Jinx took a croissant and looked back at Rat. "If Evening is really searching for something, the Revel going to be our best chance to find out what," she admitted. "I don't like letting Isola steer us, but this is probably the only time we're all going to be able to get into the Council Chambers without raising questions."

Rat glanced around at the group. "You're all going?"

"My family comes into the city for it every year," Will said. "We always get invited by Dawn. I'm pretty sure my parents have plans to meet up with Elise at the First Arrivals' reception tonight."

"My grandparents have a standing invitation from the office of Night," Jinx said. "I'm going to stay over with Cromwell and head up to Maine with them after the event."

Rat looked to Agatha.

She raised her eyebrows like they'd forgotten who they were speaking to. "Yes?"

"Forget I asked," Rat said. "Are you getting there early, too?"

"Sadly, no. You'll have to handle the intrigue on your own. My parents are letting us hold down the family home upstate. We thought it might be a chance to do a bit of research."

Rat furrowed their brow.

"The case files on the disappearances," Jinx said.

"I thought your family had those."

"They did. It turns out my granddad sent down copies."

"Fortunately for us, my parents have never trusted Evening," Agatha said. "My mother doesn't usually consult on school business, but she's taken a particular interest in some of his past cases. If he's assigned himself to investigating the break-ins, she'll have any records that have been released to the rest of the Council."

"Is she looking into it?"

"Not officially, but I think her view is that it never hurts to remind him someone is watching."

"And if there are any clues about what he's looking for in the old case files, then it's a start," Jinx said.

"Right. So. I guess it's us until the Revel, then." Rat looked at Will.

Across from them, Agatha sat up. "If you're serious about this, you're going to need to watch yourselves while you're there. Both of you. You made an enemy when you got away from my uncle last time, Rat. You're not going to be able to slip under his notice anymore."

"Yeah. I'm just not sure if we have any better options right now," Rat said.

"The hard part is going to be getting details about the break-ins," Jinx said, shifting forward. "The rest of us can ask around, too, but none of the older families are going to want word getting out if their archives were broken into. I doubt anything from the case is going to be made public." She looked at Rat. "I hate that I'm asking this, but Isola didn't tell you anything else?"

"Nothing," they admitted. "I'm not sure she knows what he's looking for, either."

"And you don't think she's holding anything back?"

Rat sighed. "She could be?"

Idly, their hand went to their compass, and then their fingers found the draub from the day before, still tucked against it. They slid the coin from their pocket, turning it as they thought.

"I don't know. I don't think she's lying about Evening. Isola has an agenda, and she wouldn't send us after him without a purpose," they said. "But she's definitely steering us. I just . . ."

Rat stopped as the draub caught the light.

"Evans?" Jinx asked.

"The lines are wrong," they said, half to themself.

Rat hadn't been paying attention yesterday. They'd thought the spellwork looked unfinished, like it was still somehow too rough, but that hadn't been right. The spell was complete. It was just that everything about it was *off*.

Harker's usual flourishes were missing, but so were the faint trace lines and markers he would have used to scaffold his work. He wouldn't have wasted good materials on a working he wasn't sure of, and it had none of his usual precision.

"What is it?" Will leaned in, peering over their shoulder. "Is that a breadcrumb spell?"

With a start, Rat looked up. "What?"

"A breadcrumb spell," he repeated, as Jinx and Agatha moved to follow his gaze. "Why are you carrying that?"

"Wait." Rat angled themself toward him. "Will. Do you know what this is?"

"Yeah. It's a type of tracking spell," he said, and everything in Rat turned cold. "It leaves a trail for whoever has the other half of the spell. My team tried using them to keep track of each other during the game on Lake Night, but there were too many of us. We ended up doing a beacon system instead." His brow drew together. "Who gave you that?"

Up close, the etching looked intentionally unskilled. Almost like someone had wanted to pass it off as Harker's work and hadn't known how much practice he'd had.

Rat's skin crawled, but they couldn't find their voice. They wanted to throw the spell across the train car.

"Rat?" Will said, a note of unease sliding into his voice.

"It was mixed into Harker's things," Rat said in a rush. "He had some of my books, and the library was supposed to release them to me. I thought it was his."

Their mind raced. Evening could have hidden the spell in Harker's things weeks ago, knowing how likely it was to get back to Rat. For all they knew, there could have been a dozen others scattered around the campus, just waiting to turn up. If Rat had stumbled onto it sooner, they might have carried it in their pocket for weeks without realizing anything was wrong.

"Evans." Jinx reached across, and Rat realized they were still clutching the coin. Delicately, she took it from their hand and traced her thumb over the etching in a counterspell. The spell broke, and the draub cracked down the middle, spent.

Rat stared down at the pieces resting in her palm. If Evening couldn't track them with it, then he would want them to be shaken and off-balance. Either way, it served him, and they hated the fact that it had worked.

"Are you okay?" Jinx asked.

"Let's just figure out a plan."

For a long moment, everyone was quiet, and there was only the low sound of the train moving over the tracks as Rat pocketed the broken coin.

They took their sketchbook from their bag and leaned in. "If we're really doing this, I need to know where I'm going," they said. "You've spent more time there than I have. Start with the Council Chambers, and tell me everything."

CHAPTER SIX

IT WAS ALREADY PAST NOON WHEN THE TRAIN PULLED into Grand Central Station. Rat spent as much of the ride as they could listening as Agatha talked them through the layout of the Council Chambers and Jinx pointed to places on their maps like she was tracing out a battle plan, but they already knew that whatever they tried to prepare for, they were heading into the maw of something dangerous.

Last semester, Evening had tried to bring Rat back to the Council Chambers as an apprentice so he could keep them there under lock and key. If they weren't careful, he would find a way to make sure they didn't leave.

By the time they made it off the train and into the main concourse, the station was packed with holiday foot traffic, and Elise was waiting in the crowd, dressed in a long wool peacoat and winter gloves. Rat's chest tightened as her eyes locked on theirs, even though they'd known she would be meeting them. They turned back to the others, then realized the rest of the group had all slowed.

"My parents are meeting me," Will said. "I'll find you at the reception?"

"I'll text you when we're on the way down," Rat said.

Rat looked at Agatha to say goodbye to her, and before they realized what she was doing, she shot forward and wrapped her arms around them. "Stab my uncle for me," she said, low enough that only they could hear. "Someone ought to."

"I'll try," they managed as she let them go.

Jinx clasped their shoulder. "Watch yourself, Evans," she said.

Rat drew in a breath. Steeling themself, they turned and started through the crowd.

Elise had come to campus once after the wards had come down, to bring Rat back home from Bellamy Arts. The last time they'd seen her, she'd been furious, but more at the school than with them. Elise had all but demanded that Rat be sent home. In the end, though, Fairchild had refused to suspend their enrollment, and there hadn't been anything else in Elise's power to do, since Rat was legally an adult and their tuition came out of an educational trust in their own name.

When Rat had told her they'd changed their plans for the break, they'd half expected her to refuse to take them along, and probably insist that they go back home and stay there indefinitely behind a dozen new wards. Rat had forgotten that as far as Elise knew, the Council Chambers was still the safest place for them. They couldn't really blame her for wanting to keep an eye on them.

"I was looking for you," Elise said, pulling them into a hug. "You made it down alright?"

"Great," Rat managed. "Sorry about the last-minute change."

"No. I'm glad you're here. I've missed you." She released them, still beaming. "I've already checked us into the hotel. We can talk more when we're there." Gently, she reached out and smoothed back Rat's bangs, and her smile dimmed a little. "We have some things to discuss, Miranda."

Rat fought back a small, internal wince. It hadn't ever felt completely right to say that *Miranda* was a deadname. They'd never specifically told Elise not to use it. They just hadn't been ready for how strange it was to hear it again, or how much they'd stopped thinking of themself that way.

"I know," they said weakly.

"Now, come on." Elise drew back, taking their suitcase. "Our rooms are waiting."

The Attwater Hotel was a short walk from Grand Central Station. Rat had been there a handful of times before. It was close enough to the Council Chambers that whenever a gathering like the Revel happened, the Attwater always became an unofficial meeting place for the old blood families who'd traveled in.

On the outside, the Attwater spoke to a kind of quiet, old-world wealth, with its unassuming gray stone facade. Once, Rat had been told that it was spelled so that anyone who wasn't a part of the magic community would simply feel that they didn't have any business there and move past it. Rat couldn't imagine that kind of trick working almost anywhere else, but New York was full of old grandeur, and the Attwater blended right in.

"I was able to get our usual rooms," Elise said, Rat following close behind her as she led them across the lobby. "I already called ahead to ask the front desk to double up the wards."

Ahead, a set of stone staircases swept up toward the mezzanine, curving along either side of the room, their bannisters wrapped in pine boughs. It was early enough in the day that it was still fairly empty, but Rat knew it wouldn't stay that way.

"A few of our allies are already in," Elise went on. "Some of them have kids in your year who you might know—were those your friends earlier? I thought I saw Will."

"Oh. I—" Rat started, but before they could finish, she raised her hand to someone across the room. Rat looked up to see Evening standing by the stairs, his white-blond hair parted crisply as always, coat neatly pressed.

All of the air went out of Rat's lungs. Their mind flashed to the last time they'd seen him in Galison Hall the morning after the wards had come down, still disheveled from the fight. They didn't care if they'd come out ahead of him. Even if Rat had technically won, it hadn't felt that way.

They wanted to bolt, and they wanted to turn the lobby to rubble just to remind him that they weren't the only one who needed to be afraid.

Elise waved him over. "Edgar! I didn't think I'd see you until tomorrow."

"I was actually on my way out. I got your call and thought I'd see if I could catch you," Evening said.

She eyed his coat. "Official business?"

He gave her a wry smile. "Unofficial. Sometimes I think more of the event takes place at the hotel than it does at the Council Chambers. But how was your trip in?" he asked. Then, almost as if he'd just noticed them, his gaze settled on Rat. He gave them a genial nod, and their magic flared protectively. "Rat. I see you were able to make it after all."

"Oh, you know. It was a last-minute thing," Elise said, resting her hand on their shoulder. "We thought it might be a nice break, with everything that's happened the last few weeks."

"Yes. I was so sorry to hear that boy still hadn't been found. I understand Rat used to know him," Evening said smoothly. "My department has been involved in the investigation, but with how these cases usually go . . . To be honest, knowing the kind of magic he was dabbling with, I'm just relieved he didn't hurt anyone else. I can't imagine what could have happened."

Rat wanted to argue, but their voice had died in their throat.

"Anyway, I need to get back," Evening said, turning back toward Elise. "You should tell me once you're settled, though. Maybe I can have one of the apprentices give Rat a tour of the Council Chambers."

"They'd love that," Elise said, almost like Rat wasn't there.

"Will I see you at the First Arrivals reception?"

"I wouldn't miss it." She shot him a wicked smile, and Rat remembered that when Elise wasn't their mother, she was a wolf.

"Tonight, then," Evening said with a parting nod. "I'll look forward to it."

Rat watched him go as he disappeared out into the street.

Elise touched their arm, and they jumped. "We should get upstairs," she said, then furrowed her brow. "Are you alright? You're shivering."

"Yeah." Rat stole a last glance toward the doors. "Probably just the cold."

Their hand found their compass as they let Elise lead the way up to their room, grounding themself. She started in again on the other families she'd already seen, but Rat let the conversation wash over them, forcing themself to relax.

You're fine, they reminded themself. *You know this place.*

The Attwater was the kind of old hotel where every suite was a bit different. Over the years, Rat had stayed in a couple different rooms, but they knew which one Elise meant before she got the door open, since it had always been their favorite.

The walls were papered in a deep midnight blue, with a marble fireplace and a set of mahogany bookshelves that were always filled with the kind of heavily illustrated coffee-table books Rat could flip through without reading. A bay window was built out of the wall in dark hardwood overlooking the courtyard below, cushions already stacked on the window seat where Elise liked to sit.

The real reason Rat used to love it, though—the reason they'd stopped coming in with Elise even when she offered—was the wrought-iron staircase set in an alcove in the corner, which no one else could see.

The first time Rat had come to the Attwater, their father had taken them up. It led to a small, octagonal turret with shelves full of star charts and illustrated astronomy books, and a row of high arched windows that looked out onto the city below, spelled to make the sky seem impossibly clear in spite of New York's lights. It had taken Rat a long time to figure out that there was another hotel suite directly above theirs, and the turret wasn't supposed to be there.

At one point during their senior year at Highgate, Rat had told Harker about the extra room. They'd always assumed they would eventually figure out a way to bring him along with them. Rat had even had a plan to convince him to let them cover the cost of the trip in exchange for making sure they didn't get lost in a subway station or wander down the wrong alley into a part of New York that didn't exist.

"You're right down the hall," Elise said as she led the way in. "First Arrivals isn't for a few hours, so you'll have a bit of time to get settled."

"Thanks. I'll start unpacking." Rat turned to go, but Elise stopped them again.

"Miranda. Before you do, we should talk."

Their chest tightened. Somehow, they'd been hoping she'd forget. "Is it that serious?"

"I realize this isn't your first time representing our family at an event like this, but things have changed since you started school. I need you to know what we're going to be walking into," Elise said. She lowered her voice, even though they were alone in the hotel room. "I don't think you understand the magnitude of the situation."

Rat opened their mouth to protest, but Elise stopped them with a look.

"I understand that you think Bellamy Arts has everything under control, but a boy is missing—a boy who used you to gain access to our family archives—"

"Harker didn't—" Rat started.

"And you are at the center of a high-profile incident," Elise finished, cutting them off. Their face heated. "I've done what I can to stop the rumors, but the other families have already begun to speculate."

"It's just talk though. Right?" Rat said, hating how hopeful they sounded.

"This isn't like when you weren't casting. It was one thing for people to wonder about your powers when you weren't using them, but you're going to be under a different type of scrutiny now. I'm afraid you need to be ready for that."

"But—"

Elise touched their cheek. "If it was up to me, you would be far away from all of this. For right now, I want you to just follow my lead and let me take care of the other families. Okay? We need to remind them that you've chosen not to cast, and it's best for everyone to let this pass quietly."

"But what if I did?" Rat asked before they could stop themself. "Learn to cast, I mean. If I wanted to take the Higher Magics track, like Dad did? I could be able to protect myself."

Elise's face softened. "You're so much like him. I don't think you realize what you'd be taking on."

"I do." Rat's voice surprised them, but as soon as the words were out, they didn't want to take it back. "Mom. You know that. The Council warded our house because Isola had already found me. That's why I was at Bellamy Arts, and she still reached me—Harker is at the tower, and I know the school told you. Not knowing isn't going to keep me safe."

They expected her to push back, but she just sighed. "The tower isn't the only thing I'm worried about. I don't think you realize what it means to be a Holbrook. The lengths your father had to go to to convince the Northeast that he wasn't his family . . . I don't want that for you."

"But what if—"

"The school told me about your casting lessons. We can talk about continuing with some more basic spellwork if you feel ready for it. I just need you to trust that I want you to be safe." Finally, Elise drew back. "I can order lunch while you start getting set up. I went to pick up some clothes this morning and had them pull some suits and dresses for you. Everything's in your closet already. Just let me know what fits, and I can send back the rest."

Rat's chest sank as they realized the discussion had ended. "Thanks," they said weakly.

They adjusted their grip on their luggage and headed toward the hall. In spite of themself, though, all Rat could think of was the tracking spell, and Isola's instructions to them in the woods, and the creeping suspicion that whatever this was, they were already in much deeper than they'd thought.

CHAPTER SEVEN

RAT CHOSE A SUIT FOR THE RECEPTION FROM THE ONES Elise had left for them. Usually, they hated to let other people pick out their clothes for them, but Elise had found one or two shops that had figured out quickly that when Rat asked for a suit, they actually meant they wanted to look like a boy. After that, the choices always fit perfectly even if most of the clothing was usually more colorful than anything Rat would have picked out for themself.

The one Rat chose for First Arrivals had a jacket in a dark shade of violet over a matching waistcoat. The silk lining was patterned with a flurry of pale moths, and the collar of their shirt closed with a set of simple silver chains. It was the kind of thing Rat thought they actually might have enjoyed wearing, if their wardrobe wasn't made up almost entirely of baggy T-shirts and flannels they'd stolen from Harker.

Rat grabbed the mirror Isola had given them from their sweatshirt and slipped it into the jacket pocket along with their compass before they turned to go.

Elise was waiting for them out in the hall in a gown with long, sheer sleeves, her hair swept up in a simple twist that only served to make her high, aristocratic cheekbones even more dramatic.

"It's just going to be a few of us," she explained as she led Rat back through the hotel. "I have some more formal meetings with our family's allies lined up over the next few days. You can come along with me to some of them so we can start getting people used to seeing you on house business, but right now we're just going to make a few introductions.

I'll handle the houses, and if you start to feel overwhelmed, just say the word, and we can go."

"Right," Rat said, keeping pace with her.

Elise glanced back, and Rat realized how tightly they were holding themself. She gave them a small smile and leaned in conspiratorially. "To tell you the truth, I always think First Arrivals is almost as much fun as the Revel. All of the groundwork for the most interesting dealings is usually laid tonight." Her eyes glinted. "Shall we?"

During the last few months at Bellamy Arts, Rat had forgotten how small being the heir to the Evans family always made them feel, like they were innately *wrong* somehow and needed to apologize to the entire arcane world for existing.

They couldn't do that tonight. They'd already let Evening see that they were scared. If they let the rest of the houses see that, too, this place was going to devour them.

Rat drew themself up, taking Elise's arm. "Right behind you," they said, more sure than they felt.

They'd reached the top of a wide, carpeted staircase, music drifting up from below. Elise smiled at them like they were in on the same secret and led the way down.

The Attwater's lounge suited the rest of the hotel in that it was grand and sweeping and looked like it wouldn't have been out of place at any time between the Gilded Age and now. A handful of guests were already milling about, but the crowd would be small tonight, and Rat suspected there wouldn't be many more people to come.

A couple sets of eyes turned toward them, and Rat drew themself up as they followed Elise down the last few stairs. They were an Evans. They belonged here.

"Elise!"

Rat turned as a woman about Elise's age waved them over.

Elise beamed. "Aurelia!" She turned to Rat. "Miranda. This is Aurelia Van Sandt. Her daughter is in your year."

Aurelia Van Sandt smiled back warmly, which might have been for Elise's benefit. "Camilla just slipped off with a few of her friends. They should all be around here somewhere. Have you met her?"

"I've seen her around. I think we have a couple of the same friends," Rat said politely, since the group of New York kids was small enough that it was almost definitely true.

"I've heard everything that's been happening up at the school. I'm sorry you've had to go through so much." Aurelia gave a sympathetic shake of her head. "That boy should have never been at Bellamy Arts."

"We've been doing our best to move past it," Elise said, saving Rat before they could speak. She drew in, taking Aurelia Van Sandt by the arm, dropping her voice to a conspiratorial whisper. "I was hoping I'd run into you, though. There was actually something else I wanted to talk to you about."

Aurelia's eyes lit with interest. "Was there?"

Elise turned to Rat. "Miranda, why don't you go find some of the other Bellamy Arts kids? I'm sure they'd love to see you."

As soon as Elise wandered off, Rat drifted back to the refreshment table to survey the room.

Over the years, Rat had been to enough parties with Elise that they could identify the heads of most of the major houses, and the guests around them were familiar, at least, even if Rat couldn't remember everyone by name.

A small group of New York kids from their year had gathered on one side of the room, sprawling on a set of couches by one of the fireplaces. Rat didn't see Will yet, but they caught sight of the two St. Augustine girls who'd been part of his Lake Night team last semester, one sprawled out in an armchair, the other with her head in Viola Nguyen's lap. Viola had also been part of the Lake Night team, in addition to being one of the handful of other trans kids at Bellamy Arts. Rat was always caught between vaguely wishing they were friends with her and having no idea what to say besides maybe flailing their arms and shouting that they were also trans, or asking how she felt about forbidden magic and the structurally questionable tunnels beneath the school. Which, was a pretty hard no.

Across from Viola, Camilla Van Sandt had claimed the better part of the loveseat, and Rat realized they did know who she was after all, since she was the girl Agatha had been trying to ask out at the Whisper Ball. That had all been right before the campus was attacked and Harker had gone missing. Rat didn't think Agatha had ever mentioned it again. Probably, like most bad things that happened at Bellamy Arts, it was at least a little bit their fault.

"I'm glad to see you made it," a voice said behind them.

Rat spun back as Evening stepped up beside them. He gave them a room-temperature smile. "We haven't had the chance to speak properly."

"I didn't think we needed to," Rat said, fighting to keep their voice neutral.

"On the contrary. You might have Elise fooled, but I know you wouldn't show up for the Revel without a reason."

"And you're here to offer me another alliance?" they asked flatly.

"A warning," Evening said. His voice came out cold and smooth. "I remember Isola coming to your aid, and I know her help isn't cheap. I can only guess you're here on an errand—unless you were actually foolish enough to come sniffing around the Council Chambers by yourself."

Rat stiffened.

He leaned in, dropping his voice. "You are a rabbit in a den of wolves. The other houses have allowed you to remain in place as the Evans heir because up until now, you've been quiet and harmless. How long do you think it would take that tide to turn if they got the idea that you were a threat?" Evening clasped Rat on the shoulder as he drew back again. He glanced out at the crowd, and Rat realized Will had arrived and started making his way toward them.

"Enjoy the Revel," Evening said coolly. "I hope your choice of alliances works out for you." He gave them a last cold smile and then swept off toward a few of the other heads of houses.

"Hey," Will said, closing the rest of the distance. "What was that about?"

"Nothing," Rat said. "I was just waiting for you to get here. I saw some of the other kids from school. We should see if they know anything."

"They always know something," Will said. "Come on." He took a plate with a piece of cake from the dessert table and passed it to Rat.

"I'm not that hungry."

"Just hold on to it so your hands have something to do. You look like you're going to strangle someone," he said.

Rat took it from him, forcing some of the tension out of their shoulders. "Is there a plan?"

"The plan is that I'm going to ask nicely because they're our friends and they like us."

"They're your friends, Will. They like you."

He raised his eyebrows at Rat. "Okay. First, they do like you. You just don't talk to anyone."

"Second?"

"You wanted my help, so I'm helping. Trust me on this, okay?"

Rat shot a breath through their teeth. They did trust Will. They just didn't trust anyone else in the room.

"I promise, it's fine. Not everything's some kind of scheme," he said. Then he started into the crowd, leaving Rat without any choice but to follow after.

"Hey." Will dropped easily onto a free space on one of the couches, and the rest of the old blood kids shifted around like he was already a part of the group.

"Oh my god, where were you?" Camilla asked at the same time Viola said, "Is Evans really here?"

He gave Rat his most charming *I told you* smile as they edged in beside him. "Last minute change of plans. What did we miss?"

Viola threw a peppermint at him as one of the St. Augustine girls started in, but Rat missed what she said. A prickling eyes-on-their-back feeling crept over them, and they glanced over their shoulder. Behind them, a couple of boys who'd gathered by the fireplace looked away quickly.

"Ugh. Don't worry about those guys," Viola said. "They're visiting from a bunch of the West Coast houses."

"Is it bad?" Will asked.

"The attack at Bellamy Arts is basically all anyone's been talking about. Everyone wants to know what happened," Camilla said with a sigh. "I don't blame them, but you two should probably brace yourselves."

Viola looked back at Rat. "I feel like we've barely seen you. How are you?"

"Fine," Rat managed.

The St. Augustine girl who'd claimed the armchair sat forward. "It's alright. We all know you weren't the one behind it."

"No, I—" Rat started to answer, but as far as everyone else was concerned, if they weren't behind it, Harker was. "It wasn't—"

Before they could finish, Will caught them by the shoulder, and Rat realized that they were gripping their paper plate so hard it had crumpled.

"Hey," he said under his breath. "Breathe."

"But—"

"Is it Blakely?"

Rat opened their mouth, but the girls were still watching, concerned. Will gave a small wave for everyone else to continue without them.

"You didn't hear how everyone was talking about him," Rat said, dropping their voice.

Will leaned in. "Alright. How badly do you want it to stop?"

"Can we do that?"

"How badly?" he repeated.

Rat hesitated. Nearby, Camilla stole a glance at them out of the corner of her eye.

Will clasped Rat on the shoulder, drawing their attention back. "I can get them to understand, but I'm going to have to tell them some things about you and Blakely. You're probably not going to like it, but it'll stop the worst rumors."

They nodded. "Okay. Whatever it is, just do it."

Will turned back to the others and let out a breath. "Alright, guys. Lay off. Blakely didn't do anything either."

The others all sharpened a little, like whatever this was, they hadn't heard it before.

"I basically had to drag it out of them, but Rat was just really close to him, and then their mom basically forbid them from seeing him and tried to get him expelled from Highgate. I'm pretty sure the whole thing about him being in their family archives was just an excuse."

"Wait, really?" Camilla asked.

"Yeah. I didn't want to believe it either, but I was with him when the school got attacked. He was only outside because he was trying to find Rat. He literally can't go forty-five seconds without making up a reason to come to their rescue. I'm, like, eighty percent sure he's just in love with them and bad at it."

"*Will*," Rat hissed.

"What? I really didn't think this was news." He gave them an apologetic look that said *Sorry, I told you you'd hate it*, and heat rushed to Rat's skin. "Okay. Forget I said anything. Evening is just letting Blakely take the blame because he doesn't want to explain how one of the best casters in our year disappeared under his watch."

For a moment, the rest of the kids around them were silent. Finally, Camilla shifted toward them. "Shit. I'm so sorry."

"Honestly, I know my parents like Evening, but he's always given me the worst feeling," Viola said. "Is there any word about Harker?"

"Not really," Rat said, but something in them threatened to give way.

They didn't want sympathy. They barely even knew these kids. Rat hated the fact that as soon as someone was nice to them, they immediately wanted to fall apart.

"It's been tough for them," Will said. "There's actually something we were wondering about, though. We don't know if it's connected, so we're trying not to draw too much attention by asking around, but apparently a couple of families had their archives broken into around the same time everything happened on campus."

"I knew it," Viola said under her breath.

"Vi?" the St. Augustine girl who'd been leaning on her asked, lifting her head.

Viola leaned in, dropping her voice. "I heard the same thing from a few of our allies. Everyone's been really on edge. Apparently it's all people with old ties to the school."

"That's like, half of New York."

"Yeah, but it's weird how it's happening right at the same time as everything at school. Especially with . . ." She trailed off, but her eyes lingered on Rat.

"Yeah," Rat said. "I thought so, too."

"Was anything taken?" Will asked.

"That's the thing. No one's saying," Violet said, meeting their gaze. "The only thing we know for sure is that whatever it is, they've all been keeping it quiet."

9

Rat stayed a little longer before they slipped away from the conversation to get some air.

The Attwater had a small study hidden away, not too far from the lounge. It was far enough from the main rooms that it wasn't the first place most people went to, but still close enough to hear the noise of the party, with a couple of comfortable reading chairs and a row of tall windows that looked out on a rose trellis in the courtyard below.

As soon as they were alone, Rat dropped down in one of the chairs, pulling their feet up onto the cushion so their back was against the armrest. They needed to breathe.

If nothing else, they had confirmation that Isola hadn't sent them to the Council Chambers under completely false pretenses. Even if they didn't trust her about anything else, there was *something* going on.

Their hand went to their compass, but their fingers brushed the mirror instead, tucked neatly beside it.

They'd tried defending Harker before, but when it came from them, it was always colored by the understanding that Rat was frightened and vulnerable and couldn't make their own choices. Maybe the old blood kids would have believed them, or maybe not. But everyone in the hotel lounge knew Will, and his word carried more weight than Rat's. If it got everyone to stop talking, Rat would take it.

Probably, if Harker had been there, he would have scared everyone off and then disappeared with a plate of hors d'oeuvres about an hour ago.

With a pang, Rat slid the mirror from their pocket. There was a whisper of Isola's magic as the image in the glass turned back to the tower.

It was still dusk there, but the sky had deepened closer to true night, and the room from before was gone now. Harker had made his way to another part of the tower, wide and open and filled with aisles of books, a will-o'-wisp of spellfire bobbing after him as he picked his way between the ruined shelves. Weeds sprouted up between the cracks in the stone floor, and in the glint of the firelight, puddles of dark water pooled on the ground.

He had found his way to the tower's library.

Rat leaned in, searching the glass. They didn't want to guess if Isola had allowed him to be there or not, but they knew the look on his face. It was the same too-sharp determination they'd seen before whenever he'd set his sights on something particularly dangerous.

"What are you up to?" Rat said under their breath. They watched as he turned down the next aisle, the light of the spellfire catching on the rows of water-damaged books.

"Evans?" someone said, jarring them back.

Quickly, Rat turned the mirror over and straightened their spine.

A boy Rat was sure they'd seen somewhere had appeared in the doorway, lanky with messy, windswept hair. "Sorry. I wasn't expecting anyone here. You're in my hiding place," he said wryly. "Allister. We met—"

"The library," Rat said remembering. "Right."

"I heard you were going to be at the Revel, but I thought it might be another rumor." He settled against the arm of the chair. "How's it going? Did you ever figure out your mystery spell?"

"Oh. That. It turned out it wasn't Harker's," Rat said.

Allister inclined his head, a question on his face.

"It's a long story. Nothing good." Rat glanced over him again, frowning. "I didn't see you with the rest of the old blood kids."

Allister waved his hand vaguely. "We don't get along. Historically speaking."

They furrowed their brow.

"Oh. Huh," he said under his breath. "You really didn't know."

"Sorry. Did we meet somewhere else? Before yesterday?"

"Not officially," he said. He flashed his teeth. "Allister Church, at your service."

Rat's stomach dropped.

They knew the Church family. Everyone did. The Churches could find the answer to any question for a price. They were known to deal in information. Rat had heard rumors that there were whole rooms of the Church archives filled with ledgers full of secrets that had been bartered from the other houses, and some that they'd come by through less overt means.

But it had been a long time since Rat had heard much about them. They hadn't realized the Churches had an heir close to their own age.

When Rat had met Allister in the library, he'd been almost purposely nondescript. Now, there was something decidedly sharper about him. He had the kind of face that was hard to miss, sharp and angular, with a crooked nose that looked like it must have been broken at least once. Which, Rat wasn't totally convinced he hadn't earned somehow. His jacket was sharply tailored like it had been made to fit him, a dark charcoal a shade off from the shoe-polish black of his hair, and he wore a stark black ace ring on one hand, a white aro ring on the other.

"So you know what we do," Allister said, reading Rat's silence.

"I hadn't realized your family was still around this area. No one mentioned you at Bellamy Arts."

"I'm not actually a student," he said. "I'm just there for an apprenticeship."

Rat's gaze flickered over him. He couldn't be more than a year older than they were, if that. But for the oldest bloodlines, the things they needed most to make their way in arcane society were a network of allies and a family archive, and college was only one way to bolster those.

"Archives," Allister said, by way of explanation. "The school has a habit of losing things, and you could say I have a knack for tracking them down. I usually try not to draw too much attention to myself though. My family isn't exactly popular with the other houses—not that it stops them from doing business with us." He paused. "I hadn't expected to see you here. I was under the impression you didn't go to these things."

"I usually don't," Rat admitted.

Allister glanced at the mirror, still resting on the chair, and Rat realized he'd seen it when he came in.

"I get it," he said. "My family's consulted with the school on a few of the disappearances. I've seen the case files. He's at the tower, isn't he?"

A chill tracked across the back of Rat's neck. "You knew already. When we met."

"I assumed you didn't want to talk about it," he said.

"Most of the things people are saying aren't true."

"I guessed. You're trying to get to him, aren't you?"

Rat eyed him warily.

"Look, Evans. I could be wrong, but I doubt it's a coincidence that you finally decided to stop by the Council Chambers at the same time the Council is investigating a disappearance you were involved in. You're looking into Blakely for one reason or another, and you could say that I'm here looking into a couple of things, too. Maybe we could help each other out."

"Thanks, but I don't think there's a lot you could tell me about the tower that I don't already know."

"I've been told I have a talent for finding things out."

Rat raised their eyebrows.

"You could call it a deal," he said. "I help you get to something you want, and you help me with a couple of questions I haven't been able to answer. Just something to think about." Then he took a pen from his pocket and scribbled down his phone number on a piece of scrap paper. "And Evans. Just between us, I get the feeling this is a good time to keep your cards close to your chest."

With that, he slid down from the arm of the chair and swept toward the door.

Once he was gone, Rat looked back down at his phone number, then folded it over and tucked it into their pocket. *Just to throw it away*, they told themselves. They weren't dragging anyone else into this. Least of all Allister Church, who knew too much as it was.

Movement flickered in the mirror, drawing Rat's gaze. Harker had moved from the library, picking his way up a narrow flight of stairs. Moonlight silvered the steps, and where the high, narrow windows of the stairwell had begun to crumble, the wall gave way to sky. His arm tightened around a book, clutched against his chest.

Rat traced their thumb over the side of the mirror as Harker glanced down at the book he was holding, the lines of his face etched in spellfire and moonlight.

"Hang in there, alright?" they said under their breath.

In the glass, Harker stole a last glance over his shoulder, then pulled the book to his chest and started back up the stairs, the shadows closing around him as he went.

CHAPTER EIGHT

RAT STARTED THE NEXT DAY EARLY SO THEY COULD accompany Elise to the Council Chambers.

The Council Chambers had been carved out of a city block, the Upper East Side's museums and rows of prewar apartments giving way to the broad sweep of the building's grounds, its marble facade pale against the afternoon sky. A row of skeletal cherry blossom trees lined the front path up to a wide set of steps and the sprawling behemoth of the Chambers beyond.

Rat had been there a few times with Elise when they were younger, but it had been years since they'd been back. They had somehow expected that the Council Chambers would seem smaller now, like they'd just built it up in their head, but as they followed her through the double doors, they realized what a mistake that had been.

Beyond the foyer, the building opened into a wide entryway, its marble floors polished to a high shine. The ceilings rose high overhead, and every single part of the room looked like it had been built to be as imposing as possible.

"I'll have you with me for everything else after this," Elise said as she led Rat through the building, past a small cluster of Dawn's Lesser Hours in the lobby, who were still in pale, morning-pink cloaks like they'd just gotten off work. "It's just a few appointments today, but I spoke with the Nguyens, and their daughter would love to show you around."

"Viola?" Rat asked.

Elise gave them her warmest smile. "Will's family was introducing him to some allies this morning, so I thought it might be nice. Her parents mentioned she might have a few friends with her. They all seem like good kids, and it looked like you hit it off with them last night."

"Right. Will introduced us. I think he's close with all of them," Rat managed.

The problem was that it *was* nice. It was entirely lovely of Viola to offer to show them around, especially since Rat had spoken to her exactly one and a half times and never been anything other than rude and weird.

Elise slowed as she came to the end of the hall. Ahead of her, the corridor opened into a wide circular clearing Rat still recognized. A set of four high archways led off in different directions, each one to somewhere deeper in the Council Chambers. The marble floors were inlaid with something that could have been a spell diagram or a map of the stars, and a mezzanine circled overhead.

The last time Rat had been here, Elise had just found out about the tower. Then, her hand hadn't left their shoulders as she'd steered them through the building, like she was afraid they would vanish the moment she let go, and Rat had been too shaken to pay much attention to where they were going.

Rat's gaze settled on an archway, engraved with the waning moon and dagger that made up the archival seal for the office of Evening. Rat thought back to his office the last time they'd seen it, with its dark carpeting and book-lined walls. They'd come to the edge of what was open to the public. Everything beyond this point was strictly off-limits.

Elise looked back at Rat, and concern flickered across her face. "I know the Council Chambers is protected, but I want you to be careful. Stay to the parts of the building you know, and stick with the girls, okay?"

"It's really fine." Their hand went to the strap of their backpack.

Elise touched their cheek, and their chest sank. "If anything happens, I want you to text me. Whatever I'm doing, I'll come find you."

"I'll be careful," they said.

For a moment, Elise looked like she might say something else, but before she could speak, a Lesser Hour appeared in the corridor.

"Elise Evans?"

Elise dropped her hand to Rat's shoulder. "I'll let you know as soon as I'm done," she said. She released them again and followed the Lesser Hour down the corridor, leaving Rat by themself.

They waited for the footsteps to recede before they turned and took in the space around them. The marble seemed to drink in the sound, and this deep in the building, everything was quiet in a way that made them think of cathedrals.

Rat stole a glance over their shoulder, then crossed to the hallway that led to Evening's wing of the Council Chambers. The faint, telltale glow of a ward shimmered in the mouth of the hallway, blocking the way ahead. Cautiously, Rat lifted their fingers to it and met a solid plane, like pressing their fingers against glass, if it was perfectly room temperature and didn't feel like anything. They reached for their magic, searching for a gap they could slip through, the same way they'd gotten past simpler spells when they were at Bellamy Arts.

A jolt pricked up their arm, and Rat yanked their hand back with a yelp.

"Shit," they muttered, working the feeling back into their fingers. The ward had pushed back on them.

They looked back at the corridor and drew themself up, determined.

They were an Evans. They were a Holbrook, and they'd been taught by one of Acanthe's seven Rooks.

Rat traced a spell on the air, reaching for their powers again. "*Open,*" they breathed.

The air split, like parting a curtain, opening into the familiar sprawl of the Council Chamber's lobby.

Rat drew in a breath and traced the spell again. "*Open,*" they said, a little louder. Their next passage opened onto the bright, cold wash of light on the widow's walk of Mallory Hall before they lost hold of the spell and it disappeared.

Frustrated, they peered back down the corridor to Evening's wing. They were used to being bad at magic, but this was different. It was the same feeling they'd gotten trying to find their way back to the tower, like they were trying to draw a card that wasn't in the deck.

Evening must have known there was a protection against wayfinding. Probably, he'd helped set it himself.

Footsteps echoed behind them. Quickly, Rat stepped backward, and before they could think about what they were doing, a dead passage swallowed them up.

They stumbled and caught themself against a rail. Rat peered down, the clearing they'd been standing in just a moment ago sprawled out below them now. They'd ended up on the mezzanine, they realized, their heart still in their mouth.

Rat sank down as they footsteps drew closer.

". . . but as long as one of the Rooks is involved, I'm afraid it falls under my jurisdiction," Evening said smoothly as he came into view.

A woman in a severe black dress swept in after him. She stood almost as tall as he did, and she was old in the way that truly powerful arcanists were, like she'd accumulated enough magic and secrets that Death had decided it was probably safer to just wait things out. Stacks of heavy rings adorned her skeletal fingers, and her fair skin was papery. Her hair, long since leeched of color, was pinned up in an elaborate twist.

"Yes," she said drily. "And while your wing of the building suddenly appears to be closed, no less. I was surprised to be turned away."

Evening gave her an appeasing smile. "I hope you'll understand if I need to act in the interest of discretion."

She dropped her voice. "There's an understanding, Cromwell. Maybe if it was one of my Lesser Hours, but doors aren't closed between us."

"I apologize if it isn't being handled to your liking, but frankly, Theophania, this isn't your case."

Rat leaned into the rail as they realized that they were looking at Theophania Aldridge, Night of the Council of Hours. Rat had seen Night maybe once in their entire life, but she was easily the longest-serving member of the Greater Hours. Rat couldn't even guess the extent of the power she wielded. The one time they'd asked Elise what her office did, they'd been told they should be grateful if they never had a case that warranted her involvement.

Below, Evening's eyes ticked up toward the mezzanine, and for the barest fraction of a second, he paused.

Rat's breath caught.

Evening's gaze lingered a moment too long before he looked back at Night. "You should go on ahead. I just remembered there was something I needed in my office. But please. If you think the others will share your concerns, feel free to tell them the same thing I said to you."

"I might," Night said coldly.

Rat tensed, waiting for something more, but Evening turned back the same way he'd come, vanishing into the hallway.

Below, Night's gaze swept the room. For a moment, Rat could have sworn that she'd noticed them, too, but finally, she took a last, furious glance at the hallway where Evening had disappeared and headed off in the other direction.

As soon as she was gone, Rat sagged against the rails. Their hand went to their compass, the metal warm to the touch, and they realized they were shaking.

"Rat?"

They whipped around to see Dawn at the entrance to the mezzanine, dressed in a pastel blue blazer patterned with winter flowers.

"What are you doing up here?" Dawn asked. "I saw your friends in the lobby and said I'd send you their way if I ran into you."

"Oh," Rat managed. "I got turned around. I must have gone through a passage somewhere."

"I see." Dawn regarded them with a kind of stern amusement, but just as fast, it was gone. "I'll take you back. Actually, it's good that I found you. I was hoping we'd get a chance to talk."

"Is everything okay?" Rat asked, as Dawn led them into a hallway.

"You don't have to pretend you didn't hear that," Dawn said, and Rat realized how long the Greater Hour must have been there before they'd noticed. "I'm not going to say anything."

Rat fought the instinctive urge to duck their head.

"Look," Dawn went on. "I don't know how much you've been made aware of, but things at the Council Chambers have been . . . off."

"Off?" Rat asked.

"I'm telling you this because I'm worried. Something is in motion here, and I don't think it's good." Dawn nodded back toward the way they'd come. "Evening's wing of the Council Chambers has been warded against the rest of the Greater Hours, and the files on Harker's disappearance have been lost twice. I know you aren't going to fill in the details about what really happened last semester, but more than a few of us suspect that it wasn't an accident Evening was able to get to the campus so quickly the night the wards came down."

"And now someone's going after the archives of families with ties to the school," Rat said.

Dawn hesitated as they led Rat around a bend in the hallway, surprised. Not by the information, Rat realized a moment late, but by the fact that they knew.

"I can't confirm or deny details about an open Council investigation," Dawn said finally, but they gave Rat a small nod.

"Why are you telling me this?"

"It's my job to see things brought to light," Dawn said. Then their expression softened a little. They came to a stop, and Rat realized that they'd reached a set of stairs back down to the first floor. "Night and I have been fighting to get him off the case, but I think you should be careful while you're here. Whatever you're doing, I don't think it's safe for you."

"Thanks," Rat said, for all the good it did them. "I'll remember that."

Rat found Viola waiting in the lobby with Camilla and one of the St. Augustine girls in tow.

"Evans!" Camilla called, waving them over.

"We were looking for you," Viola said, linking her arm in theirs. "The Merrins are hosting a lunch I've been trying to get out of since September. How do you feel about seeing all of the reading rooms? Like, all of them?"

In spite of themselves, Rat found themself biting back the edge of a smile. "Is it okay if I stop to sketch a few as we go?"

Viola gave them a wicked grin. "You're officially my favorite," she said, pulling Rat along like they were already a part of the group.

There was something easy about it. Rat had never completely known what to do around the rest of the old blood kids, but a little of the tension went out of them as they let Viola lead the way.

They started at the front of the building and worked their way back from the huge, empty expanse of the ballroom, where the Lesser Hours were still setting up for the coming Revel, to the public reading rooms of the Council Archives.

Even as they walked, though, Rat couldn't stop thinking about what Dawn had told them. Evening wasn't bothering to hide that he was up to something. He was just counting on the fact that no one could take action against him without more proof. Whatever he was up to, either he was confident that he was going to succeed or close enough that it didn't matter who suspected him anymore because he expected to be finished before anyone could stop him.

It was already afternoon when they made it back to a common area near the front of the building, and Camilla's phone chimed. "Will just got in. I said I'd meet him."

Rat moved to follow. "I should also—"

"Wait," Viola said.

Rat turned back to her as the St. Augustine girl slipped past them, following Camilla into the hall. Besides the two of them, the common area was empty. A staircase led down one side, the banister half wrapped in a garland of pine boughs, at least as far as the decorators had gotten. A couple of boxes were stacked by the windows, awash in gray midday light, and aether glinted on the otherwise polished floors, left over from a casting, though Rat couldn't begin to guess what it had been for.

Viola took a breath. "I just wanted to say I'm really sorry about Harker. I know you used to be close. I never really got to talk to him, but I just . . ."

"Thanks," Rat said, but their mind went back to the way Harker had looked in the mirror, ragged at the edges like one of the tower's creatures. "I don't know how yet, but I'm going to bring him back."

Viola smiled at them, but it was softer this time. "Will said something about that."

Before Rat could answer, Camilla appeared in the doorway, Will just behind her.

"Speaking of," Viola said, giving Rat a conspiratorial glance.

"My family just finished up so I thought I'd come find you guys," Will said. "Some of the others are heading out for lunch soon and wanted to know if we could come and join them. Evans?"

Rat hesitated, and without meaning to, their hand went to their pocket. They didn't realize what they were looking for until their fingers brushed their phone.

They'd told themself that they weren't going to use Allister's number, but in spite of themself, they'd put it in their contacts anyway.

"You should all go ahead," Rat said. "I'm going to take a minute."

"You sure?" Will asked.

"Yeah. I need to take care of something. Can I catch up with you later?"

He glanced at the rest of the New York kids.

"We've got you. If anyone asks, you're with us," Viola said.

"I'll text you where we end up," Will said.

He gave Rat a last, searching look, and then nodded to the rest of the group.

"I hope you find him," Viola said, touching Rat's shoulder. Then she followed the others to the doors.

"Yeah," Rat said to the empty room. "I do, too."

CHAPTER NINE

THE CROSS STREETS ALLISTER SENT THEM TURNED OUT TO be the most hole-in-the-wall pizza place Rat had ever seen.

"Should we be speaking here?" Rat asked as he led them inside, out of the cold.

"You really haven't spent any time in New York," Allister said, weaving through the crowded entryway.

Rat opened their mouth to tell him that they lived in New York, but they were pretty sure he knew that.

"Just trust me on this, Evans. No one here cares what we talk about, and you can get pizza for like three dollars," he said. When Rat didn't answer, he motioned for them to follow and started into the shop. "And stop looking at me like that. We're just trading information. This isn't some kind of rivals-to-whatever situation."

Blood rushed to their face. "Yeah. I got that," they said, hurrying after him. "Since when are we rivals?"

"I assume everyone is my rival for simplicity," Allister said. "People tend to get the wrong idea because they find me handsome and aggravating."

"I can't imagine," Rat said, since at least one of those things was incredibly true.

Allister flashed them a wolfish grin. "So. Toppings or no toppings?"

They both ordered and made their way to a booth near the back.

"What exactly are you asking me for?" Rat asked as Allister traced what must have been a silencing spell, his movements so casual that if they hadn't known it was magic, they wouldn't have noticed at all.

"A trade. The rest of the houses can say whatever they want about my family, but we're fair. Information for information. A favor for a favor."

"I haven't had a lot of luck with deals and favors. I'm not even sure this is something you could help with."

"Try me."

Rat hesitated.

"Here's what I think." Allister leaned in, counting on his fingers. "I think it's convenient that the last heir to the Holbrook line has no magic. I think most of the other families already suspected you were a wayfinder but were happy to let it slide so long as you didn't cast. And I think there aren't many places you can't get to, the tower included."

Hearing it out loud sent a pang of unease through them. They didn't like the fact that Allister knew all that, because then for a price, so could anyone else.

"If you could get to Blakely, he wouldn't be wasting away in the dark. Isola must be keeping you out." Allister folded his hands. "What if I could help you get in?"

"Assume that you're right," Rat said slowly. "Why would you do that?"

He held their gaze. "Like I told you, I'm looking into a few things, too."

Rat watched him, wary. They'd already learned the hard way that among the old blood families, help rarely came without strings. For all they knew, Allister was just fishing for more details he could sell.

As if he'd realized he was losing Rat, he let out a deep breath. "Fine. But if I tell you, you can't repeat this to anyone."

"What is it?"

Allister gave them a look.

"Okay. I swear," they said.

He dropped back against the booth. "My mom is sick," he said. "Really sick. The kind magic can't fix. I've been handling most of my family's records and accounting to make it look like things are still running, but everything you think of as the Church family is basically just me right now."

"Oh." Their expression softened. "I'm sorry. I didn't realize."

"That's kind of the point." Allister's mouth quirked into a small, wry smile, but it didn't touch his eyes. "It's fine, Evans. I'm not out for pity."

"No. I don't," they said quickly. "I mean, I get it."

Allister frowned.

"My dad," Rat added quickly.

"Right. I forgot. I guess that's something we have in common." A little of the tension went out of him again. "The other bloodlines can smell weakness, and a lot of them have a vested interest in seeing us fall. I'm not going to pretend my reasons for helping are all that noble, but suffice it to say it wouldn't hurt to have some goodwill from another major house."

"I'm not sure how much I'm going to be able to do for you. I don't have that much power as an Evans."

"Well, I'm not exactly spoiled for choice. I'm willing to take a bet," Allister said. "Something isn't completely right at the Council Chambers, and everyone's been tight-lipped about the break-ins. I don't like not knowing."

"Especially when the other houses want to know, too."

He slicked his hand through his hair. "I've been accused of being enterprising."

Rat raised their eyebrows. "What makes you think I'd know anything?"

"I've seen you asking around. You're not exactly subtle," he said. "So. Here's my offer. You tell me what you know, and I point you to a spell that can get you past Isola's wards and into the tower." Allister paused, steepling his fingers. "Or we finish up here, and when we get back to the hotel, this meeting never happened."

Rat's eyes flickered over him, and he took a bite of pizza, waiting for them. Probably, they were going to end up regretting this somehow.

Rat settled back against the booth. "Everyone's been pretty quiet about it, but if I'm right, whatever's going on started around the same time Bellamy Arts was attacked last semester. No one will say if anything's been taken, but supposedly it's all families with connections to the school."

"You think they're linked."

"Maybe," Rat said. "I don't have proof."

"But you have an idea."

Rat hesitated. They knew who was behind it. They had half the pieces already. It didn't matter, though, because nothing they said would hold water, and Evening knew that.

"Evans?" Allister prompted.

"If you're looking for somewhere to start, Evening has a habit of putting himself in charge of investigations he doesn't want anyone digging into. I don't know what you'll find, but I'd be interested in hearing about it, if you turn anything up."

"I'll take it under advisement," Allister said, half to himself.

He held their gaze a moment longer, in case there was anything else. Then, when Rat didn't speak, he pulled pen out from his jacket and took off the cap with his teeth.

"There's a book of concealment spells that used to belong to my family. You're going to be looking for one in particular," he said, writing something down. "It's a cloaking spell. They aren't popular anymore, but it can get you past most enchantments."

"Who has the book now?"

"You're in luck, Evans." He slid the napkin across the table to them. "It was gifted to the Council Archives a couple of decades ago as a show of good faith."

Something in the way he said *gifted* sounded like he actually meant that it was a bribe.

"If you hear anything else, you know where to find me," he said, getting to his feet.

Rat watched him leave before they picked up the napkin, studying the name of the book he'd written down for them. If it was a bridge too far, Rat reminded themself, they wouldn't have started this.

CHAPTER TEN

WILL WAS WAITING FOR RAT IN THE LOBBY WHEN THEY made it back to the Attwater.

"Upstairs," Rat said, before he could ask. "I might have found something."

"Exciting bad, or just bad?" he asked, following after them.

"Why are you assuming it's bad?"

"Is it good?"

"Probably not," they muttered.

Rat had wanted a way back to the tower for months, but it was still the tower. Whatever Allister had told them, they knew better than to mistake it for something that would be pleasant or easy.

Their suite was empty when they got back. Elise had texted when Rat was on the way over that she was staying out to have dinner with some of the other houses.

"So?" Will asked, dropping back against the arm of the couch.

Rat glanced at the window. Instinctively, their gaze went to the trees in the courtyard below, scanning the high branches for Isola's messengers.

"Not here." They motioned to Will and started toward the stairs that led up to the astronomy turret that wasn't actually there.

"Rat. You know that's a wall, right?"

They held their hand out to him. "Just come with me, okay?"

"Right. Neat," he said half to himself. "This definitely can't go wrong." He took Rat's hand and let them lead him toward the stairs.

"Just remember, you were the one who wanted to be in on this," Rat said, pulling him through.

The veil of dust broke around them, and Rat heard a sharp intake of breath as Will stumbled after them onto the narrow stone staircase.

"So, just to be clear, you have a way back, right?" he asked.

"I haven't gotten trapped yet," Rat said, and then realized that sounded a lot less reassuring than they'd hoped. "Don't worry. I've been through this one before, and it doesn't go that far. Just stay with me and you should be fine."

At the top, the stairs opened into a small room with windows on one set of walls and bookshelves lining the other, the ceiling angled to match the steep pitch of the roof. Night had already begun falling outside, and gray dusk light streamed in through the windows, slanting over the wooden floor.

It reminded Rat a little of the observatory in their house, above the family archives—not in the way it looked, but just in the way that it was always right where Rat expected it to be, like it was built into the hotel. Almost like it had been hidden away just for them to find.

Will turned, taking everything in, and Rat realized this was the first time they'd ever brought him through a dead passage. Really, it was the first time they could think of intentionally taking anyone other than Harker.

For his part, Will didn't look half as nervous as he should have. Instead, he was staring openly, like Rat had just done something incredible.

"This was just here the whole time?" he asked. "Are they all like this?"

"No, definitely not," Rat said as they settled into one of the wing-back chairs in the center of the room and slid their phone from their pocket.

"Do you get signal up here?" Will asked, peering over their shoulder, his whole face lit up with interest.

"Weakly, sometimes. It depends on the passage." Rat swiped across the screen.

Most of the dead passages didn't, but over the years, Rat had learned that some were farther away from their world than others. This one was more like an extension of the building, and even though Rat couldn't say how, the room below didn't feel very far away.

Two bars showed in the corner of their phone's display, and Rat pulled up the group message.

"Jinx and Agatha?" Will asked.

"Yeah. It's probably easiest if we all talk."

Are you both around? they typed. Then, after a moment, *I need your opinion on a spell.*

Will raised his eyebrows. "Since when do you do spells?"

"I'm not the one casting it," Rat said. Before they could elaborate, their phone rang. They swiped across the screen to answer, then realized it was a video call as an image of Jinx in an unfamiliar living room appeared on the screen.

"Hey. What's going on?" she said.

"Is that Rat?" Agatha asked, moving into the frame. She flopped onto the couch, wearing a lace dress that fanned dramatically over the cushions.

"Are you guys alone?" Rat asked. Behind them, Will settled on the arm of the chair and crowded into the shot.

Agatha gestured broadly at the empty room, and Rat realized they were looking at the inside of her house.

"It's just us," Jinx said. "Talk, Evans."

"What if there was a way I could get to the tower?" Rat asked.

For a moment, everyone was quiet, and then Jinx looked at them through the camera. "Get to the tower, like . . ."

"Past the banishment. If we could get Harker back without giving Isola anything."

"Can you do that?" Will asked.

Rat took the napkin Allister had given them from their pocket. "Here. This is the book we need. It's supposed to have a cloaking spell. There's a copy in the Council Archives, if I can get to it," they said. "It's probably past my skill level, but if one of you could cast it, could that work?"

Jinx and Agatha traded glances.

"Jinx?" Rat asked.

She turned back to them, wary. "That's serious magic, Evans. Who gave you that?"

Rat shot a breath through their teeth. "What do you know about Allister Church?"

"You met with *who*?" Will said.

"Fuck," Jinx hissed.

Beside her, Agatha sighed dramatically. "Oh god, of course it's him."

"Wait. Do you know him?" Rat asked. "Like, know him, know him?"

"Unfortunately," Agatha said.

"Better than I'd like," Jinx said. "My granddad was involved in the Council's investigations around the missing students. Once you're dealing with those kinds of secrets, the Church family is hard to avoid."

She glanced over at Agatha like it was her turn to elaborate.

"He's an old friend of the family," Agatha said. "I haven't seen him in a while, but he's rarely up to anything good."

"And you said it's a cloaking spell?" Jinx asked.

Rat straightened. "Yeah. Why? Is that a problem?"

"It's just . . . think of it like a higher-order concealment spell," Jinx said. "You're a natural wayfinder. You've been trying to get back to the tower like a Holbrook. But pretend you're a Church. And instead of spells for opening doors, what you were really good at was sneaking into places without being seen."

Rat furrowed their brow.

"A regular concealment hides you from sight, but magic can still recognize you," Jinx went on. "It's like you have a signature. A cloaking spell covers that, but it's even better for borrowing someone else's. And if you happened to know someone who the tower would remember, who's signature was already close to yours . . ."

"My father," they said, finally understanding, then hesitated. "Why is there an issue?"

"Because we're dealing with Church." Jinx shifted forward, but even as she said it, her eyes were sharp behind her glasses like she was already working through the possibilities. "I've met him. His information is good, but he doesn't do anything for free. If he gave you a spell, it's because there's something in it for him."

"I know. I paid him for it."

Jinx frowned, a question on her face.

"It's fine. Just trust me," Rat said. "He didn't want anything that bad."

"If it wasn't bad, then he isn't done collecting on it," Agatha said.

They raised their eyebrows at her. "I thought you said you were friends with him."

"Yes, which means I know he's a scoundrel," she said. "The Church family doesn't have allies the way the other houses do. They have business arrangements."

Rat looked back at Will for support.

"Why do I feel like we're going to cross this bridge when we get there?" he asked.

"What if we did?" As much as Rat didn't love the idea of owing the Church family a debt of gratitude, the way that things were going, they weren't convinced they were going to survive long enough to pay it back anyway. "If I can get the spell . . . I mean, if there was a chance—"

Jinx's expression softened, and Rat realized a note of desperation had crept into their voice.

"What?" they asked.

"Nothing. We'll get him back," she said. "The sooner we get Blakely out of there, the sooner we can cut ties with Isola and make sure she can't do this to anyone again. We're just going to have to be careful. If we strike against her and miss, I don't think she's going to give us another chance."

CHAPTER ELEVEN

WILL AGREED TO COVER FOR THEM.

"You're sure about this?" he asked Rat when they found him the next day in front of the Council Chambers. "You could come to Bryant Park with us."

"Will . . ."

"I know," he sighed. "Just . . . Be careful, okay?"

"You'll tell Elise I was with you?"

"Ice skating, hot chocolate, back to the Council Chambers to watch them decorate for tomorrow," he said. It was near freezing, but the sun had come out in force, glinting brightly off the morning frost. "Good luck."

Rat watched him go, their breath clouding on the cold air, and then they turned and headed inside by themself. They waited until they'd were almost to the doors to the archive before they drew in their focus and traced the concealment spell Isola had once taught them on the air.

The last time Rat had tried to cast something like this, it had been dark out and raining hard enough that no one would notice if the spell wasn't perfect. Rat half expected it to break apart completely, but the working slipped over them more easily than they remembered, and for a moment, they could almost taste the chill of the tower on the air, too sharp and too close.

With a jolt, Rat let it go again. They pressed a hand to their ribs, breathing hard. The low, coming-storm electricity of Isola's magic prickled over their skin, like a lingering whisper of the power she'd lent them when the wards came down, even though Rat knew that part of their bond with her had closed. Rat shoved the feeling down, the last of the magic they'd called up dispersing on the air.

They could go in without it.

They let themself in the main doors. The front entrance was mercifully deserted, but Rat was less concerned about being spotted at the front desk than the possibility of one of Evening's Lesser Hours catching them lurking in the stacks. Quickly, Rat made their way toward one of the archways that led deeper into the library.

They'd walked through the public section of the Council Archives during their tour of the building, but they hadn't actually stayed long. There was something about libraries that always made them feel particularly lost, maybe because libraries usually combined spellbooks with hard-to-navigate aisles, which were both pretty high on the list of things Rat preferred not to get involved with.

If the Drake at Bellamy Arts was a behemoth of winding aisles and hidden passageways, the Council Archives were bigger, even more labyrinthine, and about as old as the city itself. Beyond the main entrance, there were a handful of reading rooms at the front of the archives with shelves of reference texts and a section of the stacks that were open for public viewing. But that only made up a sliver of the Council's holdings.

The rest of their books were housed deeper in the building, in a sprawling maze of shelves that could only be accessed with special permission. Rat had heard rumors about holdings that even the Lesser Hours weren't privy to, where the Council kept summoning rituals and spells that pulled the stars from their orbit, and books full of the true names of lost gods that were closed to everyone but the four Greater Hours. They'd heard other rumors, still, about the burial vaults underneath that were open only to Night herself.

With any luck, the book that Rat needed would be a lot closer than that.

Rat traced their fingers over the shelves as they walked, the faint scent of aether lingering beneath the ever-present library smell of books and old leather. The lights in the archives never fully went out, but once Rat had left the main rooms, the overheads were dimmed, and a heavy silence settled over the stacks.

Ahead, the row ended, and the room opened into a wide corridor closed off by a set of velvet ropes. The faint telltale glow of a ward glinted on the air, marking the end of the public section of the archives.

Rat drew on their magic, letting the world around them open just a little. They half expected the ward to push back like the one on Evening's wing, but Rat could easily feel the seams and edges where it would give way. Like brushing away a cobweb, they slipped past it into the next room.

Footsteps echoed from somewhere on the other side of the shelves. Quickly, Rat ducked back as Night walked past, a lantern in her hand.

She glanced over her shoulder, and Rat got the same cold, watched feeling they'd had the day before, as if she'd known they were there. Their pulse beating hard, Rat retreated down the aisle in the other direction, further out of sight.

Everyone might have been busy preparing for the Revel, but Rat had forgotten that for Evening and Night, *preparing* meant they probably had spells and rituals to get in order. Tomorrow night marked a turn in the seasons, and she would be presiding just as much as he was. It was lucky Rat hadn't run into Evening instead.

Rat slipped through an archway, heading toward the section where Allister had sent them. The stacks had slowly changed around them as they walked, but there wasn't much mistaking where Rat was once they got close.

There were still shelves of books, but there were others, too, full of heirlooms and trinkets. Rat stopped at something that looked like a spyglass, inlaid with delicate sigils. Beside it, the shelves had been cleared away in favor of a simple glass cabinet, wide enough for a single cloak that looked like it had been spun out of cobwebs and moon shadows.

Rat turned as they caught sight of a row of books, their gaze tracking over the call numbers. Each of the spines had the same archival stamp. All of this, at some point or another, had come from the Church family, given freely or exchanged for services, or from what Allister had said, probably gifted to the Council to encourage the Hours to ignore some of his family's more objectionable business dealings. It would have barely been a dent in the family's holdings, but it might have been the closest Rat had come to the inside of another house's archives.

Probably, the Council had shelves of books and relics from all of the major families in the Northeast. If Rat looked for it, they already knew they would find an Evans room somewhere.

Maybe even a room of Holbrook materials.

Rat traced their finger over the shelves, pushing the thought away. The Holbrook family's archives had been sealed for a reason. They needed to find what Allister had sent them for and get out.

"Somewhere," Rat muttered under their breath. They slowed as they found the correct one and slid it from the shelf. They riffled through the pages, stopping on a spell diagram. Something in their chest deflated. It was magnificently complicated, and Rat had no idea what spell it was.

They didn't know what they'd been expecting. If Harker was there, he would probably laugh, if that was a thing he actually knew how to do.

They shoved the book into their backpack and turned to go, but in spite of themself, Rat stole a glance down the next hall. They probably weren't going to get another chance to come back to the Council Archives.

Least of all if they ended up at the tower.

Before they could think too hard about what they were hoping to find, Rat turned and started deeper into the stacks. They passed a bend in the hallway, and the shelves of books turned to glass cases filled with the bones of creatures that Rat didn't recognize. Then, at the edge of their vision, the glint of aether caught their eye.

Rat turned to see that a dead passage had opened out of the wall, leading away from the rest of the collection. The shelves were higher and narrower, the varnish beginning to wear off the wood. A thin layer of dust had settled over the floors, like even the cleaning spells couldn't fight it back, and the lights of the library seemed to dim a little further.

Rat's hand tightened on their backpack as they slipped through the passage. The room on the other side was older than the part of the library they'd been in, but even if it was hidden away, it was still built like part of the archives. More of the same high, narrow shelves lined the walls, and the scent of magic was even thicker on the air.

Rat reached up for one of the heavy leatherbound books. They slid it from the shelf, tracing their thumb over the archival stamp as they flipped the book open. Even without looking, they knew that it would be the same one they'd seen on their father's books back at their house.

Growing up, there were a few things that Elise would never talk about. Their father. Their powers. Why there wasn't a Holbrook family anymore.

Unable to stop themselves, Rat flipped through the pages and found that it was a book of maps. Rat wasn't even sure what they were looking at, except for the prickling, lightning-about-to-strike certainty that it had been made by someone like them.

They put the book back and scanned the shelves. Rat didn't know how old these books were, but their father could have been here before he'd died. Something here could have been his.

There could be something about the tower.

Rat pulled down another book, this one filled with spells they couldn't read, at least partly because all the text was in Latin. Rat leafed through it, skimming over the diagrams, even though they knew it wouldn't mean anything to them.

"Interesting choice."

Rat jumped. Quickly, they snapped the book shut and spun around to find Theophania Aldridge standing over them.

She gave them a thin-lipped smile. "You know, there aren't many people who are able to find this room. Sometimes I think the rest of the Council has forgotten it's back here. But I've always liked this section of the archives."

"You're—You—" Rat stammered. They held the book out to her. "I'm so sorry. I got lost. I'll put it back."

"Your father was the same way," Night said, taking it from them. She reached up and slid the book back into its place. "When he was your age, I think I caught him in this very room."

"You're a wayfinder," Rat said weakly.

"I like to think I've picked up a talent for it over the years, but I could live to be a thousand, and I suspect Alexander would have still run circles around me." Her eyes glinted as she studied Rat. "I was curious when I'd get to meet you. You've caused something of a stir with the old families. None of them are sure what to make of you."

"It's mostly stories," Rat said, reflexively. "I don't really even cast."

"Of course," she said, and her expression dimmed a little. "All the same, you should get back before you're missed. I suspect there's more than one game afoot in these halls, and not everyone on the Council will be inclined to let you go so easily if you're found here."

It wasn't unkind, but Rat could hear the dismissal in her voice, layered under the familiar note of warning. It was the same gentle way that

Rat had always been asked to step back and allow someone more powerful and competent to handle things.

"Wait," they said as she turned to go. "Evening is up to something. You know, don't you?"

"You may be the heir to the Evans line, but I'm afraid there are some things I can't disclose, even to you."

"But you could tell me as the head of a house," Rat said before they could stop themself.

Night's gaze flickered over them again, like she was searching for something. Vaguely, they realized that their knees were trembling. They had the spellbook, and the smart thing would be to let her walk them out so they could get back to Will.

But instead, Rat drew themself up. "I'm the head of the Holbrook family. I'm eighteen. That means I'm more than just an heir now," they said, sounding braver than they felt. "If one of the Greater Hours went after my allies, that would make the case my concern."

Night was quiet, but in the low light, she seemed to sharpen as she considered them.

"Harker kept Isola and her creatures away from me," Rat went on. "Whatever else he did, he's at the tower in my place because he tried to help me. I owe him a debt, which puts him under my house's protection, and I know that Evening wants him to stay missing. He's mine to defend by right."

Night folded her hands, and Rat realized how they probably looked to her. They still had their coat on over their hoodie, and their hair was messy from running their hands through it, their hand tight on the strap of their backpack like a runaway schoolkid. It probably didn't help that they were still shaking.

Rat squared their shoulders, forcing themself to hold her gaze. They didn't care what they looked like. If the Council wouldn't go after Harker, then they would.

Finally, after a too-long moment, Night motioned for them to follow her. "Walk with me," she said. "Do you know what it is that the offices of Night and Evening are meant to do?"

Rat hesitated as they fell into step beside her. "No?" they said slowly. If they were honest, they didn't really know what any of the Council's offices did, besides that it involved a complicated mix of magic and politics. Somehow, though, that felt inadequate now.

"There's very little magic that's all good or all bad, but some of it is . . . older. Easier to misuse. There are certain kinds of magic that flourish in the shadows that can be dangerous if they aren't approached with the proper respect."

Rat watched her warily, unsure of what she was getting at.

"Our job," she said, choosing her words carefully, "is to be stewards of the dark. We're responsible for knowing the paths through the shadows and learning each of the things that lives there by name, without allowing our own worst natures to overtake us." She gave them a meaningful look. "It isn't a responsibility that all of us are able to bear. Maybe you've already discovered this for yourself, but Edgar Cromwell has always had a talent for getting what he wants, and he's very good at making sure he isn't caught. It would be . . . impolitic, let's say, for me to openly stand in the way of one of my colleagues without the evidence to make a case."

"Oh," Rat managed. "Of course."

But instead of pulling away, Night rested a ring-heavy hand on Rat's shoulder, and her voice softened a little with something that might have been sympathy. "I know the tower well. I served in Evening's role for a number of years before I took over as Night," she said. "You have formidable eemies. I'd like to say you've inherited them, but something tells me you've managed to make them your own."

Rat winced.

"I wish there was more help I could offer you."

Before Rat could respond, Night reached past them, pulling a book from the shelf.

"The Holbrook family gave this one to the collection a long time ago," she said, dusting off the cover. "There was a story that Alexander talked about one of the last times I saw him. About a door with seven locks?"

Rat furrowed their brow.

"Supposedly, it was an old favorite of your school's founder as well," she said, passing it to them. "Perhaps you'll find a use for it."

CHAPTER TWELVE

RAT WAITED UNTIL THEY'D MADE IT BACK TO THEIR ROOM and Elise had turned in for the evening before they took the book Night had given them out again. They settled on their bed, turning it over in their hands. The cover was stamped with gold foil, some of which had rubbed away over the years, and the binding was worn from use.

They didn't know what it was, but right now, it was probably the closest thing to help that Night could offer them. Rat riffled through the pages, past an illustration of a knight in battered armor, then flipped back. An image of Isola took up most of the page, her sword in her hand and a wreath of autumn flowers in the wild snarls of her hair.

Rat's mind went back to the last time they'd seen her in the woods, the cruel weight of promise in her voice when they'd asked her to take them back with her.

Shoving the thought away, Rat flipped ahead again.

They stopped at a woodcut illustration of a set of doors, intricately carved and impossibly high, and all at once, they knew that this was what Night had meant for them to find.

"A door with seven locks," they said under their breath. Their eyes skimmed down the page. It was an old story, and as soon as they began to read, they realized they knew it. Or at least some version of it.

In it, Death was a quiet gatekeeper instead of the vicious cold that Rat had felt in the clock tower, and he kept watch over a door with seven locks to make sure no one could disturb the dead once they'd crossed over for safekeeping.

Goosebumps tracked over Rat's skin as they realized *why* they knew this story—it was the way that most of the old bloodlines built their family crypts.

For a moment, they couldn't think of why out of every book in the Council archives, Night would point them toward this one, but her words played over in the back of their mind. *"It was an old favorite of your school's founder as well."*

They thought of the doors inside the clock tower. If Night was trying to tell them that this was how Ingrid had sealed her collection, Rat suddenly regretted asking. They didn't know why, but something about it made them cold all over. Maybe because magic required intention, and Ingrid had sealed her archives like something that was never meant to be reopened. Maybe just because Isola's heart was still beating anyway, her power festering in the dark like a wound that hadn't healed, and dozens of students had died at her hands in her attempts to get it back.

Rat pushed their hand through their hair, frustrated. Nothing here actually helped them. If Night thought they could make something of this, she'd severely overestimated them.

And then, they stopped.

They hadn't asked Night how to get into the Ingrid Collection. They'd asked her what Evening was up to. If this was the spell Ingrid had used to seal the last set of doors, then it was also their answer.

He was gathering the keys.

Rat shut their eyes, remembering what Isola had told them in the woods. Four break-ins in the last six weeks. All families with old ties to the school.

"Fuck," Rat muttered.

They didn't know how Evening had figured out where to search or what kind of leads he had., but he'd started back in November. Possibly even earlier than that, if he'd been ready to move that quickly. If Rat was right about this, there was no telling how many of the keys to the Ingrid Collection he already had, or how many more he knew how to find.

The only reason Evening hadn't been trying to smash through the protective spells that were keeping him away from the clock tower was because he'd found something better. He might not be able to get any farther without Rat, but they weren't going to get in without the keys. The only difference was that Evening could afford to be patient. Rat didn't have that luxury.

Their gaze went to the window at the dark sprawl of the skyline, but they thought of the hills that surrounded Bellamy Arts. Before Rat could think about what they were doing, they shut the book and grabbed their cloak from the foot of their bed. They hadn't tried to get to Ashwood from here before, but their magic tugged at them, and already, Rat could sense the way ahead. If nothing else, Isola would be able to make something of the keys.

They slid their shoes on, then stopped themself as they grabbed their phone. They could guess what Jinx would say about taking this to Isola. Nothing that she'd said to them on the train about Isola getting her claws in deeper had even been wrong. But Jinx hadn't known that they were sworn to the tower already. There weren't any more promises Isola could extract from them because everything was already hers.

Rat could worry about whatever game she was playing later, but if they left the Revel tomorrow without the keys, they'd lose any chance they had of getting Harker back. Hating the part of themself that already knew what they were going to do, Rat went back to the story about the keys and took a picture.

Found out my dad was looking into this, they typed. *I think I might know what we're looking for.* Rat sent it off to the group. Then, without waiting for a response, they shoved their phone into the pocket of their cloak and raised their hand to cast. A passage opened ahead of them, and Rat stepped through into an empty hallway somewhere else in the hotel.

Voices drifted in from a nearby sitting room, but Rat didn't bother sticking around to listen.

"*Open,*" they said under their breath, their hand working another spell on the air. The next passage opened into a service staircase, and Rat stepped through, their hand already raised to cast again.

The third passage opened into the darkened ruins of Ashwood. A gust of cold air rolled through as Rat stepped in, biting through their cloak. They'd come out in the sprawling great room, the ceiling long since fallen away, leaving it open to the sky. Snow dusted the floors and gathered along the curve of the staircase, and skeleton vines of ivy and wisteria climbed over the walls in a brittle latticework.

When Rat had first found the tower, Isola used to meet them in the ruins, sometimes to test their powers finding lost trinkets and hard-to-reach rooms, or sometimes just to talk and wander the bones of the estate. It had always been a kind of neutral ground, even before they'd learned that once, it had belonged to Ingrid herself. That felt like a lifetime ago now.

A black bird peered down at them through the dark.

Drawing their cloak, Rat paced across the room, the soft crunch of snow under their boots the only sound.

They settled in what had once been a window seat, the glass in the window long gone now.

"I thought you didn't want to see me," Isola said from behind them, voice like clear, cold water.

"I don't," Rat said, without looking up at her.

Isola settled against the wall, her cloak dusted with snow. White flakes clung to the dark snarls of her hair, but if the cold bothered her, she didn't show it.

"It hasn't changed, has it? Half of them think you're a fragile thing that needs to be protected, and the rest see you as a monster."

"What are you really doing?" Rat asked her.

Isola inclined her head.

"Evening is halfway to finding his way in to the Ingrid Collection, and you're treating this like a game. If I didn't know better, I'd think you don't actually want me to find your heart."

"If I was aware you wanted my assistance, I would have offered it," she said, settling beside them. "Allow me to help."

"How would you do that?"

"You haven't managed to find what you're after, have you?"

Rat eyed her warily. "The door to the Ingrid Collection is sealed with seven keys. That's what Evening is looking for," they said. "The problem isn't finding out where he's keeping them—it's getting them back from him."

Isola's gaze sharpened, but not with surprise. She looked expectant.

Frustration lanced through Rat. "You knew."

"I couldn't be sure," she said smoothly.

"Oh my god," Rat said under their breath. "You left me in the dark on purpose."

"Would you have preferred I tell you my suspicions and risk it getting back to Evening? Maybe I didn't want to take a chance sending you off in the wrong direction. I'd hoped you would confirm it for me, and you have."

Rat started to argue, but they knew Isola would have a dozen good reasons she could say to them, and just as many bad ones that she wouldn't. It was their fault if they'd expected anything else from her.

"You're going to tell me what you know from now on," they said, unamused. "That's part of helping me."

"Of course," she said, her eyes bright.

Rat exhaled deeply, their breath hanging in the air. "I don't know how many keys Evening has already, but I'd guess he's keeping them close. His wing of the Council Chambers is warded off."

"That sounds like him. He wouldn't want anything that valuable where it could fall into the wrong hands, and he knows I can't cross the Council's protections uninvited." She paused, but there was something in the way she said it that made Rat's stomach twist. Her eyes traveled over them, considering. "You want a way in."

"The wards aren't the problem," Rat said, choosing their words carefully. "I think I know someone who can find a way through, but even if I could get in, it would have to be during the Revel—"

"When there will be too many eyes on you to slip away unnoticed," Isola finished. She tilted her head, considering. "Unless, of course, someone could help you distract them."

"What would I have to give you in return?"

Her eyes glinted. "A dance."

"A dance," they repeated.

"At the Revel."

"At the Council Chambers," Rat said, understanding. "No. There's no way. I can't even get you in."

"Can't you?" Isola challenged, like they were back in the field of grass with her and it was another one of her games, but a part of them understood what she was really asking. It meant taking her one more place that should have been safe from her and bringing her back into the orbit of everyone else who was close to them.

"Someone will see you," they said.

"It's the second-longest night of the year," she said. "Do you really think I'll be the worst thing to grace their halls?"

"Isola. No," Rat said.

She gave a lazy shrug. "I suppose you have your answer, then."

"I can't just let you through," they said, hating the fact that they were even entertaining this. "It isn't going to be like Bellamy Arts. The wards were already crumbling, and Ashwood was halfway on school property.

You're talking about the Council Chambers. It's under the protection of some of the most powerful arcanists alive."

"It will be different." Isola settled back, like she knew from experience. "Harder, though? I doubt it."

Rat hesitated.

"The Council's wards work by invitation. I can set foot on the grounds as long as I've been summoned."

"You've done this before," they said, understanding.

Her mouth curved. "They usually have safeguards in place, but for you, on a night like the Revel . . ."

"You mean because it's the longest night of the year."

"The *second*-longest," she corrected, but there was something sharp in her voice, as if that was somehow more dangerous. "The Winter Revel is a descent. On the other side of the longest night, there's morning. On the other side of the Revel, there's only an even deeper night." She flashed her teeth, and a chill tracked across Rat's spine. If Isola was dusk and autumn, then the Revel was the last hours before everything tipped over into true night. There was a thread of her own magic woven through all of it.

"The Council's hospitality is its own kind of old magic," she said, drawing in closer. "All that I ask is that you extend me the invitation. I can handle the rest."

"For a dance," they said.

"One dance."

Rat held her gaze, and they told themselves that the tremor in their breath was just the cold. "When all of this this is done, you're going to let Harker go."

Isola gave them a small, cruel smile. "Of course. That was our deal."

"Unharmed."

"You'll have him in whatever state he's left in."

Without meaning to, Rat thought of how they'd seen him in the mirror, bruised and tattered at the edges, shut away in the crumbling halls of the tower.

"Consider it," Isola said. Before Rat could flinch away, she brushed a fleck of snow from their hair. "You know how to find me when you've made up your mind." She drew back and tipped her face toward the sky. The moon had begun to sink, a pale sliver against the deep no-longer-black of the sky.

Then, like she'd caught the scent of the approaching morning, she shoved off, her cloak turning back to feathers the iridescent black of an oil slick. Before she finished standing, she was a bird again, her wings catching the still-crisp air.

CHAPTER THIRTEEN

WHEN RAT FINALLY MADE IT BACK TO THEIR ROOM AT THE Attwater, their sleep was fitful and shallow. In their dreams, they were in the ballroom of the sunken campus, with its weathered floors and high ceilings, except that instead of the dirt pressing in against the windows, the walls crumbled away into grass and autumn weeds and open sky.

Harker was with them, his hand pressed to the small of their back the way it had been the night of the Whisper Ball. He drew in as he led them into the next turn of the dance, but his fingers were cool under his gloves, and Rat couldn't feel his breath. In their dream, Rat knew that even if he was here until the song ended, he was already dead.

"Harker," they said, dropping their voice so Isola wouldn't hear them. "I just need you to wait for me. I can still fix it."

He lifted his fingers to their cheek. "Can you?" he asked. His touch sent a shiver racing across their skin, and he drew in close enough that for a moment, they thought he was going to kiss them.

"You did this, Rat," he said into the crook of their neck, his voice low. "Why would you think you can ever get me back?"

Rat woke up with a start, the last dregs of the dream still fading around them. Breathing hard, they touched their cheek where his hand had been. Their pulse hammered in their throat.

They were in their room at the Attwater, and it was morning. They were alone.

Rat rolled over, pulling a pillow to their chest, but they already knew they weren't going to be able to get back to sleep. They just needed to find him again. Then they could fix this.

In the dark, their gaze settled on their backpack, where the spellbook from the Council Archives was still hidden. For the first time since November, Rat had a way to the tower. If Isola came to help them at the Revel, they knew when she would be away.

Forcing out a breath, Rat grabbed their phone and slid out of bed. The room was still cold, like the heat hadn't kicked on yet, and the sky had just begun to lighten as they gathered their things and headed back up the stairs to the turret.

A layer of frost clung to the windowpanes, morning slowly beginning to break over the park below. Rat settled in the window seat and swiped across their phone, bringing up the group text.

I went back to Ashwood, they typed, and then deleted it.

There might be a way, they started. They backspaced again.

Agatha, last semester Jinx told me you'd gotten into Evening's office before. The wing is sealed, but do you think you still could?

Rat sent that one.

Then *I think I might be able to get us a distraction.*

And *One that gets Evening's eyes off us, and Isola away from the tower.*

Dots appeared at the bottom of the screen almost immediately, and then a message from Jinx.

it's 6 in the morning evans

What if I had a plan? Rat replied.

The dots reappeared at the bottom of the screen as Jinx typed something out, but this time, they stayed there for a long moment before another message appeared.

To take the keys?

Rat looked back outside at the slowly fading sky. Again, they thought of the tower as they'd seen it in the mirror, drafty and crumbling, and the ghost of Harker's touch still lingering on their skin. They had been a step behind everyone from the beginning, and no matter how good, or brave, or careful they tried to be, it had never gotten them anywhere.

They tapped their fingers against the side of the phone.

No, they typed back. *To take everything.*

CHAPTER FOURTEEN

THE REVEL STARTED AT DUSK.

Rat spent the day texting back and forth with the others while they made arrangements for the night ahead, and the rest of the guests slowly arrived at the Attwater.

"You're sure about this?" Will said when Rat showed up at his room, their cloak in their arms, the spellbook they'd stolen from the Council Archives wrapped inside of it.

"We're meeting tonight. If anyone doesn't want to help, I'll figure it out on my own."

"Rat."

They drew themself up. No one had liked the idea of bringing Isola to the Council Chambers. Rat was pretty sure that in the end, Jinx had only agreed to it so she could make sure Isola wasn't left to wander the ballroom unattended, and they knew from the look on Will's face that he'd probably been talking about the plan with Jinx and Agatha on his own.

"I'm going ahead with it either way," Rat said. Even as they said it, though, they knew that wasn't true. There were spells they needed that they couldn't cast on their own, and Agatha was the only one who'd broken into Evening's office before.

All that Will needed to do was say no. But his expression softened, and he took the cloak from them. "I'll make sure this is somewhere you can get to it tonight," he said. "Agatha's setting up a spell to get us all back to her house as soon as the Revel is over. My parents already mentioned to Elise that some of us are having an after-party. As soon as Agatha and Jinx check into the hotel, we're all leaving our luggage in their room so they can make sure it's sent back."

"Oh." As Rat said it, it sunk in that however the night ended, they weren't going to be able to stay at the Attwater. They were about to kick about a dozen different hornets' nests, and by the time the Revel was over, they weren't going to be safe here. "Right. I'll make sure my stuff is there."

When Rat finally went back to their room to get ready, they found a suit laid out on their bed, already waiting for them. A single yellow mum had been laid on their pillow like a calling card. There was no question in Rat's mind about where it had come from.

Rat ran their hand over the fabric of the suit. The jacket was a deep, shifting black, like it had been spun out of shadows, and the shirt was made from silk the color of aged bone. Shoots of mugwort and yarrow had been embroidered over the waistcoat and along the cuffs of the sleeves, lacing over the dark cloth of the jacket in a wild overgrowth.

A dangerous kind of want knifed through Rat, even though they knew what a gift like this meant. They looked at themself in the standing mirror opposite the bed, then back to the suit. It looked like it had been made for an autumn prince, cruel and terrible and touched by the first breath of night. For someone like Isola. Like Harker, when he'd still been in her service.

Carefully, Rat slipped the jacket on over their shirt, testing the fit even though they already knew it would be perfect. All over again, they remembered how many ways the night ahead of them could go wrong. Except, everything had gone wrong already. They were Isola's, and she would always be waiting for them at the end of this. Rat had known there wouldn't be any turning back the moment they went to find her at Ashwood last semester, and they knew it now.

They set the suit jacket back down on the bed and crossed to the window, settling against the wide ledge. Rat undid the latch, letting in the cold night air. Their eyes swept the empty grounds below. Then they turned their face up and whistled the notes Isola had taught them once, high and airy against the low hum of the city.

A black bird fluttered down in the high branches of a tree, its eyes glinting like beads of polished glass.

"Please tell Isola that I received her gift," Rat said, their voice crisp and cold in a way they almost didn't recognize. "I would be honored to have her as my guest at tonight's Revel."

They bird blinked at them, watchful. Then, dark wings beating against the deepening sky, it took off again.

Elise was waiting in the lobby to walk over with them. A small group of other guests had clustered around her, but she excused herself before Rat could reach her.

"There you are." She paused as her gaze flickered over them, taking them in. Frowning, she touched the collar of their jacket beneath their coat. "Did I get this for you?"

"I . . . no. I picked it out," Rat said. "I went with some friends while I was at school."

Elise's hand lingered on their shoulder, like she could sense the way the traces of the tower clung to them, but she'd relaxed a little at the mention of Rat's friends. "Of course. You'll have to introduce me to them later," she said with a small smile. Then she nodded toward the doors. "Shall we?"

The cold hit Rat as soon as they made it outside, cutting through their layers, but it wasn't a long walk, and arcanists milled along the sidewalks in packs, unnoticed in the holiday foot traffic.

Fresh snow covered the steps to the Council Chambers, and the bare branches of the cherry trees that lined the front walk had been spelled with lights, like they were full of fallen stars.

Noise drifted out like the party was already underway. Rat pushed down a wave of anxiety, letting the cold air steady them as they ran back through the night ahead.

The keys. The tower. Harker.

"Everything alright?" Elise asked.

"Yeah. Just a little overwhelmed, I guess," Rat said, which didn't sound nearly as steady as they'd hoped.

Elise gave their shoulder a reassuring squeeze. "Chin up. You're an Evans."

Drawing themself up, Rat let her lead them through the doors.

Inside, the lobby was crowded and alive with the low hum of conversation. Candles hovered on the air overhead, and orchestral music floated from somewhere farther inside, too low for Rat to make out the song.

A handful of guests turned to steal glances at Rat as they followed Elise toward the ballroom, but there was a subtle, almost electrical current in the air that Rat knew had nothing to do with them. They thought of what Isola had said, about the night being a descent.

The Revel was a night for secrets. It was the kind of event where the heads of the oldest families gathered to trade in whispers and broker deals that wouldn't be spoken of again in the morning, and it had a magic all its own.

"Miranda." Elise caught them by the arm before they could get ahead of her and pulled them to the side.

They turned back to her.

"Just . . . I know I said to be careful, but it's okay to have a bit of fun. I don't want you to worry about the other families too much. You should enjoy the party."

"Mom—"

"I know you've already learned the hard way that not everyone has your best interests at heart. You've had to be cautious for so long, and I realize how difficult that is."

A moment too late, Rat realized she meant Harker. But before they could say anything, she touched their cheek.

"I just don't want you to feel like you have to close yourself off to everyone. I know we don't always see eye to eye, and maybe I've been too protective, but I do want you to make friends, Miranda," she said. "I just want them to be the right ones. The kind who will see you for who you are and not what you can do for them."

"I—yeah. I want that, too," Rat said, but their voice came out flat and burnt.

For a moment, Elise looked like she was going to say something more, and then she caught sight of someone over Rat's shoulder. Rat turned to see Evening heading toward them dressed in a neatly tailored suit, his white-blond hair swept crisply to the side.

"It'll be a good night. I promise," Elise said. She clasped Rat's shoulder again, and they fought the urge to bolt.

"Elise," Evening said, closing the last few feet. "How are you finding everything?"

"You've outdone yourself." She gave him a conspiratorial smile. "We were just about to go in, but I'm sure you'll have your hands full tonight."

"I'm sure." His gaze slid over Rat, and then his eyes lit up in a way they distinctly didn't like as he noticed someone just past them. "Actually, this is perfect timing. I don't think I've had a chance to introduce you to my new apprentice." He nodded to someone, and Rat turned as Allister came up behind them, dressed in a charcoal suit. "Allister Church. This is Rat Evans."

For a fraction of a second, Allister looked surprised. Then, just as quickly, he recovered and dipped into a shallow bow.

"We've met," he said smoothly. "Evans. Always a pleasure."

Rat gaped at him.

Evening gave them a smug look. "I'll leave you both to it," he said. "Perhaps Allister can show you around."

"If you need anything, just find me," Elise said. She squeezed Rat's shoulder and started toward the main ballroom ahead.

Blood pounded in Rat's ears. "The tracking spell," they said to Allister. "That was you."

He smirked. "Finally. Do you want a round of applause?"

"You said you worked in the library," they said under their breath.

"With the investigation," Allister said. "For what it's worth, the school did ask me to get your books back to you."

Slowly, the pieces came together. "You knew the whole time. You offered to help me so I would tell you what I knew about the break-ins—you never actually planned for me to find the spellbook."

"That spell is useless to you," he said. "The moment Isola finds out you set foot at the tower, what do you think she's going to do to that kid?"

Rat felt like they were sinking.

"I've seen the case files. There's a reason the school never sends rescue missions." Allister clasped their shoulder. "Always a pleasure doing business, Evans. I'd say we should do this again sometime, but I actually think we're done here."

Rat stared after him as he slipped back into the crowd.

Allister had been hoping Rat would exhaust themself trying to get into the Council Archives when they could have been investigating. If Rat actually found the cloaking spell, they still wouldn't have the skill to cast. Even if they found someone who did, Allister had given them the spell knowing full well that the moment they broke Isola's banishment around the tower, she would be waiting on the other side to tear Harker into pieces.

"Rat. There you are."

Rat spun as Agatha caught them by the arm, following their gaze toward where Allister had disappeared through the doors of the ballroom.

She propped her chin on Rat's shoulder. "Oh good. It looks like things just got interesting."

Rat jumped. "You're—"

"We just arrived. Jinx already went to look for a spot upstairs, but I had a feeling I'd find you here." Her eyes tracked across the room in the direction Allister had gone. "I see that we're going to be dealing with a certain perpetual thorn in my side."

"Seems like it," Rat muttered.

"Shall we?" she asked, slipping her arm through theirs. "Before Church decides to make himself our problem."

"Might be too late for that," Rat said, starting after her. "Did you know your uncle has an apprentice?"

She shot a breath through her teeth. "God. Of course he does. How much did you tell Allister?"

"He doesn't know what we're doing."

She looked back at them.

"Evening already told him about the tower, and I told him I was looking into the break-ins," Rat said. "I didn't tell him we were planning anything."

"You didn't need to," Agatha said. "He'll be watching you like a hawk."

She led them through the open set of doors, into the ballroom beyond.

More candles drifted along the edges of the room, the faint scent of balsam and wood smoke hanging on the air, and garlands of pine and winter berries draped the balcony of the mezzanine above. Even though it was still early in the night, there was already a large crowd of people milling about the dance floor.

Rat looked over their shoulder in time to catch sight of Allister again as he went to join a few of the other Council apprentices. He nodded to them, and Agatha waved with her fingers.

"Should I tell you how he dies?" she asked Rat.

"Let's just find everyone," Rat said. They followed her as she wove through the crush of people gathered around the edges of the dance floor, toward a staircase that led up to the mezzanine above. Agatha motioned to someone in the crowd, and Rat spotted Will standing by the dessert table with a couple of the other New York kids.

It took Rat a moment to realize that Jinx was there, too, maybe because they were so unused to seeing her with the rest of the old blood kids. She'd chosen a dress made from green velvet, and she'd let her curls tumble loose down her back. Her leather jacket draped over her shoulders, and she had her full attention on Viola Nguyen, who was giggling at something she'd said.

"She's allowed to flirt," Agatha said, and Rat realized they'd clenched their jaw.

"I know," Rat said, dropping their voice.

"You're staring at her like a jealous ex. Before you start something, do you want her, or do you just want to keep her from moving on because you're still hung up on someone who isn't here?"

"I'm not—"

"You and Blakley have been chasing each since you got to Bellamy Arts," she said. "You're literally the only person on the East Coast who isn't aware that you've been dating him since high school."

Heat crept up Rat's neck. "It wasn't like that."

"Please, enlighten me, then. What was it like?" Agatha lifted her eyebrows, and blood rushed to Rat's face. "Absolutely hopeless," she said with an airy sigh.

Before Rat could protest, she slipped past them and wove her way to Jinx. Agatha leaned in and whispered something to her, and a shadow passed over Jinx's expression. She motioned to Will, and a moment later, she was on her feet, whispering to him in turn.

Rat settled against the rails of the staircase, steadying themself. Outside the windows, the sky had darkened into night, and the snow had picked up again, flurrying down in drifts.

Isola hadn't told them how she was going to arrive yet, but as soon as she got there, everything was going to be in motion, and there wasn't going to be any turning back. But they'd come this far already, and they wouldn't have another chance.

Jinx settled against the rails beside them, but before she could say anything, the music stopped as the clock struck the hour, and a hush swept over the crowd.

At the front of the room, Evening appeared at the top of the stairs in a crisply pressed suit a shade off from midnight. Rat caught sight of Night behind him in a long black gown, frowning like she hadn't chosen to be there.

"I'd like to take a moment to welcome everyone before we begin," Evening said smoothly. His gaze swept the room before landing on Rat.

Unbidden, they thought of Harker kneeling in the clock tower, coughing onto the stone floor, his clothes still soaked through from the rain. The scent of magic and stale air stuck in their memory, and for a moment they could taste it. Rat shoved the thought back down. *Harker is alive*, they told themself. They'd still come out of it, and they were going to find him again.

On the landing, Evening raised his glass, and Rat realized they'd missed his speech. A round of polite applause rose up around the ballroom. Tonight was his domain as much as it was Isola's. It wasn't a comforting thought.

The music began again as he stepped back from the top of the stairs, but Rat still felt hot and cold all over. Beside them, Jinx nudged their shoulder, jarring them back. She held out her hand and nodded to the floor below. "You still owe me a dance from the Whisper Ball."

Rat laid their hand across hers and followed her out toward the floor. "Who's leading?" they asked.

"What's easier for you?" Jinx replied, pulling them into position as she found a place.

"I can." Rat shot her a shaky attempt at a grin. "Less spinning."

"I feel like you're fundamentally missing the point, Evans," Jinx said, resting her hand on their shoulder.

Before they could answer, she nudged them forward into the first turn.

"Cromwell said we have a spy," she said, following Rat's steps.

"It doesn't change anything," they said.

"Evans—"

"You don't have to stay if you don't want to, but I'm finishing this."

"Isola already has her claws in Blakely," Jinx said. "I'm not going to stand back and watch her pull you in, too."

A feeling Rat didn't want to think about tightened around their ribs, but they pushed it down. Once they had Harker back, all that Isola had on them was their own bargain. Somehow, maybe, they would find a way to break that, too.

Jinx leaned in slightly, letting them lead her through the next turn of the dance. "I'll make sure she doesn't leave the ballroom. Just watch out for yourself, and meet us upstairs as soon as you're done. There's a common room right off the back staircase where we can set up the spell to get us all out."

"Be careful," Rat said.

"Yeah. The same goes for you," Jinx said. "If Isola gets ahold of you, she's not going to let go this time."

Rat released her hand, and Jinx spun in time to the music, her dress flaring out around her before she let Rat catch her again.

Jinx looked up, meeting their gaze. "Whatever he did, he's still ours. We'll get him back."

Rat's chest tightened. Then, before they could say anything, something shifted in the air, subtle but unmistakable, and they knew that Isola had arrived.

CHAPTER FIFTEEN

A CHILL SLITHERED UP RAT'S SPINE AS THEY CAUGHT THE faint hint of magic on the air, something older and wilder than the enchantments on the ballroom, tinged with the ever-present hint of mugwort and night air.

The music had come to a stop, and an unnatural quiet settled over the ballroom.

Rat looked up to see Isola standing at the top of the staircase.

She'd traded her armor for a dress that shifted like shadows around her, and her cloak for a mantle of raven feathers. Her dark hair hung down her back in loose, snarled curls, woven with the last autumn flowers.

The shadows seemed to deepen around her as she started down the stairs, and all of the candles flickered like they'd been caught by a cold wind. Her footsteps echoed through the ballroom when she stepped out onto the marble floor, and the crowd edged away from her, as if by instinct. She stopped as she came to Rat, and they could feel the weight of the room's gaze settle on them.

"I believe," Isola said, her voice almost too low to be heard, "we had a deal." She flashed her teeth, and for a moment, there was something about her that wasn't entirely human.

She held her hand out.

Rat took it. "One dance. And you'll leave at the end of the night."

"I won't stay a moment past the end of the Revel," she agreed smoothly, drawing them in.

With a shrill whine, the violins began again, picking up a new song.

Rat opened their mouth to speak, but Isola stopped them with a sly look as she led them into the first steps.

"I can't help you if I'm not here," she said, leaning in. "You invited me."

"You won't come back. As soon as you leave, we're done here."

"I don't think you're in a position to extract promises from me."

They looked up at her, forcing themself to hold her gaze.

"On my word," she said. "I doubt I would be able to return if I tried."

Rat caught a low murmur as Isola drew them into the next turn, sweeping close to the edge of the crowd.

"You're enjoying this," they said under their breath.

Her mouth curved. "Aren't you?"

Rat's jaw tightened.

Isola pulled them closer, speaking low enough that only they could hear. "You were never meant for this place. Tell me that you aren't the least bit satisfied, that everyone might finally have to see you for what you are. We both know your talents are lost here."

"Then why haven't you taken me back with you yet?"

"Maybe I haven't finished with you. Maybe," she said, her breath cool against their skin. "I'm waiting for you to come willingly."

"That hasn't stopped you before."

A terrible amusement played over Isola's lips.

"You promised me a distraction," Rat said, stepping back.

"Didn't I." Isola's eyes were cold and bright in the warm glow of the ballroom. "What did I tell you about tonight?"

"It's the second-longest night," Rat said, but in their head, they heard the whisper of her voice in the ruins of Ashwood again.

It's a descent.

"The Revel is the last minutes of dusk before the deepest part of the night," she said, keeping her voice low. "Illusions are always at their most powerful when the shadows are longest."

Rat fought a shiver.

"Do you remember the concealment spell I taught you?" she asked.

"If I do?"

"When I tell you to, I want you to cast it." Her eyes flickered around the room, surveying the crowd. "You'll do everything in your power to keep it up until you've left, no matter what you see. I can keep the illusion up until you've gone, but if you let the spell slip, I won't be able to take arms to defend you as long as I'm here as a guest."

As she spoke, her hand moved at their side, working a spell on the air, and they felt the faint hint of magic, like a drop in the air pressure around them.

Before they could ask what she was doing, the music rose, picking up speed. "Now," she hissed.

Isola turned them away from her, and they cast, forming the spell from muscle memory. The concealment spell slipped over them like sliding into cool water as Isola released them.

Rat spun back, bracing themself, but the dance had continued without them.

Isola had moved into the next position as if nothing had changed. Another Rat Evans had taken their place, hand still clasped in hers, their blond hair swept roughly back, every inch the strange autumn prince Rat had seen in the mirror.

The other Rat seemed to fade at the edges slightly as Isola moved them past the candles, like a shadow given form, but then they were real and solid again.

The concealment spell wavered, and with a jolt, Rat realized they'd let their focus slip. They caught themself, willing it into place as they turned hard on their heel and started toward the doors.

Rat bit back a swear as they slipped into the crush of bodies. They didn't know what kind of spell Isola had used, but they didn't think it would last long after the song had ended, and they needed to be gone before anyone realized they weren't there.

They stole a last glance over their shoulder and caught sight of Allister in the crowd, staring at the dance floor where Rat had been, his gaze sharp. Then, without waiting to see what he would do, Rat turned back toward the doors and slipped out.

CHAPTER SIXTEEN

RAT MADE IT DOWN THE HALL AND AROUND THE NEXT bend before they allowed the concealment spell to drop, their heart still in their mouth.

Agatha was already waiting for them when they got there.

"We need to go," Rat said in a rush. The noise of the ballroom had faded, the drone of the orchestra spooling out behind them. "It's Church. I think—I don't think we have that long." They didn't know how much Allister had seen, but he'd seen something. They were sure of it.

"God, of course it's him," Agatha breathed and grabbed Rat by the wrist. "Come on."

Rat stole a last glance back in the direction of the ballroom before they took off after Agatha. She broke into a run, pulling them along as she made it around the next turn. Ahead of them, the hallway ended in a set of velvet ropes, the faint shimmer of a ward just visible beyond.

"I can—" Rat started, but Agatha raised her hand, tracing out a counterspell like it was second nature to her. The ward shimmered and dissolved.

Rat stared at her. "You can cast."

"Honestly, Evans," she said, shoving past them. "How are you just figuring this out?"

They hurried after her. "But you're on bookwork."

"And? So are you."

"But—"

"I don't cast in *class*," she said like it should have been obvious.

"I know, but—" they started, and then realized they had absolutely nothing. Of course Agatha could cast. She'd earned her place at Bellamy

Arts against her family's wishes, and she'd been on track to become an apprentice for the Council of Hours before she was out of high school. She'd been the first one to identify the anchor spells last semester, and she'd been taking private lessons since the year had started.

She was probably terrifyingly good at it.

They raced after her, following her down the wide marble corridor. The lights had been left low, and the building was empty around them as they got farther away from the ballroom.

Agatha tugged Rat's hand, pulling them toward the next turn.

"Wait. Evening's wing is—"

"I know where Evening's wing is," Agatha said. "Do you want to get there or not?"

Before Rat could argue with her, she stopped at a section of wooden paneling, her hand raised to cast. Deftly, she traced a sigil on the wall, and a seam appeared. Rat braced themself for the familiar tug of a wayfinding spell, but it didn't come. However sealed off and well hidden the doorway had been, Agatha was just revealing what had been there all along.

"For when the Hours need to get around the building quickly," she said. She pushed, and the wall hinged inward, revealing a narrow corridor.

Sconces lined the walls, throwing warm light over the passage, and the floor was free of dust, even though there was something stagnant in the air, like no one had been there in a long time.

"They're hardly ever used anymore," Agatha said, pulling the panel shut behind herself. "I'm not sure if most of the Council realizes they're still here."

She slipped ahead of Rat, leading them into the hidden passageway like she'd been this way before.

"Did you and Jinx find them?"

"I knew a few. Once Jinx found out, she wanted to track down the rest," Agatha said. "I'm still not sure we have them all, but it helps having a sense for magic." She glanced back at Rat. "If we get out of here, you're welcome to find the others."

"This is how you got into his office the last time," Rat said, understanding.

"Not bad, Evans. A little faster, and you might even start keeping up."

They opened their mouth, but before they could protest, the passage ended ahead of them in another door, easier to see now that they were on the inside. Agatha pushed it open, and they emerged into a wide hallway. The floors were inlaid with dark marble, and overhead the ceiling was painted with the night's first stars.

Agatha led them to a set of heavy wooden doors. Carefully, she traced another spell on the air, then pushed.

The lock rattled and stuck.

"Your turn," she said, motioning to them.

Rat turned the doorknob and shoved their shoulder against the polished wood, expecting resistance from another spell, but the doors swung inward. They spilled through into an office. It still looked the way Rat remembered from years ago, with its dark, hardwood furniture that reminded them of a private study. Something that might have been celestial charts or intricate spell diagrams hung on the walls, and the room smelled of dusk and magic. A narrow balcony circled above them, the upper layer lined with shelves of reference books leading up to a high glass ceiling that looked out onto the night sky.

They hated how comfortably familiar it was.

Rat turned as Agatha slipped in behind them and pushed the door shut. Quickly, she produced a piece of chalk from the pocket of her dress and etched a hasty sigil on the back of the door.

"What are you—"

Before they could finish, she raised her hand to cast, and Rat felt something shiver deep in the warp and weft of the world as the spell took hold.

"It's a suspension," Agatha said. She drew another spell on the air, and the chalk markings vanished from sight. "It'll keep time from passing at the Revel, but even with a sigil, I can only buy us a couple of minutes like this, and most of the more powerful arcanists are going to notice the disturbance."

Without waiting for an answer, she shouldered past Rat, making her way toward the desk. She dropped down and ran her finger over the top drawer, tracing the shape of a sigil on the antique wood.

Then she winced.

Rat dropped next to her. "Agatha?"

"It's fine," she said, pinching the bridge of her nose. The air around her was thick with power, and Rat realized they'd never seen her try to channel this much magic at once. As powerful as she was, Agatha had to be close to her limit.

All over, Rat remembered what Jinx had told them last fall when she'd first taken them into the tunnels, about how Agatha's abilities could be overwhelmed. They'd seen what happened when Harker pushed too far and lost control of a spell, but the worst he could do was set himself on fire. In her magic's rawest form, Agatha was a seer. Rat wasn't sure what it would look like if her magic bled over, but they weren't eager to find out.

She looked down at the drawer and shut it again before reaching for the next one.

"Here. I've got it," Rat said, reaching over to pull out the next drawer.

"I said it's fine," she said, tracing the next opening spell.

"Agatha—"

"You don't know my family. However bad you think my uncle is, he's worse than that. Okay? The Cromwell family doesn't actually have any kind of affinity. The only thing they care about is power. Their archives are a mix of the worst magic you can imagine. Do you have any idea what Evening would do with the Ingrid Collection?" She pulled the drawer open and rubbed her eyes. "God, of course he anchored everything so I can't just see where the keys are," she said, half to herself.

She skimmed the contents of the drawer and pushed it shut. "Just focus on your side. The faster we do this, the better."

Quiet settled over the office as they searched. Rat stole another glance at her. For a moment, they'd forgotten what she was really capable of.

"Do you know already?" they asked. "What happens?"

"Good question, Evans. Someone should get you a Magic 8 Ball." She turned back to the drawer in front of her.

"Please," they said quickly. "I just—If there's a chance—"

"I don't know," she admitted. "It never happens this way." She pulled open another drawer and raked her fingers through the neat assortment of fountain pens, spare packages of casting chalk, and official stationary.

"This way, like . . ."

"Everything at Bellamy Arts is murky, but I have bits and pieces of it, even when I can't always put them together," she said. "I don't think there was ever a path through this where Harker made it out of the clock tower. Even as a prisoner. I think . . . I think it always ended there."

With a chill, Rat remembered the cold brush of the deathworking.

Agatha pushed the drawer shut with a huff.

"I've been scrying for him," she said without looking at them. She hunched forward as she started on the next drawer, her shoulders drawn up. For the first time, Rat realized how tired she looked. "I went back home for a few days in November so I could go through my family's archives to look for a stronger spell. Nothing works."

"Oh." Suddenly, Rat felt small. "I didn't realize."

"Well, you're not the only one who lost a friend."

Rat sank back. They hadn't actually spoken to her about what had happened last semester. After the dust had settled, Agatha had thrown herself back into searching for the Ingrid Collection, and she hadn't brought up any of it again—not Harker's disappearance, or the limits of Rat's truce with her, what exactly it meant for her that Evening had effectively laid claim to the campus.

Rat reached for a drawer on their side of the desk, the protection spells unraveling around them. They slid it open, revealing a set of files. Rat ran their thumb over them, scanning for anything important. "For what it's worth, I'm sorry about last semester. Everything, I mean. I really didn't plan for things to turn out this way."

Agatha sighed. "I know. Frankly, I don't really think you're capable of planning anything, Rat."

They looked back at her, unsure whether they should be offended, and she offered them a small, tired attempt at a smile.

"That's not—" Rat broke off as they caught sight of a glint of metal.

Beside a stack of letters and a small box inlaid with spellwork was a set of three keys on a plain steel ring. The keys were simply made, but there was the unmistakable tinge of magic about them, and Rat knew from the way they seemed to darken slightly in the light that they must have been made from arcanist's silver.

There was a sharp rap on the window, and Rat jolted.

A black bird perched outside on the ledge, nearly invisible in the dark. Again it tapped against the glass like a warning.

"We have to go," Rat breathed. They grabbed Agatha by the arm. "Like, now. Right now."

They weren't sure when it had happened, but at some point, Agatha's spell had broken, and the ambient hum of the city had crept back in. Out in the hallway, Rat caught the sound of approaching voices.

Agatha grabbed the ring of keys, and then before Rat registered what she was doing, she swept the spelled box and a handful of letters from the drawer and shoved them into her clutch. Quickly, she shot toward the stairs to the balcony, her fingers flying through a concealment spell.

Rat raced up the stairs after her, nearly tripping on the last step. They caught Agatha by the sleeve of her dress as the spell took hold, and the shadows folded over them.

Below, the door opened, and Evening stormed in, Allister close on his heels.

"They could be anywhere by now," Evening said.

Allister hurried after him as he crossed the office, looking like he'd run most of the way there. "You told me to keep an eye out. I kept an eye out."

"I gave you a job, Church." Evening spun on him, and his voice came out cold and sharp. He waved his hand, and the door slammed shut. Allister suppressed a flinch. "The only thing that you had to do tonight was keep track of one student."

"I've seen their file," Allister argued. "You know they aren't just—"

"I don't think I need to remind you how precarious your situation is. I very charitably agreed to give you a position because my support is the only thing stopping your entire house from folding."

He looked at Evening with open resentment. "You gave me a position because we had one of the keys you wanted."

"*Had*," Evening said crisply. "If you plan to be employed in the morning, I suggest you find Evans, and quickly."

Allister's jaw tightened. "Of course." His gaze tracked across the carpet as Evening turned back to the desk, the high pile still turned slightly where Rat had been kneeling. Discreetly, he cast a glance around the room, surveying the office.

Steadying themself, Rat drew up a tendril of power, and the wall behind them opened into a narrow corridor somewhere else in the building.

Allister stilled, and just for a moment, Rat could have sworn that his eyes trailed up to the place where they were standing. Then Rat took Agatha by the sleeve and pulled her through, letting the way close behind them.

CHAPTER SEVENTEEN

THE PASSAGEWAY LET OUT IN A QUIET STRETCH OF hallway.

Rat looked around, getting their bearings as they recognized the white marble floors and the long, window-lined corridor ahead of them. They were back in the public part of the building near the archives.

They were still too far from the Revel to pick out the sounds of the party, and everything was suddenly eerily quiet around them.

"Come on," Agatha said, tugging their arm. "It isn't going to take Allister that long to find us."

"Right." Rat pictured their map of the building, but Agatha had already taken them by the sleeve, pulling them down the hall toward the next meeting place. They followed her around the corner to the doors of the archives, where Will stood leaning against the wall, Rat's cloak draped over his arm, the intricate lines of a sigil chalked over the deep blue fabric.

"Rat!" He shoved away from the wall and shot toward them. "What happened? Are you okay?"

"We're good. We found what we were looking for."

"You can thank us later," Agatha said, her hand sliding to her pocket. "You have it?"

He held up Rat's cloak. "We stowed it earlier," he said, holding it out to them. "I just had time to get it back."

Deftly, Rat's hand found the clasp, fastening it at their throat. "And Isola hasn't left yet?"

"We're sure that's a good thing?"

"It's Isola. It's never a good thing," Rat said. It was just better than having her at the tower. "As long as Jinx keeps eyes on her and makes sure she stays in the ballroom."

They didn't know how long they would have. They just needed a head start, and it was going to have to be enough.

Will reached out and adjusted their cloak. "Ready?"

"Will—"

He flipped the corner of his jacket, revealing a smaller version of the spell on Rat's cloak, simpler because it didn't need to be as strong.

"I tested it out earlier with Jinx. We needed a trial run," he said. "It won't fool them for long, but it should be enough to muddle any tracking spells. Just get to the casting rooms, and I'll deal with Church if he tries to go looking for you."

"If he catches you—"

"He should hope he doesn't." He flashed them a small, lopsided grin. "Tank, remember?"

"Evans," Agatha said, tugging their arm. "We should go."

Will reached out and pushed their bangs back. "Just make sure you're safe," he said, "Okay?"

They nodded. Rat stole a last glance at Will as Agatha led them into the archives, the door swinging shut behind them.

The lights had been left low, since the archives had closed for the night, and the stacks were quiet as Agatha led them back through the familiar front rooms.

"It's this way. They're underneath the main collection, on the first floor of the vaults," she said. "They shouldn't be hard for you to get into once you're down." Agatha traced another spell on the air as they came to a closed-off corridor, and the wards gave way, allowing them to pass.

Agatha motioned to Rat, leading them between the aisles of bookshelves toward a set of doors. "Once you're in, you're going to want to draw a casting circle before you open a way to the tower, and make sure you return through the same place," she continued. "It's the same principal that's used in summonings. It makes it harder for anything to follow you back out."

Then she gave a small nod to Rat, and they pushed one door open, revealing a wide stone staircase leading down into the earth. A draft of cold, dry air rolled up to meet them.

"Rat," Agatha said, like she might stop them.

Rat looked up at her on the step above them.

"You'll find him," she said. "I know you. You'll make sure of it." Then she turned and took off the way that she'd come, leaving them alone at the top of the stairs.

Rat reached into their cloak, closing their fingers around a piece of casting chalk, then started down.

The air turned cooler around them as they descended, until the steps ended in a long hallway lined with casting rooms. Most of the lights had been put out for the night, leaving the corridor in darkness. Above, narrow windows slit the top of the walls to let the light in, but the sky outside was black.

Rat's footsteps echoed softly as they made their way toward a row of doors. They stopped at one, half expecting resistance, but the door swung smoothly inward.

Unless they counted the practice rooms at Bellamy Arts, Rat had never been in a real casting room before. The room around them was circular and windowless. Supply cabinets had been built into the curve of the wall, but the floor had been cleared completely.

Rat knelt, adjusting their grip on the chalk. Carefully, they etched out a rough circle on the ground.

It was reckless and terrible, and it was the only chance they'd have. They were going to the one place that no one would be able to follow them, and if they failed, there wouldn't be any coming back this time.

Rat drew their cloak tight and flipped up the hood as they stepped into the center of the casting circle. Their magic flickered, and they thought of the tower rising up out of the weeds, stark against the fading sky. In their mind, they named each of the stars the way Isola had taught them once.

They pictured Harker alone there.

"*Open*." Their voice echoed off the walls, and a cold draft slithered through the room, carrying the faint scent of mugwort and old stone as the wall ahead of them opened into a dead passage.

Aether curled over it in heavy drifts, like they'd peeled back the veil of the world to reveal something *else*. Tall, dry grass overtook the stone floor of the casting room, and even though Rat knew that it was snowing where they were, the deepening sky was flecked with stars they had come to know.

It had been months now since they'd set foot on the tower's outlying grounds, and never farther than the field of fallen stones, but they still knew this place in every hollow of themself. The tower was theirs, and they were always meant to end up there.

Steeling themself, Rat stepped out into the weeds, letting the Council Chambers fall away behind them. The low line of the retaining wall snaked ahead of them, the weathered stone cast in gray evening light, and the sky had deepened toward the always-falling darkness. Rat looked across the span of grass and old stone to the shape of the tower in the distance.

A black bird swept toward them, and Rat flinched back.

Uselessly, they raised their hand to cast. It would see them. The light would shift, and it would be Isola, and she would make sure they never left.

The bird landed on the retaining wall and peered up at them, watchful. It was just a *bird*. She wasn't even here.

Rat closed their hand and dropped it back to their side, their pulse still hammering. Frustration pricked through them. They knew Isola's tricks. She'd taught them.

Rat looked back at the bird, meeting its gaze. Deftly, they held out their hand to it, the fading light of the tower soft on their skin.

"You remember me, don't you?" they said to it.

The bird leapt up, coming to perch on Rat's hand.

"If Isola asks, you didn't see me here." Rat ran a finger over its wings, following the smooth grain of its feathers. It was a game they used to play, when they'd first come to the tower. Sometimes so they could try to sneak up and surprise her. Sometimes just to see if they could get away with it.

"Let the others know it's a surprise," they said, stroking the bird's head. "Our secret, okay?"

It met their gaze, its eyes like glass. Then the bird leapt up, its wings catching the air.

Rat watched as it vanished back toward the tower. Their gaze shifted back toward the shape of the broken battlements in the distance. The wind tugging at the edges of their cloak, Rat started across the grass.

CHAPTER EIGHTEEN

RAT SLIPPED THROUGH A BREAK IN THE RETAINING WALL, their steps quiet on the hard-packed earth. The overgrowth whispered around them, and the fallen rocks grew closer together as they moved toward the tower.

In all the times they'd come here, Rat had never gone much farther than this. A few times, they'd followed Isola into the grass, but until the night she'd tried to bring them back with her, there had always been an unspoken boundary they hadn't crossed, maybe because a part of them had known they might not come back if they did.

If there had ever been a line, though, they'd passed it a long time ago.

Rat stopped at the foot of the tower. The battered doors loomed over them.

Dread rose in Rat's core, but they pushed the feeling away. Drawing themself up, Rat braced their hand against one of the doors. "I'm Alexander Holbrook," they lied into the wood, willing their spell to hold. "You remember me. I've been here before."

For a moment, they felt the tower resist. Then, like it had been waiting for them all along, the door swung in, opening into a crumbling antechamber.

Sconces lined the walls where once there might have been candles or spell lights, but now the only illumination were the slats of gray twilight streaming in from the narrow windows of the stairwell.

Rat touched their hand to the wall as they hurried up the steps, their fingers skimming over the weathered stonework. Even if they hadn't been to the tower, they'd seen Harker moving between its rooms. There might have been parts Rat didn't know, but they knew his routes.

Rat took the next turn, and the stairwell opened, giving way to a wide circular room filled with bookshelves.

The tower's library. They'd seen Harker here, wandering the ruined aisles. Steadying themselves, Rat slid their phone from their pocket and switched on the flashlight.

The stairs must have picked up somewhere in the maze of shelves, since Rat could just pick out the shape of the steps curving up along the far wall, but the stonework had given way in places, leaving the room open to the elements. Dark puddles of rainwater pooled on the stones from a recent storm, and weeds sprouted up between the aisles, growing through the cracks in the floor.

Through the dim light, Rat fixed their gaze on the stairs as they started down the aisle of shelves, the beam of their phone sweeping the way ahead of them.

Their magic flickered, and Rat drew on it, allowing the maze of shelves to take shape around them. Titles caught the light as they passed, the foil worn away in places, and Rat's footsteps sounded damply on the stone floor.

As they went, something shifted in the corner of their vision.

Rat spun back, flashlight raised. The light washed over the aisle, but there was nothing there.

A cold draft rolled between the shelves, raising goosebumps on Rat's arms. Forcing out a breath, they took off again, quickening their pace.

They didn't have to be brave. They just had to finish this.

Rat took the next corner, and the shelves parted, revealing the bottom of the ruined staircase, overgrown with moss and shoots of grass.

Past the edge where the railing should have been, the staircase cut steeply away, opening onto a sheer drop-off. The stairs shifted unsteadily beneath their weight as they started to climb, and the beam of their phone's flashlight threw shadows over the walls.

You're fine, they told themself. *Keep going.*

Rat reached for their power, and something imperceptible shifted in the air as a dead passage opened ahead of them. They started toward it, and then something cold brushed past them in the dark.

Rat stumbled back and their focus broke, the spell slipping away from them. Their foot clipped one of the stairs, sending a rain of loose stones skittering down into the dark. They caught themselves against the wall, breathing hard.

They cast the beam of the flashlight over the library in a wide arc, searching the darkness. On the stairs below, a figure peeled itself away from the gloom, tattered at the edges like a shadow that had been left out in the weather for too long.

Everything inside of Rat turned to ice.

They jolted as another hand snaked out of the dark, grabbing at their cloak. Rat wrenched away from it and shot forward, their heart in their mouth, but the staircase only rose a few more feet ahead of them before it crumbled away completely, and the ground opened into a chasm.

Rat felt the dead passage before they saw it. Like a reflex, they rushed for it, letting it catch them.

They spilled through onto a high ledge on the other side of the drop-off and landed hard. Just barely, they kept their hold on the bottom step, but they'd lost their grip on their phone and it slid away from them, skidding across the stairs.

Rat's pulse kicked into their throat. They scrambled to pull themself up, and then a bony hand caught them by the arm.

"That's three, Evans."

Everything inside of them ground to a halt.

Rat looked up as Harker helped haul them back onto the ledge, a will-o'-wisp of spellfire hovering behind him. He was dressed in the same dark clothes they'd seen in the mirror, his hair hanging past his shoulders in loose snarls. Shadows etched his face, and all of his features seemed more severe somehow, though Rat didn't know if it was due to the light or because he'd wasted down to nothing.

Rat met his eyes, still breathing too hard to speak.

Harker traced a retrieval spell with his free hand, and their phone flew to him. "We need to move," he said, shoving it at them. "You shouldn't be here."

Rat fumbled to put their phone away as he started up the stairs, pulling them behind him. Before Rat could ask where they were going, the stairs rose above the expanse of the library, and the wide, curving staircase turned back to a narrow set of spiral stairs, worn but solid under their feet.

With a start, Rat realized that they'd seen this, too, when Harker had been on his way back to his room.

Harker led them into an equally narrow corridor and then pulled them inside before shutting the door behind them.

The crumbling maw of the old window Rat had seen in the mirror opened onto the night sky. A couple of books were stacked on the floor beside a pile of moth-eaten blankets, and the air smelled faintly of burnt paper and magic and something else indescribably human.

"Harker," Rat started. "I—"

He turned, pinning them against the wall. "What do you think you're doing?"

"I'm getting you out of here, you literal conflagration," Rat said. They shoved him, but he pushed them back.

"You don't understand," Harker said, his voice rough and low. "You need to leave. Rat, if Isola finds you here—"

"She won't." Frustration flared in their chest. "She's not here. The others are distracting her. I told you I would find you, and I meant it. But you have to come with me, and we have to go now."

"I can't," he said sharply. "I'm still bound here. I don't get to walk out just because you finally decided to come get me."

"Isola *banished me*, you disaster," they said, grabbing his cloak.

He drew in a sharp, surprised breath as they tugged him forward. "Rat—"

"No. Harker, you flaming wreckage, you walking fire code violation, do you have any idea how hard I've been trying to find you? I looked for you for weeks! None of us stopped looking for you, okay? I don't care what else I have to break or how hard you try to scare me away, I'm not leaving you behind again," Rat said, pulling him in. Heat spiked off of him in a ragged wave as their fingers tightened on his cloak. "This is my fault, so please for once just let me fix it!" Their voice came out harsh and burnt, and all at once, they realized how close Harker was. Slowly, Rat loosened their grip.

"Please," they said softly. "Come with me."

Harker swallowed hard, and some of his armor fell away. Suddenly, he didn't look spiteful or furious or prepared to burn them to the ground. He looked like he was on the verge of breaking. "Do you think I don't want to? She's only keeping me alive so she can use me against you. The moment I stand a chance of getting away, she'll kill me. She'll call in your promise to her, and—"

"She's killing you by keeping you here," Rat said. Slowly, they raised their hand to his cheek. He suppressed a shiver. "I promise, we're going to get out here, alright? Both of us. I just . . . trust me. Please. Just this once, and then you never have to again."

"Rat—"

"Until morning. Then you can act like this never happened if you want."

Harker let out a shuddering breath. In the half-light, they could swear they saw his lip tremble. "Do you swear we'll both make it back?"

"On everything," Rat said. "I'm not leaving without you." They brushed back a stray lock of hair from his eyes. "But we don't have a lot of time. You told me she took your bracelets for the binding spell?"

Harker looked away, collecting himself. "I . . . Right. We need them back if we're going to break the spell. She's keeping them in her room. I got in once, but I didn't have a lot of time to look before I was caught."

"But if I can deal with the doors, we can search."

"It's not that easy. If she comes back and finds us there—"

"We'll be gone before she can." Rat started toward the door, pulling Harker with them. "Show me where to go."

"Wait," he said quickly, tugging them back.

They looked at him.

"Just—I need to get something first." He slipped away from them and rushed to the pile of books next to the worn patch of floor where he slept. He pulled a sheet of paper from one and folded it over.

"Here." He closed the distance to Rat quickly and held the paper out to them. "I was trying to figure out a way to get this to you in case anything happened. You should—"

"Keep it."

"But—"

"No." Rat met his gaze. "We're done playing that game. No heroics, no putting yourself in danger to make sure I get out. I don't leave this place unless you do." They closed his hand over the page and pushed it back at him. "You can tell me whatever you found out once we're back."

Grudgingly, he tucked the paper into a pocket of his cloak. He drew his hand through the air, and the will-o'-wisps of spellfire that had begun to rove around the room came back to him, like stars pulled into orbit. "Stay with me, and watch your step."

Rat took his arm, a subtle heat still radiating off him. "Alright, Blakely. Lead the way."

CHAPTER NINETEEN

HARKER LED THEM BACK OUT ONTO THE NARROW LANDing. A few other doors lined the way, but he pulled Rat toward another staircase that rose up to the floors above.

Shadows shifted in the corner of their vision. Rat looked over their shoulder as a tattered figure drifted past, but Harker tugged them forward.

"They're wraiths," he said. A wisp of spellfire hovered after him, throwing cold, bluish light over the stairs. "They won't hurt you. They're just curious because they haven't seen you before, and they like the warmth." He held out his hand, helping Rat up. "There's a ward on the steps that stops them from going any higher."

Rat looked back again in spite of themself. The figure behind them had drifted closer, peering at them from the shadows. It had come to a stop at the foot of the stairs, vague and formless, like it had been something once but had forgotten what. A weight sank in Rat's chest as they realized how human it looked. "They were . . ."

"They're bound here," Harker said. "I don't think they're able to leave."

Rat thought of the missing students that Jinx had told them about spread out across the years, as the understanding settled over them. Their hand tightened protectively around Harker's wrist as he pulled them around a bend in the stairs and the landing disappeared below.

"We'll need to move fast once we're upstairs," he said. "I don't know where she's hidden them, so we're going to have to search. Isola has a habit of collecting things."

"You said you've been in her rooms already?"

"Briefly," he said, like it hadn't gone well.

They rounded the next turn in the stairs. At the top, a shadow-gray hunting dog lay curled at the foot of a heavy door, chewing a bone that looked like it still had bits of tendon attached.

Harker knelt down and slipped a crust of bread from his cloak pocket like he'd done this before. The dog took it from his hand, its tongue lapping over his fingers.

"Good girl," he murmured, scratching behind her ears. "That's Rat," he said, tilting his head slightly. "They're with me, okay?"

The dog let out a small whine as he pushed himself back to his feet and nodded to Rat.

"That's Phlox," he said, stepping aside to let them pass. "She bites."

Rat touched their hand to the door. For a moment, they could feel the shape of the protective workings that would hold it shut and all of the places that the spells had worn thin over the years.

You know me, they thought at the spell. *Isola invited me here. I'm a guest.*

So subtly that Rat might have imagined it, they felt the spell ease a little as it bent to them. Then, the resistance they'd felt before was gone. They tried the doorknob, and it turned smoothly, as if it had been unlocked all along.

The door swung in, opening onto a glorious ruin of a bedroom.

Outside the windows, the sky had darkened to an inky blue, as close to night as Rat had ever seen it come here, and the last gray strains of evening light poured in, etching the room in shadows. Old trunks and chests of drawers had been gathered along the walls, covered in odds and ends, and a set of dilapidated bookshelves were piled with trinkets.

Rat drew out their phone again. "I'll take this side," they said, starting toward the bookshelves. They swept the beam over the clutter. A trove of broken jewelry and still-fresh flowers covered the shelf, laid out between piles of leatherbound books. With a chill, they thought of the crow gifts that Isola had sent them, but they kept going. None of this was what they were looking for.

They moved down to the next shelf before they realized it was filled with bones, arranged like a collection.

Rat jerked back as the light fell on a human skull, yellow with age. "Shit," they breathed into their hand. Their pulse threatened to climb back up their throat.

Across the room, Harker turned to them, the will-o'-wisps of spellfire still hovering around him. He started toward them, but they shook their head.

Rat turned away from the shelves, feeling sick. Their mind went back to the missing students and the wraiths in the corridor, but Rat pushed the thought away. This place was filled with death. They'd known that before they arrived. Right now, they needed to keep searching.

The beam of the flashlight wavered as Rat swept it across the room. Isola could have put Harker's bracelets anywhere, but they knew her. She wouldn't leave those out in the open.

Rat stopped at a jewelry box on the bedside table and started toward it.

The bed at the center of the room was old, with weathered posts and a canopy that had been eaten away by moths. Rat dropped down, the mattress sagging under them. The faint scent of cold air and mugwort clung to the sheets, along with the musky, too-human note of sweat beneath it.

Carefully, they lifted the box out of the clutter, turning it in their hand. A set of metal bands were inlaid in the wood of the box, inscribed with sigils too delicate for Rat to read. A faint electrical thrill pricked across their skin as they recognized the tinge of magic.

The bed creaked, and they looked up as Harker settled beside them. He eyed the box in a question, like he'd had the same thought they had.

Rat pulled on the lid, but it held fast. Carefully, they raised the box to their lips. "*Open*," they said into the latch. Their magic rose up in answer, and they could feel the shape of the spell holding it shut. Then, just as quickly, they lost the working, and it slipped away.

Rat shut their eyes, drawing more deeply on their powers. They thought of the wards at Bellamy Arts. They'd broken those, and they could break this, too. Again, they drew on their powers, letting the protective spell take shape. Rat pushed against it, harder than before, willing it to give way, but this wasn't a ward. It was something stronger. Older.

The spell pressed back, and a faint, too-familiar magic whispered in Rat's core, full of wind and shadows.

They jerked back.

"Rat?" Harker rushed to catch them, taking them by the arm. "Hey. Careful."

"I'm fine," Rat said, gripping the box.

Blood rushed in their ears. Whatever they'd felt, it had been night air and dusk and the wild overgrowth of the tower.

It wasn't their magic.

Their bond with Isola was supposed to be gone. When they'd made their deal with her, she'd lent them her power for the night, but that had been weeks ago.

"Let's get out of here," Harker said, and if Rat hadn't known him, they might have missed the desperate catch in his voice. "We can take it with us."

They looked back at him, and their chest tightened. It wouldn't work that way. If they left with the wrong thing—if they'd made a mistake, if the binding spell didn't come undone like it was supposed to—they weren't going to be able to come back here.

The faint thread of Isola's magic rose toward the box, like it already knew what to do.

"Just hold on." Rat shut their eyes, and their hands tightened on the box.

"*Rat!*" Harker tugged them back as they cast again, but this time, Rat reached for the thread of Isola's magic instead.

Power flooded through them, rising to their call. They felt the spell on the box give way, like it had recognized the magic that cast it, and then Rat caught the low whisper of something cold and nameless in the current of Isola's power.

Rat crashed against Harker, and the box fell open as they tumbled back onto the mattress. Loose trinkets spilled out onto the sheets, but for a long moment, Rat just lay there, breathing hard. The wrongness of Isola's magic washed over them all at once. They didn't know what it was that they'd felt.

Rat shut their eyes, but before they could grasp it, something pulled on the other end of the binding spell.

They stilled.

"Evans?" Harker said, and they realized how close he was, his arm still wrapped around them.

"We have to go," Rat said, pushing themself up. "The deal I made with Isola—I felt her. She knows we're here."

"You *what*?"

"We need your bracelets. Now." They turned back toward the box, scanning the mess as they realized what they were seeing.

Binding spells.

All of Isola's binding spells.

Quickly, Rat grabbed a handful of things without looking at what they'd found and shoved it into the pocket of their cloak. Then another.

Across the mattress, Rat caught sight of a set of leather bracelets, blackened in places and covered in toothmarks. They grabbed them and shoved them at Harker.

He faltered, and all over again Rat realized how close to breaking he was. Then, like he'd caught himself, his composure slid back into place, and he took the bracelets, slipping them over his wrist.

His gaze shifted back to the bed. A quite, slow-burning fury flashed across his face, and he swept up the last handful of items.

"Come on," he said, tucking the things into the pocket of his cloak. He grabbed Rat by the wrist and whipped back toward the doorway.

Ahead of them, the door swung shut, like it had been moved by a cold wind.

"I wondered where you'd gotten off to," a voice said behind them.

Rat whipped around.

Isola perched on the crumbling window ledge, still dressed in her gown from the Revel, her sword at her side.

Instinctively, Rat took a step back, and Harker's grip tightened around their wrist.

She slid down from the sill, her landing soft in the hush of the tower.

"I have to admit, I'm impressed you made it this far. It seems I've taught you well." She let out a low, cold laugh as she closed the distance. Isola drew in, lifting Rat's chin with her knuckle, the leather of her glove cool against their skin. "Tell me, how did you imagine this would end?"

Blood pounded in Rat's ears. Distantly, they realized they were trembling. "We made a deal. You taking Harker wasn't part of it."

Rat pulled back, but Isola's hand snapped shut, gripping their jaw.

"You forget yourself," she said sharply. "Unless you've come here with my heart, your friend is mine to do with as I see fit. He's unharmed because I've chosen to keep him that way as a favor to you." She leaned closer, her fingers digging into their skin. "The fact that I haven't called in your debt doesn't change that you're mine."

"Let go of them!" Harker grabbed Rat's arm, pulling them back as the spellfire flared around him.

Rat stumbled against him as Isola spun after them, the shadows surging around her, and the full force of her magic raged across the binding spell.

Her hand shot out, and a spell tore away from her. Harker pulled them out of the way as it shredded through the air where they'd been.

A dead passage caught the corner of Rat's vision, and they shot toward it, tugging Harker after them. They spilled out into a narrow stairwell, stumbling to catch themself.

"Shit," Rat hissed. Their free hand skipped over the wall as they descended, Harker's footsteps close behind them.

This wouldn't end here. They were going to make it back.

Rat sensed the next passage before they saw it.

Quickly, they veered toward it, not thinking of where they were going, and the tight curve of the stairs gave way to the tower's outlying fields, the star-flecked sweep of the darkened sky stretching overhead.

Isola's birds leapt up around them, taking wing as Rat rushed out into the overgrowth.

They looked back as Harker raced after them. His cloak whipped out behind him as he followed them into the field.

He turned back, his gaze locked on the tower, determined. He drew his hand through the air, casting a pale will-o'-wisp of spellfire, and the dry grass flared behind them.

"Go." His breath came in hard and fast. "Open a way back," he said, keeping pace with Rat. "I know you can, I've seen you do it."

The scent of smoke rose into the air as the fire took, and Rat shoved themself forward.

The grass whipped past them as they ran, putting distance between themself and the tower. The almost-night had turned cold, but they couldn't feel the chill, and their lungs burned.

Without slowing, Rat traced a spell on the air.

They thought of the Council Chambers, with its high ceilings, and the still-crowded ballroom, and Will and Jinx and Agatha.

They thought of the last time they'd been here with Harker, pulling him back to the safety of their house.

They knew their way home from here. They'd done this before, more times than they could count.

Their magic flared and Rat felt the world open around them, like finding their way back down a well-worn path.

A passage glinted on the air ahead of them. Past the veil of aether, they caught sight of a wide marble hallway in the Council Chambers.

Rat stole a last glance over their shoulder, the field still blazing behind them. Farther out, past the veil of smoke, something moved in the grass, snaking toward them, and Isola's birds were still close behind.

Steeling themself, Rat pulled Harker forward, but he jerked to a stop. Rat stumbled, just catching themself where he'd come up short at the mouth of the passageway.

"Harker." Rat tugged him toward the passage. "Come on. We need to go."

With a wince, he touched his hand to his ribs, over his heart. Slowly, his gaze went back to the tower, like he was following an invisible thread.

"Harker?"

He looked back at Rat, but the expression on his face was an apology. Their chest sank.

"No," they said. "That isn't fair. We broke the binding spell."

"You should get back." His voice came out rough and bitten off.

"I'm not doing that. We can still—"

"I knew what would happen," he snapped. "Okay? Isola told me. I just thought I had more time. I shouldn't have come with you." But even as he said it, they could almost see the last bit of hope he'd been holding on to go out.

"But—"

"I don't remember Bellamy Arts anymore!"

Rat stared at him. "What?"

"I don't know what it looks like. I remember things that happened there, but I can't picture it. I've been forgetting more and more of it the longer I'm here," he said. "She told me by the time she released me, I would fully belong to this place."

"No." Dread settled in Rat's core. Isola's spell had been sinking its teeth into him since he'd arrived, slowly cutting away at every thread that tied him to his old life, until he didn't remember anything but this.

She'd never intended for him to go free. If she sent him back at all, it would have been as a final act of cruelty after he'd forgotten everything but the tower. He would have come back with no allies and nowhere to go, and the old families would've eaten him alive.

He gave Rat a pleading look. All of his fury and desperation died away, and something in him seemed to crumble.

"You really have to go, don't you?" Harker said, but his voice came out hoarse and broken.

Rat looked back at the birds, closer behind them than before.

Their eyes stung. They'd come this far, and they refused to let it end like this.

"I'm not leaving you here," they said. "Whatever you swore to Isola, you were still mine first."

"Rat, that isn't—"

"If an oath can keep you tied you to this place, then a stronger one can break it. That's how it works, right?" A hard, frantic edge slid into their voice. "I know you, and if there's another spell, I know you can cast it, so just swear something else!"

Harker opened his mouth, and they half expected him to tell them that wasn't the way that magic worked and that they couldn't just smash their way through everything with a stronger spell, but then he dipped his head. "Okay, I swear."

It came out fast and panicked, his voice still on the edge of breaking.

Then he squared his shoulders and met their gaze, still close enough that they could feel the whisper of his breath on their skin, warm in the cool night air.

"Rat, on all of the stars and the name that I gave myself, I swear, I'll break every other promise I've ever made. I'll follow you to the end of this. I—" Harker looked back at the tower, rising up against the dark. Heat rolled off of him in ragged waves. "I pledge myself. Whatever you ask of me, as far as this road leads us, I'm yours. I've always been yours."

Rat's heart dropped. It wasn't the same words that Isola had said to them in the ruins of Ashwood, the night the wards came down, but they knew the shape of it.

It was a binding spell.

Harker took their hand and raised it to his lips. His mouth brushed Rat's knuckles, hot and desperate against the cool night air.

The electrical thrill of the spell raced across their skin as the working took hold, and Harker drew back, their hand still clasped in his.

Then Harker traced a protective working on the air as Rat grabbed him by the arm, tugging him through the passage with them. They felt the passage push back against them, and then, this time, it gave way.

CHAPTER TWENTY

RAT STUMBLED THROUGH THE PASSAGE, PULLING HARKER along as the terrors closed behind them, and then the tall grass turned back into the marble floors of the Council Chambers. Aether curled on the air around them, the attic scent of magic hanging heavy in the corridor. The hall ahead of them was empty, and the dull glow of the city striped the way, the lights left low since it hadn't been in use.

Deep in their core, Rat felt something in the fabric of the world tear as a terror crashed through after them, skittering over the floor.

"The casting circle," they breathed. "Shit." They hadn't thought past getting away from the tower. They were supposed to come back to the casting room so nothing else could slip through.

"*Rat.*" A palpable edge of panic slid into Harker's voice. "Why are we at the Council Chambers?"

"It's fine," Rat said. "Isola can't follow us here, just go!"

He looked at them like absolutely no part of this was fine, but he was already scrambling to keep pace as they tugged him toward the end of the hallway.

Rat glanced back as Harker turned, drawing a protective spell on the air with his free hand. Heat rippled off of him in a sharp wave, bleeding out around the edges of the spell.

Behind them, another terror snaked into the hallway, its too-many legs scrabbling over the polished floors. Rat tightened their grip on Harker's arm and yanked him toward them, his skin feverish against theirs. He'd already hit his limit. Whatever control Harker had left was unraveling, and quickly. Even under good circumstances, he would have been outmatched, and he'd spent the last two months locked away in the tower.

One of the terrors snaked up the wall, and Harker flinched away from it, tracing another protective spell. A wall of force rolled away from him, stray spellfire licking at the edges. He shot a breath through his teeth as the terror was sent scuttling back, the spell scorching a trail across the ground. "Fuck."

"The Council can send me the bill," Rat said, breathless. "I'm pretty sure they owe me."

They pulled Harker around a turn in the hallway before they could think about where they were going. They needed to find help or somewhere to hide, and they needed to not lead the terrors back to the Revel.

Another terror snaked closer, the star-flecked plates of its body showing dimly in the darkened corridor. Rat drew on their magic, and the Council Chambers *opened*. They felt something deep in the structure of the building give a little, and suddenly they could feel the cracks in the world where it would be easy to slip through.

Harker drew in a sharp breath as Rat veered through a dead passage into another empty hallway, taking him with them. Somewhere down a nearby corridor, they heard the low hiss of a terrors scuttling over the marble floors. They'd gotten away, but not far enough.

"Come on," they said in a rush.

Rat ran, throwing themself around the next turn, and then a wall of force shot toward them, knocking them flat. They lost their grip on Harker and hit the ground hard.

Wincing, Rat propped themself up. All of the air had gone out of their lungs, and their shoulder ached where they'd landed.

Harker had come down next to them, his cloak pooling around him.

They looked up to see Allister standing in the hallway, his hand still raised to cast. Surprise flickered across his face as he seemed to register that Harker was with them, and then his expression sharpened into a dangerous kind of interest. "I guess that answers my question."

The low drone of the orchestra drifted in, closer than Rat had thought, and all at once, they realized where they were. It was the same hallway they'd come through with Agatha.

Rat pushed themself up. "You were waiting here."

"You're not the only one who knows the building, Evans," Allister said, stepping in. "You can call it a lucky guess, but there aren't that many routes back to the ballroom, and you tend to announce your entrance." He tilted his head slightly to the place where their dead passage had been a moment before.

Rat stared at him as the pieces clicked together. Allister hadn't noticed their concealment spell earlier—he'd seen the passage they'd opened.

They were dealing with another wayfinder.

"Trade secret," Allister said, flexing his hand. "Though I guess that makes us even, since you confirmed my suspicions first." His gaze shifted to Harker as he tried to stand, wincing. "You know, I never got how someone could be so good at magic and so bad at staying on his feet." He traced a spell, knocking Harker back down. "I'm curious, Evans. Has he ever actually won a fight?"

"*Stop it!*" Rat felt their magic slip out, even though they hadn't called it, the words taking the cadence of a spell.

A wave of power shuddered through the hallway, and Allister stilled, like he'd realized for the first time he might not be the only dangerous thing there. Quickly, Rat lunged forward, catching Harker by the arm as he picked himself up. As fast as Allister could track them, their hand cut the air, and another passage opened ahead of them.

A spell whistled past them, slicing the air. Rat glanced over their shoulder to find Allister close behind them, on their side of the passage. Gritting their teeth, Rat opened another. They didn't need to be a great arcanist; they just needed to fast enough to lose him.

Harker made a small ragged sound as he raced to keep up with them. He drew a protective spell on the air as he ran, and Allister's next attack glanced off.

"Close the way behind you," Harker said, his voice shredded.

"What?"

"He's not opening his own passages, just using yours. Either he's holding back, or he can't."

The next passage opened ahead of them, and Rat shot toward it. The sounds of the Revel were closer than before, the music louder.

Allister's next spell lashed through the air. With a sharp gasp, Harker lost his grip on Rat, and Rat staggered over the threshold, the veil of aether breaking around them.

They'd ended up on the far end of the corridor. Maybe twenty feet away, Harker had come down hard on the marble floor. One hand was still raised in a shield, shaking with the effort of holding the defensive spell, and the other clutched against his ribs like he was bracing himself. His sleeve hung in shreds, and his fingers were slick with blood, though Rat couldn't tell where he'd been cut, only that it was bad.

Footsteps sounded behind them, and Rat spun back as Allister stepped through the passageway. Aether dusted his dark hair and gathered on his suit jacket. He traced a spell, and the passage vanished behind him.

"Just let us go," Rat said, but there was a desperate edge in their voice. "You don't get a prize for finding us, Church. I don't have the keys, okay?"

"Actually," Allister said, "I'm here to make a deal."

Rat stepped back and realized they were up against a wall.

Allister drew in. "That was Isola in the ballroom with you, wasn't it?"

Rat held his gaze.

"The obvious answer is that she showed up unannounced, but I don't think that's what happened," he said. His eyes went back to the sigil on Rat's cloak, and Rat remembered the spell had come from one of the Church family's books. "I think it's incredibly convenient that one of Acanthe's seven Rooks ended up in the Council Chambers the same night that a missing student happened to return from the tower."

Rat's jaw trembled, and they clenched their teeth, hating themself for it.

"I don't think the other families see you, Evans. I think you've given them another story that's easier for them to swallow, about how you aren't a threat to them, and as long as you've behaved, they haven't examined it too closely. But I think you're slipping." Allister's gaze flickered over them. "So here's what's going to happen. You're going to tell me where the keys are. In exchange, I'm going to forget what I saw tonight and let you leave."

In the next hallway, Rat heard the low hiss of the terrors snaking through the corridors.

"Or don't," Allister said coolly. "If the Council hasn't realized something slipped past their wards yet, they will soon. I'd give it maybe half an hour before Evening has the building fully locked down." He tilted his head. "Given how fast he tried to close the investigation, I can't imagine he'd be thrilled to see either of you. If you left now, you could still be on your way out of the city before anyone knew you were gone. But it's really up to you."

A burst of spellfire shot past them, and Allister jerked back. Harker stood braced against the wall, hand outstretched in a casting position. "Drop them."

Allister whipped toward him, his hand forming a spell on the air, but before he could cast, Rat shoved free.

Their magic flared as they caught Harker by the arm, and something in the Council Chambers unhinged around them. Music and candlelight washed over them as they pulled Harker through the passageway, into the ballroom.

A spell shot after them with the low whistle of a blade splitting the air. Something sharp nicked Rat's side as they stumbled forward, dragging Harker with them.

"*Close!*" they shouted at the passage, and then their balance went out.

They heard a shout, but it sounded distant, and all of their thoughts felt far away.

With a small sound of exertion, Rat forced themself back up as Harker reached out to pull them to their feet. "It's fine," Rat said. Pain throbbed in their knees, and everything hurt. Vaguely, they realized that their shirt was plastered to their skin, but they didn't know if it was blood or sweat. "Just keep going."

Everyone was staring at them, but Rat couldn't think about it. They needed to get out of here.

Rat caught a flash of movement as Evening started toward them from where he'd been standing the mezzanine, the crowd parting as he pushed his way toward the stairs. Elise hurried after him, her eyes wide with shock. Rat met her gaze as Harker wrapped his arm around them, bolstering them, and even though it shouldn't have mattered after everything else, they felt like they'd been caught at something. Then the crowd closed behind them, and Rat lost sight of her.

At least, Rat told themself, Elise wouldn't be able to say this wasn't their fault.

The next dead passage opened before Rat could think to cast it, and they let Harker pull them forward, into the room Agatha had commandeered for the travel spell. The furniture had been pushed to the walls, and a sigil had been marked out on the floor in casting chalk.

Jinx's eyes widened. "Rat—" she started, her voice hard.

"Cast the spell," Rat said in a rush. Their voice came out so rough, they almost didn't recognize it. "We need to go, okay?"

Their head swam. The look on Elise's face was still seared in their mind.

Then the air pressure dropped like the still before a coming storm, and a frisson of energy rolled over them as the travel spell activated.

CHAPTER TWENTY-ONE

THE COUNCIL CHAMBERS DISAPPEARED AROUND THEM, and for one, horrible, weightless moment, Rat wasn't anywhere.

Travel spells weren't the same kind of magic as wayfinding. Rat didn't understand the underpinnings well enough to explain it, except that there was something about travel spells that always felt viscerally and excruciatingly *wrong* to them. If wayfinding was about finding a route along the twists and bends of the world, travel spells felt like falling through the horrible non-place in between.

The only good thing about travel spells was that they were hard to cast since they needed to be anchored on both sides, so they weren't used very often.

As fast as the spell had flared up, it faded again, and then they were standing in the mouth of a wide entrance hall, an intricate sigil inlaid in the hardwood floor beneath them.

Harker sagged against Rat, and they let themself sink onto the ground. Their heart beat in their entire body. They half expected Harker to realize how close they were and shove them away, but now that he'd stopped running, the exhaustion seemed to hit him all at once, and he just clung to them, gasping for breath. His skin was feverish even through his clothing, like he'd lost his hold on his magic completely.

"You're okay." Agatha dropped beside them and rested her hand on Harker's arm. "How is he?" she asked Rat, at the same time as Will settled on their other side.

"What happened? You're bleeding," he said.

"It's fine," Rat managed. "We're both fine."

They glanced up as Jinx picked herself up and started toward them, then stopped, like she wasn't sure how close she could get. Harker followed their gaze, watching her like a cornered animal, and all over, Rat remembered that the last time Jinx had been in the same place as Harker, he'd been an enemy.

Finally, Jinx's face softened. "We should get him off the floor. He needs to lie down."

"There's a couch in the next room until I can set up one of the guest beds," Agatha said. "I'm going to find some bandages. Can you show everyone?"

"Yeah. I know which one," Jinx said.

Harker tried to push himself up, but his arm shook.

Rat moved to help him, but Will nudged them aside. "Here. I've got it." He held out his hand.

"It's fine. I can stand," Harker said, which might have been more convincing if he wasn't still lying on the floor and doing his best impression of a furnace. Whatever was left of his strength went out, and he collapsed against Rat again, like he'd used up all the fear and adrenaline that had kept him going.

"Hey," Rat said into his hair. "Trust me?"

Harker tilted his face up to them like he really didn't, and for a moment they thought he might stay there purely out of spite. Then, before he could hide it, anxiety flickered across his face. Harker looked at the ground like gravity was a plot to personally humiliate him. "If I start to burn you, you have to let go immediately," he said to Will. "My cloak has heat resistance spells. You should keep it between us."

Rat knew that was as much about his magic as the fact that he hated strangers touching him, but Will just nodded.

"Don't worry, Blakely. I'm not enjoying this either," he said, gathering Harker off the ground.

Grudgingly, Harker grabbed on to Will's jacket, letting himself be picked up without a fight. In Will's arms, he seemed even smaller. There were scrapes and bruises on his skin that Rat hadn't noticed at the tower, and exhaustion clung to him.

As soon as Will made it into the hallway, Jinx held out her arm to Rat and nodded for them to come with her.

Rat reached out, then realized that their hands were still crusted with blood and ash.

"My jacket's been through the tunnels. Trust me, it's seen worse," Jinx said, reading their expression.

Wincing, Rat allowed her to help them to their feet. Their shirt stuck to their side where a crust of blood had melded the fabric to their skin. They were pretty sure they'd stopped bleeding, at least, but their muscles ached in a dull, far-off way that probably meant their entire body was going to be a bruise tomorrow.

"What happened?" Jinx asked.

"Basically what it looks like," Rat managed. "I'm pretty sure the entire state of New York has figured out I can do magic."

She rubbed her eyes. "You know what I meant."

"We can talk about everything tomorrow." Rat said, dropping their voice. "He's in pretty rough shape. At the tower . . . I don't know what Isola was doing to him. What matters is that it's done."

Jinx just nodded, and Rat was silently grateful she wasn't going to push.

"What happened at the Revel?" they asked.

"Tomorrow," Jinx said. She paused as Will glanced back at her for directions. "Straight ahead. It's right at the end of the hall."

He dipped his head in acknowledgment. Rat moved to follow him, but before they could get too far ahead, Jinx stopped them.

"Wait. Cromwell already told her parents we were coming back here. It's up to you what you tell your mom, but . . ." She glanced at the door. "For Blakely. Is there anyone we should call?"

"No," Rat said. "I'm pretty sure everyone's here."

Jinx gave them a look, unsure.

"He doesn't speak to his family. I don't think they even knew which school he was at. We can get in touch with someone at Bellamy Arts tomorrow if Fairchild doesn't find out sooner."

Rat glanced at the door again, and Jinx followed their gaze. Gently, she laid her hand on their arm, and when she spoke again, her voice was soft. "After everything you've done to go after him, you should at least tell him why."

"This whole thing was my fault," Rat said. "I would have gone to find him no matter what."

"Rat . . ."

"He doesn't want to hear that from me," they said, starting toward the door. "He has enough to worry about."

The sitting room had a wide bay window overlooking the yard, and all of the furniture looked antique, including the couch that Harker was currently bleeding on. Agatha had already beaten them there, and sat perched on the edge of the coffee table with a roll of bandages that were marked with some kind of healing spell. She glanced over as Rat let themself in, then said something to Will about helping her look for food and blankets and the two slipped out into the hall.

Then Rat was alone with Harker again.

Heat wavered off of him, but he'd cooled off a little, from *furnace* to *overly ambitious radiator*, and now that the adrenaline had worn off, he was shivering in spite of the warmth.

"Hey," Rat said, dropping down beside the couch. "How are you? Are you okay?"

"Rat." With a wince, Harker pushed himself onto his side so he could take their sleeve, like he needed to be sure they were really there. His gaze flickered over them, searching. "Are you hurt? I heard Jinx saying—"

"It's nothing," they said quickly. "She just needed to ask if we should call your family." He stiffened and they added, "I told her not to. I didn't know if you'd want them here."

He relaxed a little. "I don't," he said tiredly. "I don't think they knew I was gone. They'd probably think I'm just looking for a complicated new way to make things hard for them."

Rat's chest sank. "What?"

"Sorry, Evans. You're not the only one who thinks I'm difficult."

"Yeah, well. I'm pretty sure we'd both be dead if you weren't." Rat reached up to get a smudge of ash from his cheek, then caught themself.

Harker watched them, and quiet settled over the room again as Rat realized how close he was.

For the first time, it fully hit them that Harker was here. While he'd been gone, Rat had been imagining the version of him that was still friends with them. The Harker Blakely they'd brought back was one who'd clawed and scraped to survive, who was brilliant and magnificently spiteful and had never fully forgiven them. The worst part of it was that he was the one Rat wanted the most, because he was here, and real, and alive.

Their pulse fluttered. "I—here." Rat picked up a washcloth. "Can I?"

"Are we still in a truce?" Harker asked slowly.

"We agreed on morning," Rat said, and he let them take his arm. Blisters covered his hand, and underneath the soot, his skin was a mess of burns. Gingerly, Rat touched the line of his bracelets.

"Was that the Winter Revel? At the Council Chambers?" Harker asked, but Rat could hear the real question underneath it.

"It's the end of December," they said softly. "The term ended last week."

He dimmed a little. "Oh."

"Harker—"

"It's fine. I already guessed I'd missed finals. Isola came back with snow on her cloak." He winced again as Rat dabbed at one of his burns. "Sorry if I ruined your holiday plans."

"Please, Blakely. You live to ruin my plans."

The ghost of a smile tugged at his mouth. "You're right. I orchestrated this whole thing"—he grimaced as Rat moved to the next burn—"just to personally inconvenience you."

Rat stopped as they came to a mess of yellowing bruises that laced up his forearm, still too fresh to be from last semester but too old to have come from their escape.

Harker tensed, and a pleading look flickered across his face, begging them not to ask. Rat swallowed hard.

Carefully, they cleaned away the soot, as if they hadn't seen. "For what it's worth, I was kind of hoping for an excuse to skip going home this year. I don't think Elise and I are on great terms right now." Rat reached for the bandages, and his jaw clenched again as they set to work binding his wounds. "Once I'm done wrapping these, we can do the other arm, and then I'll let you get some rest."

"Wait. Rat—" Harker started, and then stopped himself.

"Hm?"

"I . . . Could you stay? After?" Harker said after a moment, his voice a bit quieter like it had cost him something to ask. "Please. Just until our truce is over."

Rat brushed their thumb over his knuckles as they finished with his hand. "Of course. You have me."

Rat worked over the rest of his burns until he'd nearly drifted off, before they got Agatha to find him a sweatshirt so he could change out of his binder. Then a bit longer, until the sky had started to fade outside, and Harker had finally gone to sleep for real.

Gently, Rat smoothed their fingers through his hair, and everything that had happened broke over them.

They'd stolen from the Council Chambers and made it to the tower and back. They'd used their powers in front of everyone, and there would already be a dozen new rumors about what had happened tearing through the last hours of the Revel. They'd found Harker.

Warmth flickered on his skin, softer than it was when he'd been awake.

"I promise, too," they said softly. "Everything you swore, so do I. I'm not leaving you this time."

Faintly, they felt the low tug of the binding spells like a pair of threads. One to Harker, lying asleep perilously close to them. One to the tower, far off and terrible and waiting for them still.

The trace of Isola's magic uncoiled in their ribs, weak but very much there, even though Rat knew that it should have faded away.

They curled their fingers around Harker's, the low whisper of Isola's magic still lingering under their skin even after they'd let it go. And like that, finally, Rat drifted off to sleep.

CHAPTER TWENTY-TWO

RAT DREAMT OF THE TOWER.

Isola stormed up the crumbling staircase, charred underbrush from the field of weeds still clinging to hem of her cloak, like she'd gone to survey the damage. The tattered forms of the wraiths peered out at her from the shadows, scuttling back from her as she passed.

Isola took the turn past the landing without stopping, her footsteps heavy on the weathered stone as she passed the wards and the shadows dispersed behind her. She let herself into her room and traced the barest line of a spell, slamming the door shut. The last strains of dusk light streamed in, and the moon outside was a pale sliver over the distant line of the woods.

In a burst of furious motion, her hand lashed out in a spell, and the sagging bookcase full of trinkets and bones collapsed in on itself with a sharp crack. She spun, already tracing another spell. The working raked across the wall of shelves like teeth, and then with a furious grace, her sword was in her hand, poised to strike.

Before she could, a cough wracked her body, from somewhere deep in her lungs. When she wiped her mouth on the back of her hand, her glove came away spotted with blood and silver. With a guttural curse in the language that only Rooks knew, Isola dropped onto the bed, panting.

Magic coursed through her, with the same too-familiar undercurrent of wrongness, except this time, Rat recognized it. They'd felt it before, when they'd brushed against the deathworking in the clock tower.

Isola took the now-empty keepsake box from its place on the bedside table, gripping it tightly. Her eyes were cold and fathomless.

"Fine, then," Isola said, and her voice was the rusted edge of a blade. "If they want a game, they'll have one."

Rat bolted awake, breathing hard. Isola's magic stirred in their chest like a living thing, and the taste of the tower's scorched air still stuck in their throat. They pressed their hand to their ribs, steadying themself as the night before came back to them.

They were at Agatha's house. Safe.

At some point, someone must have moved them from the couch, since Rat was in a guest bedroom they didn't recognize, alone in the double bed. Sunlight streamed in, slanting over the duvet, and there was frost on the windows.

Rat shut their eyes. The last of the dream still clung to them, but it hadn't felt like a dream, and Isola's magic pulled at them, the faint tinge of death almost palpable underneath it now that Rat knew what they were looking for. They would have recognized it anywhere.

Rat remembered what Frey had told them last semester, about Isola's magic waning. What Jinx had told them, about the disappearances getting closer and closer together over the years, like whatever she'd been sustaining herself on wasn't enough anymore.

She wasn't just weaker. She was dying.

"No wonder you're desperate," Rat said into the empty room, the last traces of Isola's presence lingering on the other end of the binding spell.

Rat pushed themself out of bed. Through some magic that was completely beyond them, their backpack and suitcase rested in the corner of the room, still dusted with aether. Their cloak hung from the footpost, though the remains of their suit jacket were nowhere to be seen.

Unbidden, they thought of Harker the night before, half asleep beside them with the scent of the smoke and sweat still clinging to his clothes.

There was a tug on the other end of the binding spell, and Rat realized they'd reached for it without meaning to. Quickly, they let it go.

Trying to ignore the dull ache in their side, Rat grabbed their compass from the pocket, then their phone. They had about a dozen missed texts and almost as many phone calls from Elise. Rat opened to the message thread and scrolled down to the bottom.

Will told me you're with him at a friend's house. As soon as you see this, I need you to call me. This isn't okay, Miranda. I'm worried about you.

A sick feeling slithered through them, but they couldn't think about it right now.

Whatever Elise was afraid of, anything Rat told her would just make it worse. She'd seen them leaving the Revel. Probably, Evening had already given her his version of events.

Their screen lit with another incoming call.

Rat swiped it away and went back to their suitcase to get dressed. Their ribs were too sore to bind, so they grabbed a loose T-shirt and pulled their sweatshirt over it. Then, because all of Harker's things still had to be sealed up at Bellamy Arts, Rat dumped out their backpack and tossed in an extra set of clothes for him.

They didn't actually know what came next. When Harker woke up, he was probably going to take about five showers and then burn down anyone who'd ever laid a hand on him.

Rat grabbed their sketchbook from the ground, fitting it into their backpack with everything else, and zipped it shut again before they let themself out into the hall. They hadn't gotten a good look at this part of the house the night before, but voices drifted up from the floor below. Following the sound, they made their way downstairs. Rat slowed as they came to the Cromwell Rivera family's kitchen.

Will, Jinx, and Agatha were nowhere in sight. Instead, Agatha's parents sat at the kitchen island across from Vivian Fairchild, who was holding a mug of tea in her hands. Whatever she'd been saying, she stopped as she caught Rat's gaze. "Rat. How are you?"

On the other side of the counter, Agatha's parents were already on their feet. "Are you feeling alright?" her mother asked at the same time that her father said, "Have you eaten?"

Rat was familiar with the Cromwell Rivera family. Most of New York arcane society was. But Rat could count how many times they'd been in the same room, and it was usually at events where Rat was looking to hide from the crowd.

"I'm really fine," Rat said weakly. "I just got up. I heard voices."

"Of course." Agatha's mother gave them a warm smile. "I'm glad you're awake. Agatha is up in the music room with Jinx and Will. They've been asking about you, but I told them to let you sleep."

"Harker. Is he . . ."

"He's just resting right now," she said, and a tension Rat hadn't realized they'd been holding unwound a little.

"But he's okay?"

"He isn't seriously hurt," she said. "It's going to take a bit of time for him to recover, but it's the best we could have hoped for."

"I was just upstairs with him," Fairchild said. "Actually, I was hoping I would catch you before I left. Could we talk for a minute?"

Rat glanced back at the food that had been left out, and Fairchild motioned to it.

"Please," she said.

Gratefully, Rat grabbed a piece of toast and followed her out, suddenly aware that they were somehow ravenous and also unsure if they'd actually be able to keep anything down.

"Everything that happened last night was my idea," Rat said before Fairchild could speak. "If someone needs to take the blame, it's my fault."

"You're not in trouble," Fairchild said.

"But—" Rat started to argue, then realized that wouldn't help their case.

"I'm not going to ask how Harker found his way back to the Council Chambers last night, but I suspect that you and your friends are the only reason he did." She leveled her gaze at Rat, and just for a moment, she looked almost sad. "I'm sure you know by now how rare it is for a student to return from the tower. I'm afraid he might have been lost to us otherwise."

"What happens now?" Rat asked cautiously.

"I wish I could tell you. I don't think it's going to be easy for either of you," Fairchild said apologetically. "I'm not sure if Harker is going back to Bellamy Arts."

The air went out of Rat's lungs. "I thought he wasn't hurt."

"He's been through something difficult. I've given him some time to decide, but I don't think the school holds many good memories for him, and I can't guarantee his safety if he chooses to return."

"But . . ."

"I'm sorry, Rat," she said, and the kindness in her voice cut into them. "It's not our choice to make."

Rat swallowed hard. They felt like someone had struck a match in their throat.

"That isn't what I wanted to speak to you about, though," Fairchild said. As she spoke, she drew her fingers through the air, producing an envelope stamped with Evening's seal. Rat's stomach sank. "I received word this morning. Evening has put out an order. As long as you remain at the school, he's requiring that you be kept under close watch."

"He can't do that," they protested.

"Unfortunately, he can," Fairchild said, holding out the letter. Rat took the paper from her and unfolded it, revealing the Council of

Hours' official letterhead. "All of your movements have to be reported to the Council."

"You mean he's tracking me," Rat said, understanding settling over them.

Fairchild nodded stiffly, like she didn't like it either. "The spell has already been cast. It comes into effect as soon as you set foot on school grounds," she said. "He's asking us to give you a curfew, and we aren't allowed to continue your casting lessons unless you've been reassigned *to the Council's satisfaction*."

"Is that allowed?"

"It is when the student in question is under suspicion of an unauthorized summoning, while studying under the school's foremost summoning specialist," Fairchild said, but there was a note of defeat in voice that told Rat that their lessons were over until Evening agreed to it. "I've been fighting with the Council over it all morning, but after what everyone saw at the Revel, some of the other houses are saying that he has cause."

Rat flinched. What the other families saw was the supposedly powerless heir to a major bloodline using a power they'd covered up for years to willingly endanger all of New York society, all for the sake of the boy who'd conned his way into their family archives last year.

"I think it might be best if we speak plainly," Fairchild said. "I've known Evening for a long time, and he rarely does anything that doesn't serve his own interests in some way. Dawn and Night are already pushing to help me curtail his involvement with the school, but I don't want you trying to handle this. I don't think Evening is the only danger to you right now."

Her voice was gentle and full of regret, which was somehow worse than anything else.

"By now," Fairchild said, "I'm sure you know what Isola is, and I'm sure you know she doesn't let go of things easily. As much as I wish this was over, I'm afraid it's never that simple."

"No. I didn't think it would be," they admitted.

Fairchild held their gaze, considering her next words. "When you first came to Bellamy Arts, I told you that as long as you stayed within bounds and kept a hold on your powers, I could protect you. I'm not sure if that's the case anymore."

Rat was quiet.

"If you try to take this into your own hands, I don't believe you need to be told what a dangerous path that is for you to go down," Fairchild said. "I've lost students before, Mx. Evans. Students who were more adept with their abilities, from bloodlines as powerful and well-connected as yours. I suppose you know this better than most, but there are fates that even you couldn't be pulled back from."

"I know," Rat said.

"I've taken up enough of your morning. You should go find your friends," Fairchild said.

"You said you spoke to Harker?"

"Upstairs. Left when you get to the landing, then toward the back of the house."

"Thanks," Rat said, turning to go.

"Rat," Fairchild said, taking their shoulder. In the morning light, her expression turned grim. "This won't be the end of it. Whatever you decide to do, I think you need to tread very carefully from here on out."

CHAPTER TWENTY-THREE

RAT STOPPED IN THE KITCHEN TO GET COFFEE FOR THEMself and Harker before they made their way back into the house. They didn't think for a moment that Isola would let this go. She'd always known how to play a long game, and even if they'd slipped past her for now, Rat knew better than to think she was going to let them walk away from this.

They stopped as they came to the top of the stairs. Rat had expected Harker to be in a guest room, but he sat perched in the window at the end of the hall, sunlight streaming in around him. He'd changed into a clean T-shirt and a pair of borrowed pajama pants that were long enough that he'd had to cuff them a couple of times, but his hair was still down like he didn't entirely know what to do with it.

In the always-dark of the tower, he'd made a kind of sense, sharp and vicious and tattered at the edges. In the daylight, though, he just looked small and out of place.

Suddenly, Rat didn't know what they were doing. They wanted to run across the hall to him, but when he'd let Rat near him last night, he'd been terrified and exhausted, and he'd needed them to get home. They weren't sure if the alliance they'd made with him still held. Rat took half a step back, but before they could go far, he saw them.

"Rat?" he asked, his voice rough like he wasn't used to using it anymore.

"Hi. I was just . . . Fairchild said you were up here. I had to see how you were." Rat held out the coffee. "And I got this for you. Black, no sugar. That's still how you take it, right?"

He took it from them warily, folding his hands around the cup without drinking. "Does this mean we're still talking?"

"Is that okay?"

Slowly, he nodded, shifting over to make space for Rat on the window seat.

"Fairchild told me you were thinking about leaving," they said, settling across from him.

Harker looked out the window, but something in him fell a little. "She's already talking to Dawn about helping me find somewhere to stay for the semester. She thought it might be better if I waited until next fall and started over. Maybe leave New York for a while until Evening forgets about me."

Rat's chest tightened. "And you're considering it?"

"Do you want me to?"

"Do you?"

Harker hesitated, choosing his words carefully. "I don't think what I want has ever made that much of a difference."

Rat's heart clenched. They didn't know what they'd been hoping for, but anything they were going to say died in their throat.

"I'm not going to get in your way," Harker said. "I know that no one trusts me. If you want me to go, I'll make sure that whatever happens with the binding spell isn't your problem." He dropped his gaze. "That paper I tried to give you last night. It was a spell diagram I was working on. I was trying to find a way to release the wraiths from the tower. I don't think what we did was enough to get them free, but if you have their things, there might actually be a chance that . . ." He trailed off, like even now, he couldn't make himself say it out loud.

The wraiths were already dead. Rat had felt it in the tower, in the shadowy brush of their fingers. There wasn't any coming home for them. But that didn't mean they had to stay bound to Isola.

Harker swallowed hard. "I need to get them out. So they can rest. Promise you're going to go back for them once this is done, and Bellamy

Arts can be yours like you wanted. You won't have to deal with me again."

"Harker—"

"Please." A desperate edge slid into his voice.

"Stay," Rat said before they could stop themself.

Harker watched them like he didn't completely trust that he'd understood them.

"I don't care about getting you out of Bellamy Arts. I don't want that. I—" Rat's voice caught. They'd looked for him. They'd lost him so many times in their dreams that sometimes they thought they really had. Rat wanted to set whatever was left of their dignity on fire and beg him not to leave this time, and they wanted to kick him for having the audacity to assume that after all this time, they were anything other than uselessly in love with him.

"I'm not going back to the tower with Isola," Rat said. They hadn't realized it until then, but they'd already decided. "I don't care what I swore to her, I'm going to find her heart and make sure she never lays a hand on anyone again." They drew in, holding his gaze. "And I want you to stay and help me. Not because of a vow you made when you were desperate, and not because you think I need to be protected. Because I want you here, and I'm asking you not to go yet."

"Rat—"

"It could be an alliance. A real one. Just the two of us, until the end this time." They reached out, taking his wrist. Rat ran their thumb over his bracelets, and he stilled. "We could stop her for good."

He was quiet, but he sharpened a little, and Rat could see him considering it.

"Just think about it. Please. I can catch you up on what you've missed—here." Rat reached for their backpack and dug out their sketchbook. "I brought this for you." They held it out to him.

Hesitantly, Harker took it from them and riffled through the pages, like he wasn't sure what he was seeing, skimming past maps and sketches—a bird's-eye view of the library; a rough drawing of the school's skyline, the clock tower knocked askew; a thumbnail of the War Room, etched in beside the sprawl of the tunnels.

"You told me you didn't remember the campus that well," Rat said. "I just thought maybe—while you're finding your way around, I mean . . ."

His hand tightened on the binding, and they realized he'd stopped on a picture of the Drake. "I can't take these. You need them."

"You can give them back when you're done. I've figured out my way around," Rat said, pressing the notebook into his hands before he could give it back to them. "And I have some other things for you, too." They lifted their backpack, pulling it into their lap. "It's clothes, mostly. I thought you might need to borrow some, at least until you can get stuff from your dorm."

Unsure, Harker took the bag from them and took out a shirt.

"It's big on me, so it should fit you," Rat said.

He gave them a look. "Rat. This is mine."

Their face heated. "No, I brought it with me from home. I've literally been wearing it all semester."

Harker raised his eyebrows at them.

"It's comfortable," they mumbled. They shoved the bag toward him. "I still want it back when you're done."

Before Harker could dignify that with an answer, Rat's phone buzzed.

They looked down to see a new text from Jinx.

Rat opened it, expecting time and location, but instead she'd given them a list of directions, which must have led to the music room where everyone was meeting.

Harker looked at them, a question on his face.

"Jinx," Rat said. "I think she wants to figure out what's next."

His expression fell. "Oh. You're going?"

"What are you doing right now?"

Harker hesitated again, like he wasn't sure what they were asking.

"Go get your things," Rat said. "I'll let everyone know we're on our way."

As soon as Harker went back to his room, Rat slid their phone out and scrolled down to Elise's number.

The phone rang twice, then went to voice mail, which meant that either Elise had finally given in and gone to sleep, or she was in the middle of mobilizing a search party.

"Hi," Rat said. "It's me. I just wanted to let you know I'm okay. I'm staying with a friend, and I'm not hurt." They drew in a breath. "I don't know what everyone is saying, but Harker had nothing to do with this. You can be as mad at me as you want, but he's been through enough. He was never using me. I—he told me what you did to keep him away from me last semester."

Rat's throat tightened. They should have planned what they were going to say. Suddenly, they were furious with her. "I know you care about me, but that doesn't make it okay. You can't say you're protecting me and then go after the one person I actually—" Their voice broke. "Fuck. I'm not coming home. I'm going back to Bellamy Arts, and I don't care what the rest of the Northeast knows about me."

Heart in their mouth, Rat hung up before they could make it any worse. It should have felt like a victory to finally say it, but they just wanted to sink into the floor. Rat didn't want to think about how easy it had been for Elise to go after Harker, as if he hadn't been their closest friend. As if he hadn't been their only friend who was like them.

She'd treated Harker like the terrible thing she was afraid Rat would become, and when she'd figured out he had nowhere to turn, she'd tried to use that to back him into a corner. Rat didn't want to ask what Elise would have made of them if they weren't her kid, or if she could have cut them down just as fast.

A moment later, their phone rang, but they declined it.

They'd made their choice at the Revel. Maybe long before that, when they'd first decided to chase Harker into the tunnels at Bellamy Arts, knowing that they might not make it back out.

CHAPTER TWENTY-FOUR

"HOW MUCH DO YOU KNOW?" RAT ASKED HARKER AS THEY made their way through the house. He'd changed into the clothes they'd lent him, which had somehow done absolutely nothing to make him look less like a vengeful ghost.

"Isola hasn't come back to collect you yet," he said. "I assume that means you're still looking for the Ingrid Collection."

"There are seven keys we need to get past the doors."

Harker furrowed his brow.

"Ingrid took it from an old story—I'll lend it to you sometime. My best guess is that she gave the keys to her allies for safekeeping, but Evening's been searching for them. We got into his office the night of the Revel." Rat paused. "That's how I got Isola to the Council Chambers. I told her I needed her help. Jinx was keeping her occupied in the ballroom."

A shadow passed over Harker's face, maybe because he knew exactly how close they'd come to failing. "How many are left?"

"We found three. So, four to go," Rat said.

"And do we know where to look?"

"No," they said with a sigh. "I guess that's the question now." Rat paused as they took a turn in the hallway. "I think it's this way."

They motioned to Harker, and without meaning to, they realized they'd reached for the binding spell again.

"Sorry." Quickly, they dropped it. "How is this supposed to work?"

"The binding spell?"

Rat nodded.

"I don't know," Harker admitted. "It's not a real spell."

Rat tugged the binding spell intentionally this time, and he whipped toward them, the air around him warming as his magic instinctively flared to life.

"It looks like a real spell to me," Rat said.

"It's not from a spellbook. It doesn't have that much structure. It's just intention," he clarified in a huff, like that wasn't how solidly ninety percent of Rat's casting worked. "It's not as complicated as the one I swore to Isola. I don't think it's strong enough to summon me with or compel me against my will. I think it's just . . ."

Harker tugged back, and Rat was suddenly and acutely aware of how close he was.

"What if you broke it?"

"I don't know if I can." Harker tilted his head, considering, but they could hear the frustration in his voice at not having an answer. "I pledged my intention to go with you. Spells like that usually tie up the caster's power. If it's a strong enough working, I might not be able to cast anything that goes against it, but it should go away once the conditions are met."

"Neat. So, we just, you know. Find the Ingrid Collection and defeat Isola and it's fine."

He arched his eyebrows at them like that was actually the plan, and Rat realized there was absolutely no way this was going to end well. At least Rat had some reassurance that if anyone tried to stab them, it probably wasn't going to be Harker.

Morning light washed over him as he followed Rat past a row of windows, and Rat's humor dissolved. "I'm sorry it was the only way back," they said. "I know it's not the freedom you were hoping for."

"It's nothing I hadn't promised you already. Not openly betraying you for a couple months is a small price."

"Openly?"

The ghost of a smile tugged at his mouth.

Rat stared at him, and he drew ahead of them.

They rushed to catch up. "You're joking, right?"

Rat slowed as they came to the foot of a staircase. Harker looked back at Rat, a question on his face.

"Before we go up there, I . . . my pact with Isola," Rat said. "No one else knows about it."

"Who would I tell?"

"Harker—"

"Your secret's safe," he said softly. "I know why you did it. I'm not going to say anything."

Voices drifted down from somewhere above them. Harker glanced back at the top of the stairs, the same way they'd seen him peer down darkened tunnels when they were at Bellamy Arts, and a little of the certainty went out of him.

"Maybe it should just be you," he said. "You probably have plans to figure out, and—"

"They'll want to see you," Rat said, grabbing his arm.

"I'm not sure about that."

"Sounds like a you problem, Blakely."

"Rat," he said, and a note of panic crept into his voice.

They turned back to him. "Trust me?"

Harker looked at Rat like maybe letting them rescue him from the tower had been the wrong call.

They let go of him and held their hand out. "I can still take you back to your room if you want."

Harker hesitated like he was considering it. Then, finally, he laid his hand over theirs and let them lead the way.

At the top of the stairs, the door to the music room was already open.

A full-sized harp stood in the window, the varnished curve of its wooden frame gleaming in the sun. In the center of the room, Jinx had claimed one of the armchairs, and Will had pulled over the piano bench so he could read over her shoulder, even though there were still free seats. On the other side, Agatha sat perched on the arm of Jinx's chair, also in spite of the free seats, picking at the strings of a violin in a way that struck Rat as somehow expert and idle at the same time.

A pile of books took up most of the coffee table along with a couple sheets of handwritten notes, like Agatha had already spent the morning in the archives. In the center of it all, the three keys they'd retrieved from Evening's office lay on top of the clutter.

As soon as Rat moved, Jinx was already on her feet, Will and Agatha close behind her. "Evans," she said, rushing over. "How are you? Did—" She stopped as she caught sight of Harker behind them. "Blakely."

Before Harker could say anything, though, Agatha was in the doorway.

"Finally. We were waiting," Agatha said. "It's lucky for you I prefer to take down my enemies when they're in good health."

He gave her a rueful look. "I hate to disappoint you, Cromwell, but you might be waiting a while."

"I'll make do. In the meantime, it's good you're here. There's a draft from the windows and it's freezing," she said, pulling him into the room.

Harker managed to look moderately affronted at being used as a space heater, but he let her lead the way.

Jinx caught Rat's eye with a look that they were pretty sure meant, *It's neat that he's alive, but why are we letting him near spellbooks?*

"Come on," Will said, taking Rat by the shoulder. "We were just talking about breaking for lunch soon. Agatha was going to order in. How are you feeling?"

"Like I fought a train," Rat said, biting back a wince. They looked down at the papers on the table again. "What is all of this?"

Will glanced at Jinx, and she hesitated like she was deciding how much to say.

Rat realized that there was still a small, mistaken part of them that had been hoping this would be easy. "Harker's on our side. I asked him to come with me."

"Rat . . ." Jinx started.

"I'm under a binding spell," Harker said, turning back to her. "I needed a stronger oath to break the one I had with Isola. I can't turn on Rat without risking myself, too."

"You did what?" Jinx started, then rubbed her eyes like she had no idea what she'd expected. "Don't answer that, Blakely. You don't like yourself nearly enough for this to be reassuring." She looked at Rat like she was hoping they could explain why they'd allowed any of this.

"We didn't have another choice," they said, sinking into one of the open chairs. "If he tries anything, you can blame me for it."

"Trust me, I'm going to." Jinx dropped into the seat next to theirs, unenthused. "Let's just start. We should be safe for now, but I don't think we have that long before Isola comes after us, and Evening probably isn't going to be far behind."

"He's not." Rat took the letter Fairchild had given them from their pocket and set it on the coffee table. "There's a tracking spell. As soon as we make it back to campus, he's going to know where I am at pretty much all times."

"Fuck," Jinx muttered. "Can he do that?"

"Apparently it's already done," Rat said.

She sighed. "I guess that means we're counting you out of any plans to search for the rest of the keys."

"You should probably find a place to hide them," Rat said. "The less I can give away by accident, the safer it's going to be." But even as they spoke, they thought back to Isola as they'd seen her through the binding spell. She'd sensed Rat last night. The less she could find out from them, too, the better off everyone was.

Rat looked back down at the pile of notes, then frowned as the box they'd found in Evening's office caught their eye.

"What's this?" they asked.

"I don't know," Jinx said as Rat picked it up. She reached over and tapped the side of the box. "That's the Holbrook family's seal. Whatever it is, it must be important for Evening to be keeping it."

Rat turned it to face them. After they'd split with Agatha, they'd almost forgotten about the box completely. It was just big enough to fit in their hand, and each side was polished smooth and cool to the touch. The surface was inlaid with spellwork, but when Rat looked closely, they could see the fine lines where the pieces joined together, like if they twisted it in the right way, the whole configuration might open into something else.

Rat's hands went to a loose piece where they instinctively knew the box would give. They pushed, and the face of the box turned just a little.

Like a ripple though deep water, something far, far beneath surface of the music room *shifted*, and for a moment Rat felt all the seams and edges of the world jarring against each other, like the house around them was trying to open, too. Then the box jammed, like they'd pushed too far in the wrong direction.

Jinx caught their wrist, her eyes wide. "Evans, stop."

"Sorry. I didn't think . . ." Rat lowered the box back to the table as they realized that everyone was staring at them. "Do you know what it does?"

"No," she admitted. "We couldn't figure it out. It didn't do that before."

But even as she said it, Rat could hear the unspoken, *"Because none of us are wayfinders."*

Rat weighed the box in their hand, studying it. It wasn't going to open here. They didn't know how they knew, but somehow, they were sure of it. They started to put it back, but Jinx pushed it back to them.

"Take it." She flipped open one of the books from the table and slid it toward them. "We did find something else, though. On the keys. They're an inheritance spell."

Rat furrowed their brow.

"It's a type of deathworking," she said, pointing to the page. "It imbues an object with a version of the caster's abilities. The older bloodlines used to use it to make sure that any powerful affinities weren't lost if they weren't passed down naturally. It's one of the only kinds of workings that can be cast from a natural death."

"That doesn't make sense," Rat said. "I saw the keys, Jinx. I know what a deathworking looks like. They had a wayfinding spell on them."

Jinx hesitated. "I think," she said slowly, "that your family made them."

Rat got quiet.

"Ingrid wanted to make sure that no one could get in. Hiding the collection was probably enough to keep most people away, but the only real way to lock out a powerful wayfinder . . ."

"Is with their own magic," Rat finished. Their head swam.

There were seven keys, each one with the magic of a Holbrook Wayfinder, and Ingrid had used all of them to seal the doors. The kind of power it would take to undo a spell like that without gathering all of the keys would be monstrous, if it could be done at all. Ingrid had wanted to make sure that the doors couldn't be opened any other way, even if Isola managed to get her hands on a wayfinder, and then, she'd made certain all of the keys disappeared.

Except, however Rat thought about it, something nagged at them. "How did Ingrid get them?" they asked.

"The keys?"

Rat nodded. "You said they were powerful heirlooms. The old families don't part with things like that."

"I don't know. Ingrid was a magpie. She got her hands on all kinds of things. Maybe she had something to trade for them," Jinx said, but Rat could hear the uncertainty in her voice. "Maybe the Holbrook family was already declining, and she managed to sweep in before anyone else."

Even though Rat couldn't say why, it didn't put them at ease. The whole thing felt too close to them, like at every turn, they'd managed to find themself even more deeply enmeshed with the tower.

"You said Evening was breaking into other family's archives, right?" Harker asked.

Rat looked over at him.

"If he knows where the keys are, why are there only three?"

"And one is Allister's," Rat said, half to themself. The question bothered them, maybe because they'd had a similar thought in Evening's office, even if they hadn't been able to say why it felt so off.

Now, slowly, the pieces fell into place.

Evening had been searching for the keys, but he hadn't found nearly as many as Rat would have expected. "The keys weren't there."

The others looked at them.

"Evening was confident enough to make a move against the other houses, I don't think he actually found what he was looking for. Not all of them, at least."

Slowly, Jinx nodded. "I thought the same thing. Either he was wrong about the who had them, which would be reckless even for him, or . . ."

"By the time he broke in, someone else had already gotten there," Rat finished, meeting her gaze.

As they said it, a fresh wave of goosebumps pricked up their arms.

They'd been turning it over since they'd first found the keys. A part of them had already come to the same conclusion, but putting it into words, suddenly, they felt sure.

Quiet settled over the room again.

"My father was already looking for the keys," they said. "Night told me he'd been asking about them before he died."

Their father had mapped the campus; he'd known every corner of the school. He'd been the last person to have access to the Holbrook archives. He would have known about the keys. For all they knew, he could have been quietly negotiating with the other houses to get them back for years before his death. Evening had been turning the Northeast inside-out searching, and he'd only found two keys, and traded for another. With the Council's records and the Church family's skill for tracking things down at his disposal, if there was anything to find he should have had it already.

The only question was how many keys their father had managed to get ahold of and where they were now.

It was already starting to get late when everyone split off, but before Rat could slip out, Jinx caught them. "Evans. Wait. We need to talk."

Rat's chest tightened, but they'd known it was coming. Harker looked back at them from the stairs, but Rat nodded for him to go ahead. "I'll catch up."

Jinx waited until everyone else had gone before she closed the door again.

"I asked Harker to come with me," Rat said before she could start. "He's the only person who knows Isola as well as I do. He can help."

"Rat . . ."

"You helped me bring him back. You said that he was ours."

"That doesn't mean we can just throw him back into all of this." Jinx crossed back to where she'd been sitting and settled against the arm of the chair. "I'm glad he's safe, but everything that happened last semester . . . Maybe he was bound to Isola, but he still did all of those things without blinking. He didn't want us to help him. He wanted to win."

"I know. I don't have any illusions about who he is."

Her expression softened. "He was gone for two months, and Isola already had her hooks in him before that. Even if we wanted to, I don't think we can pretend he's okay. I'm not sure if he should even be out of bed right now."

"I know," they said again. "I just . . . I don't think there's much of a choice. She's not done with him just because he got away."

Jinx sighed heavily. "No. I don't think she is. That's actually what I wanted to talk to you about."

Rat stilled.

"I lost sight of her during the Revel," Jinx said. "Isola disappeared from the ballroom for almost forty-five minutes. Almost as soon as you were gone, she was, too. She could have been anywhere in the building."

"And spoken with almost anyone," Rat finished with a pang of unease. They thought of everyone who'd been at the Revel. Will and Agatha had been there, and they'd both been left alone at different parts of the night.

Allister had been there, and he'd already proven he was desperate enough to strike a deal with someone like Evening and clever enough to deliver.

Elise had been there, and so had the heads of just about every powerful family in New York. The only ones who didn't want to rescue Rat from the tower's grasp had just been given about a dozen good reasons to want them taken off the chessboard instead.

"It shouldn't have happened," Jinx told them. "I tried to find her, but no one saw her leave."

"It's not your fault," Rat said. "I was the one who invited her."

Of course Isola had another agenda. Rat had thought she'd just wanted a way to get her claws into them a little deeper, but Isola wouldn't waste something like that. She'd asked Rat to bring her.

"It doesn't matter anymore. It's done," Jinx said, but Rat could hear in her voice that it wasn't. "Now that Blakely's away from her, we can stop pretending to work with her. From here on, the less we give her, the better."

"Right." Almost like it had been called, Isola's magic flickered cruelly in Rat's chest. Rat pushed it down. They weren't going back again.

"I already told the others, but just . . . I think you should be careful," Jinx said. "I don't know what Isola's next move is going to be, but if I know her at all, she's just waiting for her moment."

"Yeah," Rat said. "I'm sure of it."

CHAPTER TWENTY-FIVE

RAT COULDN'T SLEEP THAT NIGHT. THEY DIDN'T THINK Agatha would appreciate them wandering around her house, so they slipped their coat on and took the stairs down to the garden.

A hedge maze sprawled behind the house, trimmed back for the winter and dusted with snow from the night before. If Rat was playing by horror movie rules, the hedge maze at night was probably the worst place for them to be, but they weren't sure they were any safer staying inside. If Isola wanted to talk, she was welcome to find them.

Rat started down the path, letting the sting of the cold clear their mind. They'd known that Evening wouldn't let them just take the keys and leave, but they hadn't expected him to hit back so quickly, and it was only a matter of time before Isola made her next move.

For all Rat knew, she already had.

The idea of her alone at the Revel sent a prickle of unease racing over their skin. They'd thought they were luring Isola away from the tower, but inviting her to the Council Chambers had been her idea first. She'd wanted something. The only question was what she'd been after.

Rat's breath fogged on the air. The fact that Isola had probably known the whole time that the keys were a Holbrook heirloom wasn't reassuring.

Rat took the next turn, and the maze around them opened into a clearing, the hedges etched with moon shadows, even though Rat was sure that they hadn't gone far enough to have reached the center already. Out of habit, they reached for their compass, but their hand found the unfamiliar shape of the puzzle box instead, heavy in their pocket. They drew it out, weighing it in their hand, but like before, when they tried to turn it, it stuck fast and the world shuddered around them.

"Of course not," Rat muttered. First the keys, then the puzzle box, both with their family's magic.

It hadn't been an accident that it had been their father's sketches that led them to the tower, and it wasn't an accident that he'd been one of the only people to get close to the Ingrid Collection. Rat was sure it wasn't an accident that Isola had sent them after seven keys forged with the long-ago deaths of seven Holbrook wayfinders.

Rat didn't know how it all fit together or what it had to do with them. They just couldn't help the creeping feeling that they were already in even deeper than they'd thought, and they still weren't at the bottom of it. Their father was probably the single person who would have known exactly what they'd walked into, and he was the only one they couldn't ask.

Footsteps crunched in the snow behind them. Rat spun to find Agatha, her coat drawn against the cold. "I thought you might be out here," she said.

"I was just—"

"Wandering a darkened hedge maze while Isola and all of her horrible creatures are searching for you?"

Rat ducked their head, pocketing the puzzle box once again. "Maybe?"

Agatha looked at them like they were an actual child, then sighed heavily. "Come with me. It's freezing, and I don't think I like you enough to stay out here. You can tell me what it is while we walk."

"It's nothing," Rat said, starting after her. "I was just thinking."

"Oh. A special occasion, then." She glanced back, and mischief tugged at the corner of her mouth.

"You're not funny."

Agatha lifted her chin. "My wit is unmatched. You're just mad you can't keep up." She fell quiet as she led them around the next bend.

"I couldn't sleep either," she admitted after a moment. "I never know what to do with myself when I'm here, but this is the first time I really thought about the possibility that if this all goes wrong, we might not make it back. And things don't get any less dangerous after this."

"I don't think so, either," Rat said. Their footsteps crunched on the snow, the grounds quiet around them. "Is it that bad being home?"

"No," Agatha said. She tipped her face up to the darkened sky. "Maybe. It shouldn't be."

Rat hesitated. "A while ago, you said your parents didn't want you at Bellamy Arts."

"Well, they're fine with it now," Agatha said with obvious frustration. "At least, my mother is. She hates that I'm in danger, but she's thrilled that I'm putting my powers to use. She offered to give me a refresher course."

"And that's bad?"

"Yes!" She huffed a breath. "I don't know! She spends her whole life helping people. Most of the cases she gets called in for are averting disasters and finding missing persons. She's brilliant at it, and I just . . . There's something they say about seers. Half of us refuse to interfere and end up letting fate pull all of our strings. The rest of us interfere too much and end up pulling the strings ourselves. Either you're responsible for nothing and all you can do is watch it play out already knowing how ends, or you take it into your own hands and become responsible for every single thing you let happen. You can't win."

"There's no way you can take all of that on yourself."

"But I did," Agatha said.

Rat was quiet.

"On the train," she said, her voice soft in the hush of the snow-covered grounds. "I knew the tracking spell came from Allister. I saw him on it as soon as I touched it."

"You didn't say anything."

"Because if I told you, the possibility that we found Blakely disappeared," Agatha said. "Do you see how awful that is? If you'd been killed, I would have been the one who'd set you on that path. If I told you, I'd have to live with knowing the future I might have cost us."

Rat remembered what Jinx had told them about how Agatha didn't like to share how much she knew. For the first time, it made sense to them. They glanced over at her as she led the way out of the maze. Moonlight silvered the snow-covered lawn ahead of them. "What would you do instead?" Rat asked. "If you don't, you know . . ."

"Put my gifts to use? I was thinking of being a crushing disappointment," Agatha said. "Maybe I'll study violin and live a life full of sword fighting and debauchery."

"You can sword fight?"

"I'm a lesbian," she said primly. "We get to declare a weapon when we come out: sword, bow, or ax. Ask Viola. She's an archer."

Rat opened their mouth to tell her that they were pretty sure *debauched sword lesbian* had stopped being a viable career path sometime in the 1800s, and also that if being gay came with a weapon proficiency, they would be really, really well armed. But before they could say any of that, they came to the end of the path. They stopped a few feet from the back stairs, but they didn't feel ready to go back to bed yet.

"Are you coming in?" Agatha asked.

Rat looked up at the house. "Yeah. There's just something I needed to do first."

"Blakely is upstairs," she said. "We were back in the music room when I left him."

"I didn't—"

"I'm gifted with the magnificent burden of sight," Agatha said loftily, and Rat realized they were very obviously searching for his window.

They turned back to her, and a little of the humor went out of her. "It doesn't matter how this is supposed to go. You changed it once," she said. "You can change it again."

But there was something in the way she said it that left Rat with the unsettling feeling that whatever she'd seen ahead, nothing good was waiting for them there.

Harker was in the music room, sitting on the floor at the foot of the couch with a pile of books. The last remnants of a cup of coffee were still on the table, but all of the books around him were closed, and he looked like he'd run out of steam a while ago.

Rat knocked on the doorframe. "Hey."

Harker scrambled to his feet, one hand raised defensively. The binding spell pulled taut as he reached for it and a jolt of panic raced down the bond before Rat could process what was happening. Heat flared off of him, the air suddenly stiflingly hot and crackling with power.

"Sorry!" Rat staggered back, raising their hands uselessly. "Blakely—fuck, it's me."

Harker stared at them for a moment, and then, like he'd just remembered where he was, the tension went out of him and whatever Rat had felt through the bond was gone.

"Rat," he said weakly. He dropped his hand from its casting position, managing to look embarassed. "I didn't—I thought you went back to your room."

"No, it's my fault. I was looking for you," they said, their heart still racing. They glanced down at the books, then lowered themself to the floor. "What's all this?"

"Nothing." Hesitantly, Harker settled beside them. Residual heat from the spell wavered on the air around him. "I was just thinking about the tracking spell. Agatha mentioned you had a working you'd used to get through Isola's banishment. That was what was chalked on to your cloak, wasn't it?"

"Yeah. Will made a second one that was supposed to get in the way of any attempts to find me, but he said it was pretty weak. I don't think it could hold up long enough to keep Evening from noticing."

"Probably not," Harker said slowly, like he was still working something over.

Rat studied him. "Do you have something?"

"Not yet." He pushed the book away from himself. "But, if I'm really going back with you, we're not going to get that far with Evening watching your every move."

"If?" Rat asked.

Harker met their gaze tentatively, like he was still waiting for them to change their mind.

Rat didn't know how it had ever been a question. They knew Harker, and they knew he would set fire to the tower all over again before he let Isola get away with any of it. "Good. There's something I need you for," they said, leaning in. "If I can get you the spell I used, do you think you could figure out a version that was exact enough to fool a tracking spell without anyone noticing?"

"I might need your cloak," he said cautiously.

They shot him a dogged grin. "You'll have to be careful with it. I'm pretty sure it's a Holbrook family heirloom."

For a moment, Harker looked unsure. Then, he seemed to realize Rat was making a joke and did his best to look pointedly unamused.

"I can bring it by your room," they said.

He leaned in, and a familiar intensity flickered across his face. "What are you planning, Evans?"

"You stole my dad's notes from the school's private archive last semester," Rat said. "How hard would it be to do it again?"

CHAPTER TWENTY-SIX

THEY STAYED AT AGATHA'S HOUSE FOR THE REST OF THE break. Rat spent most of their time in the music room, flipping through the books Agatha had pulled from the archives or pacing around the grounds.

Rat had thought the tower dreams might have stopped now that they were back, but the only difference was that now, the tower in their mind was full of wraiths.

A few times, when it was still early and Rat couldn't stay in their room any longer, they found themself back in the hedge maze practicing their casting. It should have scared them to be out there alone, but they could sense every bend and turn ahead of them, the snow crunching under their boots as they raced through the maze, and the dead passages came to them like breathing.

For the rest of their stay, Harker made himself scarce, probably because Jinx had been right about him needing to rest. A couple of times, Rat found him perched in a window like he was trying to get as close to the sunlight as possible, or already camped out on the floor of the music room when Rat got there so he wouldn't have to ask to join them. The rest of the time, he was usually studying, since he'd somehow convinced Fairchild to let him make up his coursework so he wouldn't have to repeat the semester. Rat wasn't sure how he'd pulled it off, but they assumed it had taken a combination of spite, groveling, and aggressive time management.

They all left a couple of days after New Years from the train station in town.

"Why does it feel like we're heading into something even worse?" Rat asked Jinx while they entered their train time into the ticket kiosk.

She gave them a wry not-smile. "Like you said. All wolves, all the time." She reached over and grabbed the tickets from the machine. "Ready to go?"

Rat looked back at the platform where everyone else was waiting with their suitcases. Harker had Rat's scarf looped over his cloak, since his coat was still sealed up in his room at Bellamy Arts. "As much as I'm going to be," Rat said, taking their ticket from her.

They were farther along the line than Grand Central, which meant most of the Bellamy Arts kids who were coming back in through the city were already on board. Rat could swear that a couple of people stole glances as they made their way through the car. At least, they told themself, this time it was for something they'd actually done.

Harker glanced up as they slid into the seat next to him.

"Were you waiting for someone else?" they asked.

He raised his eyebrows at them. "Careful, Evans. People might think we're friends."

"They already thought I killed you," Rat said. "I'm pretty sure it can't be that much worse."

Just for a moment, something tentative and unsure whispered down the binding spell. Then, probably out of pure spite for whatever was left of Rat's reputation, he settled casually against them. "Fine, but I'm not entertaining you," he said producing a dog-eared paperback from his cloak.

Their pulse skipped in the absolute most humiliating way, and they forced themself to breathe as the train pulled away.

Somehow, Rat had expected that going back would feel like going home, but the answers they still needed were on the campus, and they weren't close to done. They'd known what they were in for when they'd left for the Council Chambers, but Bellamy Arts was supposed to be familiar territory. Now, Rat couldn't help the feeling they were fighting their way out of one patch of thorns, just to dive headfirst into another.

Evening might not have wanted to pick a fight as long as Rat was under the protection of Agatha's family, but he wouldn't wait long to strike now that Rat was on their own. And if Isola was biding her time, it was only because she was planning something worse. Rat was going to need to get the rest of the keys, and they were going to need to do it before anyone else had a chance to strike.

The sun had begun to sink in the sky by the time they made it into the station at Bellamy. Will grabbed their suitcase without asking and loaded it into his car.

"You're with us, Blakley," he said, like that decided things. "I already need to stop by Armitage Hall to unload the car before I take it back to the student lot."

"I can walk back if you just want to stop there," Rat offered.

Will glanced back at Harker, like he knew the offer wasn't really for him.

"It's fine," Harker managed. "I need to talk to the RA when I get in so they can find somewhere to put me."

"They couldn't unseal your room?" Rat asked.

He gave them a wry look. "The seal wasn't placed by the school. Apparently, the Council can't spare anyone until classes start."

"Apparently," Rat repeated.

The drive back up was quiet, and Rat felt the tracking spell slide over them like a film of grease. The unsettling feeling of being watched pricked up the back of their neck, but they fought the urge to look over their shoulder. Then Harker's breath hitched as campus came into sight, and they did turn. Some of his composure had slid away, and he stared openly at the campus like he'd never been there before. When he noticed Rat watching, he caught himself again.

From the gates, it wasn't far to the dorms. "I should—" Rat started.

"I'll stay with him," Will said. "You should go ahead."

Rat hesitated, but they let Will get their bags out of the car.

They watched as he drove off, and their gaze slid toward the center of campus, where they could just pick out the highest points of the library in the distance, and the crooked form of the clock tower rising up above the trees.

If Isola wanted a game, they could play, too.

A cold wind blew across the path, and for a moment, Rat thought they felt something whisper past them somewhere between the cracks in the world, but when they turned back, there wasn't anything there.

CHAPTER TWENTY-SEVEN

THE FIRST DAY OF WINTER SEMESTER BROKE COLD AND bright.

There were exactly two things Rat needed to do, and since they weren't getting into the school archives until Harker had found a way around Evening's tracking spell, that put figuring out the puzzle box at the top of their list.

Rat packed the box into their backpack before they headed out for classes. They already knew who to speak to, but since their lessons with Frey had been put on indefinite hold, that meant they were actually going to have to find him and ask. Which meant they had to go to their morning classes first. Which meant coffee.

The campus was still quiet, but there were already a few students out, and Rat felt eyes on their back as they picked their way up the path toward Galison Hall. They fished their phone out of their pocket as they walked and found their old message thread with Harker.

Hey, on my way to they typed, then deleted it.

Meet before class? Heading to Galison. Rat stared down at the screen. They'd been to the tower. They could send Harker a text message. Before Rat could stop themself, they sent it off.

A moment later, their phone pinged. *Already here*, it said, with an off-center picture of a to-go cup, a heating spell scrawled on the lid in permanent marker.

There in five, try not to set yourself on fire, Rat typed, and then, because they'd just woken up and shouldn't be allowed within five feet of a keyboard, they added a row of flame emojis and sent.

They glanced back to see a couple of students on the other side of the lawn quickly avert their gazes.

Galison Hall was still pretty empty when Rat got there, but the building wasn't the same kind of deserted it had been before the break. Rat stopped by the foot of the stairs in the front entrance and glanced down at their phone.

Just got in, they typed, and then deleted it again. Rat tapped their fingers against the screen.

"Well, this makes my job easy."

They whipped around to see Allister on the stairs behind them.

The last time Rat had seen him on campus, he'd been dressed to blend in, but now he wore the gray cloak that marked him as one of Evening's underlings, so no one could have any doubts about who'd sent him.

"Morning, Evans." He waved to them. "You know, I assumed I was going to have to track you down at some point to let you know you were under investigation. But there are like, what, twelve students here? How many kids are even in your year?"

"That investigation is closed."

"The *other* investigation," Allister said. "Stop me if you've heard this one, but some important evidence went missing from the Council Chambers after the Revel. The Council tends to take an interest in that kind of thing."

Rat glowered at him.

"Personally, I'd appreciate if we just made this quick. Between us, I'm not that interested in spending the rest of the semester chasing you through the woods."

"You could have fooled me."

"Believe me, Evans, there's nothing out here but bad dining hall coffee and Gothic architecture. You got your boyfriend back. Just call it a win and turn over the keys, and whatever comes next, I'll be out of your way," he said, dropping his voice. "Your choice, though."

He moved to draw back, but Rat caught his arm.

"I heard how Evening spoke to you. In his office," they said before they could think any better of it. "You realize he was responsible for the attack last semester, right?"

For a moment, surprise flickered across Allister's face, but Rat didn't know if it was the information, or just the fact that they were telling him. Then, just as quickly, it was gone again. "Save it for your friends, Evans. You can't afford me," he said, pulling away from them. "I gave you a chance to get away safely. You were the one who decided to get heroic about it."

"You *attacked me*."

"Yeah, after you broke into the office of a Greater Hour," Allister said under his breath. "Some advice, though? Maybe you had everyone convinced you were harmless last year, but the old bloodlines have a long memory, and they know what happens when wayfinders and summoners get reckless. I think this might be a good time to watch your step."

"Are you done?" a voice said behind them.

Rat turned to see Harker standing close by, cup of dining hall coffee in hand.

Since he'd gotten back from the tower, Rat had thought he'd started to recover out of his most ragged edges, but now, they couldn't help wondering if maybe they'd just gotten used to him. In the daylight, he reminded Rat of the stories they'd heard about revenants—not entirely ghost or flesh but something else that was fury and spite and horrible purpose. Someone must have finally unsealed his room since he'd gotten his coat back, but everything about him was a little too sharp, and if his magic was usually in close reach, now it coiled protectively around him like a creature waiting to strike.

Allister stepped back.

"We were just finishing up," Allister said smoothly. He nodded to Rat. "If you change your mind, you know how to find me."

☠

Their first semester casting practicum had been replaced with a second semester theory of magic seminar on the top floor of the Higher Magics building, and stares followed Rat across campus.

Jinx was already waiting in the lobby by the time they got there. She looked from Rat to Harker. "Easy on the resting villain face, Blakely. We want people to like us."

He scowled at her, like it was incredibly bold of her to assume he ever rested. "Do we?"

"It's already been a long morning," Rat said by way of explanation. "We ran into Church."

"Shit," Jinx muttered. "He's here?"

"Apparently the Council only has one intern," they said flatly.

"Rat."

"It doesn't matter what he's after. We just need to figure out the rest of the keys before he does."

Jinx managed to look unimpressed.

"He's here to draw attention," Rat said. "Evening basically told me as much before the Revel. Last semester, he wanted everyone to think I was in danger so they'd let him sweep in and protect me. Now he's sending Church to investigate me and stir up more rumors so everyone will think I'm a threat." They stopped as a group of students passed them on the stairs, whispering to one another. Harker met one of the girls' eyes directly, and she quickly ducked her head, hurrying after her friends.

"That's going to be a problem," Jinx said.

"Maybe they should think I'm a threat." Rat adjusted their hold on their backpack as they took the landing. "I had to be scared of all the other houses finding out about me. They can be scared of me for a change."

Jinx gave Harker a beseeching glance.

He took a sip of his coffee. "I think it's a great plan."

They stopped as they came to the top of the stairs. Rat had expected another room full of lab desks and supply cabinets, but the doors led to a small amphitheater and a set of polished wooden steps leading down to a semicircle of the same black slate flooring that Rat had seen in the casting rooms, the remnants of any spells that might have been chalked there carefully cleaned away.

A set of sliding blackboards took up the back wall, still covered in a scrawl of elaborate sigils from the class before, and flecks of aether hung suspended in the air from an earlier working, drifting in faintly glowing currents. A woman who, based on their schedule, had to be Professor Lindquist stood at the front, arranging papers on her desk.

Most of the desks were already full, and a couple of students turned to look as they entered. Rat didn't know if it was them everyone was interested in, or Harker, or the fact that they'd both returned from the tower bloody and covered in ash in the middle of the Revel.

Beside Rat, Harker straightened a little, a familiar chill settling over his features, and if Rat didn't know him, they might have missed the way he'd tensed. For the first time since he'd come back from the tower, he looked the way they remembered him from Highgate—cold and untouchable and sharp enough to cut. He gave Rat a small nod, and even though everyone was still stealing glances at them, Rat couldn't help a pang of satisfaction that for once, they were every bit as forbidding as he was.

Lifting their chin, Rat started down the aisle after him.

CHAPTER TWENTY-EIGHT

RAT WAITED UNTIL THE CLASS HAD ENDED BEFORE THEY headed off on their own. Frey was already in his office when Rat got there, sorting through a pile of papers.

The room was the same as they remembered it from the one time they'd been there last semester, with dark wooden furniture and bookshelves cluttered with strange odds and ends.

"Rat. I was told the Council put your lessons on hold," he said, looking up from his work.

"I actually had a question about something else," Rat said.

"And I assume that whatever I tell you, you plan on disregarding it and taking the most dangerous course of action available to you?"

Rat winced, but a small smile tugged at Frey's lips.

"I understand trouble has a way of finding you, Mx. Evans, but it seems to me you go searching for it every chance you get," he said, not unkindly.

"You heard about the Revel."

"Blakely told me what happened. I just wish you hadn't had to handle it on your own." Worry creased his face, and a little of the lightness went out of him. "It's a dangerous thing you've done, going up against Isola like that."

"I've heard," Rat managed. "I didn't realize you'd seen Harker already."

Frey sighed. "Yes. My morning timeslot for private lessons seems to have opened up unexpectedly. On the upside, as students go, he's already extremely adept at lighting candles."

"I got it to light," Rat protested.

Frey's eyes glinted with amusement, but just as quickly, it was gone again. "But I'm guessing that's not what brings you here."

Rat hesitated as they realized they weren't sure what they expected from him. Frey wasn't their teacher anymore. He probably wasn't supposed to be meeting with them at all.

"There are limits on what I can tell you," Frey said, reading their silence. "The Council has been very clear that you aren't allowed to come to me for any kind of instruction on spellcasting. But if there was something you needed to discuss, in a more advisory capacity . . ." He nodded slightly to the chair on the other side of the desk.

Rat glanced back at the door, then sat down across from him. "I came across something, and I was wondering if you could tell me about it," they said. They opened their backpack and dug out the puzzle box. "Do you know what this is?"

With a frown, Frey took it from them. He turned the box in his hand, studying it intently. "I haven't seen one of these in a long time."

"But you recognize it?"

"It's a very old type of wayfinding spell. You could think of it like a key. It's linked to a location."

"So, if you can align the puzzle . . ."

"The planes around it align, too, but they only work in exactly the right place," Frey said. "That one is your father's work. He made it during one of his last years with the school. I remember him doing the enchantments."

"Do you know where it goes?"

"He never told me. Wherever it is, I can only assume he went to great lengths to keep it hidden." His frown deepened. "Where did you find this? I always assumed it would be registered to the school archives."

Rat straightened. "What?"

"When Elise left his things with the school for safekeeping. I'd assumed this would be among them."

"Oh," Rat managed. "I found it over the break. It must have been released at some point."

"It must have," Frey said, half to himself.

"I didn't—" Rat started, but he waved them off.

"I don't think you would bring me something you'd stolen from the school archives. Maybe you'll prove me wrong, but I'd like to believe you're at least a little smarter than that." He handed the puzzle box back to them.

Rat eyed him warily.

"It's technically yours by right. I imagine there are worse hands it could fall into than yours," he said, like he suspected it already might have. "You should try to be careful with it, though. I'm sure you know this by now, but if Alexander locked something away, there was always a reason for it."

Rat closed their hands over it and returned the puzzle box to their bag, fighting a pang of unease.

Probably, Evening had slipped it out during the investigation last semester while he'd been looking into the stolen Holbrook Map. It would have put him in the same part of the school archives. For all Rat knew, he'd claimed it as evidence and never returned it.

Across from them, Frey folded his hands on the desk. "For what it's worth, I'm sorry I won't be teaching you this semester. I'm not sure how much help I can be to you, but I'll be here if you need me. And Evans. I know it won't do much good but . . ."

"I should be careful of Isola?"

"You're dealing with powerful magic, and there's a reason we don't usually teach wayfinding to underclassmen before they've had a chance to learn their limits," he said. "Doors tend to open both ways, and you can't always control what comes through. Isola isn't invincible, but she's been around for a long time, and she's gotten the better of more powerful arcanists before. You should be careful of everything."

Rat had another class to get to, but they didn't make it much farther than the back stairwell of the Higher Magics building.

They looked over their shoulder, then, satisfied they were alone, they settled on the stairs and took the puzzle box back out of their bag. Midday sunlight streamed in through the windows in dusty shafts, catching on the metal inlay as Rat turned the box in their hand.

An uneasy feeling rolled through them, and Isola's magic stirred in their core, unbidden. Rat shut their eyes, steadying themself, and an image of the tower flickered in their mind, as crisp as if they were there amid the clutter of Isola's rooms.

Gloved fingers pressed the back of their neck, cool against their skin. "What have you found now?" a voice asked them, cold and full of starlight.

Rat jerked back, dropping the puzzle, and it clattered on the landing below. They whipped around, but the stairwell was empty. They were alone.

Isola hadn't been there. Whatever she'd sensed or seen, she couldn't touch them.

Shaking, Rat forced themself up and climbed down to get the box. They closed their hand around it, grounding themself. All of this was their dad's work, Rat reminded themself. If they couldn't make sense of it, they should have at least been able to figure out where to start.

Without meaning to, they thought back to Night in the Council Archives. She might have been the only other person who would know their father's work and still have a reason to help them.

Rat slid their phone out and pulled up Agatha's number before they could second-guess themself.

How hard would it be to get a message to Night? they typed.

They sent it off, then took a last look at the puzzle, balancing it in their hand, and they hoped that Isola saw.

CHAPTER TWENTY-NINE

WHISPERS FOLLOWED RAT THROUGH THE REST OF THEIR classes that week.

When Rat had set up their schedule, Harker had still been at the tower and spring semester had been the farthest thing from their mind. They'd missed the first couple days of course registration entirely, and aside from the required theory class, the schedule they'd ended up with was probably best described as unenviable.

Rat still hadn't been planning on casting outside of their private lessons, and they'd ended up grabbing as many history courses as they could, since it was one of the only tracks that didn't involve any magic. By the time they'd registered, most of the remaining openings had been for morning classes, and Rat didn't have any days that started later than nine. When Jinx had seen their schedule, she'd visibly winced.

Rat should have hated it, except that they actually liked the campus in the mornings when everything was quiet. The History building was one of the oldest on campus, most of it still original from when the school had first been rebuilt. It reminded Rat a bit of how they imagined the sunken campus might look, if it was hauled back above ground and hit with a couple dozen coats of furniture polish. Most of their classes only had a handful of students, which meant Rat had a lot of time to try the puzzle box around campus while the buildings were empty.

It was almost the end of the week when they woke up from another tower dream to find an envelope waiting on their windowsill. The room was still dark, and the cream-colored paper showed bright in the last strains of moonlight.

The unease from their dream still clung to Rat, even though they already couldn't remember what it had been about. Just the narrow turn of the tower's staircase, and that they'd woken up gasping. Steadying themself, Rat padded across the room, the floor cold beneath their feet. A faint trace of aether clung to the paper, but it was too pristine to be from the tower. Rat picked it up, then stopped as they came to the dab of midnight blue wax stamped with Night's crest. A lily and moon.

The quiet of the dorm pressed in around them as they cracked the seal. Carefully, they slid out the letter, but it was only a couple of lines.

Galison Hall, casting room 7. Someone will be waiting to escort you. Please be there at 10 am exactly.

Rat looked out the window, but they weren't sure if they were searching for a sign of how it had gotten there or just to make sure that none of Isola's birds were watching from the high branches. Either way, there was just the dark shape of the hills and the slowly paling sweep of the sky.

Rat shoved the letter into their coat's pocket and got their things for the day.

"What do you think she wants?" Harker asked once Rat showed it to him. They hadn't discussed it, but somehow, they'd started showing him around campus in the mornings. He followed along beside them on the path, holding a cup of dining hall coffee like a hard-won prize and still inexplicably wearing Rat's scarf. Probably, Rat guessed, as part of some kind of murky revenge plot.

"She didn't say," Rat said, their breath clouding on the air. "Whatever it is, if she's scheduling it like this, she wants to make sure Evening doesn't have time to find out."

"How much do you trust her?"

"More than Evening," Rat said, which wasn't worth a lot. Their gaze went to Galison Hall at the end of the path. They'd nearly made a full circuit of the main buildings, and the last of the fog still drifted over the lawn in low wisps. "Either way, I guess we're going to find out."

They moved to go, but Harker caught them by the sleeve. "Rat. Wait."

Rat's pulse skipped.

"Your cloak." He cleared his throat. "I'm almost finished with it."

"Oh. Right," they said. "You can leave it in my room if I'm not back. I don't have any wards or anything, since—" They stopped themself short as they realized what they were about to say. *Since you always did those.* They already needed Harker a truly pathetic amount. They didn't have to remind him of it. "I'm sure you can figure out the lock. I've seen you do it before." They reached for his coffee and took a sip.

Harker whipped toward them. "Hey! That's—"

"Oh, wow. I forgot how bad that is," they said. Harker made a small, incredulous noise from the back of his throat, and they handed the cup back to him. "Wish me luck?"

"Your spell took me two all-nighters, Evans. You owe me breakfast," he said, which was probably as close as they were going to get.

The travel spell was already waiting when Rat made up to Galison Hall's casting rooms, one of Night's Lesser Hours at the door to bring them back to the Council Chambers. The spell was quick and every bit as horrible as Rat remembered before it dropped them into one of the Council's casting rooms. Flecks of aether spun around them in heavy drifts as the spell settled, and their stomach threatened to revolt. Out of habit, Rat slid their hand to their compass, letting the cool metal ground them.

"This way," the Lesser Hour said, waving for Rat to follow her.

They started after, trying and failing to orient themself as she led the way into a wide hallway in what could have only been Night's wing of the Council Chambers.

The polished white stone of the rest of the building gave way to dark marble, and the map of the sky from the main hallway extended into an elaborate diagram of the stars in their orbits, inlaid with painstaking care. A handful of Lesser Hours in deep blue cloaks made their way up the hall, looking like they were on their way home, but the wing was still relatively quiet, and Rat realized the main shift had probably ended hours ago.

The Lesser Hour who'd been guiding Rat led them through a set of doors at the end of the hall. She pushed one open, revealing a wide, circular room that reminded Rat of Evening's office, if it had been shifted a few hours further into night. The upholstery on the furniture was a deep violet, and the stairs that led up to the small balcony level were made from a dark, polished hardwood, a shade off from black. Night-blooming plants hung down from the banister and more cluttered the windows, the glass tinted to keep in the gloom.

Evening had already beaten them there, standing in the center of the room in what looked to be the tail end of a conversation. Theophania Aldridge sat at her desk, looking supremely finished with him, her ring-heavy fingers steepled in displeasure.

The Lesser Hour knocked on the doorframe.

"Ah. Thank you. Please show Mx. Evans in." Night looked back up at Evening. "As I've told you before, the Council of Hours is not a private army you can deploy in service of your personal vendettas, Edgar. No one can attest to the evidence that was allegedly taken from your office, as you failed to disclose its existence to us until after the fact. As far as I'm concerned, your part in this meeting is over. Unless you see fit to lodge a formal challenge?"

"Of course not," he said smoothly, composing himself. "I meant only to express my concerns." He gave Rat an icy smile as he brushed past them back into the hall.

After he'd gone, Night nodded to her Lesser Hour. "Thank you. I think that will be all. Please close the door after yourself."

"Of course." The Lesser Hour dipped into a shallow bow and swept out, pulling the door shut after her.

"My apologies," Night said as soon as she was alone with Rat. She rose from her desk. "I'd hoped we would be able to avoid any such interruptions, but it seems I was mistaken."

"If that was about the Revel, I—"

"I suspect I already have all of the answers about that night I need," she said, stopping them. "It's good you were able to get here. There are some things I'd been hoping to discuss with you as well."

Rat hesitated, suddenly less sure than they had been.

"Come," Night said, motioning to them. "Walk with me."

Before Rat could ask where she was going, she waved her hand, the casting so simple it seemed almost thoughtless. A panel in the wall swung out, revealing a narrow hallway like the one Rat had used the night of the Revel.

Night looked back at them, her eyes alight, and Rat pushed down a nervous twinge. She'd been their father's ally, and she didn't particularly like Evening.

She was also the most powerful member of the Council of Hours. Rat was pretty sure she handled the absolute thorniest, most unspeakable magic there was, and Rat had broken a significant amount of the Council Chambers the last time they'd been here.

Gritting their teeth, Rat stole a last glance over their shoulder and followed after her.

Once they'd crossed the threshold, Night gave a casual flick of her wrist, and the door swung shut behind them, closing off the passageway again.

Spell lights blinked on along the walls as Night led the way, casting the corridor in a soft glow. Whichever passages Agatha had shown them before, this one seemed even older, made from the same rich hardwoods as the office, but the spells kept the wooden boards polished and free of dust were still in service here, too, and the air wasn't as stale, like maybe this one had seen recent use.

It let out in an empty corridor, somewhere else in what Rat could only guess was Night's wing of the Council Chambers.

A dead passage opened out of the juncture of hallways just ahead, nearly indistinguishable from the rest save for the faint veil of aether that separated it from the building proper, and then, with a jolt, Rat realized that Night was leading them toward it.

Over the years, Rat had gotten so used to pretending not to see the dead passages, they'd let themself forget that Night was a wayfinder, too. Maybe not on the same level as their father had been, but enough that she'd found the passage like it was second nature to her. Like it wasn't strange or dangerous, but just another place that she knew.

A desperate longing that Rat couldn't name clawed at them, but they shoved it back down. Once, they'd felt that same longing to be taken in by Isola, too.

Without missing a beat, Night stepped over the threshold, Rat keeping close behind.

The passage led out into a darkened courtyard, even though it had still been morning when they left. Night-blooming flowers grew along the paths, and stalks of pale grass reached up toward a pair of twin moons that cast everything in brilliant silver. Stars flecked the sky in an array of constellations that Rat only half knew, and then they realized they were looking at the same sky they'd seen over the tower, but much deeper into the night.

"I thought it might be best to go somewhere we could speak freely," Night said. "My predecessor showed me this place before she passed. Very few people still know it's here."

Rat looked up at her, but she just continued out onto the grounds, leading them toward one of the winding paths.

Night folded her hands thoughtfully. "I've been told that Evening is keeping you under watch."

Rat hesitated. "There's a spell on the campus. He started another investigation."

"So I've heard." She shook her head. "I've been building a case against him for some time now, but he's good at getting away with things, and he knows how to make sure there's never enough evidence to act."

Rat looked up at her. "You mean for what happened at Bellamy Arts?"

"Among other things." She tilted her head, considering. "Maybe it's better to say that over the years I've noticed certain . . . tendencies. He has a knack for accumulating power and favors through his position. Investigations that might be personally troublesome for him and his allies have a way of slipping between the cracks. Books and relics entrusted to him for safekeeping go missing from time to time. He's been increasingly bold the last few months, but I suspect it's been coming for a long time now."

"He's after the Ingrid Collection," Rat said.

"He's after power, however he can come by it. For someone like him, I doubt anything would ever be enough."

"But—"

"Yes. Evening's been after the Ingrid Collection for a long time, and Isola's been after her heart," Night said.

"But you can help."

Night paused, considering.

"You said you knew my father's work," Rat said. "About the keys. Did he ever say anything else?"

She gave Rat an apologetic look that they were quickly becoming familiar with, and their chest sank. "I wish he had. Unfortunately, I'm afraid I've called you here for something rather selfish," she said. "By now, you've seen what Isola is capable of."

Rat studied her, choosing their words carefully. "I've had some experience with her."

"More than some, if I had to guess from the Revel. It's been a long time since I've seen her come into the open like that, and longer still since someone has gone up against her and won."

"I'm not sure I would call it that."

"The boy is alive. That's more than what I can say for any of the others," Night said. "Isola has been dying for a long time, but it's only made her more desperate. The keys were forged with your family's magic, and Ingrid's archive is sealed with their power. I know that Vivian Fairchild has tried to protect you, but you might be our best chance of bringing Isola to rest."

"Because I'm my father's heir."

"I saw you at the Revel. You might not have his experience, but I suspect there's very little you wouldn't do to keep your friends safe," she said.

But even as Night spoke, Rat already knew that wasn't why. Their father had been taught by the last of the Holbrook family, but Rat had been taught by Isola herself, with all of her teeth and claws. He had studied Isola, but Rat had been shaped by her hands, and they'd grown into the magnificently vicious thing she'd always known they could be.

Maybe Isola was the sworn confidant of a long-vanished god, but Rat knew her inside and out. They had her powers, and they could feel her through the binding spell, even now.

Night regarded them solemnly. "This isn't something I would ask of you lightly, but I suspect it's a road you're already too far down to turn back. Stop her, however you have to."

Before Rat could answer her, Night reached into the air and produced a small glass vial, as if she'd drawn it from the night itself. Inside, it was filled with liquid that was thin like water and silvered with starlight.

"It's an extract of nocturn," Night explained. Rat furrowed their brow, and she said something that Rat thought might be Latin. The wry edge of a smile tugged at her lips, but it didn't touch her eyes. "It has lots of names. Summoners' bloom. Breath-of-the-night. It grows in the deep planes. It illuminates the true form of things, but I should warn you that not everyone likes what they see."

Rat hesitated, and Night held it out to them.

"You apply it to your eyelids. This should be enough to last you a couple of hours. Bellamy Arts is full of dark corners. Perhaps it will help you in your search," she said. "I'm afraid the rest must fall to you."

As she spoke, Rat realized Night had already brought them back to the main doors. Night laid her hand on their shoulder. "This is one of the only entrances to the Council Chambers the rest of the Greater Hours can't track, if you have to return without being seen. And, I suppose, it's one of the only exits as well," she said, her words heavy with meaning. "I wish I could offer you more than this. I can only hope you won't ever have need of it."

After Night left, even though the travel spell was waiting, Rat stayed in the garden by themself for a little bit longer before they finally opened a way back on their own.

It was farther than they usually tried to take themself through the passages, but they didn't feel like going back into the main building, and they knew Bellamy Arts well enough to find their way back. It only took a handful of tries before they finally stumbled out into a long, deserted hallway on the top floor of the History building.

Rat brushed the aether off their coat as they started up the corridor, playing what Night had told them over in their mind. They didn't need anyone to warn them about Evening. They knew he was searching for the rest of the keys. The only thing that bothered them was the fact that even the Council of Hours knew and couldn't do anything about it.

Rat stopped as Isola's magic stirred, waking to something they couldn't see. A chill slid down the hallway, carrying with it the scent of mugwort and earth. Something brushed past behind them, and Rat spun toward it, raising their hand to cast, but there was only a stretch of empty hallway.

They reached for Isola's magic, drawing it up along with their own as they let the corridor take shape at the edge of their senses, searching it for anything that might be hiding between the cracks in the world.

There was nothing.

Whatever it was, it had gone already.

Finally, Rat let the working go again, their magic and Isola's both slipping away from them.

They looked over their shoulder one more time and started back out of the building, but even though Rat knew they were alone, they couldn't help the unsettling feeling that they were being watched the whole way back.

CHAPTER THIRTY

RAT'S CLOAK WAS WAITING IN THEIR ROOM WHEN THEY reached their dorm, folded neatly on their desk with a note. It was barely afternoon, but Rat still checked the high branches of the trees for Isola's birds. Then, satisfied that they were alone, they crossed the room.

Rat took the note and opened it, but all that it said was *For the love of god, Evans, lock your door.* Beneath it, in Harker's spindly handwriting, he'd drawn out the familiar lines of a warding spell. Rat set it aside and picked up their cloak, letting it unfurl to its full length.

The last of the mud and ash from the tower had been cleaned away as if it had never been there, and the hem had been stitched back up where it had torn, even though Rat knew it was beyond what the cloak's mending spells could take care of on their own.

Their chest twinged with a warmth they absolutely refused to name. Probably, Harker was just showing off to remind them that he could.

Another slip of paper stuck out from one of the pockets like it had been left for Rat to find. They unfolded it, half expecting an explanation, but all it said was,

The draub stays in your room to mark your location.
Not sure how long the spell will hold up, so use it sparingly.

A smaller version of the cloaking sigil had been stitched into the pocket. Inside, there was a draub, marked with the same spell. Rat turned it in their hand, taking in Harker's familiar work. They didn't know how long it would hold up, but if they were caught, they doubted that Evening would give them another chance to make the same mistake.

They looked from the draub to the vial that Night had given them. Then they tucked the coin back into their pocket and opened their phone to their message thread with Harker. For a long moment, Rat stared down at the screen, deciding what to tell him. When they finally sent the message, all it said was *when?*

💀

The night they chose for the library was cold and clear. Rat waited until it was after midnight before they gathered their things. They wouldn't need to bring much. With any luck, it would be fast, but so far, luck hadn't really been something they could count on.

They saved the nocturn extract Night had given them until they were almost ready to leave. It was clear and viscous, and as soon as Rat uncapped the vial the scent of the night garden filled the room, along with the familiar dust-and-sunlight smell of aether underneath it.

Carefully, Rat smudged it over their eyelids the way they'd been instructed.

When they opened their eyes again, the soft glow of aether lined every surface of the room in a subtle light and the edges of the world seemed a little sharper than before, as if a film had been peeled away.

Rat looked at themself in the mirror. Gold smudged their lash line where the spell had set in, and there was an unsettling depth to their reflection that hadn't been there before, like it was peering back at them.

Behind them, the shadows shifted. Rat jerked back as Isola appeared in the glass. Smoke curled away from her in dark wisps as she settled against them, her chin resting on their shoulder.

Rat whipped toward her. Their hand flew to a defensive position, even though they didn't have that many spells to call on, but there was no one there.

They stared at the empty room, their heart beating hard. A stray tendril of smoke hung in the air where Isola's reflection had been standing, like the trace of a spell, but that was all.

They looked back at the mirror. In the glass, Isola was still there, her eyes bright with a kind of predatory amusement. Her reflection flashed its teeth in something too hungry to be a grin. Then she was gone again.

Rat shoved their hand through their hair, hating how unsteady they felt. "Fine then," they said to the place where she'd been. "Watch me."

Their gaze settled on their cloak, still folded on their desk where they'd left it. Rat grabbed on to the dark fabric and unfurled it, pulling it over their shoulders. In the mirror, the glow of aether dampened around them, and the draub in their hand flared to life like a beacon.

When they'd first gotten to Bellamy Arts, their cloak had felt like one more thing they'd wanted desperately, but had been too afraid to claim. It didn't feel like something they'd stolen out of their father's things anymore. At some point over the last few months, it had become theirs just as much as it had been his.

Alexander Holbrook had been clever and brilliant and kindhearted, and he'd come closer to finding the Ingrid Collection than anyone else, with only the best of intentions. If what Elise had told them was true, he'd had to spend his whole life convincing the rest of the houses that he wasn't dangerous, anyway.

Rat wasn't their father. They were the terrible thing he'd spent his whole life proving that he wasn't. If it meant they might live long enough to finish what he'd started, they would be whatever they needed to.

Neatly, Rat set the draub down on their bed. Then, the beacon still glowing softly behind them, they headed out into the hall.

Rat half expected something to stop them as they made their way to the lobby, but nothing happened, and for the first time since setting foot on campus, they felt invisible again.

Outside, the frigid air hit them like a wall, cold enough to steal the breath from their lungs. Fog curled low over the ground, drifting over the path ahead of them as they walked.

In the dark, the campus was alive with magic. Motes of aether drifted lazily on the air around them and settled along the path, lighting the way. Figures drifted between the trees at the edge of their vision, but something told Rat not to look. This wouldn't be a good night to let themselves get lost. The whole world felt a little too open, and they knew too well that there were places in the woods it would be difficult to get back from.

Footsteps crunched behind them, and Rat spun on their heel. Their hand flew to a casting position before they realized they had no idea what they were even planning on casting.

"Hi to you, too, Evans." Harker stood on the path behind them. He'd worn his cloak, the hood turned up against the cold, but aether twisted on the air around him in swirling motes like he'd stirred up the silt at the very bottom of the universe. More of it had caught in his hair and dusted his skin, lighting the familiar topography of fading acne scars along his jaw. He glanced over as he kept walking. "Were you planning to open a passage, or was that for the spell that breaks every bone in my body?"

Rat huffed out a breath. Something that might have been a wry smile tugged at Harker's mouth, but it probably wasn't.

"Are we going?" he asked, tracing a concealment spell.

"Don't worry. I'm not afraid you're going to try anything," Rat said. "I'm pretty sure I won the last time. So."

Harker flexed his hand, and the air rippled slightly as he drew the spell into place like a veil. "Fight me, Evans."

"I did. You ended up on a roof."

Harker opened his mouth like he was going to say something, but then a shadow passed over his face.

The library lay just ahead, running long and low around one side of the main lawn at the center of campus. The crooked shape of the clock tower rose over it, silhouetted in the dark. Harker stared out at it like he'd remembered exactly how that night had ended, maybe a little too well.

"Hey." Rat touched his arm. "Are you—"

"Fine," he said quickly. "We should get inside. We only have until morning." Without waiting for a response, he started toward the steps that led up to the doors of the Drake.

"Right," Rat managed. They hurried up the front steps after him.

He paused at the door, and then his hand started on the spell for the wards, like he was working through it by muscle memory. For a moment Rat wasn't sure if it would work, but then he pushed the door open and motioned to them.

A gust of warm air rolled out to meet them as Rat followed him into the lobby. Through the nocturn, a faint dusting of aether covered the floor, built up from the years of residual magic that had passed through, and in the dark, Rat could just pick out the weave of the protective spells that snaked over the outer walls.

With a soft *thud*, Harker pulled the door shut. A wisp of spellfire sparked on the air, hovering over his shoulder, and he turned back to the door, his hands already forming the working to reseal the wards behind him.

Silvery moonlight streamed in through the skylights overhead as Rat led the way into the main reading room, etching the deserted rows of reading tables. Dozens of archways that hadn't been there in the daylight opened along the walls, and even though Rat thought they'd gotten used to their powers, their chest tightened. They'd always gotten the sense that the Drake was massive, but suddenly, they couldn't help the creeping suspicion that *massive* barely scratched the surface of it.

It felt like the kind of place that people wandered into and didn't come back from.

Beside them, Harker's breath hitch, so slightly that Rat might not have noticed if they weren't next to him. Rat turned to see him staring openly at the reading room. "Harker?"

"Sorry." He forced some of the tension out of his shoulders. "This is the room where the passage starts, right?"

Already the entrance to the stacks had disappeared outside the cold circle of light from the spellfire. "You haven't been back?"

"I . . . no. I haven't had the chance," Harker said, smoothly enough that Rat could almost believe that was all it was. Before he caught himself, a low twinge of anxiety raced down the binding spell, with something else underneath it—wonder and longing and open fury that he'd let anyone take this place from him.

Just as quickly, it cut off as Harker recovered the last of his composure. "We should keep moving," he said, drawing ahead of Rat again. The spellfire bobbed after him as he crossed the room, leaving Rat staring after him.

On some level, they'd known that Harker didn't remember the school as well as he pretended to, but they'd forgotten how good he was at putting on an act. Suddenly Rat wasn't sure how many of the buildings he'd still recognized at all when he got back.

The thought of it made them cold all over.

"We're heading the same direction I took you the last time," Harker said, scanning the room. "Before the wards came down. We weren't actually that far from the archives."

Rat turned toward where the passage had been the last time, picking it out from among the other archways that the nocturn had made visible, already open.

"Come on. It's this way," they said, taking his arm.

The air cooled a little as Rat led him through, and Harker drew up another flicker of spellfire, letting it rove after them as they made their way deeper into the passage.

Rat realized they were still holding his arm. They waited for him to pull away, but he just drew them in a little and nodded toward the shelves of the deep stacks ahead.

"Just try to stay close," he said, pulling ahead of them.

"I think I'll be able to find my way out."

"You're not the one I'm worried about."

Rat glanced over their shoulder. "Try not to ditch me in the stacks again, and we're even," they said, tightening their grip on his arm in spite of themself. "Do you remember the way?"

"It's going to be an interesting time if I don't," Harker said, half to himself. Which, Rat couldn't help noticing wasn't a resounding *yes*.

Just ahead, the passage forked, and Harker stopping at the mouth of a corridor. He traced his hand over the door frame, furrowing his brow like he was searching for something. Then his eyes lit.

Rat saw it a moment after he did. A small *X* had been marked on the door frame in white casting chalk.

It was the same thing Rat used to mark their way when they didn't want to get lost. Harker had probably seen them do it more times than they could count.

"That's—" they started.

He looked back at them, smug. He'd used Rat's own tricks, and he'd done it better than them. Probably, he'd done it on purpose.

"It's this way," Harker said. He motioned with his chin, and Rat hurried alongside him as he led them down another aisle lined with books.

For a moment, Rat caught a glimpse of relief in his expression. Then, just as quickly, it was gone again, replaced by the same razor concentration they'd seen before as his gaze skimmed over the shelves, seeking the next marker.

Rat followed after, letting him lead the way as the archives slowly became less familiar around them. Finally, the light of the spellfire spilled over the top steps of a narrow staircase that opened between the shelves like the library had been built up around it, and Harker slowed to a stop.

"It's here," he said, motioning to Rat.

He led them down the stairs into a wide, circular room. Spell lights rose to life along the walls as he passed, lighting the room in a soft glow. Cases and cabinets lined the walls, a rolling ladder propped off to the side. Between them, a set of archways led off deeper into the private archives.

"This is . . ." Rat turned back toward where the stairs had been, but they'd already dimmed. If it wasn't for the nocturn, Rat was almost sure the way back would have vanished entirely.

All over, they remembered what Harker had told them last semester, about how there were paths through the archives that even the school didn't know about anymore.

Harker knelt, drawing a small chalk X on the floor.

"Come on," he said, picking himself up. "It'll be there when we get back. Do you know what we're looking for?"

Rat stole a last glance at the wall of cabinets behind them, then followed after, rushing to close the distance. "Something about keys?" Rat asked. "Do you remember where my dad's papers are?"

"We can find them. There's a sorting system," Harker told them, heading for the ladder. He traced a retrieval spell and it slid along the track to him.

He scanned the shelves, wheeling the ladder along the track until he stopped beneath a set of boxes labeled *A. Holbrook*. He climbed up and slid a box out to pick it up. Then, with a small sound of exertion, he dropped it back into its place like he'd remembered that lifting objects heavier than fifty pounds had never been one of his talents.

"Fuck," he muttered, shaking out his hand.

"Do you want help?" Rat asked. "I mean, I can't lift it either, but I could, like, probably manage a pep talk."

"Don't talk to me." Harker drew a spell on the air, and the box slid out from the wall of its own accord and drifted smoothly toward one of the reading tables.

"You didn't, like, you know. See a ring of keys the last time that you were here, right?" Rat asked.

Harker looked down at them from the ladder, unimpressed, which they were pretty sure was a *no*.

"Just checking," they mumbled.

If there had been, they somehow doubted Harker would have been capable of leaving something like that alone.

He traced another spell, and a second box slid down from the shelves, bobbing slightly as it drifted across the distance to the reading table.

"I didn't have a lot of time to look through everything. I don't remember there being much more than this, but it's possible I missed something," he said as he climbed back down. Harker took out a pile of papers and set them on one of the reading tables.

"Isola never told you anything about the keys?"

Harker sighed heavily, and for a moment, he looked incredibly tired. "She barely told me anything. You were right. She didn't want me to succeed. She just wanted a way to you."

"She didn't tell me, either, if that makes you feel any better," Rat said.

Harker frowned, but they could see him thinking.

"She sent us to investigate Evening without telling us why, but she already knew about the keys," Rat said. "It's like there's something else she's keeping from us. Or I don't know. Maybe she just didn't want me to know enough to go after them without her giving me leads." Rat looked back down at the pile of papers, thumbing the top few pages. "Where would you start?"

Harker slid the papers toward them. "You should take the maps and sketches. You're more likely to recognize something. Or . . ." He waved his hand vaguely, which could have been Harker Blakely for *in case you stumble into something by the sheer unearned virtue of being Rat Evans.*

"You can take the books," Rat said. "I heard you read those sometimes."

Harker looked at them like he was considering incinerating the archives and calling it a night. "Remind me why I talk to you."

"I'm pretty sure you don't?" Rat said.

He gave them a last exasperated look as he settled in across from them, and then he grabbed the first book from the box and set to work.

They searched in silence, Rat shuffling through their father's papers while Harker skimmed through books that had been in the box.

When they still lived at home, Elise had never cleaned out their father's office, at least until Rat's last summer before college. Up until then, it had never occurred to Rat that the door had probably been locked, and that they weren't supposed to be there.

Most of their father's sketches had been of the campus and the school's outlying grounds, some of Ashwood, and some farther than that, of the tower itself. Those, Rat realized now, were the ones Elise had chosen to hold on to. Or maybe, the ones the school hadn't asked for her to return for safekeeping.

The sketches in the school's private archive were everything else. Drawings of the campus both old and new filled the pages. Rat flipped through sketches of Galison Hall, the old ballroom, the narrow book-lined aisles that could only belong to the deep stacks of the Drake. They found a drawing of the War Room, even though the chairs weren't there yet, and another that they recognized as the inside of the clock tower, the now-broken sigils for the wards ringing the floor like a map of the planets.

Rat tucked that one under the pile where they wouldn't have to look at it and turned to the next page, then stopped as they came to a sketch of the tower that they hadn't seen before.

They brushed their fingers along the edge of the page. All of the sketches they'd seen in their father's office had always been from a distance, but this one was of the library, with its maze of ruined shelves.

Again, Rat thought of how easily the doors to the tower had admitted them. A part of them had known that their father had a long history with the tower, but they hadn't allowed themself to think about how much time he must have spent there for the place to remember him.

They looked up and realized that Harker had stopped reading, his eyes on the drawing in front of them. Rat shuffled it back into the pile. "Have you found anything?"

He opened his mouth like he was going to ask about the picture, and then seemed to stop himself. "Nothing. Have you?"

"I don't know." Rat sighed, pushing the drawings back from them. "There's so much of it. How long did it take you last time you were here?"

Harker looked at them as if to say they really didn't want to know the answer, and then took another book from the pile.

Quiet settled back over the archive, and Rat reached across the table for another stack of papers, then stopped as they caught sight of the

Holbrook archival stamp on one of the books. Rat slid it from the pile, unsure if they were expecting a spellbook or more maps like the ones in the Council Archives, but when they opened it, it was filled with neat paragraphs of text.

They riffled through the pages, stopping as they came to a lineage chart.

They'd found a family history.

Rat flipped ahead, letting the text flicker past them. They couldn't say why, but it bothered them. Maybe because a couple of weeks ago, Rat would have been sure that it didn't belong with the rest of their father's notes on the school, and the tower, and the Ingrid Collection.

"What is that?"

Rat jumped. "It's . . ." They looked back down at the book. "I don't know. A family history."

"For Ingrid?"

"No. I . . . it's mine. For the Holbrook line."

"Why do you think it's here?" Harker asked.

"No idea," they admitted.

Rat stopped again as they came to a picture of a house. It rose out of the side of a mountain, the steep pitch of its rooftop jutting up above the trees. Rat had never seen it, but even before their eyes went to the caption, they knew what they were looking at.

The Holbrook Estate.

Before Rat could think about what they were doing, they flipped to the back of the book.

They didn't even know what they were looking for.

But of course, they did.

Too tired to stop themselves, Rat searched the pages.

They wanted an ending.

They wanted to know how the rest of the Holbrook line had fallen, if their family had dwindled away or toppled like dominoes or been felled like giants.

Something had happened that had made all of the other houses afraid of the Holbrooks. Rat had never asked. They'd spent years burying every part of themself that wanted to know.

They passed the early 1800s, still too early for anything to connect their family to Ingrid or the school or anything else, their eyes skating over the text.

They stopped as they came to an appendix and realized they'd gone too far.

They flipped back, skimming over the final page, then the one before it.

"Rat?" Harker asked.

"Fuck," they breathed.

There wasn't anything else. It just ended.

They flipped ahead again, leafing past the appendix this time in case there was something beyond it, but it was just more end matter.

Rat glanced back at the stack of books in case there was anything else on their family, and then froze. Movement rippled in the corner of their eye, like something stirring in the aether, so faint that they wouldn't have noticed it if it wasn't for the nocturn on their eyelids.

A chill tracked across their skin as they were struck by the sudden, prickling sensation that they weren't alone in the archives.

"Evans?"

Rat pressed a finger to their lips.

The same uneasy feeling of something slithering just beneath the world's surface rolled past them. Rat spun, trying to catch the shape of it, but just as quickly, whatever they'd seen was gone again.

Beside them, Harker went still, like he'd felt it, too.

Quickly, Rat moved to shove the books back into the box, but Harker caught them by the arm.

"Leave it," he said.

"But—"

"It's fine. There's a reshelving spell back here," Harker said. "We have to go."

Rat grabbed the family history off the reading table and pulled it to their chest. Another ripple rolled through the aether, closer to the surface this time, and a deep dread rooted itself in their core.

Something was trying to get through. Whatever it was, it was powerful, and it had found them.

Harker pushed them ahead, following close behind them. "Come on, Evans. Just get us back."

They reached for a dead passage, but they could feel the creature just below the surface, pushing up between the cracks.

Close.

Rat's spell faltered, and Harker grabbed them by the wrist. He pulled them back the way they'd come, and Rat caught sight of the entrance to the stacks, flickering into view between the rows of shelves like it had been there all along.

Rat rushed after him, breathing hard. They drew ahead as they cleared the passage, and then they were back in the depths of the Drake, the aisles dark and narrow around them.

They hadn't come out in the same place they'd entered, but Rat didn't have time to figure out where they were. Something brushed past behind them, closer than before, and they dodged down a row of books, pulling Harker after them.

A glimmer caught the corner of Rat's eye, and they felt the subtle shift again, like something trying to come through.

"Rat?" Harker said, a note of panic in his voice.

"This way." Rat locked on to a dead passage ahead of them. Their lungs ached. But they'd gotten out of the stacks before, and they could find their way back now.

Another ripple slithered up the hall, rolling through the place they'd been standing, and Isola's magic tugged maliciously on the other side of the binding spell.

Rat lost their footing, and Harker's hand slipped out of theirs as they stumbled over the threshold of the dead passage.

Rat's pulse skipped. They whipped back, wide-eyed, as Harker cleared the edge of the passage, keeping close on their heels.

Rat stared at him.

He'd *followed* them.

Harker couldn't see the passages on his own. He'd never been able to follow Rat when they hadn't taken him through.

Harker gave them a desperate look, too winded to speak, and before Rat could find their voice to ask him what he'd done, Isola's magic flared again.

Rat grabbed Harker by the hand and pulled him forward, but the look on his face was still burnt into their mind.

Harker had been scared. Not of what was coming after them. Of Rat realizing what he could do.

"Come on," Rat said, pulling him through another gap in the aisles.

Harker's hand tightened around theirs, his pulse beating hard and fast under their fingertips. Fever poured off him in waves, but they didn't dare let go of him again. He rushed after Rat as they tugged him down another passage, and then the stacks opened around them into the main reading room of the library.

Harker caught them as they stumbled to a stop, already raising his other hand to cast. He turned his back to Rat's, still close enough that they could feel the way the air heated around him and the low rush of adrenaline on the other end of the binding spell.

Rat's heart beat in their ears as they searched the darkness. Outside the skylights, the night had just begun to fade, and will-o'-wisps of spellfire roved through the empty reading room, throwing flickering shadows over the high bookshelves lining the walls.

The last of the nocturn had started to wear away, and the version of the Drake Rat had entered earlier that night felt more like a dream, the extra doorways gone and the thick golden light of the aether diminished to a faint glow.

Rat looked over at Harker, one of his hands still knotted in their cloak, the other poised to cast. The faint scent of books and burnt paper and something that could only be described as *boy* clung to him, and spellfire crackled at his outstretched fingertips. If Rat had been any farther away, they might not have noticed that he was trembling almost as badly as they were.

Rat reached for their binding spell with Isola, but the cold surge of her magic was gone. Whatever had been chasing the two of them, they were well and truly alone again.

CHAPTER THIRTY-ONE

A HEAVY LAYER OF FOG HUNG OVER THE FROZEN GROUND as they made their way back to Galison Hall. The lights in the dining hall were still only half-on, but breakfast had already been set out even though it was before sunrise.

Because the dining hall was empty and Rat didn't have to explain themself to anyone, they packed more cinnamon rolls than they could actually eat into a to-go box and made themself a cup of coffee with as little actual coffee in it as possible.

Harker was already waiting to go by the time they finished, his own to-go cup in hand. "Where to?" he asked.

"I don't know," Rat said, watching the doors. "Somewhere that's going to stay quiet."

He nodded like he had somewhere in mind, and then motioned for Rat to follow. "Come on."

They stopped back in Mallory Hall to drop off Rat's cloak before heading up the back staircase of the boys' dorms.

Harker's dorm was a narrow shoebox of a single room, with exactly enough space for the standard dorm furniture and one window along the back wall overlooking the woods.

Since the last time Rat had been there, the pile of books around his bed had receded a little, down to a just couple stacks of school histories he must have gotten from the War Room, and some deeply secondhand spellbooks, which might have been his own.

By some miracle, the slightly haunted, definitely spelled mirror on his dresser had somehow managed to slip past the Council of Hours when they'd gone through his room after his disappearance. Most of the half-spent votive candles he used to practice his casting drills with had been replaced with fresh ones, and Rat's sketchbook was still open on the bed like he'd been flipping through it.

Rat watched as Harker traced a spell over the door, and they caught the faint shimmer of a ward that hadn't been there before, drawing back into place like a curtain.

"Is that allowed?" Rat asked.

"I'm pretty sure I've done worse." He turned back to them. "What?" he said, and they realized they were still staring at the room.

"Nothing. It's just been a while." They dropped onto the bed and glanced down at the sketchbook, which was open to their map of the library. "I think this is the first time I've been here that wasn't, you know."

"Breaking and entering?"

"You did kind of start it." Rat took the to-go box back out of their backpack, then glanced back at Harker, where he was still hovering by the door. A little of the humor went out of them. "Earlier . . . in the library, I . . . you followed me."

Harker was quiet.

"But you can't go through passages on your own," Rat said. "Did you . . ."

He shut his eyes and forced out a breath, steeling himself. "It's not your magic."

"But—"

"You would have felt it," he said. "The binding spell isn't that complicated. It's not like the one you have with Isola."

"You used wayfinding, though."

Harker watched them, tense, and Rat realized it was the first time they'd ever seen him try to hide his own abilities.

"Does it have something to do with the tower?" they asked finally, and they knew from the way he stiffened that they were right.

Rat slid over, making space. "I still have dreams about it," they said. "About her. I wake up sometimes and I have to remind myself I didn't go with her when she offered. Whatever it is, you can tell me."

Quietly, Harker sat down on the edge of the bed, like he wasn't sure how close he was allowed to get. For a moment, Rat thought he wasn't going to talk, but then, without meeting their gaze, he said, "Frey told me it's called being star-touched." His voice came out a little above a whisper, like even now, he didn't want to say it out loud. "Apparently it's something that can happen if . . . if you spend too much time somewhere else. When an arcanist becomes untethered from their own world. A few of the older families used to try to develop their abilities that way, but it's hard to do it on purpose. It has to be severe. You basically need someone with enough power who's desperate enough to get back."

"You could have told me," Rat said softly. But even if he wouldn't say it, Rat could read the answer on his face.

The problem was never that he'd thought Rat wasn't going to come back for him—it was that after everything, a part of him had still wanted them to. And when they hadn't, he'd been desperate enough to claw his way back to Bellamy Arts anyway, even though he'd left it full of enemies.

"I've barely left my room outside of classes and meeting with you," he said, avoiding their gaze. "Whenever I'm alone, I feel like I'm putting everyone at risk if I step outside the door wards, even though I know they can't actually keep her out. Do you really think anyone would let me stay if I told them that?" He let out a small, brittle laugh. "They'd think I was unraveling."

"I don't think that would happen," Rat said.

"Of course it would. You don't get it. Jinx and Agatha actually picked you. I was always just an alliance of convenience."

Rat's chest sank a little. "But . . ."

"It's fine," Harker said quickly. "I'm used to it. As hard as it is to believe, people don't usually keep me around for my sparkling personality." He managed a wry attempt at a smile, but it looked forced.

"We all looked for you. You know that, right?" Rat said quietly. "For what it's worth, I think everyone else really did want you around last semester. What are you scared of?"

"I don't know. That I'm horrible and everyone secretly hates me because I deserve it? That everyone will find out I live entirely on coffee and simple carbs?"

Rat tore a piece off their cinnamon roll. "I like how you are."

He gave them a cautious glance. "I heard you referred to us as sworn enemies."

"Yeah, when you were looking at me like you wanted to set me on fire," they said, then sighed. "You're determined. And you care about things. And, I don't know. I like that you're ambitious. If there's an answer, I always know you're going to figure it out. Every time something happened last semester, you were basically the first person I wanted to talk to about it, before I remembered I'd messed everything up."

"It wasn't just you."

Rat hesitated.

"The whole time, I—" Harker glanced away again, and his hand went back to the line of his bracelets, picking at the tooth-marked leather. "There's no excuse for how I acted. It was cruel. I couldn't—"

"Harker." Rat touched his cheek, and he turned back to them, meeting their gaze. A shiver of longing ran down the binding spell, curling around Rat's ribs like an ache. But before Rat could even begin to make sense of it, the connection snapped shut as Harker composed himself.

He cleared his throat. "I'm sorry. I—"

"We should figure out what's next," Rat said quickly. "That's why we're here, right?"

"Right. Of course," Harker said. The moment broke, and he shifted away from them like he'd realized he was in their space.

Harker didn't want them like that, Rat reminded themself. He'd finally started speaking to them again, and he didn't need Rat throwing their feelings at his feet just because he was unmoored and shaken and the literal definition of touch-starved.

Rat grabbed another cinnamon roll from the box, then slid the box toward Harker, shoving the feeling down. They shot him a ragged grin. "Simple carb enough? I can probably run back and find toast."

"Leave me alone," he said, but he was biting the edge of a laugh, and a little of the tension went out of him again. "I spent two months in the dark. I would commit actual crimes for anything with frosting right now."

Harker picked out a cinnamon roll and traced a warming spell on it. Then, realizing Rat was watching, he held it out to them. They traded him theirs, and then tore off a piece while he traced the same spell on the one they'd just given him.

"In the library, what was that thing?" Rat asked.

"I don't know." Harker exhaled deeply, settling against the headboard. "It shouldn't have been able to get that close, even with the main wards down. Maybe if we were in the tunnels, but that was the school's private archives."

Rat looked over at him, frowning, and then understanding hammered into them. "We should've been protected."

Not just protected. The Drake was probably the best-warded place on campus, after maybe the Ingrid Collection itself. Last semester when the campus had been overrun by terrors, the library had probably been the only place that had gotten through the night completely untouched. And they'd been in the most heavily protected part of the building.

"Harker," Rat said slowly. "Could something like that get in through the library's wards?"

"Not unless it was summoned from inside." Harker paused like he was turning something over. Then he said, "What I want to know is, why wait until we were in the school archives?"

A cold stab of unease tracked down Rat's spine. Maybe Isola's creatures had slipped through the cracks before, but they'd felt her pushing from the other side of the binding spell, and it hadn't been an easy working for her. If she'd been after them and Harker, she could have waited for her moment and attacked while she had the upper hand.

She'd been trying to, Rat realized with a twinge. Ever since they'd gotten back to campus, they'd sensed her creatures following them. Rat was sure now that was what it had been, every time they'd felt a cold brush in an empty hall. But before now, Isola had still been testing the limits of the school's protections, and nothing had come this close to getting through.

Isola hadn't tried to use their bond to call them back to her. Rat wasn't sure that she could. Not until she was at her full power. But she'd been in their head. She knew their every move, and she'd made sure her creatures stayed close on their heels. And, tonight, she'd been desperate.

"She wanted us out of the library," Rat said, putting it together as they spoke. The realization broke over them like ice water. They met Harker's gaze, and he sharpened, like he'd had the same thought. "There was something there she didn't want us to find."

"Yeah," Harker said, like he was still turning it over. "I just wish we knew what."

Rat looked down at the family history on the bed beside them. They felt like they were on the edge of putting everything together. They rubbed at their eyes, trying to think.

"Sorry. It's late," Harker said. "I should let you rest."

"It's fine. I can stay up." Rat stifled a yawn, and he raised his eyebrows at them. "It's ten degrees out, and something is trying to eat me," they said, settling back on the bed. "No thanks."

Harker picked himself up. "Here. You can take the bed. I have class in an hour, anyway, and I have wards up."

"I'm not kicking you out."

"You're not." He tossed a pillow at them. "If I remember, I'm at your disposal, Evans."

Rat made a face at him.

"It's fine," Harker said quickly. "I wasn't really planning on going to sleep and . . ." He let out a breath. "I don't know. I could use the company. Even if it's not for that long."

There was an unspoken *please* at the end, and Rat felt it again through the binding spell, the low rush of want and fear that Harker was usually so good at hiding. After everything that had happened tonight, he didn't want to be alone, either.

"I might not be great conversation," Rat said cautiously.

He gave them a wry look. "Neither were the wraiths."

Rat rolled onto their side. "Did you talk to them?"

"I think they only liked me because I was warm and had news about the school," he said. His expression softened a little. "I've been trying to find out who all of them were. From Jinx's records."

"Tell me about them?" Rat asked, even though they were already drifting off.

"It's not much so far," he started, his voice washing over them, low and familiar as he began to talk.

It didn't matter if they wanted him, Rat reminded themself. Harker was finally speaking to them again. They couldn't let themself pretend it meant anything other than that to him.

Rat pulled their pillow to their chest, forcing the feeling back down.

But then, because they were tired, and shaken, and no one would ever know, Rat fell asleep thinking about Harker anyway.

CHAPTER THIRTY-TWO

WHEN RAT FINALLY DRIFTED OFF, THEY DREAMT ABOUT darkened corridors and the cold whisper of Isola's breath on their neck, and they woke with the image of the Holbrook Estate still seared in their mind and the family history open on the bed beside them. Rat forced themself up, breathing hard as they remembered where they were.

The snow had picked up while they slept, and pale gray light streamed in through the windows. Harker had headed out already, and the cold had crept back in in his absence.

Something Isola didn't want us to find.

The thought echoed in Rat's head. They reached out, their fingertips skimming the pages of the book. They didn't know if it was the clarity of morning or just the fact that they'd finally slept, but something clicked into place. The family history had been the last thing they'd found before Isola's creature had come after them. The thing she'd been so desperate to get them away from.

Rat stopped on the picture of the Holbrook Estate. Just for a moment, a pang of vicious magic slipped through their binding spell with Isola, sharp and electric.

Apparently, whatever they'd found, they'd struck a nerve.

"You're tipping your hand," they said, the air still thick with Isola's presence. They grabbed their phone off their bed to find that they already had a message from Jinx. All it said was *library* with the name of a reading room, but Rat didn't need any more than that.

Stay there. Rat typed back. *I have a lead.*

They changed quickly, stealing a clean T-shirt from Harker's things before they made their way down the stairs. A couple of boys in the lobby glanced up as Rat passed, but at least this time, Rat was pretty sure it was an *Aren't they under investigation by the Council of Hours for several serious and public crimes?* look, and not the *Wait, do they live in this building?* look.

Outside, the snow came down in heavy drifts, and the path that led between the buildings had been covered over. The grounds were all but empty, and Rat guessed that classes had probably been called for the day, if they'd been planning on going to those.

At least if they ended up at the tower, they wouldn't have to worry about failing the semester.

Jinx was already waiting when Rat got to the library, a pile of books spread out on the table like she'd been there for a while. Across from her, Harker sat curled in one of the chairs, asleep, his coat draped over his shoulders. He looked like he'd given himself exactly long enough to change his clothes and splash water on his face before heading out, and there was a cup of coffee on the table near him, which Rat would bet money wasn't the same one he'd had in his room.

"He got here before I did," Jinx said. "We've been up pretty much all morning."

"I guessed," Rat said, taking the book out of his arms. "I don't know why I assumed he'd go to bed at some point."

"Make me, Evans," Harker mumbled. "I'll sleep when I'm dead."

Probably, Harker was halfway into a formal working to make sure if he ever died, he would come back to follow Rat around as the world's smuggest, most sleep-deprived ghost.

Rat shut the book and set it on the table. "Whatever attacked us, I don't think we have time to find out what it was," they said. They knelt down, took off their backpack, and dug out the family history. "There's something at the Holbrook Estate."

Jinx's eyes widened a little behind her glasses, but before she could ask, Rat shoved the book at her.

"This is what we were looking at when Isola's creature showed up." Rat said. "Isola was trying to get us out of the archives. Something we did made her nervous enough to strike."

Behind them, Harker shifted his weight, pushing himself upright.

Rat reached across the table and turned to the picture of the Holbrook Estate. "My dad is the last person who had access to the Holbrook archives. Elise had them sealed after he died, by his own request."

Jinx was quiet, but they could see her turning it over, and something in Harker's expression had sharpened. "You think you can open them again," Jinx said, studying Rat from behind her glasses.

"I think that whatever's up there, Isola didn't want me to go looking," Rat said, but even as they spoke, they knew it was more than that. Isola knew about the Holbrook Estate. She'd been keeping it from them for a reason.

"It's going to be locked up pretty tightly," Jinx said, turning the idea over in her mind. "Knowing the Holbrooks, it isn't the kind of place you're just going to be able to wayfind into."

"Which is why it has to be me and not another wayfinder," they said.

"Do you know where it is?" Harker asked.

Rat started to say they didn't, but next to them, Jinx's eyes were bright. All over again, Rat remembered that they were dealing with the estate of a well-known bloodline. Even if the place had stood empty for a long time, it had been around for much longer, and the old families had a long memory. "Jinx?"

"Give me an hour," she said.

"But how—"

"My grandfather knew your dad when he worked here. If he doesn't have the address, Cromwell will know who to ask at the Council." She sat forward. "Trust me, Evans?"

"Whose car are we taking?"

Rat texted Will before they made their way to Mallory Hall.

It took about three minutes before they got back a *You know how dangerous the roads are right now, right?*

yes they typed as they followed Jinx up the main path.

Three dots appeared and then disappeared again.

Isola knows we're close to something and I don't think she's going to wait, Rat added. Then *I wouldn't ask if it wasn't important.*

Harker glanced over Rat's shoulder as he passed beside them. "He's right about the roads. You're sure about this?"

Their phone buzzed, and Rat held it out to him.

Looping into town for supplies. I'll text you where to meet.

Up ahead, the path forked toward the freshman dorms, the matched set of sharply pitched roofs rising out of the haze of the weather.

"We should get our things," Rat said, shutting off the screen again. "Find each other when we're done?"

Ahead, Jinx nodded to them. "I've already texted Cromwell. She's going to see if she can get Night to pull any documents on the estate to get us an address."

"Tell her to be quick," Harker said.

Rat felt a slight tug on the binding spell as he started down the path toward Armitage Hall.

Jinx put her hand on their shoulder, her brow furrowed with concern. "You're sure he should come with us?"

"It's his choice."

"Rat—"

"No. Everyone told me I was helpless until I started to believe it. I'm not doing that to him. If he changes his mind, we can figure out how to get him somewhere safe, but I'm not leaving him here if he doesn't want that."

Jinx's expression softened. "Alright."

As soon as Rat made it to their room, they locked the door and poured their backpack onto the bed.

They didn't know what condition they were going to find the Holbrook Estate in. Rat hadn't given the estate a lot of thought before now. For as long as they could remember, they'd tried pretty hard not to.

Rat threw a few sets of clothes into their backpack, then grabbed a flashlight and the new sketchbook they'd started since Harker had their usual one. They weren't sure how much time they'd have once they got there, but Rat was guessing that Isola wouldn't give them much space to work.

Her magic tugged at them, and Rat pushed the feeling away. They pulled their cloak on and set the draub back on the nightstand.

They checked their pockets to find their compass still in one, the puzzle box in the other. Then they traced a spell on the air, and a passage opened ahead of them, leading out into the woods behind the dorms.

A cold wind blew past them as they stepped through, carrying the snow with it. Somehow, even more had built up on the ground in the time that Rat had been inside, and the campus around them was a haze of white.

They caught sight of Harker ahead of them, a few feet off the path. Fog curled off of him in the cold, and snow flecked the dark fabric of his coat. There was an unmistakable tension in the way he held himself. Like an old nervous habit, his hand went to his wrist, thumbing the line of his bracelets.

Bellamy Arts might not have been protected the way it used to be before the wards had come down, but however tenuous Rat's agreement with Isola had become, she still couldn't set foot on the school's grounds. If Isola got her hands on Harker, she wouldn't hesitate to punish him for the night of the Revel. He was putting whatever freedom he had at risk by going with them to the Holbrook Estate.

Rat reached down and grabbed a handful of snow off the ground. "Hey! Blakely!" Before they could think about what they were doing, they lobbed it at his back.

Harker spun toward them. Instinctively, he raised his hand to cast, and the air shimmered with heat.

What was left of the snow splashed in his face, and he staggered back with an undignified yelp.

A small laugh bubbled up in Rat's throat, and he shot toward them.

He caught their wrist as they reached for another handful of snow. "What are you doing?" he said, breathless, but some of the tension had melted away from him.

"I told you I'd win," they said, twisting to get away.

"You snuck up on me—hey!"

Rat shoved him with their shoulder, and he yanked them back, his arm wrapped around them. Rat realized they'd miscalculated badly, since he was both fully capable of lighting them on fire and also, he was currently breathing on them, which they were pretty sure counted as a literal crime.

Behind them, Jinx cleared her throat, and all at once Rat became intensely aware that they didn't have a good explanation for why they were standing this close to Harker.

Quickly, Harker let go of them. "We were just waiting for you."

Jinx waved her hand in a spell, flicking a bit of snow from his coat. "I saw." She had a hiking backpack slung over her shoulder now, and Agatha stood a few feet behind her like an apparition, her cloak the same brilliant white as the snow.

"Will texted the group," Jinx said. "He's at the edge of the grounds. Cromwell and I got the address, but the school's main gates are closed, so we're going to have to meet him."

"We should be careful. Isola still has eyes all over campus."

"She's not our only problem," Jinx said. Discreetly, she nodded at the dorms as she started up the path. "I passed Church in the lobby."

"What?" Rat looked over their shoulder. Behind them, they caught a glimpse of Allister as he let himself outside, the wind catching the hem of his cloak.

Rat bit back a swear as Jinx pulled them around again before he could see them.

"Apparently he had some questions for you about a disturbance in the school's wards last night."

"Fuck," they breathed.

Rat ducked their head, resisting the urge to turn around again. Their hood was up and the snow was coming down in sheets, but if he recognized them by their cloak, that wasn't going to count for a lot.

Like he'd had the same thought, Harker's hand moved at his side in the concealment spell Rat had seen him use the night before.

"The spell's not going to help us much once Church notices our footprints," Harker said, drawing it into place. "The faster we can get out of here, the better." He put one hand on Rat's arm. Even through his gloves, his touch was warm on their skin, and he kept his other hand poised to cast.

Movement flickered in the corner of Rat's eye as they followed after him. They looked up as a bird fluttered down to land on the high branches of one of the trees, its gaze fixed in their direction as if it could see through Harker's spell.

Harker stiffened beside them, and his hand tightened on their arm. "Rat."

"Come on." Rat quickened their pace. Isola's magic tugged at them, but they pushed it back with a pang of unease, their free hand readied at their side.

A few steps ahead of them, Jinx turned and met their eyes with a silent nod, like she'd picked up on it, too. Her hand flexed into a casting position, and the snow picked up a little as the storm bent around her.

You're fine, Rat reminded themself. *You're here.* They were still on campus. It was still daylight.

Another bird touched down on the path ahead of them, its wings black against the white of the storm, and Isola's power stirred low and dangerous under Rat's skin.

Suddenly, they realized just how quiet the woods had fallen around them. They hadn't gone that far, but Rat already knew without looking back that they had to be out of sight of the main campus.

The bird blinked at them from the path. Then it leapt up, disturbed, and Isola's magic flared through the binding spell in a cold rush as something deep in the fabric of the world tore open.

"Go!" Rat shouted. They threw themself forward, Harker close on their heels. Then the air split and a pair of terrors snaked out into the woods, their bodies hissing over the snowy ground.

Cold air sliced Rat's lungs. Breathing hard, they sprinted up the path as one of the terrors lurched after them.

Harker spun back, but Jinx was faster. The snow rose up in a wave, crystalizing into a wall of ice. The terror smashed against it, and the ice split with a distinct crack.

The terror hissed as it scrambled to right itself. One of its chitinous plates had chipped, and something the color of starlight seeped from the wound. Then it recovered itself and veered toward Rat, the second terror snaking after it.

Harker's jaw tightened as he sent a defensive spell over his shoulder. The spell went wide, throwing up a spray of snow in its wake, and steam trailed from his fingers.

He'd let Rat go so he could cast, and they grabbed him by the wrist, wrenching him back. A dead passage opened to catch them, and they stumbled out into the snow further up the path in time to see the terror crash down where they'd been standing a moment before.

Both terrors turned and took off after them.

"Get to the road!" Jinx shouted.

Her hand lashed out, tracing another spell, and a fresh wall of ice shot up, knocking one of the terrors back. Just behind her, Agatha's fingers worked at her side like she was weaving, and the net of something that had to be a defensive spell glinted faintly on the air. Her dark braid whipped out behind her, carried by the wind, and snow flurried around her.

Rat's pulse beat hard as they turned on their heel and shot into the trees, pulling Harker after them.

"Rat—" he started. Panic tinged his voice, and magic radiated off of him in waves. Will-o'-wisps of spellfire wove after him, hissing and crackling in the snow.

"Just follow me," they said, their voice ragged.

Those creatures hadn't been after Jinx and Agatha. The terrors had been locked on them.

No, Rat thought, stealing a glance over their shoulder. The terrors had been locked on Harker. Whatever game Isola was playing, she still needed Rat to get to the end of it. She wouldn't hurt them, but he was another story.

He looked back, tracing another spell as Rat pulled him around a bend in the path, and then through the next dead passage, deeper into the trees.

Just ahead, the ground sloped down toward a dark ribbon of roadway. Will's car idled in the shoulder, headlights cutting through the haze.

Rat turned hard, shooting toward it, and then a tidal pull rolled through the aether as Isola's magic surged up again. Their footing slid, and they buckled against Harker as they lost their grip, but he braced his arm around them, keeping them on their feet.

"Rat—"

They gave him a desperate look, and then they felt it again, like the uncanny ripple of something moving just beneath the surface of the world. Whatever had tried to find them last night, it was here. Close.

"Come on," Harker said in a rush. He pushed them again. "I'm right behind you."

Rat took off, their momentum carrying them down the hillside. Behind them, a terror darted out from the trees, its too-many legs carrying it through the snow as it snaked after them.

Rat breathed a curse, their voice all but gone. They found the next passage on instinct and rushed through, catching themself in a skid as they spilled out at the road, Harker still close on their heels. They didn't know if the others had seen him follow them through the passage on his own power, but after last night, he seemed to be beyond caring.

Will pushed the drivers' side door open and jumped out of the car, already halfway through a defensive spell.

"Jinx and Agatha are behind us," Rat said in a rush, scrambling to their feet. Their knees throbbed, and their hands were numb where the snow had gotten into their gloves.

"Got it," Will called, an edge of panic in his voice. A wave of force rippled away from him, and the hillside shifted beneath the terror.

Rat had seen terrors scurry up walls before like overgrown centipedes. Maybe, under better conditions, the creature might have kept its footing, but the dirt and snow crumbled away beneath it, and the terror lost its hold on the earth, careening down into the road.

The terror writhed, trying to right itself, and before Rat could pull him back, Harker's hand shot out in a spell. Heat poured off him, turning the falling snow to steam, and Rat realized he hadn't cast earlier because this wasn't the kind of spell he could have mustered the focus for while he was running. Harker's problem had never been having the power to put behind his workings—it was keeping a tight enough grip on that power that it didn't overwhelm his control completely.

Rat felt the world open as the terror was pulled back through to wherever it had come from. Dark smoke curled in the place where it had been, already dissipating in the snow.

He'd *banished* it.

Heat pulsed off of Harker, like the air itself was ready to ignite. He looked at Rat, his expression merciless, and also a little like he might throw up.

Something moved in the woods as Jinx and Agatha made it to the road, and then another shock rolled through the aether.

"Come on," Rat said, grabbing Harker by the arm. They shoved him toward the car. Whatever else was out there, they distinctly didn't want to stick around and wait for it to catch up. They clambered in after him, pulling the passenger door closed as Agatha climbed in on the other side.

Jinx had already made it to the front seat, her face flushed and her curls plastered with melting snow. "Go!" she shouted as Will threw himself into the driver's side. He yanked the door shut and slammed the accelerator.

The tires shrieked as the car fishtailed on the ice. Will steered hard into the swerve, and the force of the turn sent Rat sliding into Harker. He caught them, his bony arm braced around them, and then the tires found traction and the car shot forward.

For a fraction of a second, Rat through they caught a glimpse of a gray cloak in the trees. Then it was gone again, lost somewhere in the snow.

Rat looked over at Harker, his face buried in their shoulder like he wasn't sure if he was protecting them or just trying to keep himself from being thrown against the window. His breath was hot on their neck, and his magic was still palpable in the air. Finally, like he'd realized he was still holding them, he shifted away and then sank down, resting his head on his knees. Fear and exhaustion rolled through the binding spell in waves, like he'd lost his hold on whatever usually held it back.

On Rat's other side, Agatha had her knees pressed into the back of the driver seat, and in the front, Will and Jinx were both still catching their breath.

Rat took Harker's shoulder, feverish even through his coat. "Hey. Doing okay?"

Harker nodded without looking up. "I banished them," he said, still sounding breathless and a bit sick. "That puts me ahead of you again."

"Alright, Blakely. You win this time." Rat gave him their hand, and Harker locked his fingers around theirs.

A memory of the tower flashed down the binding spell Rat shared with him, crumbling stones and the always-dark sky and the metallic taste of blood in his mouth.

Protectively, Rat shifted toward him, and his grip on their hand tightened a little.

Will met their eyes in the mirror. "He's managing," Rat said. "He just needs some time to cool down."

Will nodded. "Did we lose those things?"

"Maybe for now. But I'm pretty sure I saw Church," Jinx said, brushing the ice off her gloves. "He's not going to be that far behind us."

"And Isola's messengers are out there. She'll know where we're going," Rat said.

"There are wards, though. Right? On the estate?" Will asked. "Wait. Are you sure we're going to be able to get inside? Like, is the seal going to let us through?"

"It's fine."

Will's eyes met theirs in the rearview mirror again, like it was just occurring to him that Rat's entire plan consisted of being the heir to the Holbrook family and hoping for the best.

"We'll figure it out," they said, sharper than they meant.

Concern flickered across Will's face, and some of the tension went out of them.

"I don't know," Rat admitted. "I don't know what's up there."

Beside them, Harker's shoulders rose and fell as he drew in a breath. "That thing that was following us," he said without lifting his head. "It's Isola's seneschal."

"What?"

"One of the creatures that serves her. A powerful one," he said. "I thought I recognized something about it last night in the library. That's what I was looking for when you found me and Jinx this morning. It usually keeps to the ruins around the tower, but it answers to Isola when she calls on it." His shoulders had tensed, and Rat couldn't help thinking that he knew Isola's creatures better than anyone should.

But even then, they also could hear the part he wasn't saying out loud.

Isola's seneschal had found them on campus, in the daylight. Even if she had someone helping her summon it, it was a desperate move, and aside from their friends and Allister Church, no one else had been in the woods with them.

In the front seat, Jinx shot a breath through her teeth like she'd read their silence. "It sounds like you're right, Evans. Whatever's up at the Holbrook Estate, Isola really doesn't want us to get there."

"Yeah," Rat said, half to themself. "Let's just hope we get there first."

CHAPTER THIRTY-THREE

THE HOLBROOK ESTATE LAY TWO HOURS FROM THE school by car, but it seemed farther in the storm.

The low hills rose into mountains as they drove, and the woods that grew up along the side of the road dropped steeply away. Rat had been worried that the estate would be hard to find, but there wasn't anything else for miles, and as soon as they'd caught sight of it sprawling along the mountainside in the distance, it had been hard to mistake.

The car slowed as the house came into full view ahead of them, the steep pitch of the roof rising against the slowly fading sky. All of the windows were dark, and bare vines of ivy crawled over the sides of the house.

"I'm pretty sure this is as close as I can get us," Will said, pulling over. He cut the engine, and Jinx pushed open the passenger door to get out, letting in a rush of cold air.

"Okay?" Rat asked Harker.

He drew in a breath and pushed the door open before offering Rat his arm, which they knew was as much for his sake as theirs.

Ahead of them, a downed tree lay across the road ahead of the car, blocking the way. Beyond it, the pavement turned into packed dirt, before disappearing under the snow completely.

Rat glanced back as another set of headlights swept the mountainside below, cutting through the haze of weather, before the car disappeared again around the next bend in the road. "What are the chances someone else is out this far by coincidence?"

"Not high," Harker said, half to himself.

Rat eyed the distance to the house, but they didn't know where the ground wards started. Just that they were well outside of range.

"Go," Jinx said. "Both of you, get up to the house. You're the ones everyone is after. We'll follow."

Rat slid their hand into Harker's before he could argue and started toward the tree line. "Come on. You can fight with me at the house." Rat traced a spell on the air, pulling Harker after them.

Isola's magic raked at them, clawing its way through the binding spell, and for a moment they could feel the faint pressure of *something* trying to push in through the cracks in the world, like a subtle weight on the other side of the door. Then it was gone, as they spilled through on the other side of the dead passage, farther up the path.

"Shit," they breathed. "How is it here already?"

Harker's hand tightened on theirs. The spellfire flared brighter around him as he drew his other hand into a casting position, the will-o'-wisps hissing against the snow.

The house rose up ahead, but Isola's seneschal had felt close. As if summoned, another ripple pushed against the seams of the world.

"Evans?" Harker looked at Rat, and they realized they'd stopped in their tracks.

Before Rat could move, Isola's magic flared again, and suddenly the air was full of the scent of aether and mugwort like they were back at the tower. Power surged through the binding spell, pulling at them somewhere deeper than bone.

Just as fast, it was gone again, leaving them gasping. Rat sank down in the snow. "Fuck."

Whatever they'd felt, it hadn't been the distant, worlds-away trace of Isola's magic. It had been close. *Here.*

"*Rat!*" Harker dropped next to them, taking their shoulder to steady them.

They looked up at him, still breathing hard.

"Get to the house," they said, grabbing on to his coat.

"I—"

"You need to get to the house. Now," they said again. They spit into the snow, trying to clear the metallic taste from their mouth.

A gust of wind rolled past, carrying a curtain of snow with it, and Rat suddenly realized how still and quiet the mountainside had become. Ahead of them, from somewhere deeper in the woods that lined the path up to the house, something rustled in the overgrowth, moving between the trees like a shadow.

Rat scrambled back as the seneschal appeared between the trees, snaking toward them. It reminded Rat of the dragons they'd seen in old bestiaries, but whatever this was, they knew in the hollow of their ribs that it belonged to the tower. Its long body was coated in raven feathers, dusted with falling snow, and its eyes shone glassy and black like the surface of a lake.

Beside them, Harker was already on his feet. He pulled Rat up, his other hand raised to a casting position. Before they could think about what they were doing, they broke for the edge of the trees, hauling him along after them.

The snow muffled their footsteps as they ran, the cold air stinging in their lungs. Instinctively, they felt the path open before they saw it.

"Go," Harker breathed, and Rat veered off the trail, toward the dead passage. They spilled through, the edge of the woods just ahead as the seneschal snaked toward them, but they hadn't gone far enough.

Rat threw themself forward, their hand raised to form the next spell, and then Isola's magic rushed through the binding spell, drowning out everything else. They felt the working slip away from them as they lost their sense of the passages around them, swallowed up under the torrent of undirected power.

Their next step sent them sprawling.

Rat caught themself against the ground, cold melt water seeping into their cloak, and then, like a fist closing around the binding spell, they felt their magic choke off completely.

"Rat," Harker said in a panicked rush. He grabbed their arm, tugging them back. His other hand shot out in a spell. "*Leave!*"

His voice rang out harsh and low, and it took Rat a moment to realize he'd spoken in the rusted, hard-edged language of the tower. When Rat shouted their spells, they sounded frantic, but Harker's voice carried the force of an invocation even now, breathless and sharp with fear.

The spell shuddered through the clearing, and the creature reared back, smoke curling off of it in dark wisps. Then, undeterred, it shot toward them.

Harker pulled Rat to himself as the creature whipped between the trees, its massive wings unfurling so their feathers brushed the snow-covered ground.

"Fuck." Harker's arm tightened around Rat, heat radiating off of him. His breath was hot and frantic on the back of their neck.

Rat reached for their power, but before they could cast, there was a sharp tug on the end of the binding spell with Isola. Another wave of magic surged through, sweeping over them. Darkness swam in the corners of Rat's vision.

The world dissolved around them, and Rat felt themself slipping away. Distantly, they heard Harker shout as they sagged against him, and then the woods were gone.

They were back in the heavy gloom of the tower's library where they'd glimpsed Isola before, gray dusk filtering in through the crumbling walls. Isola had claimed a wreck of a leather chair, one leg slung lazily over the armrest like a rogue prince, her sword resting at her side. Her eyes trailed over Rat like she'd been waiting, and her magic tugged at them through the binding spell.

Rat took an involuntary step forward. They reached for their powers, but distantly, Rat already knew that they couldn't get back any more than they could wake themself from one of their tower dreams.

"Exactly like one of your dreams," Isola said, and her words hit Rat like ice water. They'd scraped up against the edges of Isola's mind through the binding spell before, but she was a much better arcanist than they were. She pushed herself to her feet with an animal grace. "Your body is still in the woods. I doubt your magic will do you much good, but you're welcome to try."

"You're not really here, either," Rat said, hating the panicked edge in their voice. "You're creating all of this."

"And yet." Isola flashed her teeth at them. "By the time you make it back to yourself, what do you think will happen? You still don't even know how my creatures got through, do you?"

Rat struggled against her hold, but Isola's grasp tightened, the binding spell raking at the edges of their mind.

"My seneschal is a clever thing, but it's succumbed to its own hunger before. I'm sure it'll bring your friend back alive, but I'm curious in what state."

"Let go of me."

"No," she said, and her voice was a sliver of ice between Rat's ribs. "That boy is mine by his own oath. Turn over the keys, and I'll make sure there's something left of him to give back when we're done."

Rat's pulse kicked hard in their throat. They weren't really here. They were with Harker in the woods, and they needed to get back to him. Rat reached for their power again, pushing harder, and a tide of thoughts rolled down the binding spell, faster than Rat could make sense of them.

The empty corridors of the tower. The wraiths. Isola's shelves of trinkets and bones. A ring of keys.

Then, just as quickly, it was gone again, and a sharp tug cut through the tide of Isola's power as Harker tried to pull them back. Rat reached for it, and they fell back into themself.

The woods crashed in around them, and suddenly they were lying on the ground in the snow, Harker clutching them against him. Heat rolled off of him. Mist clung to him on the cold air, and the spellfire guttered around him.

"Rat, wake up!"

"Harker?" they managed.

The creature drew in, its dark feathers iridescent like oil on water. Harker pulled Rat back to him, and his next spell was a flare of spellfire, the snow around it hissing to steam.

Isola would kill them, and she would do it slowly. She would bring them back to the tower with her wraiths, and they wouldn't see the light of day again. She would take everything.

"*Stop!*" Rat shouted, throwing their hand out. Their voice came out harsh, and even though it didn't carry the same commanding force as Harker's casting, theirs had all of the force of Isola's power behind it.

The creature stilled, its gaze fixed on theirs, and then its glassy eyes lit with a horrible kind of recognition.

On the other side of the binding spell, Rat felt a tug of awareness as Isola tried to pull away from them, but this time, they didn't let go.

Rat reached for her magic, still coursing through the binding spell in a cold rush, and then they could feel the seneschal at the edge of their senses, vast and terrible.

It drew in, bearing down on them, and Rat forced more power into the spell. Weeds pressed up through the snow around them, the woods opening to let the tower spill in through the cracks, and they felt the world threaten to unhinge. Their mouth tasted like blood and leaves and ice.

Smoke curled off the creature, and it made a horrible noise like the creak of a breaking ship before it was pulled beneath the waves.

Rat drew harder, anger coursing through them. They didn't care how powerful Isola's creature was. It thrummed with the tower's magic, and they had command of it. They had torn the school's wards to shreds, and they'd made all of the old families afraid. Isola hadn't just picked them because they were a Holbrook—she'd seen what kind of monster they could be.

Rat closed their fist, and they felt the creature bend to them, its will bowing under the weight of their own. Then Isola tore free of them, the bond snapping closed, and Rat's own magic rushed back in.

The gaps in the world closed over the creature like a trap springing shut, and with the resounding *crack* of something splintering deep in the fabric of the universe, the seneschal was swallowed up by the woods. A curtain of snow blew over the place where it had been, and Rat settled against Harker, still breathing hard.

Deep trenches sliced the snow where Harker had burned through it, and the air around him was still too warm and thick with humidity. His arms were still wrapped around Rat, and weeds pressed up through the snow like Rat had torn the world at the seam.

"Rat!" someone called.

They looked up as Will dropped down next to them, Jinx and Agatha close behind. Color ran high on his cheeks, and his breath fogged on the air. "We tried to catch up to you. Shit. Are you okay?"

"Fine," they managed, pushing themself up.

Will looked at the weeds, Isola's power still almost palpable on the air. Worry flickered across his face, but he didn't say anything, maybe because he didn't know where to start.

Shakily, Harker pushed himself to his feet. Steam curled off his gloves in ragged wisps.

Rat's gaze went to Jinx, watching them like she was trying to put the pieces together.

Before Rat could say anything, movement flickered in the trees. On instinct, Rat whipped back, just in time to catch the flash of a gray cloak disappearing into the woods.

Distantly, Rat heard someone call after them, but they were already running.

The ground sloped ahead of them as they raced into the woods. Blood pounded in their ears, and they could taste their pulse. Ahead, they caught another flash of Allister's cloak as he veered off the path, half-hidden by the storm.

"*Stop!*" Rat snapped, their magic rising before they could call it.

Allister staggered as the spell plowed into him, knocking him into the snow. He slid across the ground, but Rat was already there, still holding the threads of the working. He forced himself up, but Rat closed their hand, and they felt the spell clamp shut around him.

"Hey, don't—"

Rat grabbed the collar of his coat. "I know it was you, Church," they said, their voice harsh and burnt. "Maybe those things were Isola's creatures, but you've been the one summoning them. Was it for Evening, or did you think you could play both sides and make a deal with her?"

"Let go of me," he said through his teeth. "I'm not involved with the tower. I'm here because your stunt at the Council Chambers got me exiled to your overgrown boarding school."

Rat tightened their grip. "I don't care who you work for. The next time you try anything like that, I swear on my name, I'll drop you into a crevice so dark and so deep that no one will even know where to look for you." Their magic spilled over, and for a moment, they could feel all the places around them where the ground wanted to open.

They pushed harder, and Allister's eyes widened like he'd felt the first breath of the abyss at his back as the world began to come undone. "Wait, I didn't—"

"Rat!"

Rat caught themself as Harker grabbed their shoulder.

"Hey. You got him. It's done," he said, and they realized how much power they'd gathered. Cold fury rolled through them in waves. Distantly, Rat realized that all of their friends could see them through the trees. They opened their hand, releasing the holding spell, and Allister collapsed into the snow.

"I'm giving you the same deal you gave us," Rat said. "Leave now, and I didn't see you."

Allister's arm trembled as he picked himself up, snow still clinging to his coat. He looked at the others, and a cruel kind of understanding flickered across his face. "They don't know what you did, do they?"

"We're done here," Rat said, turning away from him.

"Isola doesn't help anyone for free, especially not you," Allister called. "If you're still walking around after last semester, it's because she already has you. You cut a deal with her without telling anyone, didn't you?"

Rat whipped back, and Allister's eyes glinted.

"Or maybe you did tell one person, but he's not going to talk." Allister flashed his teeth. "I'm curious. The whole thing where you pretend you haven't noticed that Blakely's in love with you, even though you're both obviously obsessed with each other—is that part of whatever weird martyr complex you have going, or are you actually the only person on the East Coast who hasn't figured it out?"

So faintly Rat might have imagined it, Harker's breath hitched like he'd been hit. Then he drew in, his hand still resting on Rat's shoulder, and whatever chip they thought they'd seen in his armor was gone.

"Actually," Harker said, his voice cold enough to raise goosebumps on the back of Rat's neck. "My obsession with Evans is well-documented and very one-sided. Good effort, though."

Before Rat could find their voice, Agatha reached them, and Allister's gaze shifted to her. He gave her a ragged grin. "Cromwell. It's been a minute."

She knelt down, taking his chin in her hands. "Allister. You're going to go back to my uncle and tell him you lost track of us in the storm, or I'm going to tell you the exact words that will set you on the path that closes every possible door for your family, and when it happens, I'll make sure that each thing you lose will be your own fault. Do I make myself clear?"

He looked at her with equal parts resentment and admiration. "You know, we should really catch up some time."

"Goodbye, Allister." She rose to her feet and turned to Rat without waiting to see what he would do. "Let's get inside before anything else finds us." Rat followed as she started toward the path.

"Whatever magic let that thing through, it wasn't mine," Allister called after them. "One of us is an open doorway, Evans, and it's not me."

This time, Rat kept walking toward the estate and didn't turn back.

CHAPTER THIRTY-FOUR

HEAT AND THE RESIDUAL HUM OF ISOLA'S MAGIC RUSHED under their skin as Rat made their way up to the house, Allister's words still circling in their head. *"One of us is an open doorway."*

They hadn't let Isola's seneschal through. Rat would have known if their magic was being used like that. They would have felt it. Allister was grasping at straws, they told themself. He wanted to throw them off balance, and it had worked. If it hadn't been him, then Isola could have gotten up the power to send it through herself.

"What are you thinking?" Harker asked, and they realized how tense they were.

"Nothing." They gave him their best attempt at a smirk. "What was that about you being obsessed with me?"

He scowled at them, and they didn't know if it was the cold or the fact that he'd been running, but they could swear his face flushed.

"Really, though, are you okay?" they asked, dropping their voice.

His mask slipped a little. "Fine. It's gone now."

"Can you make it to the house?" they asked.

He winced. "It's kind of a problem for me if I can't."

"I mean, I still need you alive, and I don't think I can carry you, so if it's any consolation, it's probably a problem for me, too," Rat said. Then they tucked themself under his arm, and he pulled them in a bit closer, heat still wavering off of him.

Their stomach dipped in a way they didn't really want to think about, but Rat stopped themself before they could follow that any further. The path ended ahead of them, and Rat realized the others had stopped at the edge of the stairs, waiting. They touched Harker's arm, and he let them go again.

Steeling themself, Rat made their way up the steps and traced their gloved fingers over the door. A familiar power whispered to them from somewhere deep in the fabric of the house's wards, as if the seal recognized them. Then, like it had never been locked at all, the door opened.

A draft of cold air followed them as Rat stepped across the threshold, into the foyer. Once, Rat could have imagined that the entryway had been cozy, but now dust coated everything and the scent of frozen earth hung in the air. A chandelier lay in the middle of the floor, covered in a drop cloth, like the house had been packed up neatly and abandoned with great care. Rat flipped the light switch, unsure of what they were expecting, but the sconces along the walls remained dark.

This was where Isola hadn't wanted them to go. There was something here she hadn't wanted them to find.

"Evans," Jinx said behind them. In the quiet of the empty house, her voice came out low but not unkind, and with a sinking feeling, Rat realized that she wasn't about to let go of what she'd seen in the woods that easily.

Rat looked back to see that the others had followed them in.

"We need to talk about what happened out there," she said.

"I told you, it's nothing. We should keep going before—"

"No. What did Church mean that you're an open doorway?"

"Nothing," Rat said again, hating the edge that slid into their voice. "He didn't mean anything. He's just guessing."

"I saw you banish that thing. That wasn't your magic." Jinx studied them, and Rat realized that the others had gone quiet, listening. Heat pricked up the back of their neck. "Does Isola have something on you?"

"It doesn't matter. It's already done, okay?" they said. Rat tugged out of her grasp, avoiding her gaze. "Look, let's just get to the end of this, and then I'll tell you whatever you want to know."

"Rat?" Will asked, concerned, but they brushed past him.

"I saw you out there," Jinx said, before Rat could start for the hall. "You were gone. And then, when you came back . . . I've never seen you cast like that. If there's something going on, you need to tell us."

"What did you expect me to do?" Rat spun back to her. Their voice came out hard, but they couldn't stop themself. "You were the one who wanted me to cast. Well, this is what my powers do. I summon things, and I make pacts with terrible creatures. I open doors, Jinx. What did you think was going to be behind them?"

"Hey! I'm worried about you! You're not acting like yourself!"

"Why? Because it's only *like me* when I'm too scared to do anything?"

Jinx regarded them with the same mix of pity and resignation they'd seen on her face last semester when Harker had tried to fight her, and it was a knife between their ribs.

They didn't care. Their deal with Isola wasn't the same as his. They'd chosen this. They'd wrested her magic away from her, and if that was a blade that cut both ways, they would handle it.

Harker caught their arm, and they realized they were trembling. "Rat. Breathe."

"No," they snapped, and then realized how childish that sounded. Their heart beat in their mouth. "I'm going to search the house. It doesn't matter if I have a deal with Isola or not, because I'm going to stop her before she collects on it."

There was a faint tug on the binding spell with Harker as Rat stalked off. Then, like he'd had realized what he was doing—like he suddenly didn't know if he still had permission—he let go again.

Rat made it as far as the end of the hallway before they heard footsteps follow them. They turned to see Will behind them, still in his coat, his backpack abandoned somewhere in the foyer.

"Blakely wanted to follow you, but I'm making him check the ground wards because I take it he's already in on this," Will said.

"I told you—"

"I know. Let's get some air, okay?"

Grudgingly, Rat let Will lead them farther into the winding halls of the estate. They could tell he wasn't trying to get anywhere in particular, except away from the foyer, but they followed after, forcing themself to breathe.

"Are we going to talk about it?" he asked after a moment.

"No," they said.

Will regarded them skeptically, like he was prepared to wait them out if he had to.

"It wasn't that much of a choice," they said finally. "She had Harker. I knew I was always going to end up there, but I could at least stop her from pulling everyone else in, so I made a deal with her."

Except, in the end Isola had taken him anyway.

Will chewed his lip. "What's going to happen to you?"

"Nothing," Rat said. "I'm not going back with her. If she could have stopped me from leaving the tower, she would have done it. I just need to stop her before she finds her heart or the binding spell digs in any deeper." But in the expanse of the empty estate, the quiet pressing in on them from all sides, they didn't sound as convincing anymore.

Outside, the wind howled.

"How is it, being here?" Will asked.

"Two out of ten. Drafty and definitely haunted."

He gave them a look.

"I don't know," Rat admitted. They touched their fingers to the wall. "I thought it would be familiar, but I don't know anything about this place. Elise never wanted to talk about it."

"Oh. I guess I always thought you didn't want to know."

"I didn't," Rat said, looking around. "I mean, I thought I didn't. I don't know. I'm not really speaking to her right now. I kind of just want to finish searching for now."

Will shoved his hand through his hair. "Alright then," he said. "Alright?"

"Let's search. We can at least do a lap of the house before we go back. Where are we headed?"

"I'm not sure yet." As they spoke, Rat slid the puzzle box from their pocket, turning it idly between their hands. With a familiar prick of magic, the wayfinding spell on the puzzle box woke beneath their fingers, their power rising to meet it. Rat looked at Will. "Did you feel that?"

"You mean the part where it felt like someone walked over my grave?" he said. "Was I supposed to?"

Rat turned the puzzle. Like all of the other times, it jarred against itself, like something inside of it had caught, but underneath that, it felt close in a way that it hadn't before.

They drew on their powers, letting the estate take shape around them, and then Isola's magic slithered out with their own.

Quickly, Rat dropped the working, and the puzzle slid out of their hands.

"Hey." Will caught them, and they realized they'd jolted.

Rat knelt down to pick up the puzzle, breathing hard. They shoved the whisper of Isola's power away and imagined closing a door on the binding spell, but it still clung to them like a reminder. They were supposed to be under her control. Isola wanted the keys, and if Rat wasn't ready to hand them over to her, she would be waiting to take them herself.

But just for a moment, before Rat had lost the spell, there had been something there. They were sure of it.

"Are you sure you're okay?" Will asked.

"Come on," Rat said. "There's something here."

Rat started forward, following the subtle pull of the wayfinding spell, and it felt like pieces falling into place. They slowed as they came to a set of doors, heavier than the ones they'd seen in the rest of the house. The telltale sheen of aether glinted in the dim of the abandoned corridor, not like the veil of a dead passage, but the steady glow of a ward.

The Holbrook archives.

Their archives.

Rat reached up and pressed their hand to the doors. They weren't sure how, but with a cold certainty, they knew that whatever the puzzle box was leading them toward lay on the other side of the doors.

"Rat?" Will asked, but they barely heard him. They leaned in and felt the magic in the wards give, like it already understood. Rat was a Holbrook, no matter how long they'd been away or how little of their family was left. The house and all of its books had been sealed away, but it had never been sealed from them.

"*Open,*" Rat whispered into the doors, and deep in the web of the house's seal, they felt something give way.

Slowly, the door swung inwards, opening into an antechamber. Just from the entryway, the Holbrook Archives were sprawling in a way that was wholly different from the one at the Evans place. Sometimes Rat forgot that even if the Evans Archives had felt expansive to them, Elise had only ever kept a small part of it on the premises. But now they weren't looking at an archive that had been fitted into a house. The Holbrook Estate had been built around its archive.

Rat stepped in past the threshold, Will following close behind them. A set of archways opened out on each side of the room, leading deeper into the archives. In the center, the floor had been inlaid with a labyrinth, the paths twisting in on each other.

On instinct, Rat made their way toward the middle of the labyrinth, turning the box so that the archival mark aligned with the center of the maze. Almost imperceptibly, they felt something fall into place. Rat turned the puzzle box, and the corner twisted before clicking into its new position. Deep in the aether, Rat felt the archives shift around them as the passages realigned, and the labyrinth inlaid on the floor rearranged itself beneath them.

Another archway appeared in the wall of shelves ahead of them like it had been there all along, a veil of aether curling over the mouth of the passageway.

"Rat?" Will asked quietly, staring openly at them like for once, he'd seen it, too.

"We should get everyone," Rat said. "Whatever we're looking for, I'm pretty sure it's here."

CHAPTER THIRTY-FIVE

IT DIDN'T TAKE LONG FOR THE OTHERS TO FIND THEM.

Rat met them at the mouth of the new hallway. The shelves on the other side of the threshhold looked older, the way that most of the things Rat found hidden away in dead passages tended to be, but the elements hadn't started to creep in and wear them down like they had in the rest of the house.

Almost, Rat couldn't help thinking, like the books here hadn't really been abandoned, just tucked away until the next Holbrook heir could return to claim them.

Jinx took a step forward.

"Wait." Rat caught her shoulder like they hadn't just stormed out on her fifteen minutes ago. She turned, and they dropped their hand again. "Just—not all of the passages are stable. I think this one should be, but if you get separated from me, there's a chance you're not going to be able to get back."

"Right," she said. "Duly noted."

Rat glanced from her to Agatha, then Will, and then their eyes found Harker's. He looked at them, a question on his face like he wanted to know if they were okay and didn't know if he could ask. Before Rat could say anything else they were going to regret, Agatha took a deliberate step back.

"I'll keep watch," she said, and Rat remembered how her magic had reacted to the tunnels at Bellamy Arts. Just being in the Holbrook Estate with all of its history and failing enchantments had to be straining her abilities as it was.

Beside her, Will grit his teeth, eyeing the passage uncertainly, and Rat was also unpleasantly reminded that even if they could see the passage clearly, they didn't know how it appeared to anyone else. Even the passages that seemed real and solid to Rat weren't that much more than a flicker in the corner of most people's eyes, if that.

Jinx glanced up at him. "Chen, are you okay to split up? We still need a defensive caster out here."

"You stay," he said. "I'll—"

"I'm already going," she said.

Rat looked to Harker. He hesitated a moment, and Rat realized he wasn't going to follow them if they didn't want him to. They didn't have to drag him in any farther. But he'd known the risks and he'd chosen to follow them here anyway.

Rat motioned to him in invitation. "Are you coming?"

A little of the tension went out of him as he moved to follow them, and then his composure slid back into place "After you, Evans."

Aether curled around them in motes as Rat led the way through, holding their arm out to Jinx as they crossed the threshold. Her gaze lingered on Harker for a moment, but if she realized exactly what him following meant, she didn't say. Then, the quiet pressed in around them as they left the library behind.

Rat glanced over, and Jinx looked away, avoiding their gaze. Grudgingly, Jinx let Rat lead them through.

"Jinx, I . . . before . . ." Rat started.

"It's fine," she said, even though it wasn't. "Let's just finish this."

"Wait." They said, but she'd already let go of them. "You're right, okay? I made a deal with her. Harker knows about it, but I didn't tell him. He realized what was happening when I did it."

Just for a moment, Jinx hesitated. "Last semester?"

"I promised to go back to the tower with Isola once she has her heart. She didn't mean for me to be able to use her power again after that night, but it opened up again when I went to get Harker." They remembered the faint flickers of Isola's power they'd felt before the binding spell had torn open completely. "Maybe before that. I don't know."

"You knew what she was going to ask for," Jinx said. "When you went to meet her."

"Rat didn't have a choice," Harker said. He'd been following quietly enough that for a moment, Rat had forgotten he was there. "Isola used me as leverage."

"You don't get to talk, Blakely." Steel slid into Jinx's voice. "I haven't forgotten who brought them there."

He let out a brittle laugh. "Please. Give me a little credit, Wilder."

"He didn't come with me," Rat said. "He tried to keep me from going. I had to physically stop him."

Jinx gave them a look, and they stopped at the end of the aisle as the wayfinding spell tugged at them.

"It's a long story. You were right about the door to the roof locking."

Jinx snorted in spite of herself. "What?"

"I got down," Harker mumbled.

Then Rat's magic rose in their core, the depths of the archives taking shape at the edge of their senses. "Guys," they said, and the two fell quiet again.

Ahead, the shelves narrowed and the books seemed older than before, the air thick with the scent of aether and aging paper. Rat pressed on the puzzle box, and this time it gave readily, the pieces twisting apart into a new configuration as the next passageway appeared ahead of them.

Jinx took their arm again to let Rat help her through, and for a long moment, she and Harker followed in silence.

"I've been getting glimpses of the tower—of Isola. She did something while we were fighting her seneschal. Like a dream or—I don't know," Rat said, finally. "I couldn't get back to myself. I think . . ."

The idea of Isola using their magic made their skin crawl. On some level, they'd known their bond with her went both ways, but if she'd used them to summon things—if they hadn't even known it—

"It's like you said back in December," they said instead, without meeting Jinx's gaze. "Isola's heart isn't the only thing she's after. She's always planned on taking me back to the tower, and she's going to use whatever hold she has on me to do as much damage as she can along the way."

"Then we'll get you back," Jinx said, her voice soft.

"You can't promise that. I told you. She'll use me to draw you in, and then—"

"Then what, Rat?" Jinx said, stopping them. "I think we can make our own choices about what risks we're willing to take."

"But—"

"All of us are here because we decided not to walk away. Maybe we'd be safer, but we chose this. I told you already, I'm not letting Isola have any of us."

"Fuck, I know, I just—I know," they managed.

"We're friends, okay? We wouldn't leave you." Her gaze flickered to Harker, and Rat realized he'd gone quiet again. But before he could say anything, Jinx waved him off. "I get it, Blakely. You were trying to stay alive last semester and you needed a way into the tunnels. It's fine if you don't think of me and Cromwell the same way. You don't owe us anything."

"Wait," he started, and a pang of desperate want surged down the binding spell.

Rat looked over at him as he broke off, but Harker had already caught himself, and the channel was closed again.

Jinx raised an eyebrow.

He cleared his throat. "Do you still want that? To be friends, I mean?"

"I don't know. How many more times am I going to have to threaten to douse you if you're plotting something?"

"Several?" He gave her a hopeful look, even though that was probably the wrong answer.

Jinx's mouth tugged into her wry not-smile. "Good to have you back, Blakely."

Rat followed the next turn of the hallway and fell quiet again as a high carved archway opened ahead of them, leading out into a wide circular room. Distantly, Rat realized they'd made a circuit. The path they'd taken should have brought them back to the main entrance, except now, where the labyrinth had been, the floor had given way to a wide set of stone stairs, leading deeper into the earth.

Rat drew on their magic, and for a moment, they could feel the shape of the estate again, sprawling out around them with all of its strange corners and hidden passageways. Whatever this was, they didn't know what was at the bottom, but they knew that was a long way down.

Rat stopped at the top of the stairs. Farther ahead, the light tapered off, the spells that might have lit the way long since burned out.

"Vaults," Jinx said half to herself, and Rat realized she'd come to a stop behind them.

Steeling themself, Rat slid their phone from their pocket and switched on the flashlight. The beam washed uselessly over the top steps, barely reaching the edge of the shadows. They raised their hand to a casting position. "*Light.*"

A burst of yellow spellfire flared over their hand, nipping the tips of their fingers. Quickly, Rat yanked their hand back, and the spell collapsed again. "Shit," they muttered, pressing their fingers to their mouth, then realized that Harker was staring at them, incredulous.

"Don't look at me like that," Rat said into their hand. "You weren't around to light yourself on fire. Somebody had to."

Harker drew up a will-o'-wisp of spellfire and motioned for Rat to follow. "Here." He traced his thumb over the base of their wrist in a healing spell. "If we make it back out, I'll show you one for blisters later."

"If?" Rat asked, starting after him as he drew ahead on to the stairs.

Most of the oldest families were rumored to have vaults in their archives. Supposedly, if Rat believed what they'd heard, it was a place for the kinds of magic that were best kept out of sight. The kind that even the Council of Hours pretended not to know about.

The staircase bottomed out in a small antechamber. Beyond, a set of narrow archways led on to another room of the archives, the walls lined with shelves on one side, map cabinets on the other. The scent of dust hung even heavier on the air, like wherever they were, it had been sealed for a long time, and a fine coat of aether had settled over everything.

Rat slid their phone back out and turned the flashlight toward a set of shelves, but they weren't sure where to start. They ran their thumb over a row of spellbooks. Whatever had made everyone else fear the Holbrook family—the depths of what their magic could do—it was here.

"So?" Harker asked, his voice closer than Rat had expected.

"I don't know," they admitted, turning toward him. "I don't know what anything is."

There was magic here that most of the major families would probably be willing to pay a small fortune for in loyalty and favors, and probably actual cash if those kinds of transactions weren't so far beneath most of the houses' interest. Even when Rat had been letting themself into the Evans Archives, they hadn't had access to their family's more powerful spellbooks.

"Over here."

Rat turned.

Jinx had come to a stop by a shelf of leatherbound notebooks, lit by the pale glow of her own phone's flashlight. She'd already taken one down, and she held it open in her hands.

Rat started toward her at the same time Harker did, the will-o'-wisp of spellfire burning brighter around him.

"What is it?" Rat asked, looking down at the notebook.

Jinx held it out to them by way of answer.

Rat riffled through the pages, unsure what they were seeing. Handwritten notes and spell diagrams flickered past, and then they stopped as they caught sight of the familiar shape of the tower. The lines were fine and purposeful, like they'd been drawn with a fountain pen, but it looked so close to the way Rat had always drawn it that if they hadn't known better, they could have mistaken it for their own sketch.

A chill tracked down Rat's spine.

Quickly, they flipped back to the beginning, half expecting a name or a year, even though they already knew from the handwriting that it couldn't be their father's, but instead, it was signed in the same, spindly signature Rat had seen before in about a dozen school histories.

"Jinx," Rat said slowly. "This is Ingrid's."

"Yeah," she breathed. "I think all of them are."

"Then why are they here?" Rat asked, but they already knew the answer.

Ingrid, who'd willingly spent seven years at the tower and still managed to find her way back home, with her memories intact and Isola's still-beating heart in tow.

Ingrid, who'd built a school full of passageways and hidden it away behind a latticework of wards that she'd laid along the edges of the planes themselves.

Ingrid, who's protective workings had bent to Rat's service, even when they shouldn't have.

The first time Rat had seen a picture of her, there was something sleepless and intense about her that had made them think of Harker, but they'd been wrong.

She hadn't looked like him.

Margaret Ingrid, with her bony shoulders and lank blond hair, had looked like a Holbrook.

CHAPTER THIRTY-SIX

RAT'S SKIN HAD GONE COLD ALL OVER. THEY TURNED back through the journal, skimming through the sketches of the tower, surrounded by black birds and wild overgrowth and scratchy notes that had begun to fade with time. Ingrid's handwriting was gorgeous and almost impossible to read, since it was all cursive, punctuated with bits of spells written out in a complicated notation that Rat had never learned.

They stopped at a drawing of Isola. A crown of flowers was woven into the dark snarls of her hair. A black bird perched on her outstretched glove, and her sword was at her side. Rat traced their thumb along the edge of the page, then flipped back to the start, to the date. They couldn't remember the exact year Bellamy Arts had been founded, but they knew this was earlier than that.

Long before Ingrid had gone to the tower to steal Isola's heart.

The Ingrid who'd drawn this couldn't have been much older than Rat was now.

"Except . . ." Rat said to themself, flipping the pages. They thought back to the family history they'd found in the school archives, and how it had ended before it got to the school.

"Rat?" Jinx asked.

"The story you told me last semester about Ingrid sinking the school. Why did she go to the tower?" Rat asked.

Jinx hesitated like she wasn't sure what they were asking.

"Isola was involved with some of the old bloodlines. You said she'd lined them up to fall."

Jinx's brow drew together, but when they looked over at Harker, he met their gaze with a kind of horrible understanding. What Jinx had told them last semester was that some of the lesser bloodlines that had gotten mixed up with Isola had never recovered.

"It was the Holbrook line," Rat said quietly. "Wasn't it?"

They could tell from the look on Jinx's face that she hadn't known, but in the silence of their family's vaults, the whole thing came into a kind of horrible clarity.

Isola had known their family. Not just their father. Their entire line. She'd been the reason why there was barely anything left of the Holbrooks—the reason why even now the other houses were afraid of them—and when Rat had been alone with no idea what their magic was, they'd let her take them in.

Their skin crawled as they thought of all of the times she'd offered them a place at her side.

"Fuck. Of course she's after me. It's probably some kind of twisted revenge on Ingrid. She probably thought another Holbrook would have the best chance of getting to the collection." Rat smudged their hand over their eyes and grabbed another book from the shelf, unsure what they were even hoping to find there. "God. I bet that's how she knew I could get inside the clock tower last semester. I can't believe I was so—"

"Rat." Jinx caught their wrist. "You didn't know."

They looked at Harker, desperate, even though they didn't know what they were hoping he would do.

His face softened, and he took their shoulder, steadying them. "What do you want us to do?"

"Help me search." Their voice was rough, and they hated that their lip was trembling. "Please. We came here to find the keys, so just help me find them."

"Alright," Harker said, and there was a familiar flash of ruthlessness in his voice that Rat shouldn't have found comforting. "Then we'll keep searching."

💀

It was dark by the time they made their way back to the main house.

There was still more ground to cover, but they hadn't managed to find anything else.

Will and Agatha had left their post in the library a while ago and set up camp in the cavernous expanse of the estate's abandoned great room. Like the rest of the house, most of the furniture had been moved out or covered. A ring of protection spells was chalked on the floor, a couple of Harker's spell diagrams left out in a small pile nearby, and through some magic completely beyond Rat's understanding, someone had managed to turn the lights on.

Will had moved on to setting logs in the towering brick fireplace that took up one wall, while Agatha supervised from a velvet fainting couch, the dustcloth resting in a pile on the floor beside it.

"Did you find anything?" he asked.

Rat hesitated, but Jinx just gave him a small nod and said, "We can discuss it tomorrow."

They all stayed up a bit longer, but Rat didn't feel much like talking, and eventually everyone set out some spare blankets that Will and Agatha had found in one of the house's many cupboards, then put the lights out, the last embers still burning in the fireplace.

Rat waited until things were quiet before they pulled their cloak on over their sweatshirt and slipped back out of bed, already knowing they weren't going to be able to sleep.

Once, they wouldn't have dreamt of wandering the unfamiliar corridors by themself, but the Holbrook Estate was theirs, and if there was anything waiting for them in the dark, it was welcome to find them.

Rat ended up back in the archives. At some point, the snow had turned back into rain, and a steady patter beat down on the rooftop as Rat picked their way between the aisles.

They stopped by the window and pushed back the dustcloth on an old reading chair. The grounds sprawled out below them, the mountains rising up dark and jagged in the distance. Rat dropped down heavily, pulling their knees to their chest.

Their mind went back to Isola. From the first time she'd seen them in the field of grass, she'd recognized them. Not just as Alexander Holbrook's son, but as the final Holbrook wayfinder, heir to the woman who'd stolen from her and eluded her even into death.

Even when Rat had still been wide-eyed and desperate to know about their powers, Isola had already been starting to spin her web. Rat had spent months thinking she was the only person who understood their magic, when she'd known what had happened to their family the entire time. She'd cut them off from everyone who could have helped them and then preyed on their loneliness.

They'd allowed her to train them.

Rat wanted to root out every trace of her power until they were scraped hollow. They wanted to scrub the memory of her leather gloves off their skin.

Rat's hand found the puzzle box as they forced the thought away. They drew it out of their pocket. It hadn't opened any further, but even though all of the pieces had shifted into a new place, it didn't look completed. Just different.

The bands of spellwork had changed positions, locking together into a new sigil. Something about it tugged at the edge of Rat's attention, but they couldn't say if it was because they knew it from somewhere, or just because they could feel the low pull of the wayfinding spell, telling them they weren't out of the maze yet.

It was their father's work. If anyone could figure it out, it should have been them. There was something they were missing. Rat just wished they knew what.

Lightning flashed outside, illuminating the grounds, and Rat froze. Just as fast, the woods had gone dark again, but for a moment, something had moved between the trees farther down the slope.

Dread spiked through them. Before they could think better of it, they pushed themself to their feet and rushed for the stairs.

When they reached the kitchen, Rat shoved through the back doors and then out on to the grounds. The rain came down in sheets, soaking through their cloak and into their sweatshirt beneath it. A gust of wind howled past them, tearing at the darkened edge of the tree line.

Rat stole a glance over their shoulder at the darkened house behind them and started into the trees, drawing a concealment spell around them as they went. They shouldn't have been out here alone, but they didn't care. If Isola wanted a fight, they would give her one.

The woods grew thick and close, the trees higher than the ones around Bellamy Arts, and the rain had already begun to wash away the snow. Mud and ice water flooded the trail ahead, and the cold seeped into Rat's shoes.

Under the sound of the rain, twigs crunched behind them.

Rat spun to find Harker, his cloak draped over his shoulders. A wisp of spellfire flickered in his hand, spitting against the rain. His hair was plastered down to his face, and he looked like he'd put about as much thought into coming outside as Rat had.

"What are you doing out here?" Rat asked, any grasp they'd still had on the concealment spell slipping away from them.

"What are *you* doing?" he said back.

Rat opened their mouth to argue, and he gave them a defiant look, which might have been more impressive if he wasn't soaked. Suddenly, they had no idea why they'd expected Harker to stay inside and keep himself safe. They certainly hadn't.

Farther off, something scraped along the forest floor. Rat turned toward the sound, but before they could see where it had come from, Harker dropped his spell and grabbed them by the arm, tugging them back.

"Hey—"

He gave them a warning look as the sound came again, closer.

A gust of wind tore across the clearing, carrying with it a fresh torrent of rain.

Harker shifted, his hand raised to a casting position. Rat locked eyes with him and gave him a nod, and he started up the path, toward the sound.

Rat took off after him, matching his pace. Beside them, Harker traced a spell on the air. Rat watched for him to conjure another wisp of spellfire, but it didn't come. All around them, the shadows seemed to deepen, shifting to cover them as they moved, and Rat remembered that they weren't the only one who Isola had taught. The difference was that Harker was a better caster.

A faint heat radiated off of him, taking the bite out of the air, and Rat decided this wasn't the time to think about how disgustingly relieved they were to have him there with them.

They stopped short as something moved through the woods ahead of them, just beyond the ground wards.

Through the glow of the aether, Rat caught a glimpse of Isola's seneschal, snaking through the trees, like something out of a nightmare. Dark tendrils of smoke trailed after it, and shadows swarmed through the dark around it, nearly impossible to pick out in the depths of the woods.

Automatically, Rat shifted into a defensive stance, but the seneschal hadn't gotten in past the wards. Like even now, Isola couldn't muster up the strength just yet to summon it inside.

Long, low forms slinked through the shadows behind it, and Rat realized the seneschal wasn't the only one of Isola's creatures prowling around the edge of the grounds. Maybe to search for any weaknesses in the estate's defensive spells. Maybe just to lurk around the wards and remind Rat that she'd be waiting for them when they left.

Beside Rat, Harker had gone still.

"Come on," they whispered, pulling him back. "They can't get to us here."

He took half a step backward, and then he let Rat lead the way as they took off into the trees the way they had come, the concealment spell still wrapped around them both like a veil.

CHAPTER THIRTY-SEVEN

THE RAIN WAS COMING DOWN IN SHEETS BY THE TIME they made it back to the house. The wind howled at the door as Rat pulled it shut behind them. Their clothes were soaked through, and their hair was plastered to their face.

"Fuck," they breathed, collapsing back against the wall.

Beside them, biting back a wince, Harker traced a spell on the air, and the lights went on overhead. A spell like the one in the great room had been etched on the wall over the stove, though Rat didn't know who'd set it up or when, and the counters had been dusted off.

"It's fine if you want to go back to sleep," Harker said. "I can keep watch."

"No, I can stay up."

He hesitated.

"I wasn't sleeping anyway," they admitted. "And I don't really feel like being by myself."

"I couldn't sleep either," he said, his voice soft against the steady patter of the rain.

"Sorry if it hasn't exactly been the semester you'd been hoping to come back to," Rat said.

Harker raised his eyebrows at them. "You mean the part where we're camping out in an abandoned house, or the part where you're trying to slay a Rook?"

They grimaced. "Yes?"

A ghost of a smile tugged at his mouth, and then he took a pair of camping mugs from the supplies that had been left in the kitchen. "I'll make coffee."

"Instant?"

"I brought some with me. It's vile and you'll hate it," he said. He flexed his wrist in a retrieval spell, and a couple of sugar packets shot up from the clutter. He caught them and slid them over to Rat. "I stole some creamer from the dining hall, too. It should be enough to drown the taste."

Harker, Rat decided, was absolutely welcome to add this to his tally for saving their life.

Rat climbed up on the counter while Harker traced out heating sigils, moving like he'd done this so often, it was second nature. Quiet settled over the kitchen, and for a moment, there was just the steady sound of the rain beating down on the roof of the estate.

"Those creatures out there . . ." Rat started.

Harker looked up at them.

Rat swallowed hard. "What Allister said about me being an open doorway. I let them through. Didn't I?"

"You didn't cast that spell," he said.

"But it was my magic. I've been drawing on Isola's powers. I knew it could go both ways. If she's using my powers—could she do that?" But even as Rat said it, they already knew the answer. They'd just been circling around it all day, trying not to admit it.

"I don't know. Possibly," Harker admitted. "She couldn't use my powers when I was bound to her, but I couldn't reach hers like you did either. Whatever I got from her seeped in so slowly, I barely felt it."

"I just . . . It's like everything I do puts everyone in danger, and no matter how much power I have or how much I scare the other houses, I'm just playing into her hands. If I did this—"

"You didn't." Harker reached up and touched their jaw, stopping them. "It's not monstrous to want to survive."

"What if I want more than that?" Rat said in a rush. "What if I want her to be afraid of me? What if I liked seeing the other houses fear me?"

"Do you?" he asked, but there was a terrible curiosity in his voice, like he wouldn't think that was monstrous either. Like even if it was, he knew too well what it was like to want things he'd been told he couldn't have.

Rat brushed a stray lock of hair out of his eyes and let their hand linger there. A pang of want shot through the binding spell like lightning.

God, what's wrong with me? They don't like you that way. The thought traveled down the bond, so clearly Harker's that it took Rat a moment to realize he hadn't said it aloud.

Quickly, Harker pulled back. Blood rushed to his face, but Rat was still staring at him.

"I'm sorry," he said in a rush. "I—"

"No. Wait," Rat reached for him, but he caught their wrist. Slowly, he lowered their hand to the counter.

"Don't." Harker said, his voice was barely a breath. He looked away from them, and one hand went to his bracelets, picking at the leather strands. "It's fine. I swore an oath to you. You've been clear that it's nothing more than that."

Their heart sank. "What?"

"You should go back," he said, turning away from them. "It's better if I keep watch on my own, anyway. I slept on the drive up."

"Harker—"

"*Please.*" Desperation cut his voice, and this might have been the first time Rat had seen him look so completely powerless.

Rat slid down from the counter and caught his arm before he could go. "No, you blazing trash fire. What are you even talking about, *I've been clear?*"

He whipped back, his hair still plastered to his face. "I—"

"Do you actually think this is just an alliance for me?" They grabbed the rain-damp collar of his cloak, knotting their fingers into the heavy fabric. "I barely left my room after you stopped talking to me—I didn't even want to go to Bellamy Arts, and then I followed you into the tunnels because I was so desperate to make sure you were alright! I didn't think you were going to speak to me again! The only reason I even lied about not being close to you to begin with was because I was terrified Elise would see how much I wanted to be like you and blame you for how I was, and that happened anyway! You were the one who wanted nothing to do with me!"

"Because you made it clear I'd served my purpose!" His voice came out rough. "I wasn't about to come back and make you spell it out that you didn't actually want me!"

The air went out of Rat's lungs. "But . . . No. I—"

"You were right last Halloween, okay?" Harker dropped his gaze again. "I knew if I got to the Ingrid Collection, the game would end, and I'd lose you again. I just kept drawing it out so you wouldn't go."

"I wouldn't have," Rat said, and then realized that they were still gripping his cloak, standing so they were almost flush against him. They should have stepped back, but they couldn't make themself.

Their hand tightened, pulling him in. Cautiously, Harker looked back at them.

"I've been in love with you this entire time, you burning wreck," Rat said softly.

Heat pricked across his skin. "Fight me, Evans. I was in love with you first."

Rat let out a muffled laugh. "What?"

"I—" Harker started, like he had no idea what he'd just said. Then a small peal of laughter slipped away from him, too. "Shut up. I don't know, okay?"

Rat bit the edge of a grin, and all over again they realized how close he was standing. "Harker?" they asked.

He met their gaze, and for a moment there was only the sound of the rain falling outside.

Slowly, Rat pulled him down to them, pausing long enough that he could push them away if he wanted to. But then he leaned in the rest of the way and his mouth was on theirs with the faint taste of wood smoke and instant coffee and something else unbearably familiar in a way that was just his.

Rat wanted this. They wanted *him*.

They were tired of pretending they didn't.

Rat leaned in, deepening the kiss, Harker's skin feverish against theirs in the chill of the house, and he laced his fingers through their hair, drawing them closer with a quiet desperation, like this would burn him down completely and he wanted it to.

They didn't care what creatures Isola was amassing outside, or what her intentions for them were. She wouldn't take this from them.

💀

"What's next?" Rat asked, when they'd finally untangled from him long enough to catch their breath. The rain was still coming down hard, and their coffee had likely gone cold a while ago. "We probably have to go back soon."

"Could you help me with something?" Harker asked.

Rat waited while Harker dug a pair of sewing scissors out of his casting supplies, and then they realized exactly what he was asking. His hair was already beginning to dry from the rain, and Rat couldn't remember the last time he'd actually cut it.

"I don't know what's coming next, but I think that as soon as we have the keys, everything is going to start happening fast," he said, turning the scissors in his hand. "I want to feel like myself."

"Are those going to be sharp enough?"

He lifted an eyebrow at them, which Rat was pretty sure meant *They can be if I spell them.* Then he nodded to the hall. "Come on. I wanted to get your thoughts about the keys anyway."

Rat sharpened a little. "Did you figure something out?"

"No. That's the thing," Harker said. "We assumed they'd be here, but something isn't adding up."

Rat furrowed their brow, but Harker just motioned for them to follow.

They didn't know the house well, but with the two of them together and the rain pounding down on the roof, it didn't feel quite as haunted as it had before.

A will-o'-wisp of spellfire trailed along after them, throwing shadows as they searched for a room with a decent mirror. Rat wasn't sure when it had happened, but at some point over the last few weeks, his casting had lost some of the tower's raggedness, and the flame burned brighter and steadier than they remembered.

They finally stopped in a bedroom with a paneled folding mirror on the dresser, a bit like the one Harker had hidden the Holbrook map inside of a lifetime ago. There were enough enchantments to have kept the glass relatively clean, and in the half-light, it only looked a little cursed.

"So," Rat said, flopping down on the foot of the bed as Harker took a section of still-damp hair between his fingers and made a measured cut. "What are you thinking, then? For the keys? Do you think they're somewhere else on the grounds?"

"I don't think they're here."

For a moment, it was quiet, save for the rain and the rasp of the scissors as he worked.

"I don't either," Rat admitted. "Nothing down there was my dad's. I don't think anything in this house is his." Their father might have come here for research or to look through Ingrid's journals, but even as Rat spoke, the truth of it settled over them. "He didn't do any of his work here. I don't think he ever actually lived here at all."

"No," Harker said. "I don't think anyone's lived here in a while."

They'd known, even before they could put their finger on it. Rat didn't know a lot about the dozens of maintenance and groundskeeping spells that kept most of the oldest family's ancestral homes in good repair, but they knew enough to tell that the Holbrook Estate had been all but abandoned for much longer than the ten years that the archives had been sealed.

"It doesn't make sense," Rat said. "Frey told me my father built the puzzle box. Maybe he just needed to make a new one to reopen the vaults, but . . . I don't know. I feel like there's something else. It's not finished yet."

Harker sharpened. "You don't think so?"

"No. It's like . . ." Rat slid the puzzle box back out of their pocket, turning it in their hands. It had shifted into a new configuration, but in a way they couldn't fully articulate, that wasn't the same as being *opened*. "It's different, but I don't think it's done."

It felt like a test.

Not a test, Rat thought.

It was like their father's maps—a puzzle that they were meant to solve.

The first part of it was here, in the Holbrook Estate, in the vaults, where as long as the archives had remained in their bloodline's care, no one outside the family would have been allowed to come close. It was an extra measure of protection, to make sure that whoever found the puzzle box couldn't go straight to the end without proving they could get past the estate's wards first.

"The second part . . ." Rat said under their breath, thinking.

They turned the puzzle, thinking.

"Hm?" Harker asked.

"If you need to come through the Holbrook Estate to solve the first part of the puzzle, that means the next part could be somewhere that isn't as well protected."

"Or somewhere that doesn't belong to the Holbrook family," Harker said, like he was turning the idea over. In the mirror, he frowned.

"What?"

"Nothing. It's just . . . it's the new sigil on the puzzle box," he said. "I got a look at it earlier."

"Do you know what it is?"

"No. I don't know. I think it's a seal, but . . . it's bothering me. I've seen it somewhere."

Rat sat up straighter. "Like the one in the clock tower?"

"No. It's something else." He paused, frustrated. I used to know this one. I remember diagramming it to figure out what it was, but I don't think I finished. Or it was too complicated."

"Okay." Rat sat forward, thinking. "Do you remember who was with you when you were diagramming it?"

"You might have been. I don't think we actually discussed it. I just think it was somewhere you'd seen it, too. Maybe in a dead passage."

Harker turned back to them, thinking, scissors still in hand. He'd left his hair just long enough to tie back, and it hung straight past his jaw. Rat wasn't sure when it had happened, but at some point over the last few weeks, a little of the color had come back to him, and he just looked like himself, all sharp edges and burning ambition. A tension that Rat hadn't noticed had gone out of him, like he'd finally settled back into his skin.

"What?" he asked, and they realized they were staring.

Their face heated. "Nothing," they said, but they couldn't miss the small flicker of satisfaction on his face. "The sigil. Was it college or high school?"

He frowned again, and then his gaze sharpened. "Before college. The spell diagram ended up in my notes with all of your maps when I went to Bellamy Arts."

"What else?"

"It was set in the ground somewhere. I remember it being a stone floor, but I could be wrong. I think—" He broke off. "Of course," he breathed, at the same time that Rat realized they knew exactly where the spell diagram had come from.

CHAPTER THIRTY-EIGHT

EVERYONE ELSE WAS STILL ASLEEP WHEN THEY MADE IT back to the great room. Maybe because Rat was still thinking about the tower, or maybe because of the way Harker had hesitated when they finally asked about turning in for the night, but the idea of sleeping on the floor had lost a bit of its shine, and Rat grabbed a couple of spare blankets that had been left by the door.

"Can we just take those?" Harker said quietly as Rat laid the blankets out, but once they'd thought of it, they couldn't get the thought of him in the tower out of their mind, curled up on the stone floor under his cloak.

"Yes?" Rat said. Harker watched them uncertainly, and they dropped the extra blankets on the floor where his things were. "I'm like, five monster attacks and a horrible family secret past pretending I'm going to sleep on the floor. Do you want to sleep on the floor?"

He looked at them like he absolutely didn't. Then, because Rat had already settled in his spot, he dropped down next to them, his breathing slow and even in the dark. A soft warmth rolled off him, and it occurred to Rat that thinking they could be anywhere close to him and actually fall asleep had been a horrible mistake. Rat wrapped their arm around Harker anyway, since there was no way they were getting up now, either, and like he'd just realized he was allowed to, he pulled them in close.

Rat wasn't sure when they finally drifted off, but it was still raining outside when they woke up. Harker's spot was empty, but he'd left the sweatshirt Rat usually stole from him folded on the blankets beside them, fully dry now like he must have spelled it for them before he got up. Their heart skipped.

Probably, they reminded themself, if Harker was awake, it meant he was already up to something.

Rat climbed to their feet and gathered their things, then started back toward the kitchen.

Will had taken over the stove, which must have been spelled back to life, and was making pancakes in a cast-iron pan he must have found somewhere in the kitchen. Beside him, Harker sat perched on the counter with a cup of coffee, his hair tied up in a short almost-ponytail like he'd already been awake for a while. At some point, he'd put on a clean shirt, and there was fresh mud on his boots like he'd been outside again.

His eyes lit up when he saw Rat, even though Rat wasn't sure how much sleep he'd actually gotten. "You're up."

"You could have woken me."

"I tried," Harker said. "You told me you were an Evans, and you didn't answer to me."

Rat rubbed their eyes, since that sounded exactly like something they would have said. "What are you guys doing?"

"Breakfast," Will said.

"I'm corrupting him with forbidden magic." Harker drew a spell on the air, and the bag of chocolate chips flew across the countertop.

Will gave him a look.

Idly, Harker picked a few from the bag and then offered it to him.

"I went outside for a run and found him searching the woods," Will said, exasperated. "We ended up doing a sweep of the grounds."

"Find anything?" Rat asked, coming over to join them.

Harker shook his head. "The storm cleaned up any trail we could have followed. Whatever creatures were lurking around outside the wards, we couldn't find them. Knowing Isola, she was probably scouting the area."

Will looked back at Rat. "So, I take it that means we're wrapping up the rest of the search today?"

Rat reached into the bag and took a handful of chocolate chips. "Actually," they said. They glanced at Harker, and he sharpened as he caught the leading edge in their voice.

"Wait. Did you figure something out?" Will asked, shifting forward.

Before Rat could answer, Jinx appeared in the doorway with an armful of journals. Agatha followed close behind her, wearing a flowing silk dress that might have actually been an expensive bathrobe, and had absolutely not been meant for any combination of winter, physical exertion, or exploring abandoned houses in.

"Are we scheming?" Agatha asked, making her way to the counter. She held her hand out, and Rat passed her the chocolate chips.

"Planning," Rat said. They took the puzzle box from their sweatshirt's pocket. "This pattern. It's a match for another sigil."

Agatha tilted her head slightly, and Jinx's gaze tracked from the puzzle back to Rat. "Do you know what it is?" Jinx asked.

"Where it is," they corrected her. "It's from the observatory."

Jinx furrowed her brow, but Will already got it, maybe because Rat had told him about the passages in the Evans place before.

"Whatever notes my dad left," Rat said, "they're at my house."

CHAPTER THIRTY-NINE

RAT LEFT FROM THE FOYER WITH HARKER.

They didn't have time to make a better plan, and if they knew where to go, there was only a matter of time before Isola did, too.

They waited until the others had gone back to the great room to start breaking camp and packing up to head back to the school. Then Rat shut their eyes, steadying themself.

For a moment, they thought they wouldn't know what to do, but they'd opened dozens of passages back to the Evans place over the years. That was where they'd first learned how to wayfind, even before they'd found Isola. Every time they'd gone to find her, Rat had started from that house, and it was the place they always came back to when they were finished. Maybe they hadn't tried to reach it from the Holbrook Estate before, but they'd found their way home from farther.

"This way," Rat said, nodding to Harker. Their hand found his out of habit and pulled him forward, sensing the dead passage before they saw it. A hallway winked ahead of them, branching away from the Holbrook Estate, and Rat turned down it, the veil of aether breaking around them.

It hadn't taken them directly to the Evans place, but the way ahead was rarely a straight line. All that mattered was that Rat knew where they were going.

They cut their hand through the air like drawing back a curtain. "*Open*," they said to the hall ahead of them, and another passage shimmered on the air. The dusty hardwood floors gave way to carpet, and before Rat fully understood how, they knew they'd crossed the threshold back into the Evans house.

The shelves rose up around them, familiar like the lines on their own hand. Growing up, Rat had always thought the portion of the archives that was kept in the house was huge but after being away for so long, it felt smaller than they remembered.

Through the binding spell, Rat caught a whisper of anxiety and something almost like loss, but when they turned back to Harker, he was already carefully composed, his gaze coolly sweeping over the books.

"Come on," Rat said, pulling him into the maze of stacks.

They slowed as one of the aisles opened into a reading nook toward the back of the room, well-lit but far from the windows where the light couldn't fade the books. A couple of volumes had been left out, piled on the coffee table.

"What are those?" Harker asked, keeping his voice low.

Rat took one of the sketches from the pile of papers. "They're my dad's. This was one of the sketches in his desk before Elise cleaned everything out." Rat dropped down next to the table, but they already knew that the books would be from his office, too. There was more, though—sketches and diagrams that Rat hadn't seen before, even though they were sure they'd been through everything in their father's desk.

"What do you think she was doing with these?" Harker asked.

"I don't know," Rat said, half to themself. Whatever it was, it looked like Elise had been working on it for some time. Rat stopped as they caught sight of a scotch glass, half an inch of amber liquid still in the bottom.

The floor creaked behind them, and they whipped around. Elise had appeared in the mouth of the aisle, a pile of spellbooks in one arm.

Harker flinched back, and his hand tightened a little on Rat's sleeve.

"Miranda," Elise started, but Rat was already on their feet. They stepped forward, putting themself between her and Harker.

"This wasn't his idea. Harker is here because I asked him to come with me. I—"

"I've been worried about you." Elise dropped the pile of books on a side table and rushed toward them. "Do you have any idea how hard I've been trying to reach you? What are you doing here?"

She reached for Rat, but they pulled back. "I'm just here to get something. I wouldn't be here if it wasn't important."

"No." Quickly, Elise caught Rat's shoulder before they could turn away from her. "I haven't heard from you in weeks. You aren't even trained to cast from these books. Do you have any idea how dangerous—"

"It's not something of yours. It's dad's," Rat said. Their voice came out louder than they meant it to, but they leveled their gaze at her. "I'm not asking you to help me. I have right of free passage here as an Evans, and Harker is my guest. Just let us go, and I'll leave as soon as I'm done."

Her expression softened. "Miranda—"

"No one calls me that," Rat said before they could stop themself.

Elise stared at them.

Something in them threatened to crumble. Their lip trembled, and Rat turned back toward the stairs, pulling Harker with them. "Come on. Let's just get upstairs and finish this."

"Mir—Rat," Elise called, stopping them. "Wait. I'm not going to stop you. I just . . . we should talk. Please. It's about the tower, isn't it?"

Rat looked back at Harker, but his face had gone carefully neutral. It might have been convincing if Rat hadn't been able to feel the heat pricking the air around him.

He stepped toward them protectively. "Whatever you want to do," he said under his breath, and they realized that in the last thirty seconds, whatever fear he'd had about being caught had sublimated into fury on their behalf.

Rat turned back to Elise. "Harker stays with me. He's probably the only reason I'm still alive after last year, and I'm not going to let you pretend he doesn't belong here."

For a moment, Elise looked like she might argue, then stopped herself.

Something in her expression fell. Suddenly, she looked tired. "I don't know how to do this, Rat. I tried so hard to protect you, and maybe I did it all wrong." She dropped into one of the reading chairs and motioned for Rat to sit.

Hesitantly, they did. Harker settled against the arm of the chair beside them, but Rat didn't miss the way he kept his hands away from the leather, like he was trying to keep himself from scorching the furniture.

"Your father's family has a long history with Isola," Elise said after a moment, her gaze fixed on Rat. "Most of the major bloodlines' power comes from their archives, but the Holbrook family used their talents to strike deals with creatures like the Rooks. It's potent magic, but there's a reason why most of the surviving families don't practice it anymore. Those kinds of deals need to be made very carefully, or else . . . creatures like Isola are clever. It's easy to become entangled without realizing it."

She paused, mulling over her words carefully. "They started to owe her things," she finally said. "Favors. Relics. Their heirs to train as her apprentices, so she could get her claws in deeper. The entire house was beholden to her."

"What happened?"

"They were her pawns for a long time. When they finally tried to go back on their agreement with her, she brought down almost the entire line, along with most of their allies," Elise said. "Half of the East Coast still remembers them as the monsters she turned them into, and the rest remember seeing them almost bring the entire Northeast down with them when their house collapsed. I didn't want that for you. Any of it."

Even though Rat knew Elise was skating over the details, they could still see the edges of it, maybe because they knew Isola. She preyed on desperation and ambition, and for a secondary bloodline that was feared by the other houses and never had quite enough power of its own, neither one would be in short supply.

Isola could have worked her way in over centuries until all of the Holbrook's other allies had been cut off and the whole bloodline was hers to maneuver. Maybe as part of some cosmic game she was playing with the other Rooks. Maybe just for her own amusement. And then, when they'd finally stood against her, she'd wiped the board clean, to remind them that she could.

"I just wanted you to be safe," Elise said.

"But that wasn't your choice."

"No, I—" she started, and something in her sank as it seemed to hit her what they'd been left open to. "I just didn't want you to get hurt. I wish I could do it differently, but I can't." She was quiet for a long moment, studying them. "You're going to go ahead with this whether I let you or not. Aren't you?"

Slowly, they nodded.

For a moment, they thought that she might try to stop them anyway, but then she shook her head. "I forget how much like him you are sometimes."

"We still need to talk when all of this is over," Rat told her.

"I know," she said. "Just, please. Try to be careful."

Rat knew they couldn't promise her that, but they nodded anyway. "I'll do what I can," they said, which wasn't a lie. Then they stood and held their hand out to Harker. He took it, locking his fingers into theirs, and Rat pulled him toward the archives, the same way they'd gone more times than they could count.

Rat followed the familiar path through the shelves until they came to the staircase that didn't exist, rising up out of the shelves where it always was, like another part of the house. Rat came to a stop at the foot of the stairs.

A veil of aether drifted over the opening, throwing a soft glow over the bottom steps before the staircase rose up into darkness, twisting out of sight.

A want that Rat couldn't name tugged at them, maybe because they hadn't planned to go back again.

The veil of dust broke around them as they stepped over the threshold, and a chill crept in as they made their way up, their fingers skipping over the familiar lines of the stonework as they climbed. Rat didn't stop until the stairs opened at the top, and then they were back in the wide sweep of the observatory, the glass ceiling curving overhead. Their books were still out from the last time they'd been up there, and the stars overhead were strange and bright.

Rat's chest tightened. If they were honest, a part of them had been avoiding this place. They turned as they heard Harker's breath catch.

He'd stopped at the top of the stairs, wisps of spellfire bobbing after him. His gaze swept the expanse of the observatory, and something in him seemed to waver. Rat didn't know if it had been running into Elise or just being back here, but for a moment, he was just as lost and brittle as he'd been when they dragged him back from the tower.

"I'm sorry," they said. "If you don't want to go any farther—"

"No," he said quickly. He dropped his gaze, but his hand tightened around theirs. Then, a little more quietly, "I missed this place. I was scared I'd forgotten what it really looked like."

"And?" Rat asked.

"It's incredible."

All over again, Rat remembered why they'd loved bringing him here. Then their gaze settled on the sigil at the center of the floor.

"Ready?" Harker said.

Rat drew the puzzle box out of their pocket and started toward the sigil, their footsteps echoing as they crossed the room. They were the son of Alexander Holbrook, and they were a key that opened any door. They had wandered across other worlds and sworn pacts to the left-behind confidants of long-vanished gods, and whatever had been left here, it had been waiting for them.

They raised the puzzle box to their lips. "*Open*," they said.

Rat twisted it, the pieces gliding past each other the way they'd been meant to, and the ground shifted beneath their feet.

Electricity shivered through the air, and then, like something deep beneath the surface of the world had shifted into alignment, the last piece of the puzzle box settled into place, and the seal on the floor gave way to a set of stone stairs.

Rat peered down. It should have been dark, but spell lights lit the way, throwing a dim but steady glow over the steps.

Rat closed their hand on the puzzle box, but even though they could still feel the low whisper of the wayfinding spell, they knew it didn't go any farther than this, the same way they could feel when they'd come to the end of a passageway. This is where the box had been leading them.

Rat looked back at Harker, and he drew his fingers through the air, calling up a flicker of spellfire to help light the way.

Steeling themself, they made their way down.

The stairs curved downward, ending in a small circular room. The air was cold but stagnant, heavy with the smell of aged paper and leather and dust. Aether coated everything, like a powerful spell had been cast and then allowed to settle.

All around them, the wall sconces blinked on, throwing a warm glow over the room. Bookshelves lined the walls, broken only for the high narrow windows that peered out onto the same strange stars as the observatory, except now Rat could see down to a ragged sweep of coast and the dark, lapping waters of an unfamiliar sea.

Rat touched their fingers to the glass. Twin moons hung low over the horizon, but Rat couldn't tell if they were setting or rising. Just that, wherever this was, even though Rat could still sense the Evans place, they'd found themself very far from home.

They turned back toward the bookcases. A desk stood on the other side of the room, everything neatly sorted and put away, like their father had known he wouldn't be back.

There was a story to how he must have ended up finding this place, whether he'd known it was here or he'd discovered it, long-forgotten somewhere beyond the walls of the Evans house. But whatever the story was, Rat also wasn't about to find out.

Rat crossed to the desk and trailed their fingers over the surface. They reached for the top drawer on the left-hand side without thinking about why, before they remembered that was where their father had always kept the most important things in his office.

The drawer slid open smoothly to reveal a neat pile of papers. A spare packet of casting chalk and a small pile of carefully carved draubs had been fitted into the remaining space, and then Rat caught sight of a ring of keys, half-hidden in their father's things.

The same familiar pull of the wayfinding spell that Rat had felt on the keys at the Council Chambers tugged at them, like a spark of recognition.

"Harker—" they started, then turned to see that he was already crossing the room to them. They held up the three keys. "Jinx has the ones we found in the Council Chambers."

"Which leaves one," he said.

Rat met his gaze.

They were getting close, and dangerously so. Isola might have been biding her time again, but if Rat's exit from the Holbrook Estate hadn't caught her attention, this would.

"My dad's notes," Rat said, turning back to the desk. Rat reached for the papers and spread the pages out. But they didn't have to look long before Harker leaned in and slid one out from the pile. "Look at this."

Rat glanced down at it. A list of seven surnames ran down the page, but even before Rat registered which families, they knew what they were looking at.

It was a list of the keys, with the seven original allies Ingrid had entrusted them to.

Some were stricken or crossed out, some marked found. Except, beyond that seven, there were more spaces underneath. A few with names Rat hadn't heard before. A few left blank.

Rat frowned, skimming over the list, but they couldn't make it add up. They'd found three keys at the Council Chambers, and there were three more here. One was left to be found.

But two had the word *destroyed* by them. Four more were marked only with *tower*.

Even if Isola had somehow gotten ahold of every remaining key and all of the ones their father had thought were destroyed, there were still too many.

The wrongness of it set Rat's teeth on edge, even though they couldn't fully explain why. They turned to Harker, but he'd gone still.

"You see it, too," Rat said. "It's wrong. There are only seven keys."

"No," he said like he was putting it together. "There aren't."

They furrowed their brow.

"Ingrid had seven. The first names are her allies," Harker said.

"But the other names—" Rat started, and then stopped as they caught the look of quiet desperation on his face, like he didn't want them to finish.

Then, all at once, they realized what they were seeing. They weren't looking at the names of prominent bloodlines anymore. Most of the names in front of them were minor houses.

They were looking at a condensed list of the missing students.

"How do you make a key?" Harker asked quietly, and with a horrible inevitability, the final pieces fell into place.

The years of disappearances from Bellamy Arts, and how Isola had a habit of keeping the students she took alive.

The way that Harker had come back from the tower as a wayfinder.

The keys, which took an inheritance spell to forge.

Rat felt themself go cold all over. Isola had never just been searching for the keys Ingrid had left behind. She was too desperate to get her heart back, and too cunning to play only one game at a time. Not when she might have been wasting her time chasing down keys that had been lost or destroyed, and not when she'd need to go through more powerful arcanists to find the ones that were left.

She might have been clever and patient, but she was also dying, and she didn't like to pick fights she couldn't win.

So, she hadn't. She'd made deals with students from lesser bloodlines instead. She would send them to do her bidding, and then, when they'd exhausted their use, she'd used their magic to sustain herself. But that had never been all of it. Isola hadn't just been using the students to search for the keys. She'd been creating her own.

And for that, she'd needed seven newly-made wayfinders.

Suddenly, Rat didn't think Isola had actually intended for any of the students she chose to find the Ingrid Collection at all. She'd known they wouldn't. Probably, she'd offered most of them the same bargain she'd given Harker, but it had always been a lure so she could get her claws in, to make sure that by the time she took them back to the tower, they were bound to her tightly enough that they couldn't leave.

Then she'd kept them there for as long as she could, to see if their powers would take. Most of them weren't natural wayfinders. They'd been lost kids who she'd kept shut up in the dark until they were so afraid and desperate to get home, they would have torn the world at its seams to go back.

Once she had what she wanted, Isola broke them down for parts. Their death to forge her keys, if they became wayfinders. Their magic to sustain her, if they didn't.

Their bones added to her collection, and whatever vital, human part of them was left to haunt her halls as wraiths.

Rat had always been the exception for Isola. They'd been hers from the beginning, and she intended to keep them as a prize when this ended, maybe just for the cruel thrill of knowing that she'd finally claimed the last heir to the Holbrook line.

If she'd been allowed to keep Harker, she would have taken everything she could from him and left nothing behind.

Before Rat could think about what they were doing, they reached for the notes. "There's still one left out there. I'm not leaving it for Isola to find." Their voice came out raw and frantic, but they didn't care. They needed to end this. They went back to spreading out the papers, expecting Harker to try to stop them, but he reached over and took the other half to start laying those out, too.

Rat grabbed a couple of the draubs from the drawer and pushed them at him.

"Rat—"

"My dad left these with the keys," Rat said, pressing the draubs into his hand. "They have to do something." Rat turned back to the maps, fully aware of how desperate they sounded, but they refused to let Isola win.

They stopped as they came to a sketch of Bellamy Arts that they hadn't seen before. Carefully, Rat slid that page away from the others. It was an aerial view of the school, drawn out in their father's hand, except something about it felt *off* in a way that Rat couldn't explain.

"Is that the school?" Harker asked, peering over their shoulder. "Which part of campus is that?" He pointed to an *X* marked by a building near the edge of campus.

"I don't know," Rat said. "It doesn't matter. It's wrong."

They knew the campus. They'd drawn this same map, and they'd marked the placement of all of the buildings.

It *looked* like Bellamy Arts, but it wasn't. They could pick out the familiar shape of the clock tower at the center, and they knew the line of the woods hemming in the campus. But when Rat actually looked at the buildings more closely, they didn't know what anything was.

"Rat?"

"That building." They tapped the page where the *X* was. "There's nothing there. That's past the tree line."

Not just past the tree line, they realized as they said it. *It was in the lake.*

It was like if someone who had vaguely heard about Bellamy Arts once had tried to make a map of it in their head. It might have been a version of the school, but it wasn't one Rat had seen before.

Except they had.

Rat stopped as they recognized the shape of the old library. They'd found it in school histories. They'd mapped it, at least based on the pictures they'd been able to find.

"The old campus," they breathed. They looked back. "Harker, that's the Drake. The original one, before it sank. The last key—"

He met their gaze, his expression sharp like he'd figured out the same thing, and all at once Rat realized how close he was, enough that they could smell the faint scent of magic still clinging to him from the passages.

Then Isola's magic flared, flooding out Rat's powers in a cold tide, and they realized that whatever lead they'd had on Isola had abruptly run out.

CHAPTER FORTY

ISOLA'S POWER ROLLED OVER THEM ALL AT ONCE, DROWN-ing out everything else, and for a moment there was nothing but the sharp bite of mugwort and autumn air.

"Rat?" Harker said, his voice threaded with panic.

Blood pounded in their ears. On the other end of the binding spell, far away from them, Isola was casting something. Something powerful that was taking all of her magic. Distantly, Rat realized they'd pitched forward, so the desk was the only thing keeping them up.

"Evans!" Harker took their shoulder, trying to steady them, but before Rat could speak, another wave of power rolled over them in a terrible rush.

Black marble.

Night sky.

The taste of blood.

Images flashed in their mind, faster than Rat could make sense of them. "It's Isola," they managed as Harker wrapped his arm around them, bracing them, gasping for breath. "She's—I think—"

Rat broke off again as they felt the icy tug of Isola's awareness on the other side of the spell, like she'd noticed them watching her. Then another burst of power rolled down the bond, this one hard and deliberate. If the others had been an aftershock of another spell, this was a shove, directed at Rat. The cold crashed in around them, and Rat felt their knees buckle, but their consciousness was already being swept out from them by the time their body hit the ground.

Then the study was gone, and they were kneeling in the woods. It was too dark for Rat to tell if they were seeing Bellamy Arts or the forest around the Holbrook Estate, or if this was somewhere closer to the tower.

Their throat was thick, and the inside of their mouth tasted like metal as they forced themself to their feet, still unsteady. Isola had brought them here, the same way she'd pulled them out of the fight with the seneschal. Rat had seen something Isola hadn't meant them to, and this was her way of trying to block them out.

Twigs snapped behind them, and Rat whipped around, raising their hand to cast, but there was nothing there.

"Fine! You wanted me and I'm here!" they shouted into the trees. "Show yourself!"

Their only answer was the cruel twinge of amusement from somewhere far away on the other side of the binding spell.

Dread coiled around Rat's ribs as they understood. Isola hadn't come to meet them. She was just *keeping them* here so they couldn't stop her.

Something rustled in the underbrush, closer this time, and Rat spun toward it, reaching for their power.

You're not here, they told themself. *It's in your mind.* But they weren't sure it mattered. They didn't know what kind of damage Isola could do to them here.

The images flashed through Rat's mind again in a jumble of starlight and marble and blood. They were missing something.

They needed to get out of here. They needed to think.

They felt a pull as Harker tried to call them back, but before Rat could think about what they were doing, they pushed him away and reached for their bond with Isola instead, throwing whatever they had of their own power against it.

Every other time Rat had gotten into her mind, it had been an accident. This time, it wasn't.

Isola's magic rolled over them in another vicious tide, and just for a moment, they slipped past her defenses. A flood of fear and rage and grasping need poured in, threaded with the chill of death that was quickly becoming all too familiar.

Death. Blood. Marble. Starlight. Blood. Death.

An image of a wide hallway flickered behind their eyes, the floor inlaid with a map of the night sky, and all at once, Rat knew what they were seeing.

Then Isola broke off the connection, and Rat crashed back into their body as they lost their hold on her. They were lying on the floor of their father's hidden study, their head in Harker's lap like they'd probably dragged him to the floor with them.

Still breathing hard, Rat grabbed the collar of his coat. "We need to go," they said in a rush. "Now."

"What happened? Rat—"

"I don't know. Isola's at the Council Chambers," they said. "She didn't want me to know."

Rat had recognized Night's wing of the building. They'd been there. Except, that shouldn't be possible, because Isola couldn't have gotten into the building alone.

Not unless someone had invited her.

A fresh wave of dread settled over them.

"I don't know what she's planning, I just—We have to get there. Now." They shoved themself to their feet, but their knees threatened to give out again.

Harker grabbed their hand, hauling them up. "Do it. Open a passage."

Rat didn't think. The casting was panic and adrenaline. They felt a last tug of resistance from Isola, and then their magic surged back to them, and the way opened.

They spilled through, the warm glow of the light spells giving way as they left the study behind. The stars had changed overhead to the constellations Isola had once taught Rat to call by name, but the sky was darker here.

They were back in the night garden. A path stretched ahead of them, awash in moonlight, and pale, night-blooming flowers grew up along the path, almost luminescent in the dark.

Harker drew a wisp of spellfire, throwing a cold glow over the grounds as Rat pulled him toward the entrance that would lead them back to the Council Chambers.

Their hand tightened on his as they stepped through into a deserted hallway. Rat didn't remember the way back through the building, but they knew from the dark marble floors that they'd come out somewhere in Night's wing of the building.

They cut their hand through the air, and a passage glinted ahead of them. The quiet pressed in around them as Rat pulled Harker through, and they spilled out into the corridor that led to Night's office. It should have been well into her work hours, but the building was as empty as Rat had ever seen it, and the air was thick with magic and the unmistakable scent of mugwort.

They took the next bend in the hallway and skidded to a stop. The doors of Night's office had been left ajar, and something in the silence set Rat's teeth on edge.

The horrible rush of Isola's power echoed in their core. They knew in some small, animal part of themself that whatever was behind the door, they didn't want to see it, but they shoved the feeling down.

Rat pushed, and the door swung in soundlessly.

At the center of the room, Night lay sprawled on the ground, her white hair spilling out in a halo. Blood seeped out around her, slick and mirrorlike on the polished floor, and her fair skin had turned a pale shade of gray, her gaze unfocused.

Rat's heart beat hard and fast in their throat. One of Night's hands was still outstretched, her fingers stacked with rings like the last time they'd seen her, and Rat had the desperate impulse to kneel down and search for a pulse, even though they knew they wouldn't find one. They knew death.

Somewhere outside, voices echoed up the hallway. Close.

"Fuck," Rat breathed. Quickly, they ducked back, pulling Harker toward the hidden passageway. They pushed the wall panel shut as Evening appeared in the doorway, Allister close on his heels.

"You didn't tell me you were going to make a pact with that thing," Allister said, his voice harsh. "This wasn't our deal."

"You work for me, Church. Our deal is whatever I decide on."

"You said—"

"I don't think you understand how fast I could ruin you." Evening's voice dropped to a dangerous whisper. "Imagine if the news that the head of the Church family was too sick to run her house got out. With the nature of the secrets she traffics in, I imagine there might even be a case to seize the archives for safekeeping."

There was a long silence on the other side of the door. Rat leaned in, peering through the crack in the wall panel to see Allister's jaw tremble.

"Tell the Lesser Hours I've said to close down Night's wing of the Council Chambers," Evening said coolly. "I'll be taking point on the investigation and assuming her duties in the meantime. It looks like the work of one of the Rooks. Possibly even that creature Rat Evans allowed inside our wards."

Allister looked up at him with a mix of fear and outright hatred.

Rat drew in a breath, and for the barest fraction of a moment, they could swear that Allister's eyes tracked back to the hidden doorway. Then he dipped his head. "Of course," he said, matching the ice in Evening's voice before he swept out of the office.

As soon as the door closed, Evening turned back to the desk and gave it a searching glance.

Night's case files, Rat realized. Evening was looking for the evidence she has against him, but all they could do now was hope that he didn't find it. *Come on*, Rat mouthed to Harker.

And then, maybe because Harker already knew too well that Evening was the most dangerous when there was no one else around to see it, he let Rat lead the way out.

CHAPTER FORTY-ONE

RAT CAUGHT THEMSELF AGAINST A RAIL, BREATHING hard. The familiar, jagged skyline of Bellamy Arts sprawled out below them, and they realized that somehow, they'd ended up back on the widow's walk. Weakly, they sank back to the ground, letting everything wash over them.

Harker wrapped his arm around them without a word, and they realized they were shaking. They buried their face in his shoulder and let out a muffled sob. He pulled them in, warm against the chill, and something in them broke.

"Fuck." Their voice came out choked and small. "I'll kill her. Both of them. I swear, I—" They broke off, their throat too thick to speak.

Both of them.

Isola had been in the building. Evening had invited her past the wards. Either he was desperate or arrogant enough to think that he could make a deal with her and come out ahead, and now in one move, he'd forged another key for Isola and removed the only person on the Council who'd been able to keep him in check.

Rat's phone buzzed. They drew in a shaky breath, still trying to collect themself.

"Is it Jinx?" Harker asked.

They looked down at the screen and nodded. "She's probably wondering where we are. I should—" Rat swallowed hard. Their voice threatened to break again.

Harker took the phone from their hand and slid his thumb across the screen. "Evans is with me."

Rat heard Jinx's voice on the other end, too low to pick out what she was saying. After a moment, Harker nodded slightly. "It's bad. Rat just brought us back to the school. I'll explain everything as soon as I can, but it might be a minute before we can get to you."

"Don't," Jinx said, just loud enough for Rat to hear.

"What's wrong?" Rat said, leaning over.

Harker turned the phone to speaker, and Jinx's voice came through tinny and far away, like the reception was weak.

"You can't come back here. Isola's creatures are right outside the wards."

Rat went cold. "What?"

"We've been under siege all day. It started almost as soon as you left."

"Then we'll get you out. I can open a passage, or—"

"I know. That's the problem," Jinx said, her voice firm. "She was probably sending them through the whole time and just gathering them in the woods. As long as you're here, she can use your magic. If you come back, and she cuts off your powers—"

"I won't be able to leave," Rat finished, their voice a breath.

Rat remembered the sharp tug of their bond with Isola as she'd wrested control of their magic from them. She hadn't wasted any energy getting her creatures through the wards last night because she hadn't needed to.

Either Rat would be caught outside the protections of the Holbrook Estate without any backup, or they'd try to go back for their friends and end up trapped behind the ground wards, leaving the campus wide open for Isola and Evening. Whatever they did, Isola won.

Something in Rat's chest sank a little further as they realized how few options they had. "Isola is splitting us up."

"We're not going to be able to get to you. The car is outside the wards," Jinx said, her voice grim like she'd already been turning over the options. "We might be able to rig up some kind of travel spell to get back without it, but we don't have any of the sigils we'd need and they aren't the kind of magic you can mess around with."

Rat looked at Harker, but they could see him drawing the same conclusions that they had. Even if they'd been wayfinding their whole life, Harker had always been the better technical caster, and he understood the rules in a way that Rat never spent a lot of time thinking about. If there was another spell, or a trick, or some way to twist the universe's arm into making it happen, he would know what it was.

And they could see from the look on his face that whatever it was, Isola would move in to stop him as soon as he tried.

"Don't worry about us. Just do whatever you have to," Jinx said after a moment. "We'll figure out a way down."

"Jinx—"

"Be alive when I get there. Both of you."

Then she ended the call. For a long moment, Rat stared at the phone, until Harker picked it up and handed it back to them.

"Come on. We should get inside," he said, but Rat couldn't miss the subtle tension in his shoulders. "We can figure things out from there."

He held his hand out to them, and all over again, they realized just how shaken he was. The first thing Harker always did when things were falling apart was to look for a task. He was going to crumble when all this was done, but right now, he would do whatever he could to keep everything running.

"Wait," Rat said. They knew he was right, but they couldn't go in yet. They didn't know what came next, and it would make all of this real. "I just—Please. I need to think."

Evening already knew where their friends were, and if the tracking spell had picked them up, it wouldn't take long for him to figure out that Rat had made it back to the school.

He didn't need to get to the last key. He had options. Either Rat would turn over the keys that were in their possession, or Evening would forge the final ones himself.

Rat looked out at the hills in the distance. They refused to lose like this. "Can you figure something out?" they asked Harker.

"Rat—"

"You're the one who's good at solving things. If I can buy you time with Isola's attention off the campus, could you do something with that?"

He hesitated, and they could see him thinking. "There's a chance."

"Good," Rat said, pushing themselves to their feet. "I swear, I'll come back. Just don't tell me what you're doing. As long as Isola's using me, the less I know, the better."

For a moment, Rat thought Harker would argue with them. Then he raised the back of their hand to his mouth, and his lips brushed their knuckles. "I'll see that it's done."

His voice was as cold and as clear as moonlight, but in the hush of the campus, Rat could feel the vicious undercurrent of power coiled around him in the night air.

He drew back. "As far as this road goes. Remember?"

"To the end of this," Rat said back. Their hand tightened on his coat. They pulled him in, close enough that they could smell the familiar tinge of smoke on his skin. So softly that it might not have happened at all, they kissed him on the mouth.

Then they let go again and started toward the doors that led back to the stairs, the rest of the night still ahead of them.

CHAPTER FORTY-TWO

RAT MADE THEIR WAY BACK TO THEIR ROOM ALONE.

As soon as they got inside, the first thing they noticed was a file of papers that had been left on the windowsill in the same place Night's summons had been at the start of the semester.

Rat locked the door and rushed over.

In a messy scrawl, Rat caught the words *Evening* and *The Tower*, but they didn't need to read the rest to know what they were looking at.

Night had sent them her evidence on Evening.

Rat traced their thumb over the edge of the papers. Then, carefully, they slid the file into their desk drawer. They needed to worry about Isola first. If they were still alive at the end of the night, they promised themself they would figure something out. For now, they still had another stop they needed to make.

They crossed the room again and opened the window, letting in the cool night air. Rat leaned out into the dark and whistled the same low, airy notes Isola had taught them once in another lifetime.

A moment passed, the night still around them. Then a bird swept down from the branches of a nearby tree and lit on their windowsill.

"Tell Isola I'm on my way," Rat told it. "And I'm not going to wait for her if she isn't there."

The bird tilted its head slightly, and then, like an acknowledgment, it let out a rusty caw as it leapt back up, its wings catching the cold air.

Rat watched the sky for a long moment. Then they latched the window shut and made for the stairs.

Their cloak was still at the Holbrook Estate and Evening's tracking spell would pick up their movements, but they wanted him to see. Any attention on them was attention off Harker.

They made their way back to the edge of the East Woods like they'd done a dozen times before, taking the long way through the trees. Most of the snow had already melted away in the previous night's rain, and now that they were away from the mountains, the ground had thawed, the earth soft beneath their shoes as they made their way between the trees.

"*Open.*" Rat traced their hand through the air like they were parting a curtain, and they felt the world give way.

They stepped through the passage, into the bones of Ashwood.

They hadn't been here since the night before the Revel, when everything had still been covered in snow. Now, the first stubborn weeds had begun to sprout up from the rubble, and puddles of stagnant water pooled on the ground.

Rat looked up at the sky. A cold wind tugged at their coat, and their face was still numb from the chill of the woods.

"It's always here, isn't it?" Isola said, close behind them. Rat whipped toward her as she formed out of the shadows, like she'd been waiting for them. "I wondered when you'd finally decide to meet."

Even though Rat could see the exhaustion on her, power radiated off her in a dark tide.

Night's power, Rat realized a moment late.

Isola hadn't just used her for a key. She'd taken what was left of Night's magic for herself, the way she had the students she'd brought back to the tower with her to sustain herself.

Except most of those had been fledgling arcanists who were still coming into their full gifts. Night had been a Greater Hour, and she'd had a lifetime to build up the kinds of power that even most of the major bloodlines couldn't come close to.

Isola stepped forward, and Rat fought the urge to flinch back.

"I'm here," Rat said. "You've got my friends surrounded, and I know you're pulling Evening's strings. So what do you want?"

"I think you know that already," she said. "I want only what's already mine. Nothing more."

"I know about the keys," Rat said quickly.

Isola's eyes glinted with interest, but they couldn't help noticing that she wasn't surprised. She'd known already, maybe from the moment they'd figured it out. "Do you?"

"I thought you were just taking the other students because you were dying and you needed their magic, but that wasn't it. Was it? You needed wayfinders," they said. "You were trying to wake up their abilities so you could use them. Ingrid hid the original keys from you, so you started making your own."

"Clever as always," she said, and a horrible kind of amusement pulled at her lips. "I knew I'd chosen well. You know, if you'd just turned over the keys after the Revel, we could have been finished already."

"You're working with Evening," Rat said, holding their voice steady.

"A matter of convenience." She flexed her hand. "He's made a capable ally, but then, it wouldn't be the first time someone in his office has seen an opportunity."

Something in the way she said *ally* raised the hair on Rat's neck, maybe because they knew that anyone else would have been a servant or a vassal to her. Evening wasn't prey for her. He'd dealt with creatures like her for long enough to know how this worked, and he wouldn't have promised her anything. He'd put himself in a position to close his hand around the rest of the Council, and as long as Isola continued to bolster his power, he could make sure she got her due.

And, when she finally did find a way to get her claws into him deep enough, she would have someone in power who was positioned to do whatever she wanted.

Isola's mouth curved, like she'd read the understanding in Rat's face.

"It's been some time since I've gotten ahold of a Greater Hour. I think the last time had been one of yours, actually," she said. "In fact, Evening was the one who summoned me back. He gets use of my keys so he can get the doors to the Ingrid Collection open. I get back what's mine. And if he happens to need assistance removing an enemy or two along the way . . ."

Rat thought about Night again, splayed out on the floor of the Council Chambers, blood pooling around her.

Isola reached out, tilting Rat's face up to hers. "But that's not why you came here, is it?"

A cold breath ran through the bond Rat shared with Isola, chilling them. It was like the brush of her fingers, if she'd reached out and touched the core of their thoughts. Suddenly, her presence felt overwhelming.

Rat jerked back, but something in her gaze had turned hard, and she tightened her grip. She let out a small sound that might have been a laugh if it had been sharpened against a whetstone and packed in ice. "You really thought you could lure me out again, and I wouldn't catch you at it?"

"Let go of me."

Isola dug in her fingers, and Rat bit back a wince. "You know, I've changed my mind," she said, drawing in. "I think I would enjoy having you as a prisoner."

Rat's jaw tightened.

"Everyone saw you call on me at the Revel," she said. "They already see the worst in you. Another Holbrook, falling to their own hideous impulses. I could make you into the monster they think you are." She drew the words out like she was relishing the possibilities. "Maybe I'll destroy everything that ties you here. I could come for everyone you've ever cared about, and everywhere you've ever called home, until you have nothing left to return to."

Rat forced themself to hold her gaze, fighting the shaking in their knees.

Isola stepped in a little closer. "I think I'll leave that boy you stole back for last. Did you know, he used to talk to the wraiths about you? I would hear him telling them stories about how brave and clever he thinks you are. He even used to pretend you were still there with him when he thought he was alone." Her mouth curved into something cruel. "Maybe I'll bring him back with me again, just to let him wither away in the dark."

"Stop it."

"I could keep you at the tower until you can't remember a time when you didn't belong to me. By the time I've finished, forgetting will be a gift. Maybe, when there's nothing left of who you were, I'll even keep you as an apprentice." Isola tilted her head, considering it. "Evening is already on his way to leaving the entire Northeast in ashes. I could bring you with me so we can stake a claim on the ruins."

Rat shoved away from her, reaching for their magic. "*Light!*"

Spellfire flared at their fingertips the color of sun, and Isola dodged back, startled. The moment her grip loosened, Rat pulled free from her and broke into a sprint.

She lunged after them, and Rat felt the passage open ahead of them a moment before they stumbled through it.

They came out on the other side of Ashwood's ruined great room. Isola's eyes locked on theirs, and Rat drew their hand through the air as she shot toward them. They reached for their bond with Harker, and their next spell split the air.

They just had to hope they'd bought him enough time.

Rat rushed for the passage as it opened ahead of them. A blast of raw power howled past them, splintering the floor where they'd been standing, and then the way closed behind them.

They came down in a heap on the damp earth, breathing hard. The ruins were gone, replaced by the shelter of the woods. Rat shoved themself to their knees, and a hand caught them by the shoulder.

"That's four," Harker said, hauling them to their feet.

Rat glanced back as Harker pulled them forward, his fingers laced into theirs. The campus rose up above the tops of the trees in the distance, the pathway back striped with moonlight.

"You didn't rescue me. I had a plan," Rat said, breathless, then stopped.

"Evans. Come on!" Jinx called, where she, Will, and Agatha stood a little ways up the path. On campus. *Here.*"

Hope flared in Rat's chest, but before they could ask, Harker was already pulling them forward again.

"How—".

"Travel spell. I opened it from the school," he said, his hand tightening on theirs. "Isola's creatures aren't here yet, but I don't know how long we have before she realizes we're here."

As he spoke, movement flickered in the trees, and Rat whipped toward it in time to catch sight of Allister hurrying up the path. Aether from a travel spell dusted his cloak, and his hand was raised like he was in the middle of a working, probably to find them.

"Shit," Rat muttered, ducking their head.

Harker looked back at them.

"It's Church. Keep going."

Of course he'd found them. They'd known Allister was on his way, but somehow, Rat thought they'd have more time.

They veered into the trees as Harker pulled them off the path. The woods parted, and all at once, Rat knew where they were. The map from their father's study flashed through their mind, with the *X* positioned where the lake should have been.

A gust of wind blew past as they made their way past the edge of the trees, whispering through the brittle stalks of reed grass that grew up along the muddy banks. This close to the water, the ground was soft beneath their boots, and the scent of earth and water hung on the cold night air.

Without stopping, Jinx knelt down and peeled her gloves off, the wind tugging at her curls. Moonlight silvered her leather jacket. Deliberately, she traced a sigil in the muddy bank of the lake with her fingers, the muscles in her shoulders taut.

For a long moment, everything was still. Then, with a sound like a sloshing tide, the waters of the lake rose into the air while receding from the shore, like a wave in reverse. The lakebed stretched ahead, cutting away steeply as it sloped into the ground, the murky waters towering over it in a wall.

Rat had never particularly liked the lake. Even at its most placid, it was dark and unfathomable, and there was something about large bodies of water that always gave Rat the distinct feeling that if they couldn't find their own way out, the water would gladly swallow them. Seeing now exactly how far down the bottom of the lake really was didn't help.

Harker's fingers tightened around theirs, like he hated this exactly as much as they did.

"Quickly," Jinx said, one hand raised in a casting position, and Rat realized that even with the sigil, she was still adding power in to keep the working going. If her focus collapsed, the spell would, too.

Before Rat could let themself think about it, their magic snagged on something at the edge of their senses, and they turned, pulling Harker toward it. "This way," they said to the others.

Ahead of them, set into the very bottom of the lake, Rat caught sight of a hatch, half covered in the grit of the lakebed. But more than they saw it, they could feel it pulling at them, leading down into the sprawl of tunnels below.

"Is that it?" Jinx asked, obvious strain in her voice.

"Yeah," Rat said, rushing to close the distance. They dropped down, hoping they were right about this. If they weren't, they didn't think Jinx was going to be able to hold the working long enough for all of them to get back to shore.

Rat grabbed on to the hatch, the handle still slick with algae. Their hands slipped over the rusted metal, but however long it had been left forgotten under the water, it turned smoothly under their hand, and they felt the lock give way.

"Will," they started, but he was already there, grabbing the door from them. He shouldered Rat aside, struggling to get purchase.

"Guys!" Jinx shouted. She staggered half a step back, her arms shaking from holding the spell, and then, with a screech, the hatch pulled open, and Will flung the door wide, revealing a narrow set of stairs.

"Get inside. I'll close it behind us," he said quickly, motioning to Agatha.

Agatha slipped past them, rushing down the steps, and Rat grabbed Harker's wrist as they clambered after.

Behind them, Jinx let out a small cry, and Rat spun back in time to see her eyes widen as the spell overwhelmed her. Then, like a dam breaking, there was a thunderous crash of the water as the working slipped out of her grasp.

Faster than Rat could track, Will caught Jinx by the arm, hauling her back as a protective wall of earth curved up out of the lakebed. "Go!" he shouted.

With the lake water rushing toward them, Rat lunged after the others into the dark below.

CHAPTER FORTY-THREE

WILL PULLED JINX DOWN THE STAIRS, HALF CARRYING her as he traced a spell on the air. The hatch slammed shut above them just as the lake crashed down overhead in a deafening rush.

Rat caught themself against the wall, breathing hard. The stairs stopped at a small landing before continuing down into the dark, and the passageway was lit only by the glow of the spellfire Harker had conjured. The others stood close in the clammy chill of the stairwell, and as soon as Will released Jinx, she sank down on the steps, still unsteady. Agatha had already dropped beside her, the hem of her dress caked with mud.

"Jinx—" Rat started.

"Thank me by getting us back out when we're done here," she said. In a practiced movement, she traced a spell on the air, gathering the lake water from her curls. The droplets splashed down around her muddy boots. She reached for her backpack and dug out a flashlight for herself, then passed a spare one up to Rat while Will and Agatha got out their own.

"Thanks." Fighting to keep their hands from trembling, Rat flicked it on and shined it down the staircase. Moss grew over the steps, and grass had sprouted up between the cracks in the stonework as the stairs curved deeper into the earth, twisting out of sight.

"These too."

They glanced back as Jinx held up the ring of keys she'd taken for safekeeping. "I can't—"

"They're yours. Blakely told me you found three more. You should have them."

Rat took the keys from her as the weight of what she was really saying settled over them. They were coming to the end, and there was no more advantage to keeping the keys apart.

They added their own keys to the ring and tucked it back into their pocket.

"Let's just hope nothing follows us." Jinx held out her hand, allowing Will to pull her to her feet.

Steeling themself, Rat started down the stairs.

Somehow, after the tower, they'd thought the tunnels would be easier to face, but there was something about the weight of the campus pressing in above them that still crushed the air from their lungs. Again, Rat remembered the way Isola had choked off their powers earlier. If this place collapsed on them, they could very easily be beyond help. Even the Council's tracking spell might not be able to reach them on this part of the campus.

At the bottom, the staircase opened into a cavernous room ringed in shelves. Debris littered the way, rubble and fallen books scattered across the ground, and the floors were warped with age.

"Here. Take this."

Rat turned as Harker passed them a draub, and they realized it was one of the ones from their father's study.

"I had time to look at them," he said. "You were right about bringing them." Rat's pulse skipped as he pressed the coin into their hand. "It's a seeking spell for the keys, but I don't think it'll work unless we're close."

Rat studied the draub, the aged silver catching the glow of their flashlight. Distantly, the spell tugged at them, but there wasn't any direction to it and their chest sank a little.

"We'll have to split up," Rat said. "We'll cover more ground. I don't want to be down here any longer than we have to."

"We'll start on this side," Jinx said, nodding toward one darkened wing of the sunken library. "You two take the other."

Want clawed at them, but they already knew Jinx's plan wasn't going to work. They traded glances with Harker, but he gave them a small shake of his head like he'd seen it, too.

"We can't," they said. "The binding spell. Harker and I can still find each other if different groups. It's our best chance at tracking everyone down if there's trouble."

Rat waited, half hoping someone would argue with them. They felt a nervous twinge from the other end of the binding spell, but Harker was quiet, and finally, Jinx nodded. "Alright. You're with us, then, Evans."

"We'll find you back here," Harker said, and Agatha slid her arm through his. He caught Rat's gaze before he let himself be pulled away, and then Jinx motioned to Rat.

"Come on," she said as she started in the other direction. They nodded to Will, and he took off after them, following close behind.

Rat made their way toward one set of archways, deeper into the sunken library. As they went, Rat thought back to Isola's library in the tower, the shelves sagging under the weight of their water-damaged books, weeds and fungus sprouting up along the edges of the aisles. But where Isola's had been filled with gray dusk light and the cold always-autumn air, the old Drake was the pitch-dark of somewhere buried deep.

The air around them was damp and heavy with the scent of earth, and roots had crept down from the ceiling, crawling down the walls in pale filaments. The preservation spells had been powerful enough to keep most of the books intact, but old tomes littered the aisles, heaped unceremoniously where they'd been dumped from the shelves when the library had sunk.

Rat cast their power outward, searching for the key. Somewhere far away, they felt the faint, almost magnetic draw of a wayfinding spell, and just for a moment, the seeking spell flickered with a dull, silvery light before they lost it.

"Which way?" Jinx asked.

Wordlessly, Rat reached for their magic again. And again, they found the wayfinding spell—far off, but there.

"This way." Rat turned down the next aisle, toward another set of high archways.

Something moved in the corner of Rat's vision as they made their way into the next room of the underground library. They spun back, raising their flashlight. The corridor stretched behind them, deserted save for a stray current of aether. It curled on the air before fading back into the dark of the stacks.

Goosebumps pricked up Rat's arms.

"Evans?" Jinx asked.

"Nothing," they said. "Come on. The faster we get out of here, the better."

"I'll keep watch," Will said, raising his hand to a casting position. He dropped back, letting Rat pass ahead of him.

In spite of themselves, Rat wished they hadn't split up the group. They reached for their bond with Harker, and felt a soft tug of acknowledgment on the other end.

Just finish this, Rat reminded themself. They needed to get to the key before Evening did, or worse, before he decided to forge the last two that he needed on his own.

"Wait." Jinx caught their arm, and they came up short. The beam of her flashlight trailed over the ground, vanishing as the floor dropped steeply away ahead of them, where the broken remains of a staircase sloped into the dark below.

Rat peered down. At the very edge of the light, they could just make out the floor, strewn with debris. In their other hand, the seeking spell flickered a little brighter.

A fresh wave of panic rolled through them, but Rat shoved it down. "Stay here," they told Jinx.

"What are you doing?" she hissed, tugging them back.

"It's down there. Isola can't try anything with my powers if I'm alone. She won't risk losing me as long as I'm hers."

Apprehension spread across Jinx's face, but her gaze followed theirs, trailing back down to the shelves below.

Will gave Jinx a nod, still in a defensive position, ready for anything that might slip out of the dark. "Go fast, Evans," she said finally, turning her flashlight on the ruin of the broken staircase.

Carefully, Rat lowered themselves down where the rubble had formed a jagged slope toward the level below and began to climb. At the bottom, a heavy layer of dust had settled over everything, and the stone tiles jutted up in uneven chunks where the earth had splintered when the library sank. At one point, the floor must have been filled with rows of cabinets and wooden filing drawers, but some of them had toppled or fallen in.

Rat cast their magic out toward the key again, and the seeking spell glowed in their hand. They let it lead them through the maze, drawing them up one aisle and down the next until they came to a wall of cabinets. A track ran along the top, but if there'd ever been a ladder, it was long gone now.

Probably, Harker had an advanced retrieval spell that would call the key to him. But Rat was Rat, and they were still somehow absolutely garbage at about ninety-nine percent of magic.

They set their flashlight on an exposed shelf, seeking spell beside it, then wiped their hands off on their jeans and climbed up onto the set of cabinets. Their shoes found purchase on a ledge where one of the drawers had been smashed out, and Rat pulled themself up, reaching for their next hand hold. Then the next.

The key's wayfinding spell tugged at the edge of their senses as Rat drew even with a row of drawers and they pulled the first one out, revealing a handful of translucent stones that glowed faintly in the half-light.

Rat reached for the next drawer, but it was empty.

Then another.

A glint of silver flashed in the low light. Rat surged toward it, and their hands closed around something cold and metallic.

Then a spell slashed through the air behind them.

Quickly, Rat dodged out of the way, still clinging to the bookcase. Their shoe skated over the narrow ledge of the shelf, but they couldn't get purchase, and then they were falling.

They slammed hard against the floor, their hand still clamped around the key. Their flashlight clattered against the floor, and the seeking spell skittered off into the shadows.

Biting back a wince, Rat forced themself upright as Allister slipped between the shelves. A spectral light hovered over his shoulder, casting an eerie glow over the aisle as the last of the concealment spell he'd been using slipped away. "We have to stop meeting like this, Evans."

"We have to stop meeting," Rat muttered, picking themself up.

Allister traced a spell, and a wall of force rolled toward Rat, knocking them back to the ground. "I'm not interested in this being any messier than it needs to. Just turn over the keys and we can make it fast."

The passage opened ahead of Rat before they were aware that they'd called it. Winded, Rat scrambled to their feet and shot toward it, letting the passage swallow them, but Allister stayed close on their heels.

Aether curled after them as the passage let them out deeper in the maze of shelves, and Allister's next spell sliced through the air, missing them with the wicked hiss of a blade as Rat let the next passage catch them.

Allister raced through after them, closing the distance. Then, faster than Rat could dodge, he caught their arm, wrenching them back. They let out a sharp gasp as he pinned them against a row of cabinets, knocking the air from their lungs.

"I know you didn't actually agree to this," Rat said, still breathing hard.

"It's a job. I don't have to like it. Just turn over the keys, and we can be finished here."

"And what happens when Evening wins?" Rat asked. "He was keeping you away from the Council Chambers so you wouldn't catch on, but you did anyway, didn't you? You already know there are more than seven keys."

In the low light, Allister tensed, and Rat knew that he'd worked it out, too.

"I'm almost surprised I didn't put it together sooner. After the Revel was over, Evening got you out of the way. He needed your family's key, but after that, you were too much of a liability. He knew you'd figure it out, but he still needed you on hand." Rat locked eyes with him. "You're his backup plan if he can't get ahold of enough keys. He wouldn't have dared to touch Night if she wasn't a political obstacle, but you're an apprentice from a dying house without any allies. The Council won't even have to pretend to look for you."

"Not bad, Evans. Remind me to send you a medal." Allister drew in, and whatever flicker of emotion they'd seen was already gone. "Is that all?"

In the dark, there came the low hiss, and the shelves creaked.

Allister went still, and Rat looked up as a terror crested over the top of the cabinet above them.

Most of the terrors Rat had seen in the tunnels had slipped in between the school's attempts to clear them out. This one had been living here in the dark for a very long time, probably feeding on anything hapless enough to crawl in through the breaks in the wards. It made all of the others look small by comparison.

Slowly, it unspooled itself, its massive body snaking down over the assorted cabinets and drawers.

Allister clenched his jaw like this was severely above his paygrade, and Rat shoved past him.

"Shit," he muttered, taking off after them as the terror careened into the aisle.

Rat raced forward, a dead passage opening to catch them. The passage led out at the top of the ruined staircase, and they burst through, Allister trailing after them.

Jinx whipped toward them where she and Will were still waiting, her flashlight in hand.

Below, there was a sound like thunder as the terror slammed against a wall of cabinets, sending a spray of rubble raining down from the ceiling.

"Go!" Rat shouted. They shoved Jinx ahead, but she was already off, the beam of her flashlight darting wildly over the shelves as she ran.

Rat stole a glance over their shoulder as the terror righted itself, the star-flecked plating of its back glowing dimly against the dark. Then, with a speed that seemed impossible for its size, it streaked toward the broken staircase where Rat had climbed down, its segmented body snaking over the wreckage.

Desperately, Rat reached for their magic, and then more, pulling Isola's power through the binding spell. They forced a blast of raw power toward the terror, and the creature reared back as it crested the edge of the drop-off.

"Rat, let's go!" Will said, grabbing their arm. He yanked them forward, and they staggered after him as the sunken library groaned, and another wave of rubble fell.

Rat's heart lurched as they realized what was happening. Over the last few months, they'd let themself forget that there was a reason why the sunken campus had been sealed away. It could have been the disturbance from the fight, or the force of the water when the lake had come back down, or just the fact that this part of the old campus had never been as stable, but some vital, structural part of the building had given way, and the library was collapsing.

"Wait! Harker's still—"

Before Rat could finish, Will's hand shot out in a spell as the archway ahead of them began to buckle, forcing it back into place.

"Call him! Whatever binding spell thing you have, just get him and Agatha back here and do it fast." His voice came out breathless. Without stopping to see if Rat had heard him, he drew another spell.

Rat reached for the binding spell, and Harker grasped back. For a split second, they could sense him somewhere in the ruins of the sunken library, already racing toward the doors, Agatha close at his side.

Debris rained down on the aisle ahead of Rat, and they staggered to avoid it, the spell slipping away. Their lungs burned, but they couldn't stop yet. They had the last key. They could finish this. They just needed to get back to Harker and get out of here.

Rat burst out into the reading room where they'd started and almost careened into Jinx.

Aether curled through the air in heavy gold drifts, but she'd stopped running. Deep fissures split the floor where the library had begun to come apart.

Rat's gaze snapped to the stairs, but rubble covered the bottom steps, closing the way back.

"This one's you, Evans," Jinx called. "Whatever you have to do, just get us out!"

On the other side of the room, Agatha sprinted through one of the failing archways, Harker close on her heels. Grit rained down from the passage behind him as he cleared the threshold, will-o'-wisps of spellfire darting after him. He locked eyes with Rat, and their pulse leapt into their mouth.

From somewhere deep in the building came the low groan of shifting earth. Rat stumbled to catch themselves as the ground moved beneath their feet, and their magic flared in response.

From the corner of their eye, Rat caught sight of a passageway, and they scrambled toward it.

A dead passage had opened on the wall. On the other side, Rat saw a familiar glimpse of the tunnels under the school. Isola's magic tugged at them on the other side of their bond, but Rat forced it away.

You won't. Not while you still need me, they thought at the binding spell.

If she buried them here, she'd be burying seven keys and two other wayfinders along with them. She couldn't afford that.

Rat cleared the edge of the passageway, catching themselves in the threshold. Their lungs burned, but they reached out for Jinx behind them and pulled her through. Then Will.

The floor of the reading room tilted as he made it to the other side, and Rat's heart lurched. Quickly, Will spun back, and his hand shot out in a spell. All of the muscles in his arm went taut as he cast, holding the wreck in place.

The ground had slipped down, and the mouth of the dead passage had become a ledge, jutting out over the sinking floor of the reading room. Chunks of broken masonry littered the way, and the drifts of aether on the air had turned into a violent tide.

Rat caught sight of Harker as he closed the last of the distance, Agatha just behind him. She pushed his arm, and he launched himself up onto the lip of the passageway, breathing hard. He reached back for her, and the ground gave another lurch, sending her stumbling.

Before she could fall, Allister caught her, pulling her to her feet. "Go!" He shoved her ahead as the floor shifted again, and she grabbed on to Harker's hand.

Agatha scrambled up as the library gave another groan, but Allister wasn't going to have time to follow her. Rat met his gaze, and his eyes widened as the inevitability of what was about to happen hammered into him.

Then the ground dropped away, and the ceiling collapsed in a rain of debris.

And froze.

Rat turned back to see Agatha beside them, her hand closed in a fist, gaze fixed in concentration as she held the suspension spell.

The last time Rat had seen her work a spell like that, she'd had a sigil to help her support the working. All she'd had now was her own power and will, and she already looked spent.

Without thinking, Rat rushed for the open passageway.

Allister had been thrown back in the collapse and he'd come down hard in the rubble. Aether dusted his hair, and he'd lost his grasp on the light spell, the glow sputtering weakly as he tried to pick himself up. His eyes widened as Rat grabbed his arm, but he let them haul him to his feet.

"Thank me later, Church," they said, breathless.

Rat started to turn toward the passage, above them now, but a shockwave rolled through the aether as something in the library pushed against Agatha's spell, and the suspension wavered.

"Just go, Evans!" Allister shouted, his voice sharp with panic.

Rat took off, pulling him after. Magic surged through them, and the world unhinged, all of the gaps and crevices suddenly sharp at the edge of their senses as they ran for the passageway.

They weren't aware of opening another passage, but the air split, and then they were close enough that they might actually make it back, Allister still following close behind them. Will reached down his hand for them, and Allister grabbed on to the rocky ledge of the passageway above them to climb up.

Then, like a cut thread, something in the weave of Agatha's spell gave way. Rat stumbled as the terror whipped through one of the shattered archways, its massive tail hissing over the debris.

The ground lurched under their feet, and Rat hauled themself up as the floor dropped out beneath them.

Rat and Allister heaved themselves through the passage in a heap, and they came down hard on the solid ground of the tunnels.

"Rat," Will said in a tone of voice that implied they should absolutely not do that again, at the same time Harker rushed to sink down beside them, still radiating heat, and said, "Are you okay?"

Rat wanted to answer, but for a moment, all they could do was gasp down the dusty air, so they settled for burying their face in Harker's coat. The passage had emerged into a narrow corridor that looked as if it'd been carved into the earth rather than excavated out of any particular building, but Rat wasn't about to guess where.

Agatha had sunk down a few feet away, with her head resting on her knees and Jinx's jacket draped around her shoulders. Grit from the tunnels dusted her hair, and her breath came in ragged gasps. Jinx had dropped down next to her, murmuring something low enough that only Agatha would hear.

"Cromwell," Allister said under his breath, and the closest thing Rat had ever seen to genuine worry was written across his face. "Fuck." He peeled himself off the ground and rushed toward her.

Jinx glared up at him.

"She pushed her magic too far," he said. "I—It's like psychic feedback. She can't block out what she's seeing. I've dealt with it before. Please. Just, let me help."

"Try anything and you'll wish you'd been left behind."

"Yeah. Duly noted," he said, like he hadn't heard her at all. He knelt down besides Agatha, taking her shoulders. Then, a little more softly, "Hey. Ags. Breath with me."

She drew in another hiccupping breath.

"Good. Just focus on me, alright? Whatever you saw, it hasn't happened yet. They're just possibilities."

She nodded, still gasping, and a small watery laugh bubbled in her throat. "You're a scoundrel in all of them, Church."

He managed a lopsided grin. "There she is. Breathe in for the count of four, okay?"

"Evans?" Rat looked up at Harker, still close beside them.

"I'm fine. I mean, I'm still in one piece. I think," they said.

He reached out to offer them a hand, then, like he'd realized how much heat he was still giving off, he pulled his sleeve over his palm.

"Thanks," Rat managed, grabbing on to him. He stood and they let him pull them to their feet, then froze. A moment before Rat could say why, something tugged at the edge of their senses, and Isola's magic prickled on the other end of the binding spell.

Rat raised their hand to cast, but Isola's magic rose up faster, flooding out their powers, and then a blast of force rolled through the tunnel and knocked them back.

Rat slammed against the ground hard, and the air went out of their lungs. They had exactly enough time to see Harker lunge after them before another strike swept down the tunnel, cold and sharp, throwing him and the others back.

Shaking, Rat pushed themself up as Evening appeared in the mouth of the passageway, a pall of shadows drifting after him. The corridor seemed to darken around him, and Isola's power stirred in Rat's core, like it had recognized another one of its own.

When Rat had seen him in the Council Chambers, his power had been a whisper on the air. Now, it was a brewing storm, and Isola's magic was threaded through his own.

"Isola said she could direct you here, but she did better than I thought." He surveyed the scene before his gaze settled on Rat. "She asked me to keep you alive as a favor to her. It's lucky for you that she did, because personally, I'm getting tired of this game."

Rat struggled as the shadows slithered around their wrist to pull them back, clammy against their skin. Their gaze darted to the others as the shadows spread across the ground, holding them down.

Jinx, furious, her glasses on the floor beside her. Agatha, panicked and seething. And Will, equal parts determined and just desperate.

Harker's jaw went tight as the shadows wrenched him back. All around him, the spellfire sputtered and dimmed as he lost his hold on the spell, even as a bolt of panic and desperation and cold spite raced down the bond with Rat.

Evening then turned to Allister, still sheltering Agatha with his arm. "Good job keeping them here, Church. I knew you had to be useful for something."

"The keys aren't with them," Allister said. Emotion flickered across his face, and then he forced it away again as the shadows retreated from him. He pushed himself to his feet. "Let them go. We're wasting our time here."

"I somehow doubt that," Evening said crisply.

Rat summoned up Isola's power, even as they felt her hold on the binding spell clamp shut. The shadows slithered back, their grip loosening just enough, and Rat pulled against them. The bonds holding Rat back broke apart like smoke, and they stumbled forward, their hand flying to a casting position.

Rat's first spell went wide, sending a bolt of raw, undirected power into the wall of the tunnel in a spray of rubble. They rushed to get their footing, but Evening moved faster.

His hand closed on Allister's cloak, wrenching him back. Allister shoved against him as he staggered to keep his balance, and then Evening's hand found his throat, poised to cast.

"Move and he dies," Evening said, his voice clipped.

Rat's breathing caught as Allister's eyes widened. For a moment, they were back in the clock tower, except they already knew that Evening would make sure it played out differently this time.

"I'm not going to waste time making you turn out your pockets," Evening said. "I have five keys. You can turn yours over, or I can take care of it myself. I'll start with Church and then move on to that boy you care about so much."

"Rat—" Harker started, but his voice broke off as the shadows constricted around him, forcing him down. Evening gave them a smug look.

"Don't touch him," Rat snapped.

"It's a complicated spell. I had to act quickly with Night since she was powerful enough to fight back, but if you don't have to rush, the casting can take hours. Isola kept some of hers alive for days while she drained off their magic before she closed the working with their deaths." Evening tilted his head, considering. "I could make it fast, though. Not merciful, maybe, but fast. Less of a chance for you to try anything."

Rat grit their teeth as the shadows reached for them again, slithering over their ankle.

"As always, the choice is yours, Rat."

Harker met Rat's eyes, but they weren't going to be able to reach him. Not before Evening could do worse. Close by, Allister gave them a desperate look, Evening's hand still poised at his throat.

Rat looked around, but they were out of moves. There wasn't another place they could escape to or anyone left to come to their rescue. Rat reached into their coat and drew out the keys. "You'll let everyone go, and you won't harm them."

Evening gave them a look of cold satisfaction. "I'm not sure what makes you think you're in a position to bargain."

Before they could move, Evening cast a retrieval spell, and the keys flew to him.

As soon as Evening's grip loosened, Allister clambered away from him. His hands formed a spell on the air with ruthless speed, but not fast enough, and Evening's next spell sent him staggering.

Rat rushed toward him, but Evening was already tracing another spell, and a wall of force knocked them back, sending them sprawling. Rat skidded over the floor of the tunnel. They pushed themself up, biting back a wince as Evening strode over to them.

He knelt down. "One more thing," he said. Deftly, he reached into the pocket of Rat's coat and drew out their compass like he already knew it would be there.

Rat met his gaze, still too winded to speak. They'd let themself forget how well he still knew them from the years he'd spent getting close to their family, and they hated him for it.

"The cloaking spell was a nice touch at the Revel. There was a reason that spell was at the front of Church's mind." Evening closed his hand around the compass. "I'll need something of yours for the best effect. This will do nicely."

With a dawning horror, Rat realized what was happening.

The protective spells on the clock tower still answered to them. Evening would never be allowed past on his own. Some small part of Rat had still been counting on the fact that he needed them to get through, but that wasn't the case anymore.

"Isola requested that I leave your friends for her, but I'm not interested in taking my chances." He looked at Allister. "My Lesser Hours are on the way. Make sure Rat gets back to the Council Chambers, and I'll see to it that you still have a job in the morning."

Evening waved his hand, and a pack of raven-feathered not-wolves formed out of the deep shadows of the tunnels.

"There was a summoning incident. You can let the others know Evans overreached their abilities," Evening said. He turned to the not-wolves. "Leave Rat alive," he instructed coolly.

"No—" Rat forced themself to their feet as Evening was swallowed up by the dark, but before they could reach the mouth of the passage, one of the not-wolves blocked their path.

The last time Rat had run into not-wolves, they'd been in the deep woods at the edge of the school's domain. Harker had probably made a point of memorizing the entire entry in the bestiary after that, but the only things Rat knew were that the not-wolves looked like something that had crawled out of the depths of their worst tower dreams, and they had an unnerving number of teeth.

Rat reached desperately for their magic, but it was choked out under the rush of Isola's power.

The not-wolf leapt.

Rat scrambled away from it, and then a burst of force slammed into it, throwing the creature off course as the rest of its pack shot forward, and the tunnels broke into violent motion.

Harker caught Rat's arm, already on his feet, one hand still raised to cast. He pulled Rat back as another one of the not-wolves lunged, its jaws snapping at the air, and his next spell drove it back.

"I can't cast," Rat said in a rush. "Isola—"

"Evans!" Allister called behind them. "On your left!"

They spun in time to see a wall of force roll past them, knocking another not-wolf back before it could reach them.

Just as fast, Allister had turned away from them again, forming his next spell.

Beside Rat, Harker cast again. Rat could almost feel the tug of a banishment spell as Isola's magic recoiled from it. The creature dissolved into dark smoke, tendrils curling away from the place where it had been.

Harker spun, readying his next spell, but Rat could tell that it wasn't going to be enough.

Evening didn't need to kill them to win. All he had to do was keep Rat here until he'd gotten Isola's heart, and the rest would take care of itself.

"Go!" Jinx called to them. She cut her hand in a sharp motion, and the moisture of the tunnels condensed out of the air around her. She'd ended up on the other side of the corridor with Will working a defensive spell beside her.

"But—"

"Just get out of here and find Evening!" she shouted. She met their gaze, and they realized she'd had the same thought they did. "All of you! Will and I can hold them!"

Will caught Rat's eye and gave them a nod.

Rat turned to find Agatha in the fray, but Allister already had her, his arm braced around her.

Then, before Rat could stop her, Jinx let out a shrill whistle, and the not-wolves whipped toward her, her eyes bright like she had a plan.

Jinx knew the tunnels even better than Rat did. If anyone could lose a pack of monsters or find a place for Will to wall them in, in would be her.

Rat turned on their heel and bolted in the other direction, Harker still close at their side. They reached for their magic, pushing hard against Isola's hold.

Rat caught sight of a passage in the corner of their eye, and they ducked through. For the first time, they didn't have to think about Harker and Allister following seamlessly after them, Agatha in tow. Then they were in a quieter part of the tunnels, the sounds of the fight gone, and Will and Jinx left somewhere far behind them.

The ground sloped upward, and Rat realized they were back by the door in the woods. Rat started toward the exit, but Allister stopped them.

"Wait. I—you didn't have to save me back there," Allister said. He cleared his throat. "I owe you." Rat realized it was as close to a *thank you* as they were ever going to get from him.

He started past them, but Rat hurried after him.

"Then help me," they said before they could think better of it. "Night was putting together a report."

Allister's gaze sharpened.

"Everything Evening was up to," they explained. "She sent it to me before she died. It's in my desk."

Allister studied them. "Why are you telling me this? I could destroy it."

"But you won't."

"No?"

"No," they said, more certain. "It's going to be the same as turning over your family's key. You already know that the moment you lose your leverage, he's going to find another excuse to put you back in your place." They met his gaze. "I don't think you're someone who makes the same mistake twice."

For a moment, the tunnels were quiet.

"Whoever wins tonight, Evening doesn't get away with it," Rat said.

Allister nodded slightly, like he was settling a debt.

"The Lesser Hours are on campus already," Agatha said to him. "Our best chance of making it to the dorms is through the tunnels."

She met Rat's eye, and then she and Allister split off, leaving Rat and Harker alone at the end of the tunnel.

CHAPTER FORTY-FOUR

THE TUNNEL LET OUT IN A FAMILIAR PART OF THE EAST Woods.

Harker followed close at Rat's heels as they hurried toward the center of campus, but even with the heat of his magic pouring off him, the cold slashed at their lungs.

Rat didn't slow until they were back in sight of the clock tower. The earth around it was still cracked even though most of the rubble had been cleared away, and a riot of weeds had pried their way out from the still-thawing ground.

Where the clock tower had once had an empty stretch of brick wall, the door had become a permanent fixture, like something in the building's defenses had broken last semester when Rat bent the clock tower's loyalty spells to themselves.

"It's me," Rat said softly into the wood. "I'm here to finish this." They pressed their hand to the door and pushed, and it hinged inward with a low groan, like it had been waiting for them all this time.

They stepped over the threshold, and a bolt of dread raced down the binding spell as Harker followed them through.

"Are you sure—"

"Keep going," he said, his expression steeling over. He caught their hand, leading them toward the stairs. Rat rushed to keep up as he pulled them around a bend in the staircase, wisps of spellfire roving after him.

"Harker—"

"You said both of us, Evans." He spun back to face them, stopping Rat short, and a note of desperation slid into his voice. "I swore I'd finish this with you, and you have me."

"Come on," Rat said, their hand tightening on his.

The stairs led up to a wide circular ruin of a room that was etched into Rat's memory, the ground still slanted where the building's foundations had sunk into the earth. At the center of the floor, where the seal had once been, a wide stone staircase now led down, curving into the darkness.

The last time Rat had been here, the clock tower's defensive spells had been like a living thing, imbued with magic and intention. Now, except for the echo of their own footsteps, it was silent.

Steeling themself, Rat started down, Harker close at their side. They touched their fingers to the stone wall, searching for the familiar stirring of magic, but nothing happened. All of the protection spells were gone.

Fighting back their unease, Rat rushed down the last few stairs. A long corridor stretched ahead, ending in a set of doors, but the glow of the seal had vanished, and even with Isola dampening their magic, Rat could feel the way opening ahead of them.

It was already unlocked.

Rat pressed their hands to one of the doors, and it swung open, into the mouth of the passages that lay beyond. The way ahead sloped deeper into the earth, but Rat couldn't see far before it was swallowed up by the shadows.

And then, from somewhere deep in the maze of passages, came the soft murmur of a pulse.

"Rat?" Harker asked.

"I know where we're going," they said, stepping forward. "Just stay close to me."

Beside them, Harker's spellfire flared brighter as he followed Rat down into the earth, the distant pull of Isola's heart drawing them on.

They made their way through the sprawl of corridors, moving as quickly as they could, until the passage ahead of them ended in another set of doors, heavy and inlaid with spellwork. Aether curled through the air in heavy drifts, like the last remnants of a powerful enchantment, broken now and already beginning to fade.

Rat felt like they'd plunged into cold water. Just like above, the archive's doors were already open.

Harker stepped a little closer to them, his hand raised to cast, and Rat stepped over the threshold into the Ingrid Collection.

Cramped aisles led off into the dark on all sides, disappearing past the pale glow of the spellfire. Mounds of crates and boxes rose up around them amid the maze of cluttered shelves, and spellbooks were piled on the floor.

When Rat had heard stories about the Ingrid Collection, they'd imagined the depths of the school's library or the orderly sprawl of the Council Archives, full of wide, dimly lit aisles, but they'd been wrong. It was a magpie's nest.

Margaret Ingrid had been a collector of things, and every terrible piece of magic she'd ever gathered was here.

In spite of themselves, a terrible flicker of want lit between Rat's ribs. They could turn themself into exactly what everyone else had feared and call all of the other houses to heel. It would be cruel, and monstrous, and theirs by right, and just for once they would have something that no one else could take away from them.

They knew exactly why Ingrid hadn't just destroyed this place, no matter what it ended up costing or how many other lives Isola had claimed trying to claw her way in.

"Evans," Harker said under his breath, jarring them back.

"None of this sees the light of day," they told Harker, heading toward the shelves. "We're burning this place down before we leave."

He met their gaze with a kind of grim understanding, and then they saw why he'd been trying to get their attention. In the circle of light cast by the spellfire, a set of fresh boot prints tracked through the dust, leading deeper into the archives.

Harker gave them a small nod, and Rat took off into the maze of shelves, down the narrow passageway. Blood pounded in their ears, but underneath it, the faint tug of Isola's heart grew closer, pulling Rat forward like a hook between their ribs.

Evening would hear them, or see the light of the spellfire, but they didn't have time to think. He was here, and he already knew which way to go. There wasn't any way forward without getting past him.

They took the next corner, the unnatural quiet of the archives pressing in around them, and then there was the rough scratch of something moving through the dark.

In a flash of slick, oil-black feathers, a not-wolf bounded out of the shadows. Its jaws snapped at the air, but Harker's hand shot out in a defensive spell. A wall of force rolled toward the creature, throwing it back, and it hit the ground with a snarl. It twisted, claws scrabbling over the worn floor as it tried to get purchase.

A low animal sound tore from the shadows behind it, and Rat took off. They weren't about to wait to see how many of those things Evening had summoned.

"Fuck," they breathed as Harker drew another spell, the spellfire around him flaring dangerously as he split his focus.

"*Leave!*" The word tore from him, harsh and rusted at the edges in the half-forgotten language of the tower, but the banishment went wide, rattling the shelves.

The not-wolf lurched toward him, and Rat tugged him out of the way around a bend in the aisle.

"Rat—" Harker started.

"Just keep going," they said, pulling him forward. The cluttered shelves pressed in closer as the aisle narrowed. They'd lost any sense of where in the collection they were, but fresh tracks marked the heavy dust, and the low beat of Isola's heart was still drawing them on, her magic straining to reach it through the binding spell.

Blood rushed in their ears as they raced around the next turn, the not-wolves close behind them. Ahead, the aisle opened into a clearing in the archives. Shelves and mounds of boxes lined the edges, as far as Rat could see before they disappeared from the limited circle of light.

Rat shot toward it, and a blast of force slammed into them, knocking them into a row of shelves. The sharp pain of impact pounded through them as they slid to the ground, and distantly, they realized they'd lost their grip on Harker. Breathless, Rat forced themself up as Evening dropped his concealment spell.

"You know, I had a feeling you'd try to follow me down here," he said, the shadows retreating from him. "You really can't leave well enough alone, can you?" His gaze dropped to Harker, where he'd fallen a few feet from Rat. His arm shook as he tried to pick himself up, and one of the not-wolves padded into the mouth of the aisle, blocking the way back.

Evening's eyes glinted with a kind of cruel amusement. "I have to admit, I'm disappointed. I thought by now you would've at least learned not to bring your weaknesses with you. Remind me, how did this end the last time?"

"Don't—" Rat started.

Evening's mouth curved, and they realized that was exactly what he wanted. He was toying with them. Maybe while he decided his angle of attack. Maybe just for the satisfaction of reminding Rat that they were still outmatched.

But there weren't any more bargains to strike or deals left to be made. It was just the three of them, and Isola's heart, her pulse a low murmur somewhere in the darkness ahead of them.

Somewhere close.

Discreetly, Rat looked out at the clearing behind him as they climbed to their feet. At the edge of the shadows, shelves and cabinets circled the space, forming a wall broken only by the narrow aisles that led back into the collection.

Like they'd come to the center of the maze.

"You sense it, don't you? Her heart." Evening drew in, and Rat fought the urge to flinch away from him. Magic crackled on the air around him, his own, laced with Isola's, and a heavy chill clung to him. "She really got her claws into you. I'm fascinated to see what she'll do with you when this is over."

A shadow snaked around Rat's ankle, tugging them back, and Rat's stomach lurched. They twisted away from it, but Evening had already moved, readying his next attack.

"Evans, go," Harker shouted.

Rat didn't think. They shot past him, into the dark of the clearing as the not-wolves slipped away from Evening to bound after them.

"Fuck," Rat breathed. They risked a glance back as Evening, but he wasn't chasing them.

Harker shoved himself to his feet as Evening's next spell narrowly missed him, shredding into a bookcase just behind him. The wood splintered with an earsplitting crack, but Harker was already on the move.

Urgency sparked down the binding spell, and Rat broke into a sprint. The pull of Isola's heart tugged them forward, and they let it. Isola might have lent her power to Evening, but their deal with her was an open doorway between their magic and hers, whether Rat wanted it or not.

They couldn't take Evening in a fight, but they didn't have to. They just needed to get there first.

Rat wove as one of the not-wolves snapped at the air, and their gaze locked onto a wooden box tucked away in the clutter. It was small enough that they could have held it in their hands and plain except for the bands of spellwork and engraved arcanists' silver that held it closed, but as soon as Rat saw it, a pang of desperate need ran down the binding spell they shared with Isola.

A spell shot past them, carving a gouge in the floor as Rat dodged out of the way, into the path of a not-wolf. Rat threw themselves forward, but they weren't going to be able to move fast enough to escape the creature's teeth. Dread hammered through them as they realized exactly how this was going to end.

They reached for their magic anyway, surging against Isola's hold on them. And then, maybe because there was still a sliver of protection left in this place or maybe just because her focus had slipped, her grasp on them splintered just enough for Rat's powers to slip through the cracks.

Rat felt the dead passage open beside them, and they let it catch them. They spilled out onto the far side of the clearing, their hair plastered to their forehead with sweat.

The not-wolf hit the ground in a tumble and scrambled to right itself as the other one whipped its head toward Rat. Across the clearing, Evening locked eyes with them, but Rat was already on their feet, Isola's heart just ahead of them.

He raised his hand in a spell as the not-wolves rushed toward Rat, but a burst of spellfire streaked past him, forcing him off-balance as Harker pulled his attention back.

Rat lunged.

A wave of furious power surged down their bond with Isola as she tried to pull them back, and then their hands closed on the box, the metal inlay cold to the touch.

Magic flooded through them, and it was dusk and starlight and howling wind and whispered secrets, a perfect twin to Isola's own, but somehow *more*. Through the binding spell, Isola's magic reached for it in answer, the same inevitable way that a tide reaches for the shore.

Evening's next spell threw Harker back against the shelves with a thud. Raw fear kicked in Rat's ribs, and Evening whipped toward them, firing off his next attack.

Rat took off as the spell crashed into the bookcase behind them, and the shelves collapsed in an avalanche of clutter.

Isola pushed against them, but Rat had slipped past her once now, and they caught the thread of their own magic again as the not-wolves closed on them. The passage glinted ahead of them, and Rat crashed through, pulling the box to their chest.

Harker caught them, already on his feet, and Rat grabbed on to his sleeve with their free hand.

"Go!" they shouted. They tugged Harker toward maze of old books and magic gone to seed as Evening took off after them, the not-wolves already rushing back to follow him.

Isola's magic coursed through Rat as they ran. With her heart this close, it was more than she could hold back, and the shadows drew around them, the concealment spell forming like second nature.

Rat pulled Harker around the next corner, down a row of shelves cluttered with vials, but even if he couldn't see them anymore, Evening was still too close on their heels. Another wall of force rolled through the aisle, glass shattering behind them as the spell went wide.

Glass crunched under Rat's shoe, and Evening locked on them, preparing his next spell without breaking his stride. The eyes of the not-wolves gleamed in the shadows behind him, waiting for his call, but all of his attention was fixed ahead.

Rat's hand tightened on Harker. "Light it on fire," they said in a rush. "Everything. Now."

"Rat. No. I'm not going to be able to control that. I can't—"

"Then don't control it!" Their voice came out breathless. "I'm not leaving anything here that Evening can use!"

Another spell shot past, clipping one of the bookcases in a flurry of splinters. Closer this time.

Harker spun around. "Keep going," he said, already drawing another spell. The concealment dropped as he stepped away from Rat, and spellfire blazed around him, hot and bright like the last vengeful throes of a dying star.

Evening stopped in his tracks, the not-wolves still at his heels.

Heat rippled the air, the shelves blackening in Harker's wake as all of the shadows burned away. "If you turn back now, you can still find another way to the doors before this whole place goes up," he said, but his voice was merciless. "That's more of a chance than you ever gave me."

Cold fury flickered across Evening's face as the fire spread, and then the darkness at the edges of the aisle drew over him in a protective spell as whatever was in the glass vials on the shelves around them caught, adding fuel to the flames.

Sparks drifted through the air as Rat raced toward the entrance to the archives. They glanced over their shoulder in time to see Harker rush through the smoke, the archive blazing behind him.

A spell lashed down the aisle after him, with the sharp whistle of a blade splitting the air. Harker shoved Rat out of the way as he reached them, and the spell sliced into him, sending him stumbling.

"Harker—" Rat grabbed on to him, their other arm still wrapped around the box with Isola's heart. The smell of smoke clung to him, and the air was scorched around him, his skin scalding even through his coat.

"I'm fine," he said, his voice thick with pain. "You have the heart. Just get to the doors."

Behind them, Evening stepped through the flames, the veil of shadows falling away from him again. The attack had left him disheveled and breathless, but if he'd been hurt, he hid it well.

The darkness of the archives seemed to deepen around him like a warning, and then Evening's next spell shot after them, tearing into Harker's shoulder.

"*Harker!*" Rat grasped at him, like that could do anything to help, but he pushed them away.

"Rat, get out of here. I'll buy you time, just—"

"*No! I said I'm not leaving you!*" Magic rolled off them in a shock wave even though Rat hadn't cast. They were channeling too much power, and they didn't have control of it, but they didn't care. They turned to face Evening. "*Stay back!*" Their hand shot out, and Isola's power poured out of them in an undirected wave. Rubble rained down from high above them, but Evening was faster than they were, and he was a better arcanist.

The shadows moved to his defense, and his next attack was leveled at Rat.

They went down hard, and the wooden box spilled out of their arms as they hit the ground. Beside them, Harker had gone sprawling. Weakly, he forced himself up, but his arms were shaking, and there was a deep slash across the back of his coat that Rat hadn't been able to see when he was leaning against them. The heavy fabric had torn all the way through, slick with blood in the glow of the spellfire.

Harker gave Rat a desperate look.

They struggled back to their knees as Evening strode down the wreckage of the aisle. Rat's head throbbed, and the taste of smoke coated their mouth.

Evening grabbed their coat, hauling them to their feet. They let out a small, strangled cry as he pinned them against the wall of shelves.

"You useless, sheltered child." He let out a low, ragged laugh that turned Rat's blood to ice. "All that you had to do was leave the school when I gave you the chance, but you had to involve yourself instead. You didn't even know how to cast."

"Stop it—" Rat shoved at him, but he pushed them back.

"Let me tell you how this happens, Rat," he said, drawing in close. "Everyone has already seen you for the vicious creature that you are. You made sure of that at the Revel. Of course Elise will be devastated, and the school will put on a show of searching for you, but in the end, what do you think they're all going to say when you don't come back?"

"I guess that depends on what they read in Night's investigation." Rat bared their teeth at him. "You never found it, did you?"

"Do you really think I've done anything that the rest of the old bloodlines don't know about?" His arm pressed against Rat's throat, cutting off their breath. They let out a choked gasp, and Harker forced himself off the ground, but the shadows gathered to wrench him back again. "They chose to do nothing, just like how they'll continue to do nothing when you disappear. As far as the other houses are concerned, you are another monster to be slain, and they'll live in fear of the day that Isola lets you come back."

Rat struggled against him as spots swam in the corner of their vision. They had to fight, but suddenly, they felt how small they actually were. Somehow, after everything, they were still this powerless.

"Then again," Evening said, glancing back at the flames. "Maybe you won't make it out of here at all. She asked me not to harm you, but I wouldn't have to, would I?"

Isola's power surged under Rat's skin, but their hold on the spell slipped away from them. They couldn't focus. They couldn't get enough air.

Their gaze found Harker, still struggling against the shadows. Desperate, they reached for their power, but there was only the cold and starless expanse of Isola's magic, rushing in to drown out everything else.

Then Evening reeled back with a winded gasp. Rat collapsed against the bookshelves as he released them, pulling in a lungful of air.

Isola's shadows still clung to him, but they weren't a protective shield anymore. A dark blade had pierced his side, and vines of shadow twisted around him, wrenching him back. Evening gaped, like he still didn't fully understand, and then the blade was gone, melted back into shadows, and the subtle aura of Isola's magic slid away from him. His hand went to the wound, and his fingers came away slick with blood.

A great black bird swept down from the shadows above. Then, like a trick of the light, it shifted form, and Isola was standing among the shelves. Her eyes shone bright and cold, and her gloved hand rested easily on the hilt of her sword.

"I thought my terms were clear," Isola said, her gaze fixed coolly on Evening. She curled her fingers, and her power rushed back to her. "Rat is mine by right."

Evening let out a hacking cough, the smoke heavy on the air now. Weakly, he braced himself against the shelves like it was all that was keeping him on his feet. "We had a deal."

"We had an arrangement, which I've honored to the letter," she said crisply. She paused, considering him. "You know, I remember you, from all those years ago. Always grasping at Alexander's shadow. So resentful of everything he chose over rising through the ranks with you. So insulated from the consequences of your own actions. In all this time, it's astounding how little you've changed."

Rat edged away, scanning the ground. The wooden box had skid across the aisle when they fell, out of their reach, and the flames had finally reached them, licking at the aged wood of the bookshelves.

Their eyes found Harker, biting a wince as he tried to get to his feet. He looked pale, like he'd already lost too much blood, but he glanced from Rat to Isola's heart, and his jaw tightened. His hand moved at his side, forming the beginning of a spell.

Isola's attention turned back to Rat like she'd sensed them preparing to run, and then her eyes fell to the box. "I see you've found something of mine," she said. She flexed her hand, and the box flew to her, snapping neatly into her grasp.

Harker shot toward her, and her shadows wrenched him back again, fully under her control this time. He came down hard with a sharp, pained sound.

"I—You can't set foot on campus," Rat said, as if the terms of their bargain should still mean anything to her. "I haven't called you."

"Haven't you?" Isola's mouth curved. "You've been drawing on my power willingly for weeks now. Tell me, Rat, what do you think that is if not a summons?"

Rat took half a step back, suppressing a shiver.

"You called me here, as my word is my bond." Isola stepped in. "It was always you. You know, I approached most of the other Holbrooks, but for you? I never had the chance, because you sought me out. *You* found *me*."

Rat's jaw locked as Isola stalked toward them. "I left you."

"Because you feared me, or because you feared what you could become?" Isola traced her fingers over the metal bands that held the box shut. Rat felt the unmistakable tug of their own power on the other end of the binding spell, and then the clasps fell away, and the box opened.

Isola's heart was a weak, shadowy thing. Rat didn't know why they'd expected it to be flesh, but it looked like it had been made out of cobwebs and whispers. Isola held it like it was something delicate, and for a moment she almost looked pained. Then she closed her hand around it, and in a rush of wind and shadows, its power drew back into her.

Until that moment, Rat hadn't understood how much of herself Isola had been missing. Everything about her suddenly seemed sharper and more real, like in all the time they'd known her, they'd only been dealing with her shadow.

Magic coursed through the air around her, and the darkness of the collection seemed to deepen.

Isola held out her hand, and the force of the promise Rat had made to her sharpened to a compulsion, drawing them forward.

Rat took an involuntary step toward her.

Her hand closed on their arm, and her fingers dug into their skin.

"Let them go!" Harker surged toward Rat again, straining against the shadows like he'd refused to learn. He stumbled forward as their hold on him broke, and then Isola flung him aside with a crisp wave of her hand.

The spell brought him down hard, and he slid, slamming bonelessly against the wall of shelves. He looked up at Rat, spiteful and furious and too weak to get back up.

"Stop!" Rat's voice came out ragged, but Isola was already pulling them back.

With a groan, the shelves collapsed in a rain of sparks, and Harker disappeared in the blaze. Then the ruins of the Ingrid Collection fell away as Isola dragged Rat through the passageway and into the cold night air.

CHAPTER FORTY-FIVE

THE DARK CRASHED IN AROUND RAT AS THEY STUMBLED out into the familiar ruins of Ashwood, Isola's hand still clamped on their arm.

"Let go of me! He'll die!" Rat shoved against her as she dragged them on, the passage already closed behind her.

"Perhaps you should have thought of that before you decided to take a match to the collection," Isola said, and her voice was ice.

"I'll do whatever you want, okay? Get him out, and I'm yours. I won't fight you."

"Oh, Rat," she said, airy and cruel. "You're already mine."

"*Please!*" Their throat felt raw. They needed to get back.

Isola hauled them around to face her. "Now that you've returned my heart to me, I think this concludes our bargain. You've run enough. It's time that you return with me as promised."

Rat grit their teeth against the pain as her hand tightened even more.

"That boy's always had a talent for surviving," Isola said, "If he makes it out, I'll let you be the one to destroy him."

Desperation rose in Rat's chest. If they tried anything, she would kill them. She would kill them, and they didn't care. They just needed an opening so they could get back to Harker.

Rat pushed away from her, reaching for their power, but the spell choked off as Isola's magic overwhelmed them again. A wall of force slammed into them, knocking them to the ground, and Rat slid across the broken floor of the ruins.

Isola knelt, grabbing the collar of their coat to pull them up. "You were right when you guessed that I hadn't collected you because I couldn't without my full power at my disposal. Not without you slipping past me again. But now . . ." She drew in, and Rat suppressed a shudder.

"Let go of me," they said, but their voice barely came out.

"By the oath that you swore and the debt that's mine to collect, I bind you to me," Isola said, her voice a cold whisper in the silence of the ruins.

Rat struggled against the spell as her magic curled over them in shadowy tendrils. Their own magic flickered weakly, and then Isola's power rolled through the binding spell in a current, too violent for them to grab on to.

The binding sank its teeth into them, slicing deep into the core of their being, like it was digging itself into everything they were. The thread of Isola's magic rose in answer, growing thorns and roots.

Everything inside of Rat threatened to revolt. They pitched forward, gasping, but they could already feel themself losing whatever ground they had left. Isola's mouth curved. "Rat Holbrook Evans, I call you to my service."

Rat reached desperately for the bond they still shared with Harker. He'd sworn to follow them to the end of this.

Rat had never let themself say it out loud, but he was supposed to be there *after*, to finish out the rest of their time at Bellamy Arts once the dust had settled, so he could hoard overdue library books and scare off all the new freshmen with them next year. Rat wasn't supposed to lose him again after they'd come so close.

They felt a faint pull on the other side, but then it was gone, drowned out by Isola's power, and Rat was alone.

All around, the ruins had fallen still, the stars clear and bright overhead. Rat collapsed, bracing themself against the ground as her magic retreated again, leaving them shaky and hollow as they fought to catch their breath.

The binding spell was complete. Even now, the faint pressure of Isola's will pressed on them, drawing them toward her. Toward the tower.

It couldn't end like this. Rat wouldn't let it.

Rat shoved themself to their feet and rushed for the edge of the ruins, drawing a spell on the air as they moved. They didn't care what Isola had done or what bound them to her. They'd shredded through powerful enchantments before, and they would do it again. They were heir to the Holbrook line, and Isola herself had trained them.

The air shimmered ahead of Rat, and they caught a glimpse of the still-burning stacks of the Ingrid Collection.

Then the full force of Isola's will slammed down on them, and the spell snuffed out again.

Deliberately, like she was deeply enjoying it, Isola curled her fingers in a fist, and Rat sank back to their knees as all of the strength went out of them.

"So determined," she said on a sigh. She strode across the ruins, the overgrowth whispering around her as she knelt down across from them. The air around her was thick with magic, but underneath there was still the faint, familiar tinge of death.

Isola had been dying for a long time. She'd been weak without her heart, but her heart had grown weaker without her, too.

But it didn't matter that she hadn't come back to her full strength. She was still one of Acanthe's seven Rooks, with a long-ago god's whispered secret for a heart. And Rat was on their own against her.

Rat suppressed a shudder as Isola's gloved fingers brushed their bangs away from their face. "It doesn't have to be a punishment," she said, tilting their face up to hers. "I've seen your dreams about the tower, and they aren't all nightmares. You can still go willingly."

"Don't touch me."

Isola drew back, but her gaze was cold. "I promise you this, Rat. When you take your place with me, every choice you make will be your own. I'm going to turn you so slowly, you won't feel it happening, and when you bring this place to ruin, it'll be because you wanted to, gloriously wicked thing that you are."

Wind whistled through the ruins of the old house as Isola rose to her feet, her armor clattering softly. She held her hand out to Rat, like she had so long ago, the first time she'd offered to bring them back to the tower. "Come," she said. "The night grows short, and we still have a long way ahead of us."

Rat closed their hand in a fist as the binding spell weighed on them. Everything in them ached, and they could feel themself losing ground.

"*Come with me*," Isola said again, slipping into the language of the tower, her words rusted at the edges. It was an invitation and a command, and it resonated in the hollow of Rat's bones.

In spite of themself, they stepped toward her.

They made a last desperate grab for their binding spell with Harker, but Isola reached for their magic, and whatever hold was wrested away from them as she opened the passage and the tower shimmered into view.

Then a burst of spellfire tore through the darkness, and Isola lost her hold.

Rat whipped around, their pulse racing.

Another passage had opened like a curtain, and Harker spilled through, a torrent of spellfire raging behind him. "You're not taking them!"

Rat stared at him. They hadn't opened the passage—he had.

Smoke billowed after him, breaking apart on the night air as he rushed toward Rat. Fresh burns marked his hand, and blood and aether matted his sleeve where he'd been cut. His jaw clenched, like he was in pain and trying not to show it, but another will-o'-wisp of spellfire flared at his fingertips anyway, burning steady and bright.

Isola's eyes lit dangerously, and the shadows gathered, deepening around her. "It seems I spoke too soon," she said, low in Rat's ear. "Tell me. Should I tear him apart now, or would you rather I leave him for you to finish?"

Rat shoved away from her as Harker sent another blast of spellfire toward them, blazing across the ruins to drive Isola back. The force of her will pressed in on the other side of the binding spell, but Rat felt her grip on them loosen as she dodged back.

Rat locked eyes with Harker, the finality settling over them. There wasn't any escaping this. One way or another, it would end here.

Then Isola spun toward Harker and unleashed the full force of her magic on him. Power rushed on the other side of the binding spell, terrible and deep as the sky itself.

Rat shot forward. "*Open!*" Just barely, they caught the thread of their own magic and felt the world give way. They weren't going to be able to get back to the school, but they didn't need to. They only had to reach Harker.

The first passage carried them to where he stood, already working a defensive spell on the air. They caught him without stopping as Isola's power tore across the ruins in a wall of wind and shadows, shredding everything in its wake.

The next passage took them to the foot of the staircase of the ruins, leaving Rat breathless from the effort. Isola's power had rushed in with their own, and weeds pushed up through the rubble around them. Rat met Harker's eyes, their pulse still pounding in their ears.

"You're welcome, Evans," he said, fighting a wince, his hand already forming another spell. Faster than he could complete the working, a great black bird swept toward them, and then Isola's form shifted back, human again as she touched down on the splintered floor of the ruins.

She grabbed the collar of Harker's shirt, hauling him toward her. Rat lunged after him, and then the full force of her will came down on them again, slamming them against the stairs.

"You never could resist running to their rescue," she said, pulling Harker in close. Roughly, she shoved him to the ground, and he landed hard. With the low hiss of steel, Isola drew her sword. Moonlight flashed on the blade as she angled it at his throat, pinning him.

Rat couldn't breathe. Isola's magic rushed over them, holding them in place as they tried to get to their feet.

Isola looked down at Harker, considering. "I was starting to wonder when you'd claw your way back." She tilted his chin up with her sword, and helpless fury thrilled through his bond with Rat. "But then I suppose I have you to thank for how things turned out. Rat really would do anything to get to you."

"*Stop!*" Rat reached for her magic, and whatever door still separated them from Isola's power hinged wide open.

Power flowed through them, sending a ripple of cracks through the weathered stone floor, and Harker twisted out of her reach, spellfire flaring at his fingertips as he regained his footing. Weeds sprouted up from the ground, like Rat had torn through the veil between their world and the tower, and the faint scent of mugwort hung on the air.

Isola's gaze darted to Rat, and then Harker's next spell shot toward her, drawing her attention back. She whipped after him, sword raised.

Dread curled around Rat's ribs. Rat was already hers, but Harker was the last thread that tied them to this world, and one of the only people to ever escape from Isola. She wouldn't let him walk away from this.

Rat reached for Isola's power again, before they could give themself time to think through what they were doing. The ruins shifted on their foundations as the tower forced its way in, splitting the ground, and then their control was wrenched away again by the binding spell.

Rat's power choked off as the air went out of their lungs, and they caught themself on their knees.

Harker drew Isola's attention back to him again with another blast of spellfire, but Rat already knew it wouldn't buy them much time.

Spots swam in Rat's vision. They weren't meant to channel this much power, but they kept going anyway. Isola still wasn't used to being at her full strength. If Rat let her bring them back to the tower now, the next time they fought her, she would be, and she'd make sure they never had another chance to strike at her.

The spell tore away from them, shredding through the ruins, but Isola had already sensed it coming, and it broke harmlessly around her.

Harker's hand flew up in a defensive working as Isola brought her sword down, the blade slicing the air, and through the faint thread of the binding spell they still shared with him, Rat felt his spell fail. Then a shadow passed in front of Harker, catching Isola's strike.

A wraith.

Isola's eyes widened, and then she locked her jaw. She drew back, and a hand snaked out of the dark of the ruins, grasping at her. Isola flexed her hand, drawing in her power. Wind howled through the ruins as she flung the wraith away from her, but another was already there, reaching for her from the shadows.

Blood and liquid silver trickled down Isola's cheek where the wraiths had clawed at her. She touched her gloved fingers to her lips, and her gaze locked on Rat, sharp with understanding.

The wraiths were bound to the tower, more tightly than even Harker had been. Rat couldn't pull them away from the tower, but they hadn't tried to. Rat had simply shredded through the veil, until the ground they were standing on was as much the tower's as it was Ashwood's.

Isola struck out at the wraiths with her sword, driving them back, but another shadow caught her arm, and the blade flew out of her grasp.

The sword skittered away from her, and she raised her hand to a casting position instead. Power emanated off of her in cold waves, and all the shadows in the ruins seemed to deepen, the air heavier around her like a coming storm.

Harker drew up another will-o'-wisp of spellfire, the flames flaring bright and hot around him.

Isola stepped forward, and her next spell knocked him back with an explosive burst of force.

She knelt as the fire around him guttered out. "You've always been a pitiful little thing, haven't you? So desperate to prove yourself, yet so scared of your own power. Determined to keep it in check so you won't hurt anyone." She drew in. "Even now. You pretend to be so ruthless, but you can't really do it, can you?"

"I wasn't going to," he said.

Rat grabbed Isola's blade from the ground, and a familiar rush of power surged through it, an echo of Isola's own. Their hands tightened on the hilt, and they lunged forward, struggling against the weight of the sword.

The blade slid between Isola's ribs from behind with a soft, wet sound that Rat felt in their bones. Pain shot through the binding spell, but Rat drew it in, calling Isola's magic to them.

"*Close*," they breathed, and like shutting a door, they felt her heart shudder.

Isola reached up to the wound as Rat drew the blade back. Dark blood and the runny silver of starlight seeped out, spreading between her fingers. Her eyes lit, like this was something fascinating and new. It was the same way she used to look at Rat in the field of grass when they managed to sneak past her birds unseen or open a door somewhere interesting. Like they'd figured out a particularly clever new trick.

She let out a small, winded laugh, her breath ragged. "Of course, it's you."

It felt too plain, too human an end for her, but Rat knew the cold brush of death, and they could feel it, seeping out through the tide of her magic. Already, the binding spell had begun to unravel its hold on them.

Isola's knees buckled. She staggered against them, and Rat sank under her weight, letting her pull them down to the floor of the ruins.

"One more time," she said, looking up at them. "The names of the stars."

It was already beginning to get light out, and the stars overhead weren't hers, but Rat wasn't sure that it mattered anymore. One by one, Rat named the constellations she'd taught them as her breathing slowed.

Rat wasn't sure when it stopped, but by the time they came to the last one, Isola was still and quiet.

CHAPTER FORTY-SIX

THE SKY WAS NEARLY LIGHT BY THE TIME RAT FINALLY opened a way back to Bellamy Arts, but it was still early enough that the buildings were dark and the campus was mercifully quiet. They hadn't thought about where they would go once they were back, but Dawn's Lesser Hours had already arrived at the school. It didn't take long for someone to find Rat as they staggered out from the mouth of the woods with Harker, underbrush and the scent of smoke still clinging to their coat.

Not for the first time, Rat let themself be escorted across campus as the sun came up, too exhausted to argue. At least this time, Harker was there, his arm wrapped tightly around them.

Protective spells shimmered faintly on the air as they approached the clock tower, marking off a perimeter around the edge of the lawn. A small swarm of Lesser Hours and about a dozen faculty members moved frantically around the grounds, weaving new protections over the building and organizing what Rat could only guess was an attempt to bring them back.

Dawn saw them approach from where the Greater Hour had been pouring over a hastily set-up folding table covered in spell diagrams, and then before Rat and Harker had even crossed the edge of the lawn, everything was a flurry of motion.

Rat was still too tired to think of how to explain themself, but in the end, maybe because it was clear that they and Harker were barely staying on their feet, Dawn said a few words to Fairchild and then split off from the crowd.

"Thank god," Dawn said, half to themself. They were dressed immaculately as always, but weariness clung to them, and Rat could only guess that it had been a long night at the Council Chambers, too. "How badly are you hurt?"

It didn't take long after that for Dawn to call over a Lesser Hour to get Harker to the infirmary. By then, his injuries had caught up with him, and he'd put off enough heat that he was beginning to shiver, which meant he'd passed the point of exhaustion a while ago.

Rat brushed their fingers through his sweat-mussed hair. "Get some rest, you disaster. I'll find you, okay?"

"You'd better. You owe me breakfast," he mumbled.

Rat wanted to go with him, but they knew they weren't finished quite yet, even if they wanted to be.

After Harker had gone, Dawn motioned to them, leading them away from the clock tower. "I won't keep you long. Fairchild's already agreed that she can speak with you after you've had some sleep, but I thought we should talk."

"My friends," Rat started. "Are they . . ."

"Safe." Dawn gave them a small smile, but it faded just as fast. "We couldn't allow them to stay out here, but they're waiting up. I promised we'd get word to them."

Rat hesitated. "How much does the school already know?"

"Only the broad strokes," Dawn said, but they forced out a breath like even that was too much. "Evening's being held at the Council Chambers for the time being. But . . ."

"There are going to be questions," Rat said, understanding.

Dawn nodded, but their expression softened. "The collection was opened, and no one knew where you'd gone. I don't want to guess what you've been through tonight, but if Isola's still out there—"

"She won't come back to the school," Rat said, their voice hoarse and burnt.

Dawn furrowed their brow, and Rat met their gaze.

"I see," Dawn said quietly.

A breeze blew across the path, and Rat swallowed hard. "What's going to happen now?"

Gently, Dawn rested a hand on their shoulder. "That depends. What do you want to happen?"

Rat wanted a lot of things. They wanted to spend the next three years at Bellamy Arts, the way they'd been terrified they wouldn't get to, and they wanted all of the other houses to know exactly what they were. They wanted to go to their friends and make sure everyone was okay, and they wanted to keep their word to the wraiths.

They wanted to be back with Harker.

"The Ingrid Collection burned," Rat said after a moment, choosing their words carefully. "It was mine by right, and I made the decision. I think it would be best if the rest of the houses knew."

Dawn nodded. "I think that can be managed. We're putting up new wards on the clock tower. Fairchild wants to make sure the way down is sealed off to keep out anyone else who might be curious. And, before I forget—" They slowed, reached into their suit jacket, and drew out Rat's compass. "We found it in Evening's belongings when he was taken into custody. I assumed you might want it back."

Rat took it, balancing the familiar weight of the compass in their hand like they'd done a thousand times before. "Wait," Rat said, before Dawn could turn back. "Night's case files. Did you . . ."

"It's interesting you should ask," Dawn said, but in the early light, they seemed to sharpen a little. "No one's sure what prompted it, but the Church family had copies released to the offices of Dawn and Day. And to Elise, the Rivera-Cromwell household, and about a dozen of the Cromwell family's most powerful enemies."

Rat sharpened a little. The old blood families would always do whatever served their own interests. Allister had known that, and he'd made certain that everything Night had gathered had made its way into the hands of whoever would be the most motivated to use it, while keeping his own name out of the official proceedings.

"It's not going to be neat," Rat said.

"I wish that it was." Dawn shook their head. "The Cromwell family's alliances run deep, and too many of the heads of houses are afraid of setting a precedent that can be held used against them in the future. They'll do what they can to pull their punches."

"But his enemies won't."

"No," Dawn said. "And he's made quite a number of those."

Rat half expected that Harker would have gone straight to bed as soon as the Lesser Hours let him go, but he'd found the others, and he was still waiting outside on the path that led to the dorms.

Will and Jinx were in the middle of comparing battle scars, but not too much worse for wear, and Agatha had already cleaned away the grit from the tunnels, looking like she'd come back to herself again. Allister Church was nowhere in sight. Rat could only guess he'd had the good sense to vanish.

Harker turned as he caught sight of Rat, and even though they knew he was tired, his eyes lit up like he'd been waiting for them. He'd tied his hair back and gotten most of the ash off his face, and fresh bandages wrapped his hands. "Rat—"

Rat rushed at him, and he staggered back as they crashed against him, wrapping his arms around them to stay on his feet.

The last remnants of the binding spell tugged at them, maybe because whatever this was between the two of them, they hadn't reached the end at all. Then it was quiet again, and Rat knew that whatever was there, it was little more than a promise and a thread of intent now.

For a moment, they weren't sure what to do. Then Harker pulled them closer, and his mouth pressed against theirs, warm and desperate in the cold morning air. They grabbed on to his coat and pulled him in, his breath feverish in the chill, and it was something more fervent than an oath and more desperate than any promise he'd made to them yet.

Behind them, Agatha let out a shrill whistle.

"*Finally*," Jinx called, and Will let out a wordless shout, which really wasn't any better.

Rat's face heated, and they could swear that a wave of flustered warmth rose to Harker's skin, even though he still didn't let go of them. Rat pulled back, resting their forehead against his. Sooner or later, the events of the night were going to catch up with them again, but for now, they didn't want to think about anything else.

"So," Harker said. His voice was still hoarse but his eyes glinted. "I take it I have about ten minutes before one of the major houses tries to stab me for standing too close to you."

"Five," Rat said. "It's New York. We're not that big on small talk."

"Alright. Come on, you two," Jinx said. "I've been awake all night and it's literally freezing out here. You can scheme inside."

Harker gave her a look, but Rat just tucked themselves under his arm and started after the others, pulling him along as the morning slowly broke over the school.

EPILOGUE

THEY TOOK ISOLA BACK TO THE TOWER TO LAY HER TO rest under her own sky.

A couple of days had passed, and things at the school quieted down enough for Rat to slip away to Ashwood with Harker. But what felt like a lifetime ago, Rat had sworn to return, and they still had one more promise left to keep.

Isola's body lay where they'd left her, surrounded by the wild overgrowth of weeds, a small flock of crows standing sentinel. She hadn't started to decay, but aether dusted her skin and gathered on the ground around her, like she'd already begun to break down back into the same magic she'd been drawn from once, a very long time ago.

Rat covered her face with her cloak, her body cool to the touch, and then stood back to let Harker work the spells they needed to bear her to the tower, since neither one of them could carry her.

This time, when Rat tried to open the way to the tower, it came to them easily.

Harker left them at the top of the tower alone, in the ruin of her bedroom. They didn't blame him for not wanting to go any further than that, but it wasn't for Isola.

"Knowing you, you'd just find some way to make even more trouble if I left you there," Rat said quietly, laying her sword beside her on the bed. "This makes us even. I'm not yours anymore."

Just for a second, there was a soft flicker on the other end of the bond that they shared with her, so faint they might have imagined it. Then it was gone again, like it had never been there at all. Rat wasn't sure that something like Isola could truly die, but whatever she'd been, there was only a shadow now.

When Rat finished, they made their way back down the stairs.

Harker knelt on the ground, etching out the last lines of an elaborate sigil, the wraith trinkets already scattered in the center. The wraiths flocked around him as he worked, drawn to the warmth of the casting, and he spoke to them just low enough that Rat could only pick out a couple of the names from the files on the missing students as he told them about the school and who some of them had been.

Already, the wraiths seemed a little like smoke that was beginning to dissipate, thready and translucent in the dusk.

"Will this work?" Rat asked, kneeling beside him.

"If it doesn't, we'll try another one," Harker said, determined as ever. "But I think so. This place is already different. The spell hasn't completely broken yet, but it feels like we're just cutting the last few threads."

Rat knew he was right. Something in the air had shifted. Isola was all but gone from this place, and whatever power had held it under her sway was slowly coming undone.

Harker finished the final mark and tucked his casting chalk back into his pocket. In a practiced motion, he pressed his fingers to the stone floor, and magic flared off of him as he completed the casting, warm in the chill of the tower. Aether glinted on the air, glowing softly in the dim as the tower's enchantments unraveled a little more. Harker sat up, the spell finished, and Rat held their hand out to pull him to his feet.

"Alright, Evans. Your turn."

"Right." Rat drew in a breath.

The passage opened into the woods outside of Bellamy Arts. It was still morning there, and light streamed through the trees, the air thick with the smell of rain from the night before. The first early shoots sprouted up out of the ground, even though the trees hadn't gotten their leaves yet, and aside from the low sound of the wind on the lake, everything was quiet.

Rat didn't know how long they could keep a passage open for. As long as they kept watch, it seemed like it would last. They looked back at Harker, who spoke to the wraiths in a voice too low for them to hear. Most had clustered around him, but a few had already noticed the doorway. Then, with nothing else to do but wait, Rat settled on the steps of the tower to hold the passageway as the wraiths slowly began to depart.

It was still early when they made it back to campus. The last of the morning's fog had begun to break apart, but the main paths were quiet. They'd made it in sight of the library where the others would be waiting for them when a voice called out behind them.

"Evans!"

They turned to see Allister. Aside from a couple of cuts and bruises that hadn't been worth healing, he was back to his usual windswept self.

"Your assignment is over," Rat said. "You can stop following me."

"Lucky that we're heading the same way, then." He nodded to the library ahead.

Rat glanced at Harker. "I'll meet you?"

Harker gave Allister a look that Rat was pretty sure meant *Try me, Church, I'll set your cloak on fire.* "Don't be too long," he told Rat, then turned to go.

Rat watched as he receded up the path before they turned back. "Allister. In the tunnels—"

"Save it," he said. "I was paying back a debt. We're not about to hug or anything."

Rat snorted. "You're safe there." Ahead of them, a breeze blew across the path. "So. What now?"

"I haven't decided. The Council invited me to stay on. Apparently, word got around that I had something to do with helping to bring down Evening."

"I can't imagine how."

His mouth twitched, but just as quickly, it was gone again. "They're offering me a spot as a Lesser Hour after my apprenticeship ends. I guess the rest of the old families decided that it might be advantageous to keep me around after all."

"That's not a bad offer," Rat said slowly.

"I don't know. I was kind of thinking I might try being self-employed for a while," he said. "Either way, I'm heading back to the city after this. You should find me if you ever need a favor. I'm pretty sure I still owe you one."

The others were already upstairs in one of the reading rooms when Rat got to the library. Midterms were coming up, and in another week or two, it would be impossible to secure a space in the library. But for now at least, the rest of the school was still giving them a wide berth.

Since the Ingrid Collection had gone up in flames, there was a new rumor that Rat had unsealed a legendary archive that was theirs to claim and burned it to the ground. In some versions of the story, it was because they'd unearthed something so horrible, it had to be destroyed. In others, they did it out of sheer arrogance. In a few, it was to send a message to the rest of the old houses that Rat was already powerful enough to tilt the Northeast off its axis, with or without Ingrid's magic.

Rat might have minded more, except that it guaranteed them one of the good armchairs in the Drake. And at least this time, some of the whispers were true.

Viola leaned against the side of the couch, Jinx's leather jacket draped over her shoulders. Rat wasn't sure how many of the details she'd gotten, except that whatever Jinx had told her, apparently, her interests did involve structurally questionable tunnels.

"Later?" she asked Jinx.

"Text me once you're free," Jinx said.

Viola waved to Rat as she slipped past them, back toward the hall.

"She's been around more," Rat said as she disappeared back into the building.

Jinx raised her eyebrows at them. "And?"

"Just an observation."

Harker shifted over where he'd perched on the arm of a chair, and Rat dropped down next to him.

"What's all this?" Rat asked, surveying the maps spread out on the coffee table, between pages of notes and their half-finished application for the Higher Magics department.

"Nothing yet," Harker said, but he said it like he was already turning something over in his mind. Even now, there were parts of the tunnels they hadn't managed to reach, and Rat somehow doubted that Bellamy Arts was the kind of place that ever ran out of secrets, or that Isola would be the last one to come looking for them.

Out of habit, Rat's hand found their compass, and they turned the cool metal in their fingers as the needle swung toward north.

"Tell me?" they asked.

In the morning light, Harker's gaze sharpened a little, and Rat settled against him as their friends started to talk.

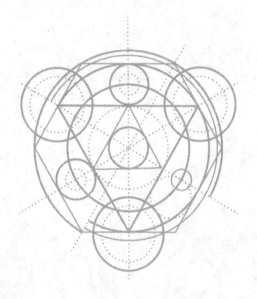

ACKNOWLEDGMENTS

I genuinely couldn't have asked for a better team to see this story through, and I can't express how much I've appreciated getting to work with them.

A huge thank you to Jordan Hamessley, always, who's championed this story from the beginning (and occasionally reminded me to take a much-needed breath). She's done so much to make this book possible, and I've been ridiculously lucky to have her in my corner.

I also owe a ridiculous amount of gratitude to Emily Daluga—for connecting with the story so deeply, for her willingness to take on the absolute roughest of drafts when I was fighting to keep it together, and for seeing what all the jagged pieces could be and helping to guide this story to its vicious, hopeful, and gloriously queer conclusion that's beyond anything I'd originally imagined.

Also, my most genuine thanks to the brilliant Corey Brickley and Micah Flemming for the cover illustration, and cover and book design respectively. It's been an absolute privilege to work with both of them, and I still can't express how absolutely floored I've been at every stage of the process.

Sincere thanks to the rest of the team at Abrams who worked on this book—Marie Oishi, Maggie Moore, Maggie Lehrman, and Lily Rosen Marvin—and to Margo Winton Parodi, for all of their support, attention to detail, and effort in getting it to print.

Thanks as always to my critique partners Hayley Stone, Maiga Doocy, and Karen McCoy, for being generally wonderful, and just, literally everything.

Thanks once again to my parents for all of their enthusiasm and occasional moral support.

And sincerely, thank you to everyone who's read and supported these books—who has cared for these characters as much as I have, and chosen to come along with them through all of this story's darkened corners and hidden passageways. I can't say how much I appreciate it.

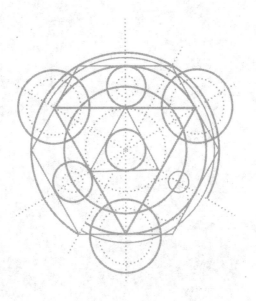

ABOUT THE AUTHOR

Lee Paige O'Brien (he/they) is an author and literary agent from New York, where he writes queer fantasy books about strange magic and monsters of all kinds.